MADNESS AND GODS

RESTORED I

V. S. HOLMES

AMPHIBIAN PRESS

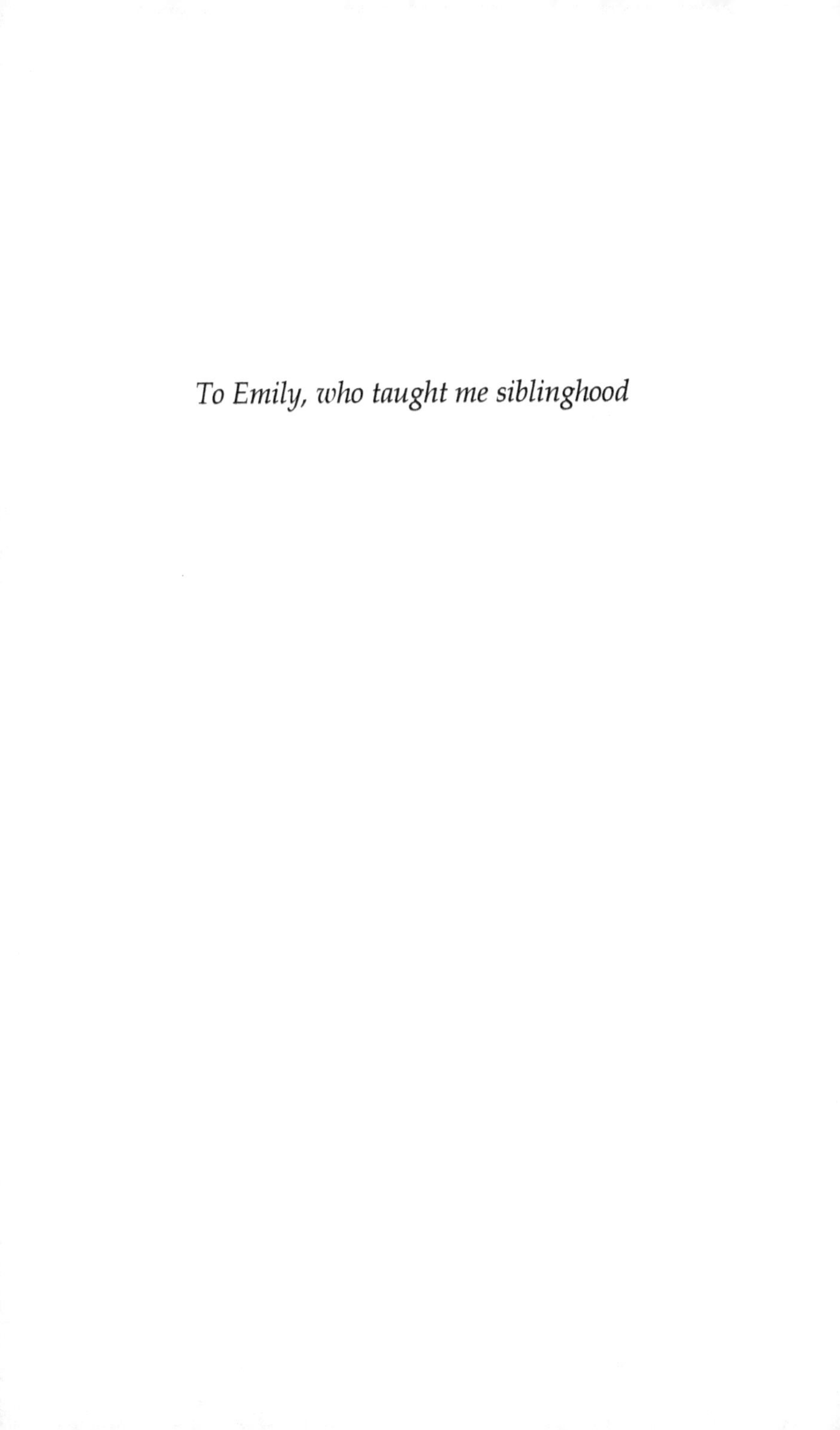

To Emily, who taught me siblinghood

Incredible praise for the world of
BLOOD OF TITANS

Smoke and Rain

International bestselling fantasy and winner of NewApple Literary's 2015 Excellence in Independent Publishing Award

"Holmes weaves a tapestry of the forthcoming events with the skill of a thaumaturge…In [the] seductive opening few lines so much of the nidus of this fantasy tale is hinted…Wade deeply into these waters for a fine curtain raiser for REFORGED. V.S. Holmes quite simply demonstrates that she is an artist of significance"

- The San Francisco Review of Books

"A well developed and subtly-layered world…filled with compelling characters and dangerous magic"

- Aurealis Magazine

"The very first page hooked me with the simple yet elegant narrative…The characters' dilemmas were revealed in perfect timing yet kept me wanting more, and Holmes didn't disappoint with dropping tidbits of emotion, character growth, and internal struggle among all the the action and war-time maneuvers."

- Kathrin Hutson, author of *Gyenona's Children*
and The Unclaimed Trilogy

"I couldn't put it down to save my life and I couldn't turn the pages fast enough. The plot line was incredibly unique … Holmes gave me a lot of the things I look for in a wonderful story and so much more."

- Cassandra Carpio, *The Bookish Crypt*

Lightning and Flames

"The atmosphere surrounding this saga is intoxicatingly real…Very highly recommended… This REFORGED volume elevates the reader even more, adding to the obvious stature of V.S. Holmes' literary presence. Very Highly recommended."

- The San Francisco Review of Books

"Holmes' prose perfectly illustrates the incredible, world-shaking horror unleashed when Alea and Arman's magic clashes with that of the gods."

- Aurealis Magazine

Madness and Gods

"…This tale focuses on the political struggles of its characters with few traditional trappings of the fantasy genre…it takes fantasy's ability to explore complex issues such as gender, mental health and human rights through allegory, and refocuses back on the issues themselves…while new and secondary characters now take centre stage. The new protagonists are interesting and richly drawn…"

- Aurealis Magazine

"Following this fantasy experience is addictive and thoroughly satisfying."

- The San Francisco Review of Books

Blood and Mercy

"The series excels in using allegory to mirror contemporary issues and explore them in a unique, thoughtful manner. Frustration, hope and the transformative power of righteous fury ooze from the...The underlying optimism of the series, balanced with unflinching realism regarding the difficulty of change at personal and systemic levels, is a testament to the possibilities of the fantasy genre—and a worthy read for our times."

- Aurealis Magazine

Books by V. S. Holmes

BLOOD OF TITANS

REFORGED
Smoke and Rain
Lightning and Flames

RESTORED
Madness and Gods
Blood and Mercy

REBEL
*Treason's Tears**

STARSEDGE: NEL BENTLY

Travelers
Drifters
Strangers
Heretics
Fugitives
*Emissaries**

SHORT FICTION

"Nowhere Fast" (*We Came to Dance*)
"Starfall" (*Vitality Magazine*)
"The Tempest" (*Out of the Darkness*)
"Disciples" (*Beamed Up*)
"Familiar Waters" (*Love and Bubbles*)
"Mere Primordium" (poem, *Mystic Blue Review*)

**forthcoming*

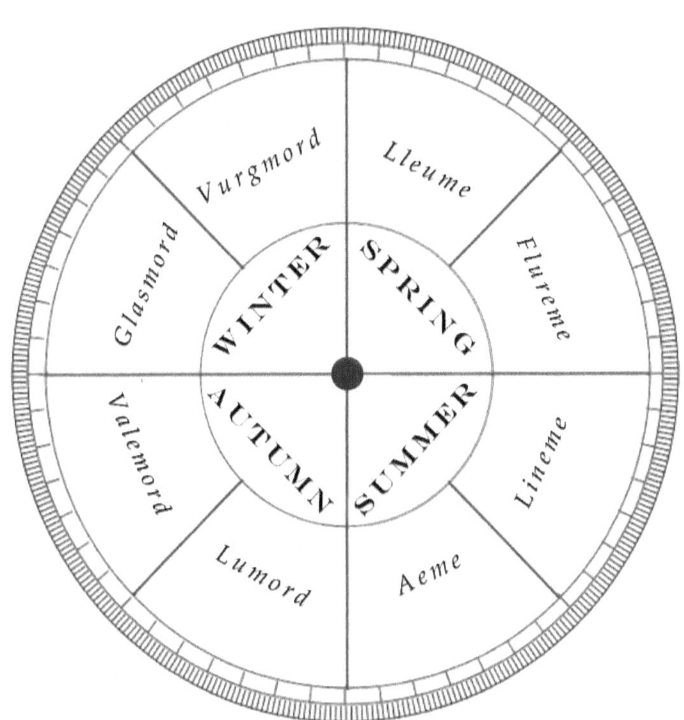

Vurgmord
Lleume
Glasmord
Flureme
WINTER
SPRING
Valemord
AUTUMN
SUMMER
Lineme
Lumord
Aeme

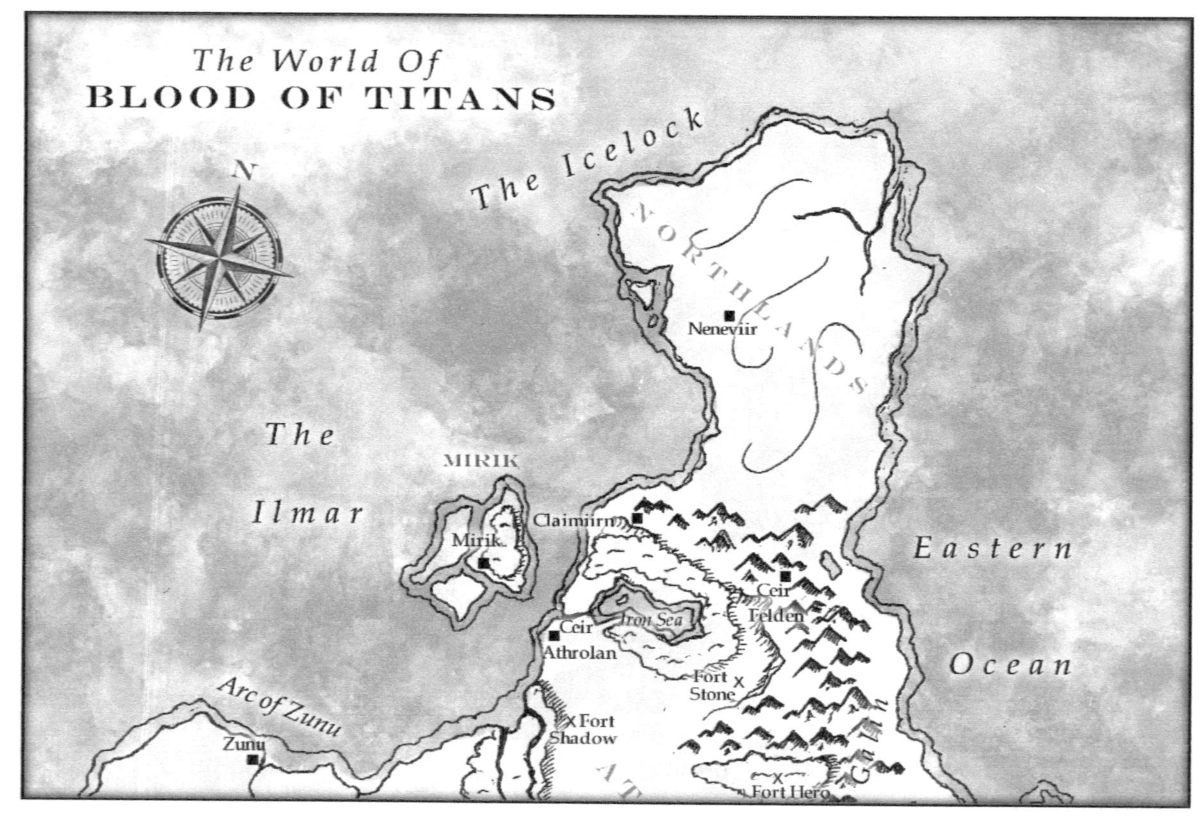

The World Of
BLOOD OF TITANS
N
The Icelock
NORTHLANDS
Neneviir
The
Ilmar
MIRIK
Mirik
Claimiirn
Ceir
Felden
Iron Sea
Ceir
Athrolan
Fort
Stone
X
X Fort
Shadow
Eastern
Ocean
Arc of Zunu
Zunu
X
Fort Hero

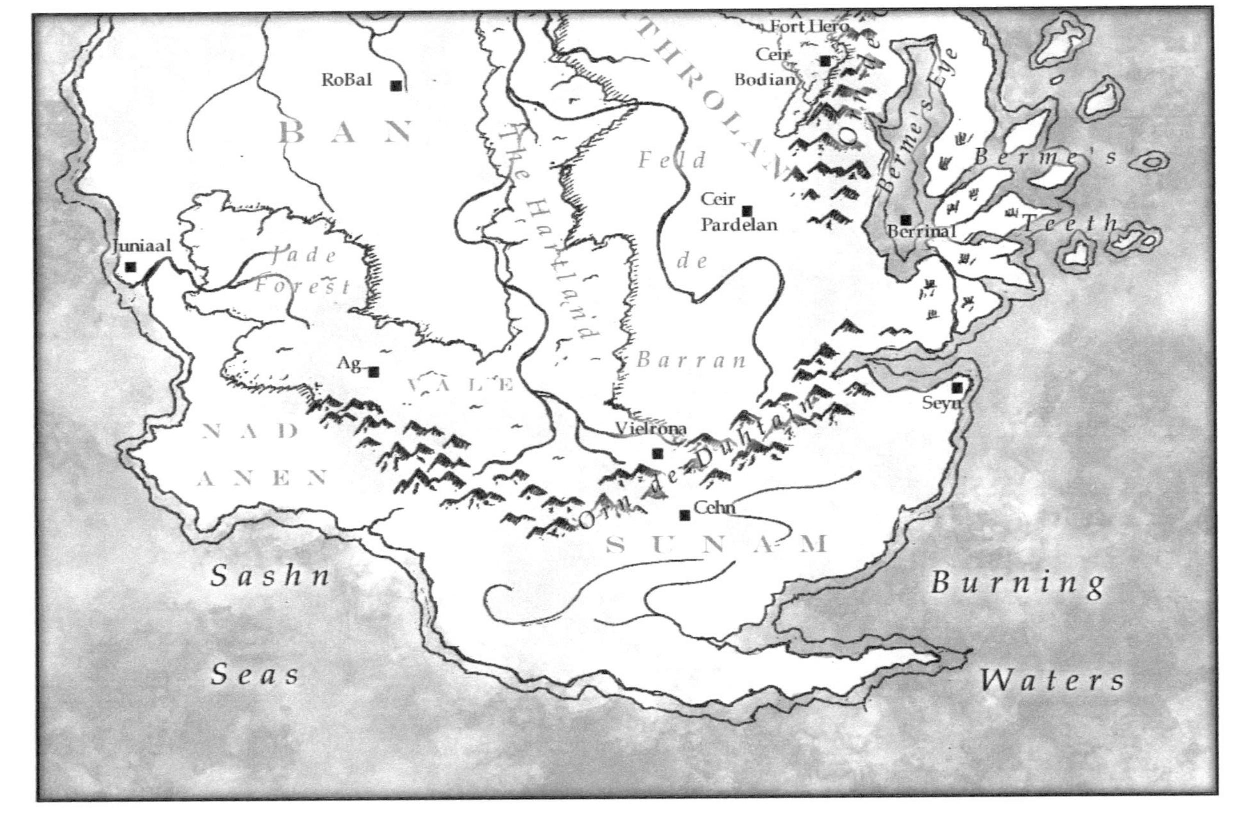

BAN
RoBal
THROLAN
Fort Hero
Ceir Bodian
Berme's Eye
Berme's Teeth
Feld
Ceir Pardelan
Berrinal
de
Juniaal
Jade Forest
The Hartland
Barran
Ag
VALE
Seyn
NAD ANEN
Vielrona
Fotn de Dunlana
Cehn
SUNAM
Sashn Seas
Burning Waters

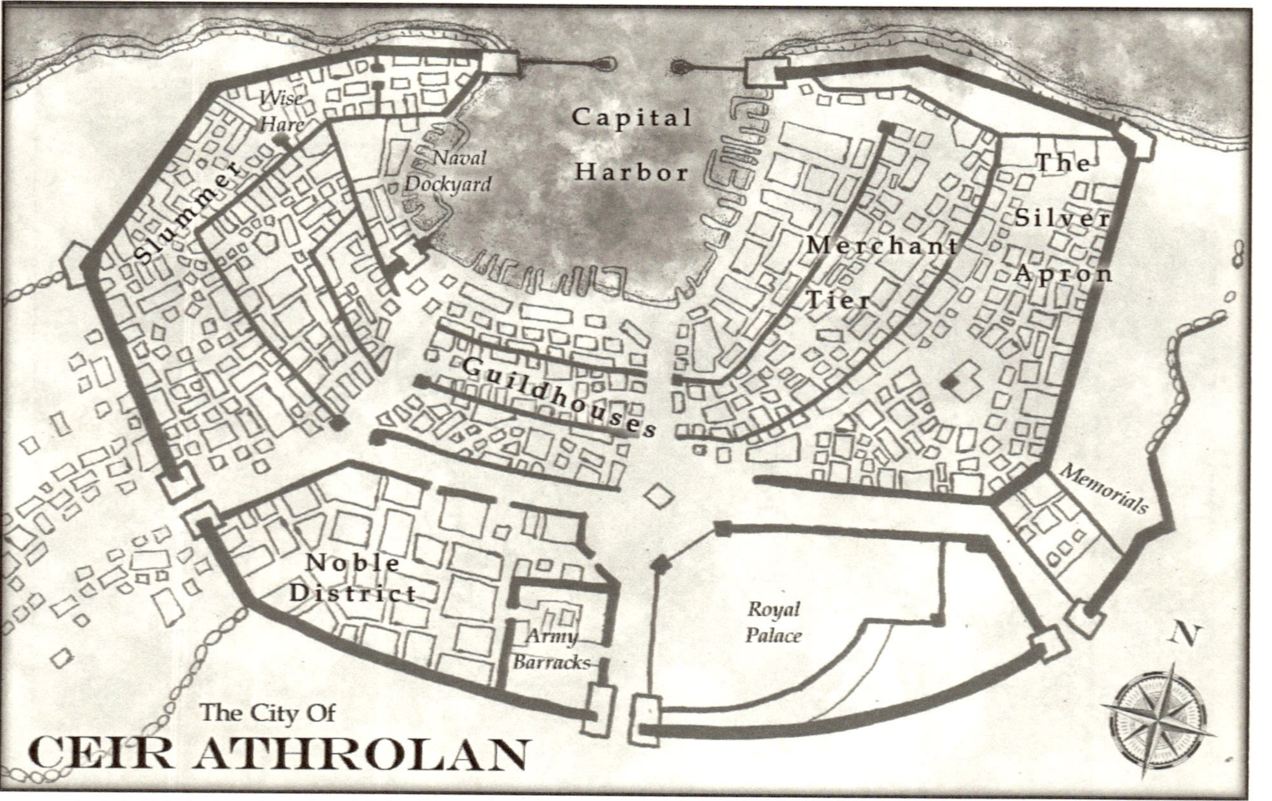

Wise Hare
Slummer
Naval Dockyard
Capital Harbor
Merchant Tier
The Silver Apron
Guildhouses
Memorials
Noble District
Army Barracks
Royal Palace
N
The City Of
CEIR ATHROLAN

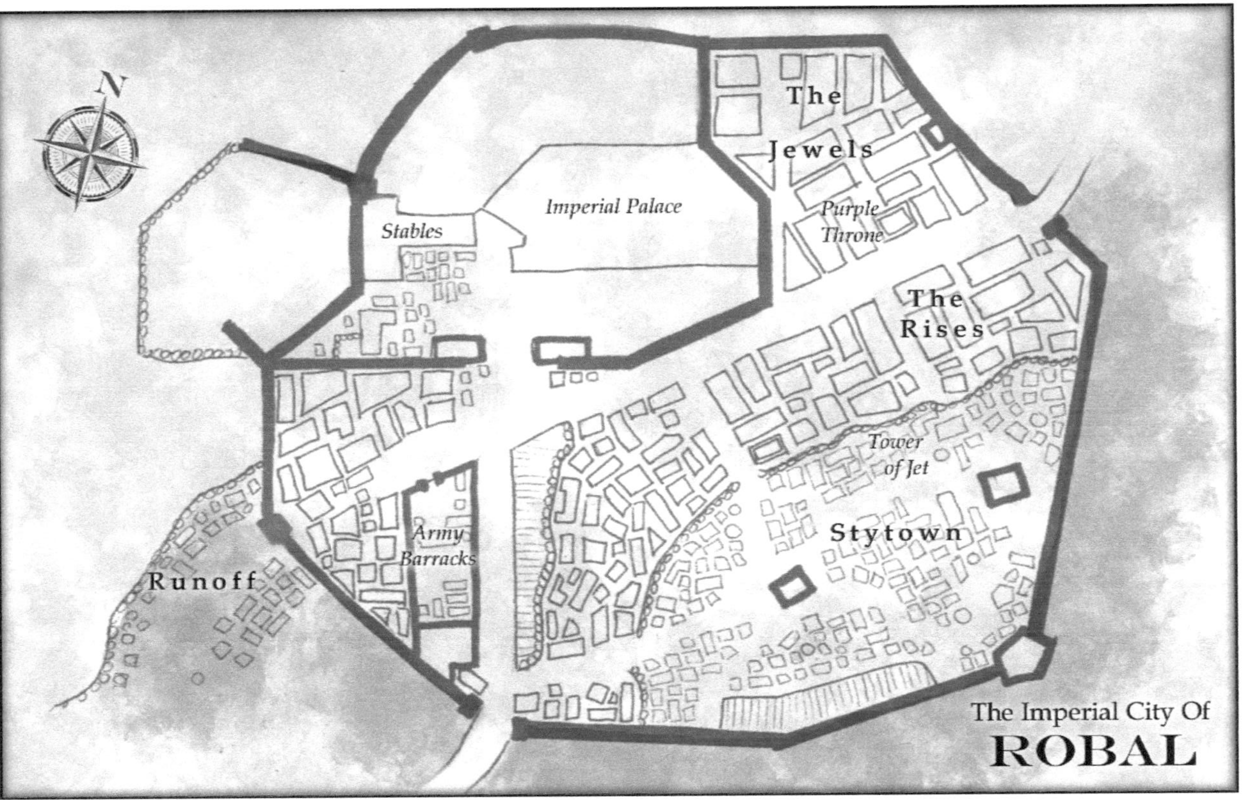
N
The Jewels
Purple Throne
Imperial Palace
Stables
The Rises
Tower of Jet
Army Barracks
Stytown
Runoff
The Imperial City Of
ROBAL

The Marks of Violence

CHAPTER ONE

The 27th Day of the Month of Rainfall, 1272
The Forest of the Hartland

THE ROOM WAS DESERTED. Arman felt the absence before he opened the door. His gaze roved from the made bed to the hook by the door that no longer held breeches. *It's all wrong.* They kept the truth of their bloodlines from their son, hoping he would live the life they could not. One of peace. Of anonymity. *Perhaps it was a mistake.* Pain gnawed at Arman's gut. He thought Alea would panic, and he would comfort her. Instead, it was his body thrumming with fear and guilt.

He wavered on the threshold, unwilling to allow the last person to enter be someone other than Keplan. The part of him that heard too many legends expected a note on his son's pillow, explaining he left for some adventure. There was none. The ragged parchment protruding from the desk drawer spurred him into the room. It was a letter, but not one from his son. It was one he had kept secret, even from Alea. Underneath lay a series of sketches, drawn in Keplan's quick, haphazard hand.

Arman took both and retreated to the kitchen. His eyes remained fixed out the small, soot-stained window above the kitchen washbasin, waiting for the water to boil. Soft footfalls sounded behind him as he took the muttering kettle from the fire and poured two mugs of tea.

"Has he come back?" The circles under Alea's eyes spoke to how well she had slept. "It's not like him to spend a night in the forest without telling us."

He jerked his chin at the teacup waiting on the table before her. Concern erased his usual compassion. "I don't think he'll come back for a long time."

"How can you say that?" Her voice rasped with tears and fatigue.

Arman heaved a sigh. "Alea, when I left home I packed my bag, made my bed, swept my floors. Trust me when I say I know what running looks like." The words replaced his despair with understanding. Fear, though, still burned through his body. "I found something. Though perhaps you should finish your tea."

"All the tea in the world will not help if my son is missing."

Arman winced. *He's my son too, Alea.* Instead, he set the letter and sketch between them. "I received a letter on my last visit to Namus. I hoped ignoring it would work. I realize, now, I was wrong."

Darkness filled Alea's eyes, an expression he had not seen in years. Decades. "What does it say?"

"It's from An'thor." He held the letter up.

"'Alea,

I don't know how this letter will find you, in all senses of the words. I've spent precious amounts of what's left in the kingdom's treasury to find you. I think, finally, that I might have. Namus. A tiny town, unremarkable save for its proximity to the Hartland.

I understand the value of peace, more than many, I think. You've looked in my eyes and you know this to be true. I remind you of this, so you understand the gravity with which I write this letter.

She is dying. Perhaps she will be gone by the time you read these words. She never revoked her dismissal of Daymir. Instead, she named your child, should you have one.

We need you. Ceir Athrolan needs you. Just once more. This is my last resort.

I won't beg, though I want to.'"

He swallowed. It explains the news we've gotten, the patrols we've seen. I knew Ban was on the verge of war with Mirik, but this is different. This is our fault."

"He uses no names—"

"That was to prevent rumors of the queen's death should this letter fall into other hands. You and I both know to whom he refers. This was in Kep's desk. Fates know what he thought. I assume, like us, he left looking for answers. And I don't think our power ended with us."

Her winter-chapped hand touched the ragged edge of the sketch. "You found this with the letter?"

Arman let her regard it in silence. He already knew the scene. It was a battle, their battle, above the cliffs of Clai'miin, half a dozen armies locked in a divine fight of lightning and fire. It was not just accurate. It was perfect.

When she looked away, he cleared the emotions from his throat. "Somehow he knows. Maybe not all of it, maybe nothing but this, but he knows."

"You told him?" There was as much confusion as accusation in her tone.

"No! You all but forbade me. I may have disagreed with your choice, but I respected it. That sketch, it's not him drawing a story I told him. It's as if he reached into our memories and drew exactly what he found."

She rose, tea forgotten, and paced the tiny room. "How could he know?" It was a question, but they both already knew the answer. The power that drew lightning from her skin, pulled fire from his hands now told him, unwavering, their son was not human.

"Alea, we denied him the truth. You did exactly what your mother did to you."

"I was trying to protect my child!"

"So was she!" Arman's hand shook, but it was no longer from panic. It was rage. *Our son ran from us because he couldn't trust us to tell him the truth.* Arman was tired of secrets, tired of protecting. "Keplan may not know what we were, what he is, but he damned well knows someone wants him in the capital. And I'm willing to bet he knows they won't lie." Arman's fist rattled the counter. "There are thousands of leagues between here and Athrolan. I'm damned if I know where he is."

Alea trembled, eyes frantic. "Arman, what have we done?"

Her words made him pause as he tugged on his cloak. "I protected you both. You blinded him." The words he threw over his shoulder bit sharper than the draft blowing past him. "You better hope he forgives you." He slammed the door. "I'm not sure I can."

CHAPTER TWO

The 35th Day of the Month of Rainfall, 1272
The Banis Prairie

GRASSES HISSED IN THE wind, rolling in waves of green and gold as the air scuttled across the hills. Keplan drew up at the crest of the hill. But for the dark line of trees far to his right he could have been anywhere. The prairie had a sentience, a quiet draw that threatened to swallow him if he met its eyes for too long. Still, the adrenaline and confusion that drove him from home still echoed in his limbs, and he could not help the laugh that bubbled from his throat when the wind tugged his long brown hair from its tie. "Pity Ma and Da had no true maps, eh Moly?" The gray horse flicked one fuzzy ear back then forward again, cocking one hoof as if to remark that she was confident they would find their way.

He pulled out a tattered piece of deerskin and held it open against the wind. His penmanship left much to be desired, and his knowledge of geography came only from his own mind and stories pieced together from childhood. His gaze traced the woods stretching north from his home. The rocky fields in the east were Athrolan, and while the capital was his goal, the Banis plains were a shorter road, he hoped. "Besides, Da was always touting their beautiful horses. Don't you want to see your cousins?"

Moly's snort drew a smile from him. He preferred animals to people and preferred Moly best of all. He pushed away guilt that his parents would search for him. He realized now, the sanctuary of his parents' house became isolation. His mind was quieter since leaving. The barrage of information and voices had not come again. *I still won't turn about.* Hard choices must still be made, even if they hurt.

The steady rattle of insects heralded the dry season on the plains.

Keplan looked up from the map, tucking it back into his bag as he scanned the sky. *There.* Sullen smoke inched upward from a hollow in the plains. It was too thin to be a grass fire, too regular to be a cloud. His heart hammered, fingers tightening in Moly's mane. The Hartland forest received fair few visitors, and though he occasionally rode into the neighboring town with his father, the idea of other people still sparked his imagination. "Campfire. Or a house." *Rel. Banis houses are called rels.* It may be quieter, but his mind was far from silent.

He shook the unsolicited information away and nudged Moly faster. He was hungry, and though he could use the bow strapped to Moly's rump, curiosity lit in his gut. Waving grasses hid the curves of the prairie, smoothing them into a featureless plain. In another hour he paused atop a hummock. The *rel* squatted in a shallow cleft below him. The roof barely reached Moly's withers, the door leading into the dark depths of the sunken dwelling. A low shed served as shelter for some animal. Keplan lifted his nose to the eddying breeze. *Oxen. Maybe a goat.* Smoke curled from the hole in the peak of the round roof's shallow curve.

His stomach muttered to itself. Keplan urged Moly down to the bare, hoof-trodden area that served as a yard. He cleared his throat, unsure. He knew serviceable Banis, but was unfamiliar with their customs. "Hello?"

The silence sharpened, and after a breath the form of an old man appeared in the shadow of the doorway. The black eyes rested calculatingly on Keplan's gangly form. "Ho, the traveler."

Relief washed over Keplan. "Evening, Farmer. I've been riding alone for a time. Might I share your fire? Perhaps I could tend your animals for the night."

The man's eyes flicked to the hills behind Keplan, to the beaten track running north. "Just the night. I'm not a rich man."

Keplan smiled brightly. "Then I would be happy to share the grouse I caught earlier."

The farmer's smile was faint, but warmed his eyes. "Get your mare stabled and clean the stalls. I'll have supper ready when you're through."

The heat of the stable was comforting, as was the familiar smell of animal. Tending their horses had always been Keplan's favorite chore. Now it was a bittersweet reminder. *Before things changed.* He shook away the shadowed thoughts and slid the stable's door home. The chill of winter was almost absent here, echoed only in the dampness of the ground.

He ducked under the eaves and trotted down the few stairs to the sunken door. The house was warm and smelled of a sweet spice. *Cinnamon?* He shucked off his boots and stepped down into the tiered single room. The farmer crouched by the central hearth, watching the grouse sizzle. His robe was stained and tucked up into a tattered rope belt.

"What is your name?"

The man's eyes flicked over, but he did not turn his head. "Hi-taln."

"Well, Hi-taln, you have a fine house." He offered his hand. "I'm Keplan. Have you lived here your entire life?"

"I was raised just east of the Vale. I came out here after the revolution."

Keplan nodded, though he had no idea to which revolution Hi-taln referred. "I was born east of here, in the Hartland." He suspected it went by a different name in Ban, though it was not one he knew.

"And you're traveling north? Times being what they are, I'm surprised a man of your color would brave it."

Keplan looked down. It was obvious his pale skin was far from the warm brown of the Banis. He had not thought to look into the political state before traveling. *Did I tumble into a war?* "An old family friend asked me to visit. This was simply the quickest route." It was not, strictly, a lie.

Hi-taln hummed in response. "I suppose your coloring could be Athrolani. Besides, your accent speaks of the south, not Mirik." The man tested the meat with one calloused finger, then tugged the grouse off the spit. He handed Keplan a wicker plate and a wooden stick with a prong on one end and a blade on the other.

"Thank you." Silence fell, interrupted only when they tore meat from the bones. Keplan struggled to master the dual-ended utensil, managing to barely shovel the meat into his mouth.

A wry smile hovered over the older man's mouth at the display, but he said nothing. When the food was gone, Hi-taln snugged a broad pan into the coals and removed the lid. He jerked his head at the thick mixture when it began to bubble. "Some tea there, if you'd like."

Keplan eyed the pan warily. Tea was thin, black and bitter in his house. This looked closer to something left over from frying meat. "Perhaps just a little."

Hi-taln's chuckle rolled low and soft, but he poured a single ladle's worth into a clay mug and handed it over. The drink was both savory and sweet and rolled down his throat like gravy. A night bird trilled outside, echoed by another, closer. The man's eyes narrowed on the small window, then glanced at the locked door. "I'd best be off to bed. You can sleep here." Hi-taln nodded to the rush pillows left a few tiers higher. His brown eyes refused to meet Keplan's. "I'll be out by dawn, and so should you."

"Thank you." Keplan curled his back against the earthen step, face to the fire. Uncertainty fluttered in his chest, and he missed home. Images and words flickered on the edge of his own thoughts. When the breathing from the other room was even, he opened a scrap of parchment from his bag.

An'thor, Daymir.

The only two names mentioned in the letter. He had not meant to snoop, but found it tucked in his father's writing kit while searching for charcoal to sketch the alien images bombarding his mind. Nights of poring over the words before leaving helped him memorize the lines. "*Ceir Athrolan needs you. Just once more.*" So Athrolan's capital had needed his parents before. Maybe more than once. *Were they warriors? Spies?*

Keplan knew Ceir Athrolan, but there his understanding stopped. He did not know what he had been named, or why this person would choose him. Perhaps his parents had owned a business. Stories of his father helping in the inn as a boy were always his favorite. *I could do that.* He hoped, too, the city might hold an answer as to why he saw things not his to see. In a place as great as Athrolan, a city as perfect and legendary, surely even a madman could find peace.

Φ

The 36th Day of the Month of Rainfall, 1272

The wealth of Ban was not in the gold of the empire's fields, or the jewels glittering on the hands of the nobility. It was in the sleek muscle of horses and the long strides of the army. Rih crouched in the grasses, her brown fingers tracing tracks in the rain-softened ground. The prairie in spring was always her favorite. It bore a potential that the summer sun burnt away in later months. She picked out the nuances of the trail through the grass. The prints were those of a heavy horse, not one of the Banis beauties. Boots, not sandals, marked the ground where the rider had dismounted.

Rih flipped the camouflage of her woven hood back and scanned the scattered soldiers. The patrol numbered eleven women if she included the two trainees. Captain Gali was wrapped in what seemed a fervent conversation with another soldier. Rih tucked her head down to blow the clay whistle tied to the shoulder of her leather breastplate. She wondered, briefly, how annoying it was for her fellow soldiers to hear it. From the little she could hear, it was the same tone as theirs.

The older woman glanced over and nodded an acknowledgment. A moment later she jogged over and knelt beside Rih. Her gnarled fingers curled, her head tilted. "What?" she signed.

Rih pointed at the track, hands twisting in the same language. "One horse, not ours, with a light rider."

The captain traced the tracks herself, following the direction toward a dip in the hills. Rih watched her mouth as the woman called orders to the others. This close, Rih picked up enough voiced words to make lip-reading easier. "Pack up! We move northwest in five minutes. Ji-alt and Yana, flank us, Rih-elte: take up the fore." She turned, catching Rih's eyes and switched to signing. "Front."

"I saw, thank you." Rih fell into place at the head of the group. Her long legs stretched easily to keep stride with the other soldiers. While the male generals and commanders might be mounted, as were the male cavalry, the female infantry relied on their sandaled feet and the steady endurance built by years of training.

She traced the grasses with her eyes, picking out tiny depressions the others might miss. She rarely envied them their speech and perfect hearing now, though it might have made her life easier. *Stronger shoulders may make the dart fly further, but they lack the flexibility for precision.* She honed her vision to find tiny nuances in faces, to read mouths and features as well as any other could hear tonal differences. Now, as a soldier, that skill made her an unparalleled tracker.

The grasses thinned, and the soft earth was trampled into hard mounds. Rih slowed and raised her fist. An old rel was tucked into the hills. By the barn and tracks surrounding the buildings, it belonged to a farmer. The captain gestured for the others to fan out, surrounding the home.

She sent Rih and two others into the barn. It smelled sweet and dusty, the way a barn should. The two oxen stared at them, brown eyes distant. A Banis horse watched them curiously, golden head bobbing as he scented the air. The stall at the end, however, held a pony. It was not the beautiful gold or cream of a Banis horse, and it lacked the tell-tale dorsal markings.

Rih glanced over the half door at the hooves. *Unshod. Small.* She snapped her finger to get her captain's attention and jerked her chin at the foreign horse. The older woman's lips pursed, and she slipped outside. Rih followed, watching the other women circle the house. She crept up to one of the windows. The smell of smoke was faint, and the air eddying from within was only slightly warmer than outside. *No one is up yet to tend the fire or start breakfast.*

She drew a steadying breath and peered inside. As she had guessed, the central fire was low, sullen embers shedding orange across the tiers of the main room. A boy sprawled a step above the fire. He lacked the coloring and height of a Banis man. His pack pillowed his head. His fingers flexed in his sleep, and a strange expression crossed his features. Rih met the eyes of her captain who crouched just outside the house's door. The captain held up a finger and tapped it on her wrist, held up another and tapped her throat. *One prisoner, one traitor.*

Rih sat back on her haunches to watch. She was too much of a liability in ambushes, her captain claimed. The woman raised a fist, then brought it down. The soldiers swarmed the house. The door broke, splinters flying. Rih leaned against the clay. She felt the reverberations as a body fell. She closed her eyes. Their orders were clear. They were always clear. *"You are to hunt down any who might betray the Banis Empire and by extension, His Eminence the Emperor. Any who seek to spy upon us or bring ill will through our borders from our Eastern neighbors shall be detained and questioned. Any who aid them are to be slaughtered without delay."* Acrid smoke billowed across her face as blood doused the fire.

Φ

The sky was still dark and bruised when the door exploded inward. "Ji-alt, check the stables!" Keplan scrambled to his feet, adrenaline scouring sleep from his mind. The tall figure of a soldier was silhouetted against the blue of fading night.

Leather armor scaled shoulders and chest, tassets swaying over a silk tunic. Hi-taln appeared in the bedroom doorway, hands peacefully open beside him. The soldier thrust her spear into the fire-lit room, drawing a knife from her sash. Her dark eyes pinned Hi-taln against the far wall. "You're the master of this house?"

Keplan strained his ears. He heard the Banis words, but understood them, or at least the essence.

Hi-taln jerked a nod. "I am."

Three more soldiers entered, similarly dressed, but without the crimson wrap around their skullcaps. The first soldier's eyes flicked to Keplan. "And who is this?"

"He is a guest, a traveler, Ma'am."

"He's Mirikin."

"I'm not. I'm from the south," Keplan interjected. *I should have looked into the politics.*

The soldier descended the tiers in two strides. Brass rings on her left hand split the skin over Keplan's cheek when she smacked him once, twice. "Silence, barbarian!" Her brown lips curled in a snarl, and she glared down at Hi-taln. "I ask you again: who is he?"

"I just met him today—yesterday. He offered to tend my animal in exchange for a fire and bed."

"You let a foreigner touch your horse? Idiot," the soldier scoffed, large black eyes rolling. She kicked Keplan's bag dangerously close to the fire. "Check this."

A subordinate crouched, upending the bag onto the floor before rifling through the contents. "Change of clothes in the eastern style. A personal letter written in Trade. Old bread. Half a dozen coins—old, but Mirikin."

Pain bloomed across Keplan's face with her third blow. He was too frozen to protect himself, or even panic. His teeth gouged the inside of his cheek, and blood flooded his mouth. "Ma'am, I'm just a traveler."

"You're a damned barbarian spy." Her hard fingers bit into the back of his neck and shoved him to the floor.

Behind him, Hi-taln's shouts of protest guttered into wet silence. A thick trail of blood dribbled down the stairs and hissed against the coals. "Bind and drug him. He's coming to the capital. Burn the rest." The earthen smell of the floor was replaced with that of an acrid rag that stank of urine. Keplan's vision narrowed then went black.

CHAPTER THREE

The 38th Day of the Month of Rainfall, 1272
The City of RoBal, Ban

KEPLAN WOKE TO DARKNESS and pain. He blinked rapidly, focusing his mind as much as his vision. It was dark, the kind of dark that pressed against his eyes.

"Moly?" Pain bloomed in his lower left ribs. *Broken ribs, bruised collarbone.* Blood matted his hair, and his temples throbbed. *Concussion.* What puzzled him was the stinging in his right palm. He tried to flex the hand, but the skin was tight and stiff. *I must have scraped it when I went down.* He gently felt the walls with his other hand. It was not a room, but a cell the size of a coffin. Straw stuffed in a bucket served as a privy. He returned to his curled position and cradled his hand against his chest. He was hungry, but not painfully so, not yet. *Must have only been here a day.* Keplan rested his head on a scuffed knee. *Where's Moly?* The past weeks seemed like a lifetime.

Three weeks ago his woodsman's life melted with the snow.

Three weeks ago I went mad.

The images were like remembering pieces of a dream, but these were things he had never dreamed. Some events he recognized from stories, recalled with such detail it was as if he witnessed them. Now he need only focus on a topic or place, and fragmented information tumbled into his mind. He closed his eyes, focusing on the city around him. *Ban, empire to the west of Athrolan. The only kingdom that rivals its size. Civil to its neighbor.* He swallowed hard. *Apparently close to war with Mirik.* If only he had checked, if only he had stuck to the winding road through Athrolan's rocky fields. *If only I had left a note.* His thoughts fled at the sound of a key in the lock of his door.

Light poured in. After the darkness of his cell, even the dim hall lights were blinding. He shrank back against the wall, away from the rough hands. His back met stone, however, and he was hauled out. His adolescent frame had not filled out, and even his best attempts to flail free did nothing. He caught glimpses of stone floors and dark, wooden walls, but nothing else. The way was short, and after a moment he was pulled into a small office at the end of the hall.

The guards shoved him into a seat, standing just behind him. Keplan's vision finally began to return. The desk before him was utilitarian and covered with papers. A small rack of wooden rods held a collection of the stone, metal, and clay beads of Banis currency.

"Banis?" The man behind the desk was lean, his brown face lined from a life on the sunny, dry plains.

Realizing the man was asking if he knew the language, Keplan nodded, ashamed of his obvious trembling.

"Name?"

Keplan swallowed the dryness from his throat, but his voice was still a croak. "Keplan Wardyn, sir." He was still curious enough to note the planes of the man's face. Besides the few trips to Namus with his father, he rarely saw people other than his parents and the face that stared back from the tarnished mirror in their kitchen. Like Hi-taln and the soldiers, these men were brown and their hair black. Their eyes were large and wide, like his own, but darker.

"Height?"

Keplan opened his mouth to answer, but a sharp rap on his shoulder stopped the words.

"He's a hand under two paces."

"Coloring?"

"Sickly."

"I asked for coloring, not constitution, El-Jak."

"Pale. Hair brown, like dead grass. Eyes colorless."

"Features?" The man behind the desk looked up, eyes narrowed. "Birdlike. His journey here must not have gone to plan. He looks like a wretch."

Keplan glanced up. He had never been muscled or wiry like his father, but neither had he cared or questioned it.

"Nationality?" The man's eyes pinned Keplan.

"What do you mean?"

"Are you an idiot? Nationality—to what nation are you pledged?"

"I don't know—I grew up in the Hartland. My father is Vielronan. I'm not sure about my mother."

"See, this is where we disagree." The guard leaned forward. "You are a spy sent from Mirik. You traveled from the capital through Athrolan—perhaps you did come from one of the southern cities. And you came to what? Bring down our slave trade? Free our property?" All composure evaporated from the man's eyes at Keplan's stammering attempt to argue. "Well, I'll tell you what—you're our property now, and if you don't die in the next three weeks, you'll wish you had."

Φ

The 40th Day of the Month of Rainfall, 1272

Swollen wood screamed as the guards jerked the door open. Keplan scrabbled toward the back of the cell, but a pace of space was precious little for escaping. Sleep was a generous term for the drifting state of mind he adopted in the cramped, dark space, but it was dear to him. Landmarks slipped from his exhausted mind when he tried to memorize the turns down a set of stairs. The room they dragged him into was low, beneath the street level. Locks clicked shut when the door slammed.

A barred tunnel at the top of the wall opposite the door shed light from a window far above. He whirled, dropping into a crouch, but the two guards were broad and practiced. They dropped him into a heavy chair bolted to the stone floor. His wrists were shackled to the arms. His heart thundered as if trying to escape the cage of his ribs.

One of the guards, the one with several bronze earrings, bent to look Keplan in the eye. "What is your purpose, son of Mirik?"

Mirik? They still don't believe me? "I have never been to Mirik. I am a traveler from the south." A misunderstanding, a perceived small crime, those were easy to rectify. This was different. He heard the other guard moving about behind him, and he craned his neck to see. The man laid out tools that looked like those used to carve wood. *Not wood. My skin.* He glanced down at his shackled right hand, only now seeing it was not scraped, but newly tattooed. The design was a red handprint over his palm. *Enemy. Slave.* Dread was the cold spread of frost in his stomach.

The session was short, and while it brought little pain, there was the promise of much worse. He guessed less than an hour had passed when he was returned to his cell. He did not rise from where the guards dumped him. He curled in on himself, hoping he would wake, and it would be a terrible dream.

CHAPTER FOUR

The 42nd Day of Lleume, 1272
The City of Ceir Athrolan

AN'THOR'S HOBNAILED BOOTS CLACKED against the flagging of his room, the buckles clinking softly in the silence. Outside, the servants' shoes were muffled and the conversations whispered. *As if the queen will recover if her sleep goes undisturbed.* In truth, he wished she would wake. Her eyes had not opened in a week, and hitching gasps replaced her breaths. An'thor knew the signs. A soft knock paused his steps, and he jerked the door open. The queen's lady of honor stood in the hall, trembling hands hidden in the folds of her skirt.

"General, sir. The healer says you should come."

An'thor did not even dare nod. The knot tied around his chest tightened and sank to somewhere beneath the flagging. He followed her to the royal wing in silence. A single, dim lamp lit the royal chambers, where Raven waited. The commander was pale.

"Raven, is she—?"

The commander's glare cut the Ageless man's words short. An'thor ducked under the curtain across the door,

Raven close on his heels. The bed was in the center of the room. Incense fogged the air and, save for the crackle of flames in the hearth, silence reigned. The doctor leaned on the mantle, staring at the fire.

An'thor stepped up to the bedside. The queen was still, her skin yellowed and waxy. Someone had brushed her hair across the pillow in a thin, snowy fan. He laid a hand on hers. "When?"

"Not five minutes ago," the doctor answered.

Raven dropped to his knee in the doorway, jaw clenched as his fist met his brow in a salute.

An'thor ignored the dramatics. "Who else knows?"

"Her Lady of Honor, Countess Fiena of Felden. That is all. Servants gossip, of course, but no one has been in." He wavered for a moment. "And I will say nothing, of course."

"I will expect to see you here tomorrow morning to discuss things further. Send the countess in when you leave." An'thor's gaze did not waver from the queen's face. He finally turned when the curtain's rustle announced the countess's arrival. "Have you told anyone?" When she shook her head he asked again, black eyes pinning her. "Anyone, even your husband?"

"I have not left the room save to fetch you, sir. I met no one in the halls."

"You will keep this from everyone—including family—until I say. I don't have to explain what this will do to the country. Do you understand?"

She nodded, but An'thor crossed the room and gripped her hand, splaying the fingers so the firelight caught the wedding band on her middle finger. "Swear on your country."

"Sir, is this necessary?" the doctor interjected.

An'thor loosened his grip, but only slightly. "You understand me, Countess?"

"I do. I swear on my country, my life and that of my family, I will tell no one." When An'thor released her hand she tipped her head toward the door. "Now if I may go? I haven't seen my family in days."

"Of course."

"What should I tell them, sir?"

An'thor glanced back at the queen's body, half-expecting her to stretch and wave away his dour mood. *Tell them the world has ended because she no longer graces these hills.* "Say the doctor has brought his own nurse to help care for the queen. You've been given leave as thanks for your dedication to the Xain house." An'thor paused, unable to meet her eyes. Alcohol and a century of heartbreak had cauterized his heart, but Fiena was his queen's dear friend. "Thank you for your care of my lady queen, may her spirit rest with those—" his voice faltered. "Good evening, Countess."

When she was gone, An'thor glanced at Raven, and his mouth thinned. The man still kneeled. "Get up."

Raven stared at the flagging. "She was as precious to this kingdom, and to me, as she was to you. Have some mercy."

"You realize we face civil war." An'thor's boots rattled against the stone as he paced from window to hearth and back.

"Write to Daymir, to Brentemir, even." His face twisted in scorn. "You don't still hold hope for Dhoah' Lyne'alea's promise that Athrolan will not fall?"

An'thor jerked his head at the door. "Out. I can't think with your nationalism hanging over my thoughts."

"You're an ass."

"Raven, please, not in front of—"

"She's dead, you fool." Raven lurched to his feet and stalked from the room without another word.

An'thor sank onto the window's broad sill with a ragged sigh. Uncomfortable emptiness filled the room without Tzatia's sharp wit and quiet laughter.

Or her breath.

"I wrote to Alea already, your majesty," he spoke to the air, whatever faint energy was left of his queen. "She never replied. There are no gods, no Laen, no Rakos."

Φ

The 45th Day of the Month of Rainfall, 1272
The City of RoBal, Ban

Stagnant air lay in the bottom of Keplan's cell, but the close space was no longer maddening. Instead, it was a sanctuary. Pain shot through his palm when he felt his face for stubble. His cheeks never boasted a beard like his father's, but it was his only way to judge passing time. Images of Moly, free on the prairie filled, his mind. It was less painful than thoughts of her put to work or imagining his parents searching. *Do they know? Did they search the road to Namus or follow my trail here?*

His empty stomach clenched. He kept careful stock of his injuries thus far, but hunger clouded his thoughts. *Five meals since I arrived. Is that two days or five?* He pressed his bruised face to the cool relief of the stone floor. Faint light under the door showed him two rats hunched at the edge of his plate. Loneliness made him imagine they were the same ones each time.

"That piece looks far too rotted, Aud." He named them after heroes in his father's stories. "There's far better food on the prairie. Seeds and grasses and places to burrow down by the river." He barely recognized his own voice. The scratching of his throat aged his tone. A laugh hitched and bubbled between the words. *If I wasn't mad before, there's no doubt I am now.*

Morose thoughts clattered to a halt as the door jerked open, bringing a flare of torchlight. Weakness made his struggle little more than a jerk of the shoulders. He recognized the gray in one guard's brown eyes, and the other's lock of beaded hair. As much as he tried to force the questioning from his mind, he noted the guards were always the same two. His eyes closed when the belts tightened over his limbs. He hated the weakness, the exhaustion. Each time he planned escape he was met with the same dilemma—in the middle of Ban his pale was a beacon, and all the knowledge in the world could not lend him the strength to run.

"Why are you here?"

"What have you learned?"

"Who are you informing?"

"What are their plans?"

"Why did you ride from the south?"

Keplan understood now they were not seeking the truth. They were seeking a confession. Burning pain followed a blade down his sternum. The world tipped. Roaring blood muffled any other sound. It was as if he stumbled in a dream, but he did not fall into wakefulness.

A city burned, perched on soaring cliffs. Survivors clung to boats, to debris bobbing in the harbor below. Above, the clouds themselves ignited. Keplan searched the ruddy faces and copper eyes. These are the gods. *Wind gnawed his cheeks as he spoke, but it was not his voice, just as his hands and body were not his own. "This is where we end. This is where we must end." Time unraveled before Keplan's fading vision.*

Long grasses and gentle wind brushed his mind. It was silent. Pain still writhed, persistent, into his unconsciousness. Aching pounded the tattered skin of his chest, thumped in his bruised bones.

"Hooves of Faco-il, you killed him."

Rough fingers pawed at the boy's eyelids and he slid back from wherever he had been. The face before him lurched into focus through the bruised skin and blood-laced tears. He met the guard's gaze. *A rel burning to the ground. Mirikin soldiers dancing atop the smoldering wreckage. Receiving commendations from the Lord Interrogator. Pride. Frustration. Terrible dreams of his sister dying in the fire. Honor. Confusion. A storm approaching.*

Keplan's pupils blew wide, and he was promptly sick all over himself. *I don't have a sister.* Somewhere, thunder growled a warning. His eyes found the copper square pinned to the guard's sash. "They killed your sister."

The guard straightened. "Excuse me?"

"The Mirikin took your sister." Clotted blood splattered the floor with the effort of his words. "But I'm not Mirikin. Doing this to me won't fix your dreams." Foreign memories flickered between memories of peace, of pain.

The man with the gray-laced eyes scoffed from his perch on the countertop. "Now he speaks?" Another boom of thunder rolled through the city.

"Quiet." The guard's eyes narrowed on Keplan's for a terrible minute, then he spun away and rummaged through a drawer.

"What're you doing?"

"The rains were over weeks ago."

"Your meaning?"

"I trust my gut, and it's a warning. We are through questioning him." He unclipped the wooden lid of a squat jar and drew a thin stick from a toolkit. *Poison? More pain?* Adrenaline fired up his arms, but it only gave him the strength to strain the straps.

The guard with the light eyes pursed his lips, muscled arms crossed. "The Lord Interrogator will have your hair for this."

"Then let him take it. You know this is a fool's chore. If this boy were a spy, he'd be the worst I know." He dipped the needle on the end of the tool into the pot and spread Keplan's left hand out. His gaze flicked to Kelplan's face, then returned to his task.

Blood and pearls of dark ink followed the pricks of fire across Keplan's palm. His head flopped back onto the hard wood of the chair's headrest. Red blood and green ink dribbled down his wrist from the new handprint on his palm. He did not smile with relief or at the meaning of the new mark, or its irony.

Innocent.

Φ

The 47th Day of The Month of Rainfall, 1272

At least this cell had a window. Keplan followed the pool of sunlight across the earthen floor. Stillness in the wake of agony was its own kind of pleasure. The ache in his chest could not be described as homesickness. It was grief. His mind drifted on the piece of knowledge he earned, rather than inherited: he had power. *I looked that man in the eye, and whatever he saw there stayed his hand.* He did not understand it, not by a league, not yet, but it gave him hope. If he kept his head he might just survive Ban.

The door scraped open, and the guard with the braided hair entered, then shut the door behind himself. His hand rested on a long knife, but he did not draw. He would recognize the large, dark eyes for the rest of his life.

"What are you doing?" Keplan's weakened heart thrummed against his ribs, loud enough the man must have heard. His mind screamed at him to fight back, but the guard was armed. *And he hasn't been starved for days.*

"How did you know?"

The question lit something in Keplan's mind, something too hot to be fear, too large to be anger. *How did I know?* "I just did." He swallowed hard. "I know things. Nothing useful. You said yourself I'm not a spy."

"Then what are you doing here? Pale boy, in the middle of war? That's got to be the worst mistake you've made." His tone was not friendly, but curious. "My mother was in the war. The Gods' War. I know the gods are dead." It was his turn to swallow. His eyes darkened, hand relaxing its grip around his knife. "What you said made me wonder, though, if that were true."

"I'm not a god." If Keplan were on level with the man, he would have rolled his eyes. He only dared a sigh. "I'm just a madman."

The guard did not answer. Instead, he tossed a woven sack on the floor between them.

"Put that on."

"Why?" It did not seem like death was imminent, but Keplan was in no mood to gamble.

"I don't care what you are, cursed or touched or something else entirely. But I'm not having it on my head."

Something burned in the man's eyes, but it was not hate. Keplan would not even say it was fear. Keplan hauled himself to his feet and pulled the sack over his pounding head. The two days since his ordeal did much for his spirits, but walking was a chore. Locks clunked, and the door creaked open. Dry hands twisted both arms behind him and guided him out. A stumbling march up two flights of stairs and a winding path through a cool, still hall brought them into a muggy space that smelled of dust and urine. The bustle of the streets was strange after the peace of the forest and the cloying stillness of the cell.

The first step was faltering, sunbaked brown clay burning Keplan's tender feet. Shouts arced through the crowd. Slapping sandals beat dust from the red road. Thundering hooves sent Keplan cowering, but the guard's hands tugged him forward. Cooking meat and overripe fruit overpowered the baking smell of the prairie grasses. The guard was quiet for the twenty minute walk, speaking only to warn Keplan of a stair, or swear at a poorly driven cart. After several minutes, neighing and bustle replaced the clamor.

Someone tugged the sack, from his face and stinging sunlight flooded his eyes. They stood in a stableyard, tucked in the shadow of the looming palace. The guard and another man conversed just out of earshot.

Run. Trembling legs told him he would only make it to the street before someone caught him. The sun was almost at its zenith, and he had lost all concept of east or west. The short walk taxed him enough. He already knew that a single false step would at least send him straight back to the interrogation room. *More likely I'd be killed.* He lowered his head, colored palms tucked close to his body, and tried to get his bearings. The massive mound of the city dropped away to the right. Roads switch-backed up the red earth. Slatted wooden rooftops and brightly dyed silks were an apron around the crooked towers and bridges of the tiered palace behind him. It was as if the city climbed to the clouds. Keplan was impressed in spite of himself. *Whatever their customs, this is beautiful.* RoBal was stunning as it was cruel. Gold and crimson opulence dripped from the hungry, grandeur built over suffering.

Shrieking of an angry horse shattered his thoughts. As much as he loved Moly, the creature in the stableyard was wind made into flesh. Banis horses were a legend, one his father mentioned often. Their build was closer to that of the prairie gazelle, and their dorsal stripes and markings seemed like royal signets. His heart twisted at the thought of his pony. He missed her mutter and the tickle of her coarse whiskers.

"Come on, we'll get you sorted."

Keplan whirled, dizziness clouding his vision at the movement. The other man held a hand out. He was of middle years, and his stable uniform bore an insignia on the chest. The interrogator had already disappeared back into the street.

He caught Keplan's glance back to the street. "I wouldn't. Come talk with me, and I can get you fed and clothed." He gestured to an office built between the stable's two broad aisles.

Even if I made it out of the city, I have weeks of travel on foot. He had no horse, no clothes, and no food. His body ached, and desperation gnawed at his bones. This was a better chance than any he could have planned. The adrenaline drained from his limbs, and he staggered into the office.

The stable master settled himself behind a broad desk and motioned for Keplan to take the chair across from him. He did not speak for a moment, taking in every inch of the false stable boy before him.

Keplan forced himself to keep the man's gaze. If he was someone who believed in luck, or anything at all, he would have prayed.

"The filth will wash away, but you look starved. And we'll have to do something about your hands and the Kisses."

Keplan frowned. "Kisses?"

"The marks on your face. We call them Interrogator's Kisses."

Keplan looked down at his palms. "But green means I'm innocent."

The man sat back with a snort. "You must know by now 'guilty' and 'innocent' are meaningless here. Everything is at the discretion of the Interrogator. Green simply means they've released you. We'll find you gloves."

"Sir, I'm sorry, but why am I here?"

"You will work for me. I don't know what you said to my nephew, but he was adamant. I don't often take released prisoners, but we have a few indentured. You will work for me for six weeks. In return, you will receive clothes, a place to sleep. Food. After you have served your time, should you wish to stay, you will be given wages."

Keplan stared at his bare feet. The offer seemed too simple, too perfect. "The last man—other than your nephew—that showed me kindness bled out into his own hearth."

"I'm not showing you kindness. The care of our horses costs much. I'd rather not spend more on labor than I must. You're doing me a favor in exchange for your life." The words were hard, but his eyes were steady and soft.

He's kind. Keplan forced words through his abruptly tight throat. "Aren't you afraid I'll run? That I'll escape?"

The stable master's mouth thinned, but his displeasure did not seem directed at Keplan. "No one escapes." He briskly drew out a wax tablet. "You'll find clean, suitable clothing in the room beside the bathhouse, which you will visit first. The yellow shelves should suit if you fasten the sash tight enough. You'll be a mucker, and only handle the drafts in the evenings." He etched a few more marks onto the tablet before brushing ink over the wax and pressed a thin piece of cloth over it. After a moment he drew the cloth off and passed it to Keplan. "Read and sign, please."

Keplan glanced at the symbols. They were curled and riddled with hard stops. "Would you mind reading this?"

"You cannot read Banis?"

"Only speak it. My father knew some but had never learned to read it himself."

"You speak it well, for a foreigner." He peered at the paper and read the words aloud. It reiterated the details of the contract with set dates. "Any questions?"

Keplan signed where he was told. "Only one. What happens to the horses of those taken by the Lord Interrogator?"

"Ah." The stable master's expression closed. "If you give me a description, I'll do my best."

"A mare—a barbarian mare—red roan and old. She's just over 14 hands of stubbornness with tufted ears and nose. Her name is Moly."

The man jotted down the description, glancing up at Keplan when he was through. "Anything else?"

"Why are you doing this?"

"This city is complicated." He pulled a cord hanging on the wall behind him. A gong rang outside.

A moment later a boy not much younger than Keplan himself stepped through the door. "Afternoon, sir."

"Afternoon, Fer-hil. I have a new mucker here who needs to get washed and outfitted. I trust you can show him to the bathhouse and then to the stock-shelves? He will need gloves."

The boy frowned, tucking a loose strand of black hair behind his ear. "He's a barbarian, sir."

"Fer-hil, I do not pay you to be either political or rude." The stable master had already turned to a pile of scrolls awaiting his attention.

"I'm sorry, sir. I'll show him about."

Keplan pushed himself to his feet, suddenly conscious of his bare chest and legs. He followed the silent Fer-hil down the broad aisle. Keplan caught a few curious stares, but nothing that made his skin itch with fear. The entire building smelled of horse sweat, leather and grasses. It was a safe smell, Keplan decided. Still, the longer he stayed in the city, he could not shake the feeling he was crawling down the gullet of a beast.

"Are you even listening?"

Keplan glanced over and realized Fer-hil had been speaking. "I'm sorry, it's a very impressive stable. What did you say?"

"I'll take you to get your bath and uniform first, then we'll talk about the schedule. It's still early enough we have time before the afternoon rides. Most of the rich folk go for a jaunt after they have lunch, and the stable is busier than a brothel at midnight."

Keplan frowned at the analogy, but did not comment. The long, low barracks hall ran along the rearmost wall of the stable, like an afterthought. The bathhouse sat at the end.

"I'll wait out here." Fer-hil settled on the floor and pulled a set of game tiles from his shirt.

Keplan ducked into the dim bathhouse, blinking in the humid, scented air. Brown stone slabs covered the floor surrounding the yellow tiled bath. Oily lanterns hung, unlit, from the low ceiling. Keplan stripped off his tattered loincloth and plunged into the warm water. He kept his still-tender right hand as dry as he was able and took stock of his other injuries. Scabs covered all but the shallow line down his sternum. A few were angry and ached with heat, but none oozed with infection. *A small mercy.* He allowed himself a moment to drift in the comfort, swallowing his relief past the lump in his throat. Only when the blood was gone from his matted hair did he haul himself from the water.

He dried quickly and peered through the door. Fer-hil appeared to be losing his solitary game. "I'm done."

The boy glanced up. "You really are pale."

Keplan looked away, embarrassment burning on his cheeks. His own nudity did not bother him, but without the layer of dust and grime, his wounds and emaciation were a stark reminder.

A narrow room beside the bathhouse was seemingly comprised only of shelves. Fer-hil paced up and down a few times, shooting a critical glance at Keplan's body. "Start with these." He tugged a pair of knee-high sandals from a low shelf and tossed them over.

Keplan held them up. The shins and toes were reinforced with wood, held against his skin with leather straps. Manic laughter bubbled from his chest at the thought of sauntering through the stables naked save for a pair of boots.

Fer-hil looked over and finally cracked a grin of his own. "There's more to the uniform." A loose brown tunic joined the sandals, and Fer-hil found a red sash that would denote Keplan's status.

Keplan cinched his pocketed leather work belt a bit tighter and caught a glimpse of himself in the copper mirror by the door. The face that stared back was unrecognizable. Something burned deep in the ice-chip blue of his eyes, and it seared his gut. He shook himself and stepped quickly out into the hall. "Did I forget anything?"

Fer-hil stepped back to give his uniform a cursory glance. "Seems fine to me." He jerked his head at the curtained doors of the barracks. "You'll get one of these later. We get up at dawn, dress and eat in the mess hall across from our rooms. Slaves take away the night soil, but we tidy our own space. We take rolling lunches—a third of the muckers and stable hands at a time, so the stable is never left untended. You'll be in the third group with me."

Fer-hil frowned suddenly. "Where are you from?"

Keplan's heart thundered into panic. *Why are you here? Where are you from?* "The south. In the forest. The Hartland."

"You're not Mirikin?"

"No. Never even seen it."

The other boy hummed in response.

Keplan pointed vaguely up the aisle, desperate to change the conversation. "What are our duties?"

He barely listened as Fer-hil detailed the mucking in the mornings. Keplan knew how to clean a stable. The only part that seemed complicated was the afternoon handling requests for renting draft animals. Like the rest of the city, everything was built of wood and leather. There was no metal, not even in the hooks for the horses' harnesses. Two main halls connected with the lower one that housed the drafts. *Four hundred horses. Maybe more.* He hoped, if Moly had been taken, she was in a stable half as nice as this.

Keplan stared at the warren of halls. This was not the life he wanted. This was not how he pictured leaving home. *One step at a time.*

CHAPTER FIVE

The 2nd Day of Flureme, 1272
The City of RoBal, Ban

IT WAS WARM IN the barracks. The winds and rain of winter had finally dissipated, with the exception of the sudden storm two days before. Rih eyed the square of light on her wall. It was just below the darker board halfway to the ceiling from her top bunk. *Almost time for breakfast.* She rarely joined the other soldiers in their mess hall. The atmosphere was too close, and keeping track of even one conversation was exhausting.

She rose with a soft breath and stretched, shoulders popping as she rolled them. Finally, she shucked off her blankets and swung herself off the bunk. She landed easily. Though her muscles were stiff, she was strong, and the warm weather did wonders. She grinned as she jogged, naked, through the halls. Morning was one time she had no need to make excuses or find an interpreter. She was gloriously alone.

The bathhouse was empty, save for the afternoon training master. The older woman stood before the broad copper mirror, peering into a cleared space on the fog-hidden metal. She scraped a straight razor over her scalp. Wiry gray hairs dusted her shoulders and the tiles around her broad feet.

Her eyes met Rih's in the mirror, and she lifted the razor to nod good morning.

Rih signed a greeting, punctuating the gesture with a brief smile. Il-fald was her favorite of the trainers, a woman she hoped to one day become. *Perhaps by the time I'm old enough, another will have ascended the Holy Emerald Throne of Emperor and the empire will have changed.*

She shoved the private wish into the tiny, secret place of her heart before sliding into the hot water. It was a luxury to bathe twice a day, and she knew it, but there was no better way to awaken her body. Sudden waves lapped at her back, and she turned to see who had entered the pool.

Il-fald smiled and dunked her hair-covered shoulders into the clean water.

Rih wrinkled her nose playfully and made a show of escaping the floating clippings. She flicked a finger up her right jaw. "That's disgusting."

The training master tilted her head back, shoulders shaking with mirth. Even with just the two of them, the room's tiles reflected and altered what little Rih could hear.

"Will we practice the staff today?"

Il-fald shook her head and flicked her wrist. "Atlatl."

"I'll practice before then," Rih promised. After a quick scrub she stepped out of the bath and moved to the adjoining dressing room. Atlatl was her favorite weapon, but not one at which she excelled. If she was ever going to become proficient enough to train anyone older than a child, she would have to learn.

The training court was deserted for another hour until the morning training began. Rih would rather stay for the entire day. She felt the twang in the atlatl's supple wood when she released a dart properly. The darts were of two sizes — the standard hunting darts and the larger, heavier war darts. Her body was lean and long. At twenty, she already reached close to two paces in height. Still, her range on the hunting darts was poor, and her control of the war darts was laughable.

She collected a quiver of each and went to stand at the throwing line before the central target. Her back straightened out of habit, her shoulders rolling back and her eyes closing. She drew a breath and cleared the dark thoughts. *A warrior has a single mind. She wakes for the Empire. She rides for the Empire. Her blood and heart and mind are Ban, breathing and alive. A warrior has a single mind.* When the litany was through, her spirit was steady and her hands sure.

She settled one of the war darts into the notch at the end of the atlatl. Most soldiers started with the lighter missiles to warm their muscles, but Rih preferred the foundation of strength the heavier ones provided. Her hand curled around the handle, forefinger and thumb steadying the dart as she drew her arm back. Her left arm rose, guiding her sight to the center of the target. Warm air filled her lungs as she twisted. Her arm coiled past her shoulder, loose and smooth until the last moment when her wrist tightened, launching the bolt into the air. It was a clean throw, the wood passing through the target's edge and skittering over the ground behind for several paces.

She raised the next dart, but a hand pressed against her shoulder. She suppressed a gasp and turned. Enif raised a hand. She was a palace guard of middle years, tall and with an angled face. "You're summoned to the palace where you will be honored by His Eminence's presence." Her fingers were deft, and she knew most of Rih's signs, as several of the Emperor's male cousins were also born unable to hear, either completely, or, like Rih, only under the most ideal circumstances.

Rih watched the lines on the interpreter's face, hoping for any clue as to the nature of the request. Nothing. She had not made it so far in the palace by being careless. "Is he angry?"

The guard pursed her lips. "Always."

Rih would have smiled, had it been a joke. Instead, she drew another breath. Most of the emperor's many children were brought before him yearly. This was several months too early. No amount of reciting the Woman's Code would prepare her for a meeting with the Emperor. She put the atlatl and darts away and followed the interpreter at a jog. Her tassets tapped against her legs, and she was glad she donned her full uniform early, instead of practice clothes. *This will present better before His Eminence.* She momentarily wished she could wear the silk-bordered cap of an officer, carrying her head high under the weight of duty. *Perhaps then I would be taken seriously.* She scoffed at that thought, as well.

A woman was never taken seriously.

The road sloped up to the massive arched doors. The city was picked out in the reds and browns of the earth from which it was built, but the palace itself was a vicious green sore at the capital's peak. Green tiles and verdigre decorated the doorway. A winged horse leapt with emerald coat and hooves across the black jungle wood of the door. Enif's mouth moved, but Rih's angle was poor. The other guards seemed to understand, however, and stepped aside to let them pass.

The palace was a warren Rih never understood. She seemed to take a different route to the throne room each year. This time they took a winding stairway she was certain she had never seen. The windows were open to the air, save for a picture made of colored glass suspended in the center of the opening. The grandeur was sickening. Enif led her down a dark, richly painted hall and to a set of double doors made of the same dark wood as those at the main entrance. These, however, were emblazoned with the emperor's crest.

This is his personal receiving room. Rih heard the room beyond was filled with more riches than all of Ban combined. She straightened her shoulders and lowered her eyes, waiting for the press of the guard's hand on her elbow before she stepped through. The floor trembled when the doors shut behind her. She knelt, hands spread on her bare knees. She never caught more than a glimpse of the emperor—it was forbidden for someone not of the court to look higher than his jeweled feet.

Her eyes found the copper surface of the gong at the foot of his dais, however. In the gleaming metal, his image was reflected from the mirrored surface of the doors behind her. He was a warped sea of jade and emerald silks and golden jewelry. The black draping his shoulders told her his long hair was down.

Enif reminded the emperor which soldier stood before him and began to sign his words to Rih. "We have allowed you to entertain the role as soldier for these years, but the farce has gone on long enough. You are unable to be a proper soldier, and you are useless to the army. If anything, you are a liability."

Rih's face flamed with anger. *Useless? I've patrolled. I brought in that Mirikin boy. My tracking is some of the best in the army.* "I've bled for you!"

Enif laid a hand on Rih's knee, gaze piercing the younger woman's. She shook her head. Even though the words were Rih's, the punishment would fall on them both. "The Mirikin barbarians might consider a treaty to avoid war. Though defeating them on the battlefield would be easy, treaties look better to our Athrolani neighbors. You are my blood. You will be the bride in this peace marriage."

Rih's shoulders slumped. *No.* Before, he never acknowledged he sired her. *Along with a quarter of the officers and court women.* It was no coincidence so many bore the same striking high and wide nose of the emperor himself. "I don't know anything about court," she argued, forcing her trembling hands to form the words, "let alone the court of a foreign kingdom."

The guard grabbed her hand to halt the tirade. "You cannot speak, so you cannot betray Ban by telling secrets."

Rih's stomach heaved, then tightened somewhere near her lungs. She was just a tool, a replaceable factor in a very long equation. The lowest soldiers were always female, for women were disposable. This was different. She did not watch whatever the interpreter signed for the Emperor's closing statement. Her tiny, silent world curled tighter on itself. In Ban she had people who understood her language. In a barbarian country she would have nothing. She did not even know enough of their tongue to read their mouths.

Φ

The 5th Day of Flureme, 1272
The City of Mirik

The wind off the sea bore too many teeth for summer, but its bluster was now mostly show. Brentemir shrugged deeper into his cloak with a sigh. Twenty years ago his body would not have noticed the change in weather. *Now I run for the hearth at the balmiest of winds.* He leaned on the ramparts, eyes narrowed on the open ocean to the west. The island of La'yne still glowered across the channel, its shores barren. He refused to meet the caverns in its black cliffs that seemed like the isle's eyes.

War. He had avoided it for twenty achingly beautiful years. Now it slavered at his doorstep again. He scraped a hand through the stiff gray-brown of his receding hair.

"Pa, the steward says there's a warrior here to see you." The young man was as tall as Bren, with a slighter build.

Bren glanced over his shoulder. "Can it wait, Al?"

Alleanthus shrugged and jogged up the remaining steps to lean on the wall beside his father. "Is it the war?"

"I'm not ready to go back to that life."

"You're an ambassador, not the Military Commissioner. You don't have to."

Bren laughed softly. "You were always as direct as your mother."

"Don't call her that."

Bren's mouth tightened, but he allowed the retort. "I don't fear war just because I think I'll be called back. I know I won't. Your Ma will do fine. War destroys things, things you don't see or miss until it's far too late to reclaim them."

"If I wanted dark thoughts I would have written to An'thor."

Bren snorted wryly. "Insolent boy."

"Old man."

Bren smiled at the familiar banter. "Where's your brother?"

"Training. He's got it into his head he'll be champion at the head of an army."

"Toar, I never should have read you both those legends."

"I doubt it was the legends in the books that inspired him." Alleanthus leveled his dark eyes on Bren. "It's the ones you lived." He shoved off of the wall with a sigh and ran a hand through his thick black hair, his fingers echoing the path of his father's. "Best not keep them waiting."

Bren followed his son down into the modest manor. "When Azimir's through with training I want to see both of you over lunch." He waited until the young man had disappeared before stepping into the study. The light was stark, but strong. He smiled at the warrior perched on the window sill. "I wondered if it was you."

Reka answered his tight embrace with her wiry arms. "And I wonder if you're mad. Last summer in Athrolan you seemed set on peace." Her eyes, one dark, one clouded, narrowed on his gray ones when he finally pulled away. "I leave Mirik for two months, and you start a war."

"I didn't start this one. And it's been five. Azimir is almost sixteen."

Her features softened for a moment. "Are they well?"

"Yes, though you don't seem to care." As long as they were trading barbs, he would start their old argument again.

"Bren, they're your children, and the children of your wife, even if she couldn't birth them. I only bore them for her. I care about them because you do, but I'm not their mother." She slid off the window sill and sank into the chair across the desk from his. "Please, I'm not interested in this argument. I actually came to bring news."

"From Athrolan?" Bren shucked off his cloak and propped his head on his clasped hands.

"Partly. I'm hungry, though."

"Toar, of course." When Bren had ordered food for her and drinks for them both, he returned to his desk, a battered officer's log open before him. He maintained an extensive intelligence network, many branches of which were unaware of others. Reka would always be the best of his officers, though she hated her title of Spy Master.

"Athrolan's shifting. The queen's illness changed things. There's violence and darkness on those streets I haven't seen before. I have a theory, but it is just a shadow."

She fingered the faded butterfly tattoo on her scarred nose. "I think Tzatia is dead."

Bren gaped at her, dark brows advancing on his graying hair. "You can't be serious. She wrote me just two weeks ago. It wasn't as keen as her usual letters, but she's weak. Surely we'd know if the city was suddenly grieving."

"Bren, I don't think the city knows either."

He sat back, arms crossed over his chest. "Explain yourself."

"I saw An'thoriend often. He is a drinker, but his habit is usually nursed in privacy. It was late in the evening, close to midnight. The queen's Maid of Honor—the one attending her night and day for weeks—was dismissed. She looked frightened, not worried. Not even an hour later, An'thoriend emerged. He was drunk and weeping. He sat on the stoop of the Royal mausoleum until close to dawn."

"And that told you Her Majesty had passed? I think An'thor just fears it. From what little he shared, they are quite close."

"Brentemir, you pay me to understand people, to see into their minds without a single word shared. Trust me, what I saw was not fear, not anxiety, but cold, fathomless grief."

Bren frowned at his log, thin lips twisted. He did not look up when Reka's meal was brought, or when his serving man delivered a steaming mug of tea. "I hoped they would back us," he finally murmured.

"In a war against Ban? They will be pressed to stop civil war, let alone a pretentious argument over another man's business."

"Slavery is not another man's business."

"When you blunder in and kill most of the people who are slaves, it should be. But you and I will never agree on politics."

Bren smiled at the softness in her eyes. "I'm glad you keep me focused. I never could do this without your friendship. You said 'partly,' do you bring news from Ban?"

"No, and I won't until Yun reports back. He's already three weeks overdue, and I fear the worst. I bring news from the south."

"South?"

Reka put her fork down and leaned forward, her eyes holding his unwaveringly. "Bren, I think I found them."

Bren wordlessly reached into his desk drawer and poured a generous portion of wraith into his tea. He took two deep sips before meeting her eyes. His heart hammered with something between betrayal and relief. "You 'think.' If you say you found Alea, you damn well better have spoken to her yourself, or I'll never believe it. You've thought you found them twice before. My heart can't take another."

"This time I'm certain, Bren."

"Where?"

"There's a village a day's ride from the Hartland. Townsfolk mentioned a man who trades with them a few times a year. I waited for weeks, but he finally arrived. I did not speak to him, but I saw him. It's Arman. He seemed healthy and happy. Old, like the lot of us. He shared banter with several shop-keeps. He bought a beautiful pin, one fit for a woman with gray eyes."

Bren scrubbed his face with his shaking hands. *Twenty years. Twenty years without her and now I've finally found her.* His pulse clattered in his neck. "Toar, she's alive. After so much time I had started to fear...."

"There's more." Reka's mouth curled. "They have a child, and he's on his way to Athrolan."

Φ

The 7th Day of Flureme, 1272
The City of RoBal, Ban

Keplan was already late to breakfast. He hoped to avoid the ordeal all together, but going without food until the afternoon made him irritable and fog-minded. Now he risked making a spectacle of himself by entering late. The din was caustic. Boys from ten to eighteen shouted over each other. Insults and jokes were tossed with food and coins to pay up bets from the week before.

Keplan edged up to the table. Several bowls held honey-covered fruit and oats. Two vats steamed with porridge, and another held a thick tan substance that many of the hands and muckers drank by the mugful. He collected a small portion of everything onto a wooden tray before finding a quiet table. He knew better than to try and find Fer-hil in the chaos. The boy was his guide, not a friend. The table's other occupants glanced at him, but said nothing and returned to their rapid conversation. He wondered briefly if he would get lonely. It was a familiar, but comfortable emotion after growing up alone. Now he was too focused on surviving the next few weeks.

Peppery spice followed each bite of the sweet fruit, and the plain porridge reminded him of the kind his mother cooked in winter. He wiped fruit juice from his chin and pushed the tray away. Confident they took no notice of him, he watched the boys carousing at the end of the table. They were mostly muckers, and their hair was long, like his, braided or held back in wooden and leather clasps. His eyes found the wide ones of the current speaker.

A family of close to a dozen children, raised on a farm. Hot days spent on the prairie, evenings by a river. Too poor for any masters' craft training, save for the eldest boy. Five sisters, all sent to the military or neglectful marriages. He loved the stables, the loud boys like his family, and the importance of working with horses in the capital. He had dreams to travel to the rainforest in the southwest as a horse trader.

Keplan's head ached at the barrage of information. His trembling hands spilled the thick drink as he bent to take a sip. Sweet butter rolled over his tongue, replacing foreign memories with those of Hi-taln's rel. *Somehow, I can see their lives.*

His own childhood was spent learning survival, history, and legends from his father. His mother taught him nature, politics and economics. Neither mentioned anyone having such an ability. He stumbled on a second realization. *They never discussed their own past.* He knew the antics of his father's childhood friends, the names of his mother's sisters and brothers, but nothing about how they met, or when, or anything of their adult lives before his birth. *Who were you?*

A distant gong rang. He scrambled up, discarding dishes and tray on the stack by the door before grabbing his pitchfork. He preferred to be early, to pick his hall before the others. It gave him the illusion of control. He opened the first stall, blocking the door with his barrow before stepping inside. "Hello there," he murmured to the horse within. Like their people, the Banis mounts stood impossibly tall and proud. This one had a cream coat, her markings a warm beige. She muttered at him and shifted the weight on her rear hooves.

Accepting that as a "good morning," he set about his work. He told her about his breakfast and a story about Moly. He continued down the line, stalls emptying as the morning wore on. The gong for third lunch startled him from his discussion of the weather with a placid brown draft.

Lunch was similar fare as breakfast, cold fowl stew replacing the porridge. By the time the sun hung low over the city, staining the walls of the stable red, his body ached and his mind sputtered with exhaustion. Supper was disinteresting, and he ate little before slipping off to the bathhouse. Most of the boys had yet to return from their meals, and he had the baths to himself. It took the past few days to fully work the mats and blood from his hair. He took cursory stock of his wounds, as he did every time. Scabs were becoming dry, preparing for scar tissue. Hooked marks on his cheeks stiffened his expressions.

Before the others arrived, he was tucked in the curtained sanctuary of his room. The hammock in the corner was comfortable, and he lay watching the candle on the shelf beside his head.

"Oi, anyone seen my tunic? I lost it days ago." The voice drifted over the curtained walls, answered by a series of puzzled or disinterested negatives.

Keplan grinned, hoping the banter would keep him awake. Exhaustion dragged at his eyelids, but nightmares were only a matter of time. He sat up after several precarious moments drifting on the edge of consciousness. When he struggled to sleep as a child, his father would play tiles with him by the hearth.

"If you win, you can stay up." Keplan always won the first two games, but at the third Arman would try moves that Keplan had never been taught and invariably beat his son in the game.

Keplan's eyes fell on the broad woven slats of wood that made up his wall. A piece was loose in one corner. He slid off the hammock and bent the strip away. His knife was in the Lord Interrogator's drawer, but the edge of the shelf made a decent fulcrum over which to break the strip. In a minute he had the 17 pieces of a basic tiles game. The pin from his sash scratched the symbols and soot from his candle turned them black.

He lay back in his hammock, pieces laid out haphazardly on his thin chest. He was asleep by the third game.

Φ

"Ah, that's a good move." Keplan's eyes narrowed on the tiles spread across a bare path of floor among the stray. "Someday you'll have to tell me where you learned to play so well."

The horse puffed air at him as if in promise.

"Of course, you must have studied hard. It would be difficult to play with hooves." He slid a tile over and tapped another. "I've got you in four counts if you're not careful."

A whistle shot down the hall, and the horse's head popped up, ears flicking forward. She was on her feet in a moment, dark hooves scattering the carefully laid game Keplan had played by himself for the last half hour of lunch.

"That's a dirty trick." Keplan pocketed the tiles and rubbed a gentle hand down the horse's neck. "I'll get you for it tomorrow." He ducked out of the stall and jogged down the hall. He was supposed to meet Fer-hil at the lower halls.

Sure enough, the boy leaned against a door in the main hall. His brows curled together as Keplan approached. "You were supposed to be here a minute ago."

Keplan ducked his head. "I'm sorry, I got caught up in a game of tiles."

The boy's eyes brightened. "I didn't know you played. Most barbarians don't." His expression faltered at the slur, but he did not apologize.

Keplan ignored it. Being called "barbarian" was a small price to pay for conversation. "I'm not a master, but I enjoy it." He hoped for an invitation to the games the other muckers and stable hands began in the dining hall after supper, but again, none came. "You are teaching me about the drafts?"

Fer-hil jerked his head and took off at a jog. One of the side halls led out to the east of the stable. The double doors were smaller and plainer than those in the main courtyard. Racks of painted wooden beads hung against one wall. Most were slid to the side, but others had been arranged carefully in some pattern Keplan could not decipher. "Are these codes?"

"They're requests. Someone will come in and slide the beads explaining how many drafts they need, for what, when, and for how long. They ring a gong, and one of us will come to check. We collect payment upon their arrival."

"No one ever steals them?"

"Horse-thieving is punishable by torture and slavery. Few have been so foolish."

Keplan's shoulders tightened at the thought. He glanced over to see if Fer-hil had noticed. The other boy's eyes were fixed on the beads. "Looks like we've got a request coming in shortly." He took a stone disk from his belt and hung it on a peg above the rack he indicated. "This shows that I'm taking care of this specific request. It can be competitive since most of the renters tip well."

He pointed to the colored beads. "Can you figure out what this says?"

"One yellow — one draft. Two red?"

"Pulling a ware's load."

"Two plain — this afternoon?"

"Yes, morning is one, afternoon is two. Three is tomorrow morning and so forth."

"Four of the green — is that rented for two days?"

"Yes. Follow me, I'll have you harness him up."

Φ

The 20th Day of Flureme, 1272
The City of Ceir Athrolan

"I think we're past the point of claiming this is political, An'thor." Raven glared at the locked door of queen's bedchamber. "This is sick and born only of your own selfish ties."

An'thor glared at the other man. "You were worse when Eras died."

Raven's face twisted into an ugly sneer. "She was my lover."

An'thor's brow quirked. "Only sometimes." He brushed a hand over the empty desk before him. They announced the queen's worsening illness the week before. The city knew any day might bring news of her death. "Death and illness can look so similar, but yet the greatest gulf lies between them. Odd that. She has not spoken to her subjects in a month. If I told them today that she was dead, everything would fall into chaos."

"Maybe in your eyes."

"And what do you mean by that?"

"I mean you're on this pathetic search for a murderess' spawn when there is a man of Tzatia's blood who spent thirty years training for the position."

"She disowned him, Raven."

"She was scared."

"And so are we all." An'thor jerked his head at the door. "I'm upholding her last wish."

Raven rolled his eyes. The stress showed in the thinning of his hair at the crown and the white streaks in his formerly dark beard. "Daymir has more support than you realize."

"This fanatic, Peraan?"

"Contact him. Just hear what he has to say," Raven reasoned.

"I have no idea who he is."

"He has influence. Several of the lords—most those who worked closely with Daymir when he was Treasurer—have made it known their swords are for him."

"How many is 'several?'" An'thor's shoulders tensed. Whispers in the city were dangerous. Lords who commanded troops were worse.

"Five at least. And I command the navy."

An'thor's white brows shot up. It was a blatant threat, and one he hoped to never hear. "It won't come to that. Fates, Raven, don't make it come to that."

"Get your head out of your arse, and it won't." The commander slammed the queen's chamber door on his way out.

An'thor slumped against the desk. He thought finding their child would be the most difficult piece of the complicated puzzle Athrolan had become. Putting down dissenters was not what he wanted, but he could handle the task. *A war between Athrolan's navy and army would rip the kingdom apart.*

He checked that the main chamber entrance was locked before going to the bedroom door. Dust already lay thin over the sigil. He wiped it carefully clean. Over-sweet rot drifted from under the door. It was insidious under the thick incense and bowls of dried flowers he placed in the foyer each day. He had wrapped her tightly and dressed her in her best robes. The room was far from the rest of the palace, and her windows faced the forest. His morning ride told him the windows were still shuttered tight. He pressed a hand to the door hiding his gruesome secret.

"I'm sorry, Tzatia. You deserve so much better than this. And you'll receive it, I swear. Just a few days more. You'll have the finest funeral anyone has ever seen."

Inside, he heard the buzz of flies.

Φ

The 25th Day of Flureme, 1272
The City of RoBal, Ban

The clattering gong echoed through the stable. It was the rougher, low sound calling a mucker to tend a draft animal. Keplan propped his pitchfork against the wall and hurried up to the lower entrance to check the request. *Two drafts to pull a military wagon for two days.*

A hand stopped him as he turned to fetch the horses. The soldier was tall, even for a Banis woman, and Keplan stumbled back a few paces. His skin crawled at the sight of her. He preferred an arm's length between them. "Is that your request?"

She jerked her head at something down the road. Her fingers curled, and she tapped her badge, pointed at the sky then made a complicated gesture around her throat.

"Excuse me?"

"The soldier Rih-elte says she will return for the mounts shortly. She needs a harness for both that will fit a flat two-wheeled cart." A youth stood a pace behind the soldier, watching her flicking hands carefully.

"Of course. Right away." Keplan left the courtyard at a jog. His nerves still ignited at the soldiers' shaved heads and brightly wrapped helms. This was only the second time he dealt with them directly, but it was two times too many in his mind. He grabbed harnesses from their hooks and found two of the larger animals, both well fed and alert.

He clipped the animals to the cross-ties in their hall and set about grooming them and settling the harnesses over their worn, striped skin.

Keplan waited outside the lower gate when the soldier returned. He accepted her payment and signaled thanks before rushing from the building. It would be another few minutes before his absence was noticed. His body buzzed with the memory of pain, and his heart seemed determined to crawl up his throat and lodge itself between his clenched teeth.

Large paddocks bordered the rear of the stable, surrounded by high wooden fences. The side of the building there was low, and Keplan easily pulled himself up onto the flat roof. Blazing sun warned of summer's heat. It was far from silent, but the sounds were distant, softened across the rooftops.

He was not given to panic, not before Ban, at least. Now his blood screamed in his veins, every inch of his flesh crowing for movement, to run, to scream, to do something, dammit! His father suffered explosive rages. Once, when Keplan was five, his mother went missing. Though not old enough to understand, he heard rending wood as every chair and table in the house broke and burnt before Arman's fear and anger. She stumbled from the woods close to midnight, shivering and with blank, too-dark eyes.

"I took a walk."

He understood his father's anger better now. The need to go, to move, the surge of energy commanding he break something. He could not stand a world continuing on when so many were broken down to their very souls. His hand groped at the space beside him, searching for Moly's warm flank.

The Hartland and Athrolan seemed a world away. It occurred to him that, were he to die in RoBal, his parents might never know. He scrambled down, stumbling back through the stable.

His fist almost split when he pounded on the stable master's doorframe.

"One moment." A muted conversation wrapped up, and then Hi-et's voice came again after a new mucker emerged from the office. "Enter."

Keplan could not school his hands into stillness or remove the quaking in his voice. "Master Hi-et."

"You look ill." The man gestured at the seat. "Before you fall down, please."

"Forgive my suddenness." He swallowed some of his fear and perched on the chair. "I was wondering how one might send a letter."

"A letter?" Hi-et's glanced at the doorway as if someone might hear. "To whom?"

"My parents. They've not heard from me since I left. I told them I was going to Athrolan. They don't even know where I am."

"I'm sorry, Keplan, but I can't help you."

"What do you mean?" Keplan's stomach was a yawning chasm threatening to swallow him.

"The Lord Interrogator will see it as correspondence to your masters, whoever sent you here. And don't even think about asking me to send it in your stead. You said yourself they killed the last person who showed you kindness."

"But I'm innocent. I work here. That must count toward something. Please." It was hopeless, and he knew Hi-et was right. *I have to try.*

"You are a mucker now and under your gloves you have a green palm proclaiming your innocence." He leaned forward. "But you bear a white face. Your eyes are as blue as King Azirik's himself. And your other hand is red. You may not be a spy, but under the Banis sky, you will always look like one."

Φ

The 30th Day of Flureme, 1272

Summer heat drifted in through the window. It was cooler than outside, but the air was stale. Rih watched the bustle of the courtyard outside the captain's office window with longing. Last year at this time she was returning from the Emperor's Progress March across the nation. Now she waited for the next decree that would further cripple her future. *And outside, my sisters are the wheat before the millstones of war.*

Air wafted past her, heralding a door opening. The captain entered with a nod, followed by a soldier Rih had never met and a woman swathed in silks.

Rih caught the captain's eyes and signed, "What is this?"

The captain motioned for the robed woman to sit. "This is Ki-elte, Mistress of the Hall of the Purple Throne. She is here to take you to your new quarters."

Though the captain tilted her chin so Rih could better make out the spoken words, it still took far more effort than she realized, and often much was mistaken. "I thought I was to remain here until a suitable marriage was arranged."

"I'm sorry," the captain said, switching to signing, "His Eminence has decided you should learn your role as a wife before you are wed."

Fear flooded Rih's mind. *I thought he would forget about me. I thought I would have months, perhaps a year, to prepare myself.* "No."

"I'm sorry." This time the captain used Rih's signs. Her eyes flicked to Ki-elte, and Rih's gaze followed.

"We should leave now, so we have plenty of time to get her settled." Ki-elte spoke quickly, which was not always a problem, but she spoke to the captain, and Rih had trouble deciphering her voiced words.

Rih's fear and anxiety flashed into anger, and she reached out, snapping her fingers before the woman's face. "You will be teaching me. Learn to talk to me, not over my head."

The captain hid a smile and relayed Rih's words to her new tutor. "She's not stupid or touched, Ki-elte. She just cannot hear or speak the way we do."

Rih's anger faded for a moment. It was nice to be defended. She assumed her captain was indifferent to her existence. *Frustrated, if anything.* "May I say goodbye?"

"I don't think you have the time, but if you give me names I'll pass along your farewell."

"Just Il-fald and Jih-alan." Her chest ached. It was like she was a tumor, an infection they neatly excised from the world she inhabited for so long.

"I'll let them know. Gather your things. As of now, you are dismissed from duty." The captain rose, shoulders rolling back, and touched her fingertips to her breastbone. She waved them upward, a salute to an equal. Her dark eyes bore into Rih's, brighter than Rih remembered them ever being.

"Thank you, Captain. It has been an honor." Her feet took her to the barracks. She was aware of Ki-elte beside her. Perhaps the woman tried to speak, to comfort her, but Rih could not bring herself to look at the woman's face. She threw open the chest at the head of her hammock. Most of her belongings were on loan from the army. She tied her few personal things into a bundle and slung it over her shoulder before turning about the room. It was deserted, but she had few enough friends that it did not matter. She closed her eyes, fingered the rough, worn fabric of her hammock, and turned to Ki-elte. The woman's calm face would have looked expressionless to anyone else. Rih caught the tension around her eyes, the clenched jaw.

She did not bother to ask why the woman was worried. *She wouldn't understand me, anyway.* Instead, she jerked her head toward the door and followed her out.

She expected to be brought to the palace, or the hall for dignitarys' wives and daughters. Instead, Ki-elte turned right as they exited the barracks. She expected a male guard, or to be stopped and asked her business. No one even looked at them twice. *With anonymity comes freedom.* The barracks and training halls stood across from the trade markets. Downhill, the lower city was a tangled mass of color and smells. Through the haze of midday, Rih picked out the red clay guard towers looming over the piles of buildings and throngs of people. *Not so much to keep us safe, but to keep the rabble from rising.*

They skirted the edge of the city, winding through the larger buildings of state and commerce. It was not the most direct route, Rih was certain, but the mess of carts and traffic, with war approaching, were easier to avoid than navigate. She glanced at the woman leading her. She afforded her grudging respect—Ki-elte hardly broke a sweat, despite the nearly hour-long walk. A massive building rose before them, the center of a smaller square. Like the others, it was mostly clay and built in rising concentric circles. Instead of the baked red and orange, however, the clay was washed with a deep purple. She collided with Ki-elte's silk-covered shoulder. "Forgive me, I was distracted by the building."

Ki-elte watched her fingers, but looked back to Rih's face and shrugged. "I can't understand your hands. I'm sorry."

Rih slowed her breathing as if preparing to launch a dart. She gestured for them to continue on. Instead of heading toward the women's wing of the Dignitary's Hall, Ki-elte turned into the courtyard of the burgundy building. A small stable curled around one side, and a gilded door led into the bulk of the building. There was no emblem on the larger door or hanging over the arched entrance to the courtyard. There did not need to be. Heavy pungent flowers, undulating tiles on the ground and walls—everywhere Rih caught glimpses of purple. *Hall of the Purple Throne.* Ki-elte pointed toward another door. It, too, was built in a pointed arch, but the pillars and vines afforded some privacy.

Ki-elte pulled two circular keys from her sash and fit them into the large locks on the door. It swung inward, and she stepped aside., gesturing left. "This way."

Stepping through the door was akin to emerging from the cool training hall into summer's heat. Still, warm air brushed Rih's bare arms. Musky jasmine underlay sharp sandalwood, echoed by eucalyptus. Instead of windows, glass sconces shed rich light across the dark draped walls. She followed the woman down the low hallway and up a series of stairways. Each woman they passed nodded to Ki-elte and offered Rih a smile or greeting.

After the third, Rih stopped to stare. Their faces were not lined with soldiers' creases. *Their eyes bear the wisdom this life forces upon us, but their mouths are framed by smiles, their eyes by laughter.* She glanced back to Ki-elte, stopped at the top of the stairs. *Even Ki-elte carries herself differently.* It could have been lack of soldier's training; it could have been the layers of silk wraps and robes. Rih suspected it was something else.

They arrived at a room at the end of the third-floor hall. The rolling silk screen bore wooden lattice and a simple lock.

Ki-elte handed her a silver key hung on a braided purple cord. Rih ran a calloused thumb over the bright metal circle.

"You can read my mouth?"

Rih nodded, though the reality of her actually understanding was more complicated, especially as Ki-elte was not used to accommodating Rih. *We'll start small.* "Yes."

Ki-elte watched her hands and then mimicked the gesture. It was clumsy, but correct. "Yes?"

Rih nodded again.

"Bathe, change, unpack your belongings. I will be by in a few days for your first lesson, but for now, you may adjust in private. Someone will bring you supper at sundown. Clothes and books will arrive tomorrow perhaps. You have a tub, but the bathhouse is downstairs."

Rih twirled a finger, asking her to repeat several phrases. When she was sure she understood, she smiled. "Thank you."

Ki-elte cocked her head. "'Thank you?'"

"Yes."

The other woman smiled. "Good night."

Rih slid the door shut behind her and rotated the lock until she felt something click. The room was dark but boasted a shuttered window. Deep shelves ran along the left wall, flanking a mirror. Behind the desk on the right were empty racks for scrolls and tablets. A straw-filled mattress in the far corner was larger than any she had slept in, since her mother's death. She slumped onto the bed and tucked her face into the soft sheets. Other women might speak her signs, and she hoped to find them soon. It would be a long few months if she could not talk to anyone. The room was still, and the fresh straw of the mattress smelled of freedom.

CHAPTER SIX

The 34th Day of Flureme, 1272
The Forest of the Hartland

DARKNESS WAS SOOTHING, A lack of sensation enveloping Alea's mind. Her lungs billowed silently. Thoughts slid through her mind like a leaf on the surface of a placid pool. This was where she escaped from the war.

A face blossomed from the darkness. It was a woman's, lined with an impossible tangle of wrinkles and scars. Eyes too bright silver to be anything but Laen rolled with madness. "Gods' blood!" The words were furtive, whispered. Her gaze locked with Alea's, and the woman screamed. Her lips cracked, bleeding, as the sound went on and on.

Alea hauled herself out of meditation with a gasp. Sweat drenched her back and chest. Her pulse thundered in her throat. *What was that?* She raked a hand through her graying hair, wincing as chapped fingers caught in a tangle. Only the wind hissing through leaves broke the silence. The house was far, out of shouting distance. The war was distant enough for her to feel safe, even out of earshot. She put a shaking hand to her mouth, wondering if nausea would do more than threaten.

Arman stood at the clearing's edge when she looked up again. "What happened?" Resignation, rather than fear, lined his face. Since Keplan's departure they had spoken little.

"How did you know?"

His features softened, brows relaxing. "It's you. I'll always know." He gestured to the grassy patch under the largest of the beech trees. "May I?" He rarely came to her meditation spot and never entered.

She leaned back against the beech's trunk, nodding. Her limbs were heavy and her eyes ached, but she did not yet trust the darkness when they shut. "I'm afraid, and I hate it."

Arman sighed as he sat before her. His rough palms scratched at her breeches when he placed his hands on her knees. He did not speak, only rubbed circles on her legs with his thumbs.

"I was happy here. It was beautiful and peaceful and ours. Even when Keplan was small it was perfect. I feared for him, but only in the usual ways — I feared he would trip, or find an animal in the woods. I feared he would fall sick. Now I am afraid of everything." She raised her head from the trunk and looked at him. "You were right. We should have told him."

Arman looked down. "I know. But I had just as much a part in his raising." He squeezed her hand. "Are you having dreams, too?"

"Dreams of pain and fear. And every time I see this woman's face."

"Laen?"

"Yes."

"I thought they were all dead."

Alea shrugged, staring at their entwined hands. "I'm not. The world is whole, and yet the winters grow colder, the summers shorter. After the war something powerful and beautiful was supposed to replace the Laen and Rakos, the Gods. I fear I missed something. What if I was supposed to die?"

Arman's hands tightened on hers. "Please don't walk that road again. After the war was terrible. Neither of us knew how to live without fear and pain and running. Please don't go back there." He brushed a strand of hair away from her clammy cheek. "Have you thought about what the woman wants? Does she say anything?"

"She says 'Gods' blood.' Sometimes she says that it's everywhere, or spilled. It doesn't feel like she's damning me or threatening. If anything, it's a warning."

"Gods' blood. In your reading, where did the gods come from?"

"There were as many theories as there were books. The Laen created them. The Rakos created them. They were the children of the Rakos and the Laen." Her eyes met Arman's, silver and gold luminous in the shade of the clearing.

"What if they were right?"

Φ

The 42nd Day of Flureme, 1272
The City of Robal, Ban

"Keplan?" Hi-et's voice cut down the hall.

Keplan glanced up to see the stable master silhouetted against the brightness of the main doorway. "Yessir?"

"When you're through with that request, I need to see you in my office."

"Of course, sir." Perhaps it was the man's refusal to help him send a letter, or maybe the four military requests he filled that day, but his stomach flipped at the words. *What did I do wrong?* He shoved the thought into the back of his mind and headed to the man's office. Keplan hovered in the doorway until the Stable master gestured to the seat across the desk. He forced his legs into stillness as he sat. "What did you need, sir?"

"You know what today is?"

"I believe it's the 42nd day of the month, sir. The final week of Flureme."

He slid a scroll across the desk.

Keplan unrolled it, frowning at the symbols. His gaze fell to the date beside his signature at the bottom. He could read the numbers now. "Oh."

"Your servitude is up, should you wish to leave. We also found your horse. She was set up in a stable in the lower streets. She is thin, but otherwise unharmed."

Keplan stared at his feet. Surviving did not include thinking of freedom.

"Will you stay?"

Keplan glanced up. "I can't. Not here."

"Collect your things, then. Your horse is in the seventh draft hall. You may leave in the morning."

Keplan did not rise right away. "I wish I could have learned about your city in a better way. I feel there are beautiful people and customs."

"There are. Perhaps one day you'll return. Keplan," Hiet's voice stopped the boy on his way through the door, "I had a brother. There was a misunderstanding. He was dragged from our house, and I never saw him again. That is why I agreed to hire you. I don't want more innocent men to meet the same fate."

Keplan looked down. "I'm sorry." When the stable master said no more, Keplan bid him a good night. Excited relief exploded once he turned down the side hall. Sawdust skittered from under his sandals as he took turns too quickly. He stumbled to a halt outside a dim stall. His heart hammered between his ribs.

A familiar gray and red head bobbed over the door. Moly's face was thinner, but she looked healthy. She nosed him once, then again, letting out soft whickers of happiness as she lipped his tunic.

"I missed you too." He swung over the door and wrapped his arms tightly around her neck. "Tomorrow, girl. Tomorrow we'll be out of this place and on the road to Athrolan." Moly must have slobbered on his face because his cheeks were suddenly damp.

Φ

The 47th Day of Flureme, 1272

Dawn broke slowly. Sunlight bloomed through the haze already clouding the horizon. Keplan was awake before the sky was fully light. The hammock creaked as he rose and donned his mucker's uniform. He buckled on his sandals, folded his blanket and pillow. There was nothing to pack. His bag was taken, perhaps destroyed when he was captured. Now his only belongings were borrowed from a man too kind for Ban.

The stable was just coming alive. Night Hands made a final round before bed, extinguishing the dangerous lanterns and unlocking the side doors. Moly's ears perked when he arrived at her stall. He handed her some dried fruit from his pocket and checked her over. "Tomorrow we'll wake in a new place."

She bobbed her head at him, and he smiled before leading her down the hall. The rear door of the stable opened into a dimly lit and poorly guarded area of the city. The road leading past wound down and through the eastern gate. Fer-hil and the other muckers had not considered

Keplan a friend, but it was odd not to say good-bye. Leaving was easier, more joyous, with good-byes, even if it was from a place of pain. *I never said fairwell to my family.* He promised himself he would write when he arrived in Athrolan. "Though what could I possibly tell them?"

Moly snorted and nosed his pocket. He scratched the bristles at her poll. Dawn bleached the sky when he pulled his stiff body onto her back. He did not pause at the gates and nudged her into a trot as he passed the guard house. Something rose in him as he left the city, cracking the thin, numb shell helping him survive. Anger roiled in his chest. Ceir Athrolan was a terrifying unknown, but it was a fear he welcomed.

Keplan stopped to rest Moly often, but there was no way to put the endless waving grasses behind them swiftly enough. Wind that seemed a thoughtful hum when he first emerged from the Hartland was now a sinister hiss. Despite her own weeks of work in the city, Moly was strong and the pace affected her little. The dark band on the horizon became a brown smudge and soon grew into the green tangle of a forest. Left with his one-sided conversation with the mare, Keplan was uncertain which were his own thoughts and which were the strange new memories collecting in the corners of his mind.

The crack of an ax jolted Keplan from his stupor. Moly's ears perked with curiosity. A cluster of sunken houses abutted the dense copse. Raw wooden stakes ringed the village, jutting out at an angle. Keplan shuddered. *Perfect height for riping open the bellies of attacking cavalry.* With the majority of the Banis military consisting of infantry, most cavalry would be an enemy. He counted almost two dozen houses. Cooking meat sparked his hunger into an audible growl, but he could guess the nature of his welcome.

He swallowed hard and glanced about. It was almost dusk. Snares were simple, and Keplan knew how to make a snare and shoot a bow, but he had neither the materials or patience to make them. But a growing man could survive only so long on bruised fruit and dried berries. He urged Moly off the road and into the shelter of the trees to wait until dark.

Birdsongs he recognized rose from the black tree boughs. Lanterns bloomed in the village. Furtive talk and hurried steps told Keplan he must be close to the border. What seemed like an inn at the edge drew his attention. Rough walls encircled the rear yard. *Inns mean trash, trash means food.* He slipped through the crossed stakes and moved along the fence, listening to the pattern of the noises and talk within. Adrenaline stung in his veins at each crunch of soil under his sandals. Music swelled as a group of young men emerged from the inn carrying a drunk companion. Keplan ducked behind the privy. When they stumbled down the street, he edged farther.

Compost filled the corner furthest from the building's door. Most of the food was rotten, but a few fresher pieces dotted the top. He stuffed half an eggplant and a bruised pear into his shirt before the door behind him banged open. He pressed his back against the wall, hoping the shadows would hide him. Newly sawn wood dug into his back, and the scent of spoiled meat threatened to make him sneeze.

A boy stood on the steps, dark eyes wide. After a moment he stepped down. One brown hand gripped a bucket full of scraps. His free hand trembled, raised. "I'm just getting rid of these. I won't tell, just don't hurt me."

Keplan realized he looked like a thief, one much larger than the boy. He cleared anxiety from his throat. "I'm just hungry."

The boy inched closer to dump the bucket over the pile. "There're some good pieces in there, just stay clear of the pork." He peered into the dark, as if waiting for Keplan to emerge, before turning back to the inn. "If you're here in the morning, I'll leave a bag of food by that tree."

Keplan murmured his thanks but waited. No shouts or running feet indicated betrayal. He grabbed what he could and dashed back to the safety of the trees to examine his finds. Spoiled parts were easily pared away, and his red sash made a good sack to hold the leftovers. With the promise of a breakfast in the morning, he settled in for the evening. He curled against the dip between roots and closed his eyes.

A nightbird's warning shriek sent adrenaline burning down his limbs. Then Moly's hoof falls as she grazed shook him awake. He untucked his hands from his chest and removed his gloves to peer at his palms. Moonlight turned the red of the right into a rich purple. The left was still tender in a few places, where the needle pierced too deep. The green ink was nearly black. Both were already marred with callouses. If someone asked, he would have denied thoughts of vengeance.

Φ

Keplan's stomach drove him to the village just before dawn. Gold bled across the wooden slats of the low rooftops. Keplan hung back, crouched where the shadows still clung. The boy emerged. He was younger than Keplan first thought, perhaps twelve. He slipped across the yard and tucked a parcel from beneath his arm into the compost pile.

Just as he turned to leave, Keplan stepped out and raised a hand. "Thank you."

Whatever the boy's response, it was interrupted as the door to the inn swung open.

"I thought you were Banis, Kola-ih." A young man strode down the steps.

Kola-ih's shoulders fell. "He was just hungry."

"Da said he saw a stranger last night. You taking the Mirikin side? Traitors are worse than barbarians. They're not even human." His lilting speech was calm, almost friendly, but his words cut. "You want to be a dog, brother?"

Kola-ih had not moved, save to close his eyes. Now he looked up at Keplan, and his hands fisted. Keplan wanted to grab the food and run, but his feet rooted to the earth. The mocking tone echoed the words of the interrogators and Kola-ih's tiny rebellion burned in Keplan's chest. *That's right. Fight him.*

"You eat like a dog, you're no better than one." Kola-ih's voice was small, but his mouth snarled the words an instant before he leapt forward.

Keplan's eyes widened. This boy showed him kindness. Now his small fists rained on Keplan's head and ribs. His sight darkened. Pounding filled his ears.

A groan drew him back to the confrontation. He crouched in the dirt, the boy's face pressed to the ground, his impossibly bent wrist gripped in Keplan's bony fingers. He blinked and staggered back. The older brother seemed too stunned to act. Keplan ran. A whistle brought Moly racing through the grass. He kept pace with her for a few staggering steps before dragging himself onto her back. It would take minutes for the village to muster. Even if they never gave chase, he held Moly at a run.

Φ

The 1st Day of Lineme, 1272
The City of RoBal, Ban

Footfalls rarely shook the floor. Though Rih could not hear the press of silence, she noted the stillness of the air. At first, she relished the space to stretch and bathe in private. After several days, however, the solitude felt more like isolation. An alcove by the window boasted a wooden tub hidden by a dressing screen. In the army she shaved her head once a week, less if they were on patrol. Now it was every other day, mostly out of boredom. Rih swept up the tiny hairs from that morning and smoothed the coverlet across the surface of the straw-stuffed cotton. The cords of muscle in the small of her back bunched and cramped. Adjusting to a mattress after almost two decades of military hammocks played havoc with her body.

Sunlight through the lattice of the window painted plaid across the ceiling and down the opposite wall. The light warmed her naked skin. Ki-elte would arrive after breakfast, and Rih was unfamiliar with traditional women's clothing. *I am a warrior, not a wife.* She perched on the dressing stool and fingered the silk shift and draping wraps. *My mother made dressing look like a dance.* Each morning Valin-elte would scrape her scalp bald with deft fingers, thread jeweled wires through the half-dozen holes in the shell of her ears and brows and nose. White and lavender, sometimes pink, wraps drifted down on her shoulders like gossamer. *Like wings.* Rih sighed and just donned her kalas.

Ki-elte arrived with a smile and a wooden tray of fruit and yogurt. She set the tray down as she caught Rih's eyes. "I thought our first lesson would be best over food. Are you hungry?"

Rih nodded and sat at the desk—the only surface large enough for two in the small room. She piled her plate high with fruit and took several deep sips of the thick tea. She wished there was time to eat before concentrating on Ki-elte's distracted speech. The tutor had a habit of talking through every action, and it was impossible for Rih not to miss most of the words. Now Ki-elte discussed Rih's outfit, it seemed.

Ki-elte settled in the seat across from Rih and looked up expectantly. "I hope you will teach me some gestures so we might better understand one another."

Rih smiled. The offer seemed genuine, but teaching others her signs was an endeavor. Whatever else the woman had said was a mystery.

Ki-elte winced. "Can you read and write? It would make this easier. I'll try to speak slowly."

Rih pushed her food away with reluctant hands. She found a wax tablet from the desk drawer and carved hasty marks into it.

> *Yes, I can read and write, any soldier can. Long phrases and not seeing your face are worse than speaking quickly. Long speeches are almost impossible. What I speak is a language — not gestures to punctuate speaking, and it will take time.*

Ki-elte's smile faded at the rebuke, but she took the advice. "I'll try my best, and please, stop me when I'm being unclear. Writing will help until I know enough to read your hands." She helped herself to breakfast and settled into the chair across from Rih. "Do you have any questions?"

Rih looked away. She had hundreds. Some she simply did not like the answers to. *I'm here because I'm the smallest liability to the Empire. I will never see my friends, and when this marriage is final, I will never see my home again.* She scratched another line onto the wax, pointing at each word and showing Ki-elte the signs for key words. "You, and the others, you look happy. How can a woman be happy in an empire such as Ban?"

"Perhaps we should start your lesson now." Ki-elte's eyes burned, an expression Rih saw in her training mistress's eyes more than once. "Do you know why you are here?"

Again, Rih wrote and then signed her answer. "Because His Eminence believes I can't hear plots or speak secrets."

"Because we are at war. His Eminence wanted to send one of the women trained here because we understand politics like we breathe air. He considers us well-trained. We consider ourselves soldiers of a different war. The way you dress tells the world something, whatever you wish. Just as armor protects you in battle." She finished her food and pointed at Rih's plate. "If you're through, let's begin."

Rih cleaned the last of the fruit from her plate and tucked it under the others on the tray. As much as Ki-elte tried to liken dressing to armor and battle, Rih hesitated to believe her. *Armor protects against blows, against darts and arrows. There is nothing that protects against words.* She brushed a hand over the shell of her ear. *Not even being deaf to them.*

Ki-elte rummaged through the shelves beside the dressing screen. Often she turned and repeated whatever comment she spoke first into the baskets so Rih could see. Rih refrained from rolling her eyes, but only just. "We'll have to do something...only soldiers lack rings and studs." At Rih's wrinkled nose, Ki-elte laughed. "Just like with clothes, each one means something. We'll find something you like, and you don't have to decide right away." She straightened, a stack of folded silks in her arms. A pile of fine, gleaming chains topped the fabric.

Rih smoothed the front of her kalas. It was longer than her thigh-length soldier's tunic and made from lighter cotton. There were short sleeves, and bright blue bordered each hem. Ki-elte babbled again, and Rih grabbed the tablet.

Show, don't tell me. It might be easier if you write too, unless you are sitting, looking at me.

"Of course, I'm sorry." Despite her distracted energy, she seemed to genuinely want to do better.

The pieces don't change, but the colors you wear say much. Several bright colors make one statement, while shades of a single tone make another. The first implies passion or mirth, the latter control, dedication.

She draped a shorter lavender wrap across Rih's front and back over her shoulders where she fixed it with a pin. The second, gray wrap crossed only one shoulder and folded at the waist to create a pocket before falling to the floor in front and behind. Ki-elte stepped back so Rih could look at herself. "What do you think?"

Rih plucked at the twisted belt holding everything in place and shrugged. *I don't look like a wife either.* She glanced at Ki-elte's gleaming head, stained a deep rose to match the woman's usual color palette. A burgundy silk net stayed in place with delicate chains clipped to the woman's ruby studded earrings, and the weight of the tiny gems hung at the edges. "I like your net." She added extra gestures to help convey her point.

Ki-elte's eyes crinkled at the corners. "I can find you some." She pointed at the outfit. "You like blues?"

"And purple." Rih brushed a hand down the lavender wrap and turned to see how the fabric fell in the back. *I'll snag on everything I walk past in this.* She heaved a sigh.

Ki-elte frowned, began to speak, then wrote instead.

I know this is a change. I'll try to take things as slowly as our time allows. We're also going to meet with one of the ambassadors to learn the politics and customs of the kingdoms you might marry into.

"I thought it would be Mirik?" Rih leaned over to repeat the question in writing.

"Probably. But we aren't certain they'll listen to reason."

Rih winced. "I don't want to marry a barbarian on a salt-stained pauper island. At least our other allies know our tongue." *I don't want to marry at all.* "I want control over something, even if it's only my own body." She didn't bother to write the second half. Sometimes she appreciated the privacy of speaking a language few understood.

Ki-elte gestured for Rih to take a seat by the window, her expression bare of its usual playful smile lines. "I am Mistress of the Hall of the Purple Throne. You know what this is?"

Rih's gesture was rude, borrowed from the barracks, but unmistakable.

"Yes, a brothel. The palace brothel, to be exact. We are paid in amenities, rather than beads so we can keep up this lifestyle." She repeated a few phrases before continuing. "There may be shame in being a woman in Ban, but whores are the best off of all."

Why did they send a Mistress to train me? And one who doesn't even speak my language?

Ki-elte looked down for a moment before meeting Rih's eyes. "You're being traded in negotiations as a wife. I cannot guess to whom, or when, but you will be married. You do understand a woman's role as wife?"

Rih slashed the air with her hand and made the rude gesture again.

"It is unlikely you'll have a choice to bed him."

Rih squeezed her eyes shut. Being sold to a foreign man was frustrating, but she could study another culture, learn to read another language. She could not replace her body. A gentle hand settled on hers.

Compassion brightened Ki-elte's dark eyes, and Rih realized the woman was not much older than she. "I know what you feel. I felt it too. We do not have a choice in this, but you must remember you have power."

Rih rolled her eyes. Her only power now was whether or not she wore a blue robe or red.

"Listen to me." Ki-elte winced at the poorly chosen word. "I'm sorry, I misspoke. I need you to understand. A man might—"

Rih handed her the tablet.

A man might bed whom he wishes, but you will be his wife. You will bear heirs. I will teach you skills to impress him, to control when you bear a child, but more than that, I will teach you how to navigate court, how to manipulate the people around you without them seeing. The Language of colors and dress isn't just to pass the time. The right dress will force people to listen, even if you don't speak.

"Tell me, who rules the people of Ban?" she asked.

"His Eminence," Rih replied.

"Yes. And what rules him?"

"He is as a god here." The answer was one they all memorized as children.

Ki-elte stared out the window for a moment before rising. "I'll bring you a net tomorrow. For now, there is someone you must meet." She nodded toward the door. "We're meeting him in the Lapis Room."

Rih fell into uneasy step behind her teacher. There was something she missed, something between Ki-elte's question and her answer, but she could not place it. Now her fingers trembled with nerves. The Hall's corridors twisted through rooms lit with low screened lanterns, and the heavy scent of flowers clung to the myriad draped silks. Ki-elte paused at the top of a flight of stairs and swung open the heavy door that separated the women's personal quarters from the Hall of the Purple Throne itself. "We are meeting an ambassador. He will help explain fashion and dances of the kingdoms you might marry into."

Rih forced her pace into calm, steady steps, rather than the strides she trained to do in her sleep. Anxiety fluttered high in her stomach. Even the windows were covered with dark blue and lavender silk screens. Each door bore elaborate inlays of specific colors and stones. Ki-elte directed Rih to the Lapis Room.

I could buy enough horses for my entire patrol with the gems on this door and still retire in a palace of my own. Rih shook the dream away and watched Ki-elte unlock the door and slide it aside.

The room beyond was awash with blue silks. A broad bed sat in the center, draped with more curtains and pillows than Rih had seen in her entire life. The window shades were thrown open. Ki-elte's tap on her shoulder brought Rih's attention to the man seated on a shelf beside one of the windows. His face was smooth, but his eyes held a spark that said his patience took effort. His gaze slid over Ki-elte and fixed on Rih. His lips flew into action too quickly for her to catch more than a few words.

She turned away and waved a hand at Ki-elte. Some bothered to learn her gestures in the army, but there her future had not been at stake. Now the isolation tasted bitter in her throat. She remembered the faint condescension in Ki-elte's eyes the week before. A warm hand touched her shoulder, and she turned.

The man lowered his head, dragging her gaze up to his black eyes. "Forgive me. I did not know." He made a few halting signs. "You, I young play." He offered his hands, palm up, in greeting and switched back to voicing. "I am Ambassador Mosil-ten-Ebal, third nephew of His Eminence."

Her eyes narrowed on him. There was something in the thick brows, the angle of his eyes and cheeks that tugged at her memory. *A boy, when my mother still lived in the Women's Wing.* Warmth burst in her chest, swelling out to her fingertips as they flew into action. She could not keep the smile from her lips. "Yes! You were my mother's friend's son," she shrugged, "and, I suppose my cousin."

He raised a hand. "Slowly, please, I am out of practice." He glanced at Ki-elte. Rih realized she must have spoken. "I can understand it, yes, though I speak it poorly." He gestured to the two chairs by the window seat. They did not match the rest of the decor. "Please, both of you, sit. We have much to cover." There was a shadow to his face, something another might have missed.

Rih trained herself to learn how faces changed. It helped when she inevitably missed their spoken words, but, moreover, she found it useful in navigating the complicated Banis hierarchy. "You seem sad."

"I did not know you were the bride I was to brief. It makes this more complicated." Mosil's chest hitched in a laugh Rih could not hear. Though his lips curled up, his eyes were still dull. "Politics make slaves of us all." He turned to include the teacher in their conversation.

Rih took the chair closest to the desk, perched on the edge. As a boy, Mosil was kind, and judging by the lines about his mouth he was a man who still smiled often. "Do you know whom I am to marry?"

"There are two possible matches. One is the son of Ambassador Brentemir Barrackborn—the man descended from Azirik." He paused to clarify the latter to Rih before continuing. "The other option is a man of forty, a son of a wealthy former lord across the island. Of course, both will fall through in the face of outright war."

A shred of hope fluttered in her stomach. "Could I return to my duties as a soldier?"

"If we're at war, we will need allies more than ever. Our eyes will turn to Athrolan perhaps. Maybe Sunam."

"What do you need to teach me?"

"I have books you are to read. Brief histories and etiquette I can teach you myself. For now, we will focus on Mirik." He looked to Ki-elte and began discussing their teaching schedules. "I regret that I'll only be able to teach her every fortnight—the very work that makes me a perfect tutor also pulls me away."

Rih looked away, unwilling to process more. Her future stood on the auction block like an underfed heifer. After a few moments, Mosil turned back to Rih. "Perhaps we might write, so your questions are answered more readily." He unrolled two scrolls and opened a rare book, clearly bound in the east. "Mirik is a small kingdom, but not without its traditions." He detailed the government, the lack of king, and the roles of the commissioners.

It must have been close to an hour later when both Ki-elte and Mosil turned to the door at some unheard interruption. The former opened it after a moment. A wide-eyed woman stood outside, her face pale. Rih could not follow her rapid speech, but Ki-elte's face sobered further. The teacher turned. "There's been an accident. I'll continue my half of your lessons tomorrow. In the meantime, I'll have someone bring you two scrolls to read." She flashed a faint smile and disappeared down the hall.

Rih turned back to Mosil, determined to learn. She would never command armies, she would never rule an empire. *But I might influence the man who does.*

Φ

The 5th Day of Lineme, 1272
The Banis Coastline

Brown rocky fields surrounded him. Here, the unbidden flood of information did not scare him. Athrolan was still barely more than a precocious city-state to the north. Building clouds darkened the horizon behind him. The ground broke apart ahead, and a city rose up, stark and sinister. A man stood at the gates, swathed in green and bone white. Dust rose from the pile of bones on which the city perched. The trim of his tunic was deep red, dyed with blood seeping up from each footfall.

Keplan tried to turn Moly about, but her steps continued, unchanging. He glanced down. Her fluffy coat shed, changing into the stripes of a Banis mount. The stripes became ribs and spine. Putrifaction burnt in his nose. The skeletal horse brought him ever closer. Nausea rose, and the world spun. Ahead, the man's face split into a gaping chasm that swallowed him whole.

Cold, damp wind hit Keplan's face. Salt and something else he could not name tickled his nose. He groaned and blinked. It was dark, and the air held a chill that was absent in Ban. Warm breath and long whiskers brushed his cheek. He sat up. Moly stared, as if puzzled why he had chosen such a strange way to dismount. The sound of water rushed nearby. His sore hands clenched, dry leaves crunching between his fingers. Stars glimmered through the trees' canopy and a thin smattering of clouds. He smiled at the sight.

"Apparently I need to rest." Rain whispered louder on the leaves, and he noticed they were like those from home. It took a moment for him to gather a few branches overhead and brush damp leaves away from the still-dry ground. Moly settled with a graceless thump behind him, and he leaned back on her flank. His gaze roamed the sky.

His dream was strange, but he supposed it was just that, a dream. "You know," he began softly, "in RoBal they think of their horses as great wealth. Like a gold vase or intricate tapestry. They aren't friends like you are to me." He reached up and brushed his colored palm against her downy chest. "It was strange, down in the dark. I never knew the time or when to expect food or pain." His words faltered as he recounted imprisonment and the weeks that followed. Her ears flicked forward and back, large eyes lidded and content at his voice after so long.

Dawn showed him the stream he heard the night before was, instead, a large cobbled river, running north from the hills. The water was clear enough to see the pale rounded stones littering the rocky sand of its bed. He sniffed the air. *Salt.* Keplan brushed dirt and leaves from Moly's burr-like coat and mounted up. The river's edge was broad and gentle on his side, sloping easily down to the river from the trees. He guided Moly carefully, watching ahead for places she might turn her hoof. Summer made the waters shallow, and the other bank grew farther as he rode north.

The trees dropped away to his left and they stood amid the waving beach grasses of the ocean. He sat back, and Moly stopped at the change in his weight, her ears flicking back to listen for a further command.

Keplan patted her shoulder absently. He could not find the words worthy. Green waves lapped at the rocky strand. The horizon was a vague gray strip where the water merged with the colorless summer sky. White birds swooped at fishes in the brackish water of the delta, black speckled counterparts dappling in the foam with earnest, pattering strides.

The noon-day sun struck orange and gold from the white-caps, smarting Keplan's eyes. He raised a hand to shield them as he looked a moment longer before dismounting. He stripped and tied his sandals and clothes into a bundle on Moly's back before leading her out into the delta. The tide was just beginning to turn. The crossing took the better part of an hour, Keplan, then Moly losing the bottom for several minutes in the middle channel. The far bank was steep and higher than the other, but Keplan kept his footing. He was glad for the warm summer as he spread his clothes on the hillside to dry. He lay down beside them, staring at the wisps of clouds scuttling past. Moly nosed his wet, salt-thick hair then turned her attention to the grass.

"This is it, Moly. That was the border. We're in Athrolan." His heart fluttered with something too pained to be happiness and too resigned to be relief.

CHAPTER SEVEN

The City of Mirik

"ANYONE HOME?" THE DOOR rattled closed as Kemmer stepped into the foyer.

Bren emerged from the parlor, mug of tea in his hand. His brow furrowed as it often was in the past weeks. "Hello, love. How did the meeting go?"

She hung her cloak on the hook on the wall and heaved a sigh. Her smile was exhausted but genuine. "Long. And we spoke in circles for about three hours. Please tell me Janna saved some supper."

Bren nodded his head toward the parlor. "It's in here. I was keeping watch, making sure Azimir didn't eat any."

Kemmer snorted, kissing him on his bristled cheek. "You'd be as likely to eat it as he. You look as tired as I feel. How was your day?"

He followed her into the parlor without answering. He leaned onto the long table that held a collection of alcohol. Wraith splashed into his cup. The shaking in his hands gave away that this was far from his first drink of the evening.

Kemmer allowed him the dramatic silence as she set about eating. After a minute she pointed a piece of chicken at him. "Brentemir, you haven't been my commanding officer for seventeen years. I'd like an answer." Her brown eyes softened, and she leaned forward. "What's wrong? I've scarcely seen you in the last week. Is it the war? You missed the meeting tonight. I know an ambassador doesn't need to be at every one, but this is a perilous time. It's not like you to miss a war council."

His bloodshot gray eyes flicked up to hers. "So, it's war then?"

Kemmer sighed. "It has been for a while. You know that. I hope to hear from Athrolan within the week on an alliance."

"But for certain? Mirik can't go to war again, not so soon after the Gods' War. I just finished rebuilding her."

"Oh, for fate's sake, Brentemir. You did not single handedly swing each hammer and write every law. Mirik going to war is no longer your decision. It's actually mine."

He glanced up. "You're acting queen?"

She sighed, twirling her empty glass by the stem. "Yes. Tonight the council named me Hetmir."

He turned away. His chest hurt, and his head already pounded. He was too old to drink this much. His hangover started before being tossed. The thought of Kemmer as queen so soon after Reka's news of Tzatia made his skin crawl. It was stupidly superstitious, but he could not shake the unease.

"Do you wish you were in my place?" Her voice was suddenly hard.

"Yes, love, but for an entirely different reason than the one you imply. Reka came to visit."

"When? I never saw her."

"That's rather the point. She'd be a rubbish spy elsewise." His wife did not laugh. "Right. She brought news from Athrolan. Her Majesty Tzatia is dead."

Kemmer's glass shattered against the far wall. "When were they planning on telling us?"

"They don't know. An'thor and the Commander are keeping it from the kingdom to stall potential civil war. Reka happened to see An'thor's reaction and made an astute deduction."

"I supposed we can't expect an alliance for a while, then."

"No, but I do have some hope. I'm sailing for Athrolan in the morning. Alea's son should arrive there soon."

Kemmer fell silent, her face unreadable. "So you're leaving us in a time of war to chase a nephew you've never met."

"Don't make it sound like that. I'll bring him here. Having the son of the Dhoah' Laen on our side will make the Banis think double before attacking us. They were there. They saw what she did at Claimiirn."

"You don't even know if he has abilities, let alone whether he wants to be roped into a war."

"He's her child. There is no question."

Kemmer slid her half-eaten plate away. "I'm going to bed. If you're not too preoccupied, perhaps you could spend some time with your wife before you leave."

Bren hummed in response, but did not follow when she swept from the room. After a moment she called down the stairs to him. He did not hear, staring into his drink long after the hall lamp was extinguished.

Φ

The 9th Day of Lineme, 1272
The City of Ceir Athrolan

Bells shook the earth. Moly's head bobbed up, ears pricked at the sound. Keplan drew up at the crest of the hill, pulse thrumming. Afternoon light bathed the city pink. The road wound through the villages and farms smattering the surrounding foothills. Buildings crowded against the city walls as if to press themselves into the protection. Keplan kept his jaw from dropping, but only just.

Rolling foothills replaced the broad river banks from five days before. White cliffs plunged hundreds of paces to the ocean, and Ceir Athrolan perched on the edge, an ancient white bird protecting its harbor. Legends betrayed him now. It was easy to run from home seeking a stranger based only upon a cryptic letter. With Athrolan's vast capital sprawled before him, how could he hope to find a man with nothing but a single name?

"Move along!" a guard barked.

Keplan dragged his attention back to the packed street and pressed forward through the tide of color and noise. Massive gates stood open, their archway muffling sound before he emerged into the city din. A square opened from the main road, boasting performers and stands of finer wares. He stayed firmly seated on Moly's back, wincing each time a shoulder brushed his leg or eyes paused on him overlong. Damp stone and salt underscored the scent of timber and lantern oil.

"The General will force our army against us!" The shout came from just beside him. He whirled, heart hammering. A man of middle years perched atop an overturned crate. His clothes were tidy and bright, worn to catch the eye. "The greatness of Athrolan will fall to these foreign warmongers. Already she rots from the top! We will be fodder for Ageless war machines if we do not take our rule into our able palms. Prince Daymir, rightful heir to our throne was exiled when the general arrived!" The man brandished a sheaf of papers. Catching Keplan's eye, the barker raised a fist. "You, capable Athrolani, do you not agree Lord Daymir is your true king?" He shoved a paper into Keplan's shaking hand.

"I'm not Athrolani." Keplan pulled Moly away. *Is Athrolan under martial law?* Tension tripped along Keplan's spine. He shoved the drawing into a pocket of his sash and searched for a quieter street. Tiled roofs of manor houses jutted above the wall to the right. Most streets angled down to the harbor and crisscrossed the tiers. The chipped and rust-stained palace dome reared above the rooftops.

By evening, his eyes were tired and his back ached from his stiff stance. *I'll need a place for the night.* A street to the left skirted the city wall and curved around to the towers above the naval barracks. It was dirty and its storefronts dark and poor. He headed down the narrow road, relieved when the bustle lessened. A few establishments made his stomach churn with their cleanliness, or the haggard eyes staring from stained windows.

"Copper for a bag, silver for a box." The croak twisted from a stoop in the shadow of an aqueduct's pillar.

Keplan edged away. "What?"

"Dust, lad, it'll turn your nightmares into nothing."

He gripped Moly's reins and shook his head. "I don't have nightmares," he lied. He was about to turn back when a small inn caught his eye. It sat at the end of the street, tucked between a derelict cotton mill and what may have once been a brothel. Stale alcohol and the bite of rotten food hung in the air.

Old wood had faded to gray, but the windows were clean and the lantern out front polished. He dismounted by the door, fiddling with the reins. He loved the woods, but his body ached from so many days sleeping on the ground. *They might take Banis beads, or know where I could exchange.*

"If you're looking for a place for the night, you can shack your pony around back. We've got a barn of sorts."

Keplan's hands tightened in Moly's mane. A bearded man peered from the ally beside the inn. His clothing and body matched the condition of the inn — worn, but clean.

He jerked his head down the alley. "We've no stable boy, but I trust you can care after your own. Elsewise you can find a place more to your liking." He flashed another smile before disappearing up the narrow stairway on the building's side.

When he was gone, Keplan led Moly around the back where a dingy barn haphazardly hung off the rear of the inn. It allowed for barely enough space to dump the rubbish. He put Moly into one of four stalls, avoiding the vicious teeth of the draft horse beside her. He checked her coat, fingers running over and over scars and rough patches he had long since memorized. It was only when he smoothed his hands down her legs for the third time that he admitted he was nervous. *You blend in here, at least more than in Ban.*

He wished he had the letter to vouch for him, but in a city of thousands, he doubted he would stumble into an inn that knew the sender. He straightened his tunic and swung open the door between the barn and the inn. It moaned audibly, but the three patrons in the corner did not look from their mugs. Keplan slid onto a stool at the end of the bar.

"What can I get you?" The woman paused beside him was a darker, female version of the man from the alley.

After weeks of communicating solely in Banis, his native Trade was almost awkward in his mouth. "Just water, please."

Her lips pursed, but she brushed past him without another word and ducked into a room that, by the heat and smell, had to be the kitchen. He leaned back on the wall. His gaze flitted from corner to door, to patrons, to door. One leg bounced soundlessly on the wooden rung of the stool.

The low ceiling was swaybacked as a nag's, and the fireplace shed more light than the dim lanterns. Carved pillars caught his attention. They were made in the shape of rabbits in scribes' garb, some holding outstretched tomes and maps serving as tables and shelves. One's raised iron quill held a cloak by the door. Most bore marks of hasty repair from bar brawl damage. Despite himself, a smile tugged at Keplan's mouth.

"I don't trust a man who orders nothing but water in a tavern, noontime be damned." The man from before leaned on the bar and slid a mug over to Keplan.

Keplan gestured at his clothing. "The only money I have is Banis." He took a slow sip of the water, wishing his stomach was not so empty.

"So you came here to rest from the sun?" His brown eyebrow arched playfully. "You staying in Athrolan long?"

Keplan lifted one boney shoulder in a shrug. Who knew how long it would take to find the man who sent the letter? "For a while, yes."

"If you sweep up the place in here, and tidy the back you can stay the night and have some supper. And nevermind Mirrel. She bites a bit at first, but that's just her way."

Keplan watched the dark-haired woman bustle from the kitchen. Her green eyes shot a hard look at the two of them. "She's your sister?"

"Older by two years." The man stroked his thick brown beard. "I'm the prettier though."

The joke startled a laugh from Keplan, and he looked down. "I'd like to stay the night." His stomach punctuated his words with a low rumble.

"When was the last time you ate, my man?"

Keplan paused, counting back. "It's been a bit. I was traveling, for a time, and lost my bow."

The man's eyes darkened only for a moment, and Keplan wondered at the expression. "I'll fetch you something now. We can talk clean-up details when Mirrel's through. She works mornings, I do evenings. I'm better at bar-talk anyway." He patted the bar before Keplan with a smile. "Firas."

Keplan frowned. "Excuse me?"

"Firas Smytheson. My name."

"Ah. Keplan Wardyn."

Firas's grin broadened before he slipped into the kitchen. "Well then, welcome to Athrolan, Master Wardyn."

"Thank you." Keplan looked away, nervous at the attention and the kindness. He wished trust was more durable, wished it took more than weeks in a cell to rip it from him. He smoothed the barker's paper on the bar, eyes scanning the crude sketch. Two military figures grappled, one with horns, the other broad and gripping a ship's tattered flag. They stood on a pile of dead officiates. At the top of the mound lay an older woman with a crown.

"Here you are. Not much, but Mirrel would be ticked if I gave away our best." Firas slid over a bowl of greasy sauce and a plate of toasted bread and meat strips.

Keplan glanced up. "Thank you. Might you have a fork?"

Firas snorted. "Not from Athrolan, eh?" He jerked his head at the other patrons. "Fingers are fine."

Keplan flushed and looked away. "Forgive me."

"Nothing to forgive." Firas's hand tapped the parchment. "I see you've met Peraan's group."

"Who?"

"The barker who heads this train of thought that General Domariigo plans to destroy the nation."

"Is Athrolan at war?"

It was Firas's turn to shrug before pushing off from the counter. "Not yet. Who knows what will happen when Her Majesty passes?" He waved at the food. "Eat up before it gets cold."

Keplan shoved the paper away and set about eating. His parents told him of Athrolan, of her might and beauty. Her palace's glittering pearl of a dome, the queen's grace, the joy and bustle of her streets. *Can that much change in twenty or thirty years?* He fingered the tattoos on his gloved palms. He supposed it could.

Φ

The crowd grew in the evening. Lanterns bloomed with the setting sun, and it seemed every moment the door banged open again. Keplan sat on the rear stoop for a moment, broom in hand, and looked up at the stars. Ban was interesting for its differences, but Athrolan fit around him. It was not the people or the language, for he imagined under different circumstances Ban could be beautiful. *This is familiar.* The purpose of his journey seemed so distant in the dark Banis cell, in the dim heat of the stable. With every borrowed memory from those inside the inn, he felt a step closer to whatever set his feet on the path to this city.

He rose with a silent sigh and finished sweeping the makeshift courtyard and alley. Disused tools and hay filled the barn, which he set about tidying. It was close to midnight when Firas coughed politely from the doorway.

"I was beginning to think we'd scared you off." His eyes lit on the state of the barn. "You did well in here."

"I worked as a mucker for a bit." The words slipped out, startling Keplan.

Firas did not seem to notice his embarrassment, nodding instead at the door. "Most of the patrons are gone to bed if you want to start the common room."

Keplan followed his host inside, closing his eyes for a moment to enjoy the flood of firelight and swell of warmth. It took a few minutes to straighten unoccupied chairs and stack dishes and mugs by the kitchen door. The last customer left by the time the common room was clean and Firas dimmed the lanterns. The bearded man leaned on the counter with a tired smile. He pushed a full mug over to Keplan. "Have a drink. You earned it."

"I only earned the one meal."

"Nonsense. You earn what I say you earn." He tugged off his apron and tossed it onto a hook by the door to a narrow stairwell. "So, what brought you to Athrolan? Your clothing says you're from the west, but your coloring and accent certainly don't." His eyes narrowed in mock suspicion. "Are you a spy?"

Blood roared in Keplan's ears, drowning whatever else the bartender might have said. *"Worthless barbarian spy!"* He choked down a gulp of whatever was in his mug, but it tasted of blood. "I'm not a spy." He spat the words, ale misting the bar before him.

Firas straightened, hands still planted on the counter. His brows met over his green eyes. "I'm sorry. Mirrel's forever saying my mouth is too fast for my head."

Keplan glanced up, and the whirling of his thoughts slowed. "You meant nothing by it." He took another deep sip of his drink. It was too acrid for his liking, but filled his gut with pleasant warmth. "I'm from the south. I came here to find someone my parents knew before I was born."

"Ah. Many come here looking for something and never leave. Maybe they find something better." His smile was softer this time, kind and shadowed with patient curiosity.

"You probably just want some quiet. I can show you to your room."

"I would appreciate that." Keplan drained his mug and trudged upstairs after Firas. Half a dozen rooms lined the narrow hall above the common area. Keplan took Firas's smoky candle and ducked through the door with quiet thanks. The room was as bare and small as his barrack in the stable, but in the style of his room at home. A low window sat above the bed. He crawled across the thin coverlet and pushed open the shutters. Cool air brought the sounds of sailors, ships, markets, the smell of lanterns and fish and old stone.

The neighborhood may have been poor, but the view was spectacular. The row of houses across the street were low and Keplan could see over the brown battered tile of their rooftops to the bowl of the city. Glinting lanterns painted the twisting streets and outlines of buildings in golden light. Aqueducts ran through the city like ribs. The reflection of dock lamps swelled like starflies with each wave in the black mirror of the harbor. Torches cast guards' exaggerated shadows on the dome of the palace.

Keplan stripped off his Banis clothes and let the air cleanse his body of prairie dust.

Φ

The 11th Day of Lineme, 1272
The City of Robal, Ban

Summer's heat was a cloying blanket. Overripe fruit covered the scent of sweat and baking soil. Rih flung open the wooden slats of her window with a sigh. It was a useless gesture, hopeful of a breeze that would never reach so far within the walls. The Hall was tucked into the heart of the city, away from any proper prairie wind. She unrolled the scroll in the stand on her desk and paused at an image. It was a dance. Mosil gave her instructions to read accounts of his time in Mirik before the threat of war. He expected her to memorize every move and phrase of introduction. Today, when they met in the heat of afternoon, she would learn to dance. *At least the first part was easy.* She neither knew the language nor could she speak it, so her introduction was entirely reliant on her cousin or another state official.

She ran a finger down the detailed painting. Mosil was taller, but something around his eyes and the set of his mouth told her it was intended to be her cousin. Traditional loose pants and a silk wrap covered him. The knots and draping of the fabric were the same as Ki-elte taught her and she smiled. *I'm learning.* Beside him was a young man she presumed to be Mirik's king wearing a quilted orange vest layered over a longsleeved gray-green shirt. Tight breeches were tucked into high boots. She shook her head. Mirik may have been a more eastern nation, but she could not fathom being cold enough to warrant so many layers of wool and leather. *If it's so cold, then why do the men cut their hair so short?* She glanced at the caption:

> *Ambassador Mosil-ten-Ebal of RoBal meeting Alleanthus A'hane of Mirik, son of Military Commissioner Kemmer A'hane and Ambassador Brentemir Barrackborn.*

Her heart raced. Everyone knew of Brentemir Barrackborn—Azirik's son and the brother of the Dhoah' Laen. That meant Mirik's Military Commissioner was female. Did that change negotiations for the Banis Emperor? *Does it irk His Eminence to sit eye-to-eye with a woman?* She pushed away the ache in her chest. A soft breeze brushed her cheek, and she turned.

Ki-elte stood in the door, bright smile in place. Her usual pink clothing was pale in an effort to ward off the heat. "Good morning!" Instead of joining Rih, she gestured to the door. "You can take lunch during a break in your lesson. Dancing takes time even when...." She tried to hide the falter with a smile, but Rih saw.

"Even when the student can hear the music?" Rih signed.

Ki-elte paused and mimicked the gesture of a bow on strings. "Music?"

"Yes." Rih tried to use signs Ki-elte recognized. The woman was a fast learner when she focused, but often fell back on writing out of impatience.

Ki-elte smiled, made the gesture again, then signed crudely, "Yes. Even when hear music."

Rih grabbed her tablet and asked:

> *Couldn't they just tell the Mirikin boy I cannot dance?*

> *Dance is a part of so many Eastern rituals, especially for a figurehead of court. I can't imagine them agreeing to a marriage with a woman who couldn't dance.*

Rih sighed and followed her teacher through the Halls. It soured her stomach that she was learning dance before Trade. *Teach me their language. Teach me to read their mouths, their songs, their legends.* As it was, most myths she knew involving the Eastern lands were of the Dhoah' Laen and the asai. When Ki-elte knocked at the door to Rih's lesson, fatigue dragged the other woman's movements.

Rih touched her shoulders. "Are you alright?"

Ki-elte smiled again, but this time Rih saw the shadows underneath. "I'm tired," she signed before switching back to voicing. "The threat of war is heavy. Its weight falls on us first."

Rih rolled her eyes. She knew about war. Ki-elte had never seen the true frontlines of battle.

I'd think it falls on the soldiers' first.

Ki-elte's chin jerked in a derisive snort. "Then you haven't been listening." She waved the conversation away when Mosil opened the door. "I have other things to take care of. I'll return to show you back to your room." A rare frown curled her thick black brows, and she wrote on Rih's tablet.

War kills the nobles, the rich last. But the soldiers are never first. You want to see whether war will come? See if the poor are dying, if the invisible are dying. War isn't coming, Rih. It's already being fought.

She smoothed her words from the wax once Rih read them. Her honey-colored eyes hardened to amber, and she disappeared down the hall.

Rih stared after, wondering why her stomach had turned to stone. A hand on her arm startled her from the dark mood.

"Morning, Rih-elte." Mosil punctuated his signs with a frown. "Is everything alright?"

Rih offered a false smile and pointed to the room. It was clear in the center with a small dais for musicians, meant for private gatherings and performances. "You are going to teach me to dance?"

"I will. Usually, I can just say 'it will make sense when you hear the music.' Today will be a learning experience for both of us." He paused. "Can you hear at all? I know many can only hear certain tones."

"Only very loud noises or in a very quiet space. Often, I simply know something made noise, but it's not clear. A ballroom is neither of those. I can feel, but with dancing, my steps will cause more disturbance than a faint tremor from music." She repeated some signs, exaggerated, for him, but it was a relief to use her own language. "If I can see the musicians, I can read their rhythm and that of other dancers. And my partner." She stopped. "Do Mirikin dances have partners?" Banis dances began as great patterns with partners growing closer and closer, the music ending when hands finally touched. If the pictures were any indication, formal Mirikin—and most Eastern dances—were often paired.

"These are paired. You can follow your partner, but be sure you don't trip over his feet." He held out his hand and switched to verbal speech. Standing so close, face to face, she could see enough of his words to understand. "Let's start with positioning and steps. We can worry about music later." He moved her hands, one against his and the other featherlight on his chest. "Feel the pressure in my hands and body as I move." The steps were mostly back and forward with a few rotations returning them to where they began, albeit facing the opposite direction. The count seemed to be of three.

When they paused for a drink, musicians filed in. Two were white and bore the marks and clothes of slaves. Rih frowned. "Where are the cellos? The violins?"

He laughed. "Mirik has none. Eastern lands rarely use them, though some of their songs adopted our instruments." He made a face. "They play them poorly. Instead, there are drums and wind."

She resumed the starting stance. Over his shoulder she watched the musicians bend into their first notes, one man tapping the drum. Mosil's hand pressed on hers, and she tripped over the beginning step.

His lips thinned, and he waved for the musicians to start again. "The first steps are the most important. The rest just follow."

Another hour passed before Rih mastered the first half of the dance to music that she could never hear. Her cousin called a stop and dismissed the musicians with a sigh. "We'll meet again soon to do more. There are four other dances you'll be expected to know. For now, that's enough for you to think on and practice."

Or you're too frustrated to continue. "I'll practice."

"Good." He gathered his things, his guard falling in step behind him. "I'll see you soon."

Rih laid her glass aside and turned to look for Ki-elte. The seat in the corner was empty. She checked the hall, but only a guard stood beside the sliding door. Long shadows stretched outside the window. It was afternoon, and their lesson ran late. *She should be here.* Rih waited a minute longer, then slipped out on her own. The hall was crowded, but she managed to find her room without mishap. It, too, was empty, the lamp unlit. She settled in to read more while she waited. The sun set and her supper arrived, but Ki-elte never came.

Φ

The 14th Day of Lineme, 1272

The letter arrived with breakfast. It was one of the three days of the week Ki-elte spent teaching her, but the woman was already late. Rih helped herself to a bowl of fruit and tea, one hand peeling the seal from the scroll.

R-

Forgive the sudden nature of this letter and my absence. News came from the west, news that bodes poorly. I will elaborate further in person and when I know more. I hope to return to the city in time for our next meeting, but until then, please study your books. I asked, too, for some advertisements on fashion to be sent to you from the city jewelers. I thought you could decide on which style rings you wanted.

I wish you well,

-K

Something churned in Rih's gut. This felt like the hour before a raid, pulled from sleep to creep through the darkness, for once, her companions as silent as she. Despite Ki-elte's words during their first lesson, Rih did not consider the woman any sort of warrior. *She was called away on an emergency, something about politics and war, no doubt.*

Ki-elte was as much a soldier as any who carried an atlatl or armor.

Rih pushed her food away, stomach a knot of nerves. War was less terrifying when she bore a weapon. She fingered the edge of the reed cards on her tray. They bore images of impossibly beautiful women, each dressed in intricately patterned robes, bedecked in skull nets and gemstones.

The figures' expressions were vacant, faded eyes gazing at some distant point. The women in the Hall of the Purple Throne, however, were different. Rih had been contemptuous of the life of a courtesan or prostitute over a soldier's. She realized, now, she missed a large piece of the story. Her gaze slid to the doorframe. A silk thread bedecked with wooden beads hung through a small hole there, presumably attached to a bell somewhere on the other side. She tugged it firmly and turned back to the cards on her desk.

When a serving woman arrived a minute later, Rih handed her a roll of paper.

The woman scanned the words. "You want someone to come pierce you?" She glanced up at Rih's bare face and ears and smiled. "She will be by shortly."

Rih offered a nervous smile and returned to perusing the variety of rings on the cards. She thought the decorations were pretty, if impractical. Curiosity sparked in her mind the more she learned how much women conveyed without speech. Body language and expressions were universal, even for her. This was new. *And something men may not even notice.*

A hand touched her shoulder, and she whirled. The serving woman stood behind her and a woman, tall even by Banis standards, waited in the doorway with a box in her arms. Rih penned a quick explanation for why they would communicate through writing. The woman smiled in response and gestured for the serving girl to be on her way.

When the door shut, the piercer turned. She bore laugh lines and gray in the stubble on her head. Her hands flew into motion. "I'm Hi-alan-Kan. I do most of the ring work at the Hall. I understand you're new here?"

Rih's heart thundered at the signing. "I was a soldier before I was chosen to marry. My teacher tells me each ring means something."

"Yes." Hi-alan opened the box. "Unlike with clothing, where color carries the most obvious meaning, rings are more about placement." She laid a sheet of silk on the desk and unpacked a series of needles, a bottle of dark liquid, and several tiny boxes with jeweled rings. "A ring in the nose indicates strength, in the brow, intelligence or power. Lower in the ears shows kindness, empathy. Higher is for philosophy. Some women prefer a bead, like the one in my nose, here." She tapped the tiny pearl stud on the right side of her nostril. "These are often seen as playful, rather than elegant rings."

"And left and right—do those have meaning too?"

"Wives and teachers tend toward the right side, while courtesans prefer the left. The gems are chosen to match our outfits." She turned to look at the shelves of Rih's clothes. "Blue?"

"Purple, too." Rih pointed to the deep purple wrap Ki-elte brought the other day as a gift.

Hi-alan opened one of the boxes and handed it to Rih. Inside were rings and studs of varying sizes, each bedecked with amethyst, lavender chalcedony, or lapis.

Rih grinned. "These are beautiful." She peered into the small mirror Hi-alan produced. Her features were strong as it was, and she did not want to damage what little she could convey to others who did not know her language. *This is just another way to communicate.* She pointed to her left brow, both her nostrils and her left earlobe.

"Both sides?"

"Is that wrong? I'll need all the strength I can muster."

Hi-alan smiled. "I think it'll look good on you."

Rih eyed the needles while the other woman cleaned her skin with the dark liquid. Pain from a pulled muscle or twisted ankle was familiar. Pain by choice was entirely different. The first punch through her ear burned. The second ached. Pinching accompanied the hoop through her brow. Tears flooded her cheeks, and she glanced down at the bloodless knuckles of her hands on the chair's arms. The needle through her nose was a hornet's sting. The ground disappeared, her body falling forever, leaving her stomach far above. Darkness receded from her vision a moment later.

Hi-alan's smile was kind, if amused. "The first time I received my rings I fainted dead away. Ripped my lobe in half." She turned her head so Rih could see the fine white line bisecting the flesh.

Rih shuddered, stomach still flipping in the aftermath of the pain. She checked the mirror. Though red and still dotted with blood, the new jewelry was striking on her face. "Thank you." Her eyes met the reflection of Hi-alan's.

"Keep yourself clean, and take care with your new hoops. You'll forget and catch them on all sorts of things if you aren't careful." She set about cleaning and packing her tools. When her box was fully packed, she touched Rih's shoulder, expression soft. "This life is hard. We are expected to be everything and ask for nothing. Be perfect without the respect. It isn't easy. I wouldn't know how different the soldier's life is, but I know the fire in your eyes, in mine, is the same in most women in this city. Ki-elte is a good teacher, but she only sees the happiness it seems sometimes. Perhaps she has to, to survive this." She paused and finally met Rih's eyes properly. "You did not ask advice, and I don't know if you need it, but my suggestion is to learn. Learn everything you can. What we know is our power." She squeezed Rih's arm and bowed her head. "Good luck."

Rih caught Hi-alan's hand. "Thank you."

The woman smiled. "I wish more women spoke your language. Some men know it, but not many. It'd be nice not to hide half of what we say anymore."

A frown bloomed on Rih's brow as she watched her go. She always viewed her lack of speech as a frustration to others—if not always herself. Silence was often isolating. *I never thought it could be freeing.* Her body hummed, wanting exercise, wanting to jog the open prairie with her patrol beside her. Energy filled her limbs as her body countered the pain of piercing. Instead, there were scrolls to read if she was going to do things properly.

She heaved a sigh and went to the cluster of scrolls beside her desk. Half a dozen were those Mosil lent her. During their first week together, Ki-elte urged her to read a smaller, darker one. Rih tugged it from the vase and settled herself by the window.

> *There is a colorful history to Ban. Drenched deep with red blood from wars and slavery and the betrayal of emperors. The darkest blood, however, the coldest drip of gore across the pages of our people is what we have done to our own. There was one day when we were as city-states — warriors and warlords eating upon one table. Women commanding beside their men. But there is one way, the easiest way, to command an army, to drag warlords under a single banner and make them think it is for their own good.*
>
> *To command the horse, you break its will. To turn its road you rein its head. Humans are no different than horses. Bloodier, perhaps, but just as simple. The empire was not always an empire. There was a time when we were but cities, sisters and brothers to the Vales. The men who ruled were not always great or even good. The first emperor broke his people and cut the will from their hearts. He reined their generals, killed those who opposed until the only officers were loyal.*
>
> *But even a horse may break free when he learns the whole of his will and the might of his body is greater than the strength of the man who seeks to ride him.*

Rih sat back. What did Ki-elte mean? If the people of the empire realized they were stronger than the emperor, than the generals and nobles, it would destroy Ban. *He must live in fear of that, for to have power is to fear its absence.* She grinned and scrabbled from her seat. The tablet from her first lesson with Ki-elte lay nearby, where she read it before bed, hoping the answer would arrive in dreams. *What commands the Emperor?* She rummaged through her desk until she found her stylus and scratched one word across the wax surface:

Fear.

CHAPTER EIGHT

The 10th Day of Lineme, 1272
The City of Cier Athrolan

SUN POURED THROUGH THE open shutters, dripping over the coverlet and onto the floor. A particularly insistent ray crossed Keplan's face. One hand flopped over his face, and he groaned. His eyes shot open when the noises of a city registered. *Not at home, then.* He rolled from his bed and stretched. The city was beautiful in the morning, though not as magical as the night before. The folded tunic brought a frown to his brow. Looking out of place was dangerous, but a new set of clothes would be expensive. He needed food and a room too. *I need money.* The common room was quiet, and as he feared, Mirrel perched behind the bar, dark head bowed over a tattered ledger.

When she did not look up, he cleared his throat. "Miss?"

She ignored him a moment longer before glancing up. "Why are you still here?"

"Your brother let me stay."

She snapped the ledger shut with a disgusted look. "He's worse than a dock-whore. I couldn't count the number of times he's tupped patrons, not even if I used my toes."

Keplan blanched. "No, I mean in a separate room. In trade for cleaning up the common room and courtyard."

She snorted at the term. "You mean the alley?" Her expression slipped from annoyance to contemplation as his words registered. "You tidied up?"

"Yes."

Her eyes scanned the room before returning to him. "You did well. Better than Firas ever has."

Keplan bit his lip, something close to hope blooming. "You own this inn?"

"I inherited it from our mother."

"I would like to continue to work for you."

"We can't pay you. I just looked at the ledger. Trust me when I say you'd have to pay us to make it worthwhile."

Keplan squared his thin shoulders. She was clever and, moreover, she was stubborn. "Miss, how many rooms are let at a time? Two? Three? You have six. I won't take up valuable space. This tier is above the docks—"

"As is the whole city if you hadn't seen."

"Right, yes, but I mean the naval docks. Do you have a courier? Do you have a proper barn? I'll help you. I promise I'm good with my hands, quick on my feet. I spent time fetching horses, so I know errands. You both are too busy to worry about those small jobs."

She did not turn, but she was listening. "You act courier and errand boy, tidy the place, mend things what need fixing. In return, we offer you meals and bed?"

Keplan glanced down. "And I'll need something to wear."

Mirrel's eyes fell to the ledger, her full mouth twisted in frustration. "I can run this business myself."

"Of course you can, sistermine, but for fate's sake, listen to the boy's sense." Firas stood on the last step, leaning on the doorway. His beard and hair looked wild, and fatigue narrowed his eyes. "If he helps, we could bring in a bit more coin. You're busy enough with cooking and the books."

"Two weeks. I'll give you two weeks, and we'll see how things go." She jabbed a finger at him. Despite her small stature, Keplan retreated a step. "You steal from me, boy, and I'll bake you into our sailors' pot pie."

Firas tossed Keplan a tired grin and nodded up the stairs. "Come on, I'll see if I can find something that fits you."

At the end of the second-storey hall, another set of stairs led up to the attic. The space was divided in two, the other side presumably for Mirrel. Firas's room was cramped, and Keplan ducked his head to avoid hitting the gabled ceiling. The view, however, was a fantastic one.

He patted the slight paunch from his nights of drinking. "Hard to believe, but I was once almost as slender as you. My shirts might fit, though I'll have to search to find suitable breeches." He dug through a chest at the end of his rumpled bed. He tossed two tolstovka over his shoulder. "Try these."

Keplan turned away and tugged off his tunic. He was not modest, but he did not want to discuss the obvious pattern of scars across his body. The shirts fit well, though the sleeves were shorter than the current fashion dictated. The cloth belt allowed him to tighten it over his narrower waist.

Firas's eyes lingered on Keplan's bare legs before handing over a pair of dark, loose breeches. "Your build does not lend itself to being that thin. I know Mirrel's a hard woman, but please eat as much as you need. I'd rather have a healthy bar boy."

Keplan's cheeks flamed, and he tugged on the breeches quickly. "I eat fine."

"Of course. If you wear boots over those no one will notice they're too short for you. Mirikin folk tuck their breeches still."

"I'm not Mirikin."

Firas frowned at the hard tone. "Well, no. Of course not. Neither are you Banis, but you wear that thing." He pointed at the discarded tunic on his floor. "Let me see your feet."

"Excuse me?"

"Boots, you idiot." His grin, bright through the brown beard, softened the mock insult.

Keplan flushed again and held out a bony foot. "My father promised I'd grow into them, but I haven't yet."

"You're what, sixteen? You've got some years left."

"Seventeen. I was born during snowmelt."

Firas laughed and dug deeper into the chest. "I was too, though I'd say a fair few years before you. I was a wartime babe." He drew out a pair of worn boots. They were old and far too large for the short Firas, but recently polished. "These were my Da's. His boots and armor came back from the battle at Claimiirn, but he didn't."

Keplan eyed the dead man's boots. "I don't want to intrude."

"Nonsense. I'm a sentimental man, but I'd like to see them used. They do no good collecting dust."

Keplan shoved his feet into the boots, almost toppling over in the process. He righted himself with a soft laugh and tucked the short legs of the breeches in. He glanced up at Firas, curious. "Think I'll pass?"

Firas nodded in appreciation and flopped onto his bed gracelessly. "Rather well. Now get down to the common room. I'd like to sleep for another two hours before I deal with Mirrel again."

Keplan found the man's kindness contagious and left the room smiling.

Φ

The 14th Day of Lineme, 1272

Stone buildings ringed the harbor, marked by crests and signs. Anvils, ships, coins, cloth marked their trade, but none were actual workshops. *Guildhalls*, Keplan realized. The largest bore coins and scales above the arched double door.

The cool room was dim, and he blinked to adjust his eyes after the sun-bleached city outside. A counter ran across the cool room, topped with heavy iron bars. It was quiet, despite the two dozen people in various lines. He found a shorter wait and clenched the paper in his hand tightly. Surprisingly, Mirrel trusted him, but he supposed she knew he would get nothing from stealing a delivery note.

When called, he approached the clerk and slid the note through the bars. "I'm here from the Wise Hare. Miss Mirrel Smytheson requests her coin retrieved on her usual day." Seeing the well-armed guards outside, Keplan understood why it was far safer to have the bank retrieve her money.

"You're a new face."

He glanced up at the clerk, puzzled.

"I've seen the Smythesons come in for years."

"They've just hired me to help out a bit." He took the stamped note stub with a faint smile and hurried out the door. The clerk meant well, but Keplan's skin crawled when singled out, even if it was just through common talk. The commotion in the harbor as he exited overcame his worries.

Fishing boats long since sailed, and the sparse docks were shadowed by a massive vessel. It was not the long, armed naval ships clustered near the harbor's entrance, but tall and fine, built to weather the storms of the open ocean, if not battle.

Keplan's steps stalled. He knew little about ships, but he enjoyed the way the hull slid through the water, the rigging swarmed with sailors as they made ready to dock. Deep green lacquered the wood, accented by vermillion rails, both shining with layers of resin. The stiff sails were bright white, save for the flying jib, emblazoned with a vermilion serpent and crossed keys.

Mirik. People swarmed the docks, but Keplan was heedless of the jostling. *Their flagship, no less.* He shouldered his way to the edge of the dock, clambering onto a piling. The ship was secured and the gangway lowered for the first wave of cargo and mail, including two horses fine enough to rival the Banis mounts. A man of middle years disembarked, flanked by clerks and guards. Faded auburn striped his short gray hair. An older boy followed, his darker features too akin to the man's to be anything but a son.

Something strange writhed in Keplan's stomach. Mirik's ambassadors should fill him with anger. *Shouldn't I be blaming them for what happened in Ban?* He hardened his eyes, leaning forward on the piling to catch a glimpse of the dignitary's eyes. They were a pale gray, almost colorless. No foreign personal history flooded his mind, however, only vague images from the war. The boy was the same. *Why can't I see?* One fact forced itself through his cluttered thoughts: Mirik somehow silenced his madness.

Φ

The 15th Day of Lineme, 1272
The Forest of the Hartland

Arman smoothed a hand over the rough countertop, staring into the distance. Alea believed hers were the only thoughts twisted with ugly darkness. He let her, but it was a lie. His mantle of protector was heavy after so many years. Anger was heavy too. She meditated now, and had been more often. It was a way to seek answers, but it worried him. *What if she sees only what she wants?*

A blank sheet of parchment lay before him. Writing to An'thor would seal Keplan's fate. The vague letter from the general was damning enough. Instead, Arman carefully scribed Bren's title and name before pausing again. *What does one say after twenty years of silence?* He shook the dark thought away and set about his letter. It was long, but not nearly long enough to encompass all that changed. Black ink dried to charcoal while Arman wondered if he made the right choice.

Keplan's birth was unplanned. Alea thought she was unable to bear children, and Arman was content to love only her for the rest of his days. Their son was a beautiful surprise. Now he wondered if it was coincidence. Power begat power. They were the most powerful creatures the world had seen in aeons. *How could our child be anything but miraculous?* Alea predicted something came after the war, something she could not name or understand, but more powerful than she.

What if it's Keplan?

"What are you writing?" Alea leaned on the door frame, arms crossed over her chest. Her body was relaxed, but her eyes tired. "A letter?"

Arman stared at her, wondering how long he would lie to protect her from her own thoughts and fears. Should he even bother? "Alea, I don't think you missed anything."

She moved to sit across from him, brow furrowed. Her eyes lingered on the parchment, but made no move to read it. "What do you mean?"

"Whatever you saw predicted in that book. I don't think you got anything wrong. I think you just don't want to see it."

Her frown deepened, following the familiar paths of wrinkles. "I don't like your tone."

He closed his eyes and shed the weight of protector. "I don't like your blind idealism, Alea. You are the most powerful Laen in centuries. I'm an Earth Shaker."

"Was. Were. We're just people now, Arman."

"No, we're not. We never will be. Alea, we're barely human. What hope could we possibly have that our child would be normal? Something changed in Keplan. We both saw how preoccupied he was. Within a week he was riding north looking for An'thor. He realized something."

Alea looked away, lips in a tight line. "What are you suggesting?"

"I'm suggesting he's something incredible and powerful and alien that this world has yet to see. What if our son is what you saw?"

Her eyes flicked to the letter, head still turned away. "You're writing to him?"

"I'm writing to Bren. We tossed Keplan into the world without any tools, without the knowledge of what we are. Someone has to help him, and I don't trust An'thor not to make him a pawn."

Unreadable darkness filled her eyes. She had been simply Alea for so long, calm and quiet, writing poetry and gardening. The woman who looked up at Arman now was not Alea. Softness fled her features and shaking hands clenched. "Pack your things. We'll leave tomorrow."

Arman watched, incredulous, as she strode into their bedroom. Anticipation tightened his chest. "What are you doing? What if Keplan comes home?"

"You know as well as I do he won't. I'm finding Daymir and convincing him to take the throne instead. I'll find this woman who haunts my thoughts and learn what she means by 'gods' blood.'" She appeared in the doorway, fingers braiding back her gray hair. "I don't care if he's the most powerful thing this world will ever see. He is my son, and I'll be damned if he rides into this alone."

Φ

The 18th Day of Lineme, 1272
The City of Ceir Athrolan

Unlike Ban, Athrolan's summer weather varied. Heavy, fluffy clouds filled the sky, and breezes curled through the streets carrying trash and leaves. Travel's momentum kept his mind busy, but now uncertainty plagued him. Errands and chores filled his mornings, but his afternoons were free.

Now he moved along the edge of the market in the paved circle near the western gate. Each time he met someone's eyes, he cataloged the information to explore later. It was strangely intimate, and he struggled with the morality of his actions. *The man with the bead on his beard plans to leave his wife next week. The woman by the apple stall works as a half-dressed barmaid in a love-house. The smith across from me runs a smuggling and spy route to Mirik.* Keplan paused at the last one, peering closer at the man and memorizing his face. Information and discretion were good skills. He turned down a smaller makeshift alley between stalls. A young man admired the tooling on a leather sheath, tanned face lit with an open smile. It was the Mirikin dignitary's son.

Keplan's thoughts were silent.

Why is your family the one thing I can't see? He moved to tap the other boy on the shoulder. Hard fingers twisted his wrist, and he sank to his knees to avoid breaking the bones. White-hot pain burst behind his eyes. Ban flashed through his mind, and it took all his will to clear his vision and focus on his attacker's words. A burly, older soldier held him. "Sorry to disturb you, Master A'hane. This scum was angling for your purse."

The dignitary's son stared, confused, at the proceedings.

Keplan shook his head violently. "Sir, you have it wrong. I was trying to get his attention, not pick his pocket. I thought I knew him."

His last words were cut off as the other boy waved the soldier off. "Thank you, but I know this man. I was supposed to meet him here, but this knife smith's ware distracted me."

The soldier paused, his gaze going between the two. "Are you sure, Master?"

The boy pressed a hand to the man's shoulder. "Quite, Captain...?"

"Sousa," the Captain offered.

"Here, for your trouble." The boy handed Sousa a gold coin, one of the square ones from Mirik, before turning to Keplan. "Come on then, we ought to be moving on."

Keplan hesitated only a moment before dusting himself off and hurrying after. After rounding a few corners, the boy leaned against the stone of the building at the head of a narrow street. An uncertain giggle bubbled from his chest. "Were you really going to pick my pocket?"

"I was trying to get your attention." Keplan fixed him with a hard stare. "Why did you lie?"

"You don't look like a pickpocket. My pa always said I'm too trusting, but you looked horrified, not guilty. And I have few friends here who aren't nobles." He shifted his feet. "Why are you staring at me like that? Why did you want my attention?"

Keplan looked down. Lying came easier to him now, and truth did not bring safety. "I saw the snake pin on your shirt—I had a saddle blanket with the same mark."

The boy laughed, the sound light and loud. "Fair enough. Who are you?"

"Keplan Wardyn." He held out his arm in greeting, then remembered he addressed a noble, and tried to bow, only to realize he did not know which to use.

"I'm Azimir." His smile brightened his dark face. "Azimir A'hane of Mirik. My father is here on business and agreed to take me along." His eyes narrowed playfully. "I'm the son of an ambassador and the Military Commissioner of Mirik. How do you know nothing about me?" Without waiting for an answer, he rattled on. "Well, if you've never been here, would you like a tour? Where are you staying?"

Keplan stumbled over the stream of questions. *Nothing good comes from favors.* Yet something loosened in his chest, not strong enough to be hope or happiness, but it unfurled at the younger boy's words. He looked up at where Azimir waited with barely hidden impatience. Firas did not need him back for another few hours. "If you aren't busy, a tour would be nice. I'm staying at the Wise Hare in the slums."

Azimir jerked his head toward the east side of the harbor, grinning. "You have to see the Thread."

"Thread?" Keplan asked as he followed the boy's easy, confident stride.

"It's where all the merchants unload their warehouses for their stores. It's named for the silks and fabric they ship in, but they have everything there!"

Though Keplan knew many of Athrolan's streets angled down to the harbor, the city's plan was more complicated. The main streets did indeed lead from the highest points of the city to the docks, but on the tiers of buildings roads twisted, the whole looking like dozens of interconnected, tangled strings. Each "knot," Azimir explained as he hurried through the masses of people, was a district with its own name.

"The streets were built before anyone used carriages, so they're a mess. The three biggest streets are named, but most people navigate by tier and district. Waves' Crash is the street along the navy yards. Lane of the Sun connects the Guildhouses to the square where we met. Tzama runs straight to the palace, following the biggest aqueduct."

Azimir's excited chatter reminded Keplan of a squirrel. Though he could gain knowledge when looking at someone, he realized information was vastly different from understanding.

"What about yours?"

Keplan realized Azimir had been talking. "I'm sorry, I was distracted."

"I said my family comes here often. My father and brother at least. We're a small family. What about yours?"

Keplan turned sideways to let a two-team wagon lurch past. "Just my Ma and Da. I'm not sure if they ever visited."

Azimir turned to stare, but whatever questions were about to spill from him stopped when Keplan caught sight of the street before them. Ropes were strung between the upper storeys of the buildings, draped with fabric and skeins of thread. The colors were brighter even than the streets of Ban. The smell of dye and wet cloth hung heavy. The combination of metal, gems, silk, and carvings made the street seem like the hall of an opulent palace. Even the white paving stones shone from the boots, sandals, and slippers that polished them each day. City and private guards dotted each storefront. Sunlight filtered through wood screens and cotton awnings. Lanterns glowed from the warehouses of the glass merchants from Mirik, and the smell of oil and sawdust drifted from the ebony imports from western Val. Each stall of wares was an organized pocket within the general chaos. He grinned. "This is what my mind looks like."

Azimir's brows rose, but he did not respond, only going on to detail where each shipment hailed from. Keplan listened absently. They wound through the Thread, then up the Tzama and back across to the Market. Keplan learned each district had a distinct smell and sound as well as a name. By the time they returned, his stomach rivaled the rumble of the cartwheels on the cobbles.

"Would you like lunch? There are fantastic meat vendors, and I know a place to eat with a view of the harbor."

In truth, Keplan wanted to go back to the Wise Hare. His feet ached from pounding cobbles in his thin-soled boots, and his mind was exhausted from the press of people.

Azimir caught the hesitation and gnawed on his lower lip. "I'm sorry. Da says I talk too much. Did you want to do something else?"

"I'm tired, but food sounds nice. I don't have any coin, though. I eat at the inn where I work."

Azimir waved away Keplan's words and led him to a vendor on the corner. He bought them each a stick of rolled meat, bread, and vegetables roasted over a greasy fire. He handed Keplan the meal before nosing through the crowd to one of the aqueducts. A narrow, rusted ladder led up the side of the stone. The top was not much wider than a footpath, but it was cool, and the noise of the street below lessened. Keplan sat on the edge, enjoying the thrum of the water rushing beneath him.

"So, the Hartland, eh?" Azimir spoke around his large bite. When Keplan nodded the darker boy continued. "How long did you live there? What brought you to Athrolan?"

"My parents lived there since before I was born. I know my da was raised in a city called Vielrona. He says it's gone now. My mother never said where she came from, but her accent is different from his." He took a bite of the meat while he thought about the answer to the next question. The food was good, the spices more earthen and herb-based than the intricate flavors of Banis seasoning. "I came to Athrolan to learn."

Azimir glanced over with admiration. "You're young to be a journeyman. You must be talented."

Keplan stared at the stones. *I want to stop my mind from spinning and understand the images I keep seeing.* "I'm seventeen. I want to study history and politics."

"You're a year older than I am. The worms can have history, in my opinion. It's too slow for me, but I suppose if you like it well enough...." He shrugged, a gesture that accompanied the boy's every answer. Azimir stared off, silent for a rare moment.

Though he claimed to only be a year younger, his features were far more open than Keplan's. His nose was not as strong as his father's and his skin several shades darker. Warm brown highlighted his black hair. "Your father was in the war, wasn't he?"

"You want to study history, and you don't even know that?"

"My parents told me nothing of the war. I think it was a dark time for them."

"War's a dark time for most. The Dhoah' Laen was my Da's sister. Younger sister. She and the Rakos won the war, bound the world. She disappeared after that."

"My da had a book on the Rakos—they have the stone plates and the fire in their hands. She disappeared? The binding killed her, I suppose."

"No." Azimir's face was uncharacteristically serious. "She rode off and didn't come back. I never met her, but sometimes Da's face gets sad. I think that's when he misses her."

Φ

Warm purple bathed the sky, orange clouds scuttling after the setting sun. Keplan finished sweeping the courtyard and ducked through the rear door. His tasks were easier with daily maintenance, though the common room was always hopeless after the patrons got their boots and hands everywhere. There were still several hours before he would have space to himself, and he tried to sidle past the bar to his room.

"Keplan!" Firas grinned from his perch on a stool. "I was going to go dancing. Would you like to come?"

Keplan frowned. "I thought you work evenings?"

"Ah, but Mirrel does sometimes so I can go out and shirk responsibilities for a bit. Besides," he flicked a hand at where his older sister toiled in the kitchen. "I worked her morning today."

Keplan's brows rose at the lengthy response. The man was clearly well into his mug. "I'm afraid I have no knack for dancing." He grinned sheepishly. "Ma said I have crooked feet, and Da told me I was note-deaf."

Firas laughed. Drink flushed his cheeks, and his eyes sparkled with mirth. "You'd still probably dance better than most there, but suit yourself." He paused in the doorway, head tilted to the side. "Keplan, how long will you be staying?"

Keplan shrugged. Late at night, with the air soft through his window, he wanted to stay forever. "I don't know. I have no plans, no other place to be."

Firas's smile broadened, and in a whirl of blue shirt and patter of boots he was gone.

Keplan closed his door and flopped onto the bed. There was no use trying to nap. *Is this where I'll stay?* Home was faded and childhood gone. Returning would only be a jest of what once was. Firas and Azimir were so bright, finding happiness even in dark corners of the city. *How can they be happy? Is it as simple as ignorance?*

Keplan was still awake when the bartender returned hours later. Keplan was about to open the door to talk when he heard another, deeper voice laughing and muffled talk through the ceiling after the upstairs door shut. Other noises followed a few minutes later, softer ones, that made Keplan's cheeks flame.

When bells tolled midnight, he shoved on his boots and hurried down the stairs. The common room was warm, and the fire crackled in the hearth. He placed the chairs up on the tables and bar before thoroughly sweeping the rough wood clear. He had almost memorized which spots were burn marks rather than spilled food. The task cleared his mind. When Mirrel emerged to set out washed mugs he was already hanging the broom and mop in their place behind the counter.

"Do you need supper?" Her voice was low, more tired than usual.

He turned, unable to hide his surprise at the offer. "I ate in the city, thank you though."

Her brows rose. "With what coin?"

"I made an acquaintance. He bought me food."

Her mouth thinned. "Be careful, Keplan. Not everyone is out to pay you favors." Her face softened. "Though I imagine you know that better than most. I have a bit of cider leftover. Care to finish it with me?"

He sat wordlessly, afraid if he spoke she might change her mind. The steaming half-mug warmed his heart as much as his hands. "I like the spices you use. They're rich."

She grinned, the expression very like Firas's. "It's our da's recipe. He taught our mother to make it too, but it was never quite right."

"Firas said he was in the war."

Mirrel looked down at her mug. "He never met our da. I barely remember him. Both of us look more like my mother's blood. I miss him, sometimes. More, I miss what moments we could have had." She glanced over. "Both your parents are still about?"

"Yes. They lead a simple life, but I think they're content. They don't mention their lives before me, though. Perhaps that is what keeps them happy."

"I wish I knew their secret." Melancholy shadowed her smile. "It's lonely, working all the time."

"You have Firas."

"He doesn't like serious talk. Besides, he is scarcely still long enough for me to speak to him."

Keplan snorted into his cider. "I heard him come home before I came down to clean."

"I doubt he was alone."

"He wasn't."

She grinned at his dubious tone. "Now you know why I put you in that room. None of the paying patrons would be able to sleep with his ruckus."

"Perhaps I'll forget to mop tomorrow after having such a poor night's sleep." He twirled his near-empty mug slowly. "I wish I knew their secret too. Firas's and my parents'."

"Then I'd have no one to talk to." Mirrel nudged him with her shoe. "Go head up to bed. Perhaps they'll pause in their lovemaking long enough for you to catch some rest."

He rose with a soft groan and stretched the stiff muscles of his back. "Thank you for the cider. And the talk."

She toasted him before draining her own mug. "And you."

He wound his way quietly up the stairs and locked his door behind him. Loneliness still weighed on his heart, but his mind was still. He might have been alone, but he took strange solace in knowing he was not the only one.

Nightmares woke him just before dawn, sending his heart thundering with the echoes of pain. He rose, rough palms brushing the still-tender scars on his chest. They were bright red against the tawny skin. He tugged a shirt over his head, angry at the Banis and at himself. His mornings were usually quiet, but his mind needed distractions.

He hurried downstairs, nodding a good morning to Mirrel as he passed. Her scowl was back where it belonged, and she waved his greeting away. Trash and broken furniture and fates knew what else crowded haphazardly under tattered canvas in the stable. Keplan winced. *I hate messes.* He rolled up his sleeves and began with the bins.

Mist burned away as the sun marched up the sky. The sounds of the city changed. Constant wagon wheels and hooves on cobbles grew louder, replacing pockets of low laughter and conversation. Keplan paused to wipe sweat from his brow and perched on the stoop to survey his work. Moly wickered at him from over the stable's half door. The courtyard was clear, the bins neatly lining the small space behind the stable where they would be out of the way. He had untangled the jumble of leather piled by the rear door. It was an old harness for a horse-drawn rickshaw. The vehicle itself he had moved from a disused stall and parked beside the stable under the canvas. He brushed the wood with a hand, smiling at the smooth warm grain on his skin.

A young man with Firas's smile drove a woman home to the Wise Hare. Stolen kisses and a promise before war. He jerked his hand away with a frown. He glanced back at the rickshaw as he retreated to the common room. Objects had never given him memories before. He pushed the thoughts aside and found a thick piece of parchment behind the counter. He was bent over the bar, pen in hand, when Firas stumbled down the stairs.

The bartender's eyes were bleary, narrowed even in the common room's dim light. His neck was scraped red from someone else's beard, and love-bites dotted his collarbone. He offered an incoherent groan and tottered into the kitchen. He reemerged a minute later with a mug of something that looked better suited to a privy floor. He slumped onto the stool beside Keplan and peered at the parchment, only one eye focused. "What's that?"

Keplan turned the drawing so the older man could better see. It was a sketch of the rickshaw pulled by the bad-tempered gelding. A few lines topped the drawing.

"I can't read, lad."

Keplan's cheeks flamed. "I didn't realize. It's an advertisement. I found the little wagon in the stable while I was cleaning, and with some care the harness could be made usable again. If you provided service to the docks and markets, you might draw more customers. I'd be happy to be the driver."

"You cleaned the stable?" Firas's frown deepened, though Keplan did not know whether it was from a headache or thought. When Keplan nodded, the older man looked down at the picture. "That thing hasn't been used for years, but we kept it for sentimental reasons."

"It was a reminder after he died in the war." The words were out before he thought better of them.

Firas glanced up sharply. "Mirrel tell you that? It's not the kind of story she'd share unless she was warning you not to mess about with it."

Keplan grasped onto the excuse only to be interrupted by the inn door banging open. Visitors in the afternoon were uncommon, patrons not arriving until their duties elsewhere were finished for the day. Azimir leaned on the bar, watching Keplan with a bright smile.

Mirrel bustled out of the kitchen, glowering at Firas, who seemed happier to sit. "Welcome, lad, what can I get you?"

"I'm Azi, Keplan's friend, actually."

Her suspicious gaze eyed him from toe to top. "Will you stay long?"

Azimir glanced at Keplan. "I've got a few errands to run, and I thought you might want to come along."

"We'll head out, thank you, Mirrel. I'll be back for supper and to tidy." Keplan led the way out the door, breathing deeply when he was safely out in the street. "I'm sorry to rush you out of there, but I needed air."

Azimir glanced back through the window at Mirrel. "Why, when you have her to look at?"

Keplan stared at the younger boy, confused. "What?"

Azimir rolled his eyes. "That woman, she's a pretty one. Let's go to the markets. I need to find a gift for my brother."

Keplan snorted and fell into step beside him. "Her words are far from pretty. She bites worse than a snake. Firas is kinder."

Azimir glanced over curiously. "Do you prefer the saber to the shield?"

"Excuse me?" Keplan frowned.

Azimir's laughter bubbled from his chest. "Are you more for the menfolk? Are you courting your own?"

"Fates, Azimir, I understand now." The euphemisms tugged a smile onto his face, however, and he felt his steps lighten. "I haven't given it any thought."

Azimir stopped and stared at Keplan, incredulous. "You're seventeen and you've not had a lady or a fellow?"

"Azimir, I lived alone in the woods with my parents until just several weeks ago. What chance, really, would I have had? I wasn't about to jump into the trees with the squirrels."

Azimir doubled over at the thought, his raucous laughter drawing stares.

Keplan's nerves flamed at the unwanted attention, and he nudged the boy with his foot. "Come on, I thought you had errands to take care of."

Azimir's laughter trailed them to the market and Keplan scanned the crowd. Between Azimir's curious questions and his slip about the wagon with Firas, he felt exposed. His legs tightened with the instinct to run. Facts flooded his mind each time he glanced sidelong at the crowd, as if heightened by his anxiety. Azimir paused by a table of jewelry, and Keplan waited for him a pace away. His narrowed his eyes at his new friend's back. *Still nothing.* He shook the curiosity away and focused on his surroundings.

It was close to evening. Sailors and barmaids replaced housewives and children. Cooking meat and pipe smoke underscored ale and burning lamp oil. Keplan may have felt out of place on the streets during daylight hours, but nighttime brought security. He could be anyone. The scars on his cheeks were simply shadows in the low light, and he was one of many foreign young men.

A raised voice arched over the crowd, and Keplan glanced over. It was the same barker he had paused to listen to his first morning in the city. He stopped again. The litany was much the same, with added portions about how trade would fall and the city folk would starve. It was tailored to a poorer, working crowd.

"Azimir," he drew his companion back from his pursuit of a gift. "What is this talk of civil war?"

"I'll explain while we eat. I'm tired and Alleanthus is hard to buy gifts for." He insisted they eat at a bar stall, buying them both a mug of ale and platter of chicken to share before he spoke. "Her Majesty Tzatia is ill, and she disinherited her only heir years ago during the war. Many worry she'll pass without naming a new heir, though who knows who it could be. It would pitch Athrolan into civil war."

"Imagine being thrust into that fate?" Keplan shuddered. "If they do exist, I pity them."

CHAPTER NINE

The 20th Day of Lineme, 1272
The City of Ceir Athrolan

AN'THOR GLANCED UP WHEN Bren opened the door. The general frowned and shuffled his papers into order. "I thought there was another day before we met."

"I'm not here in any official capacity." Bren slid into a chair across from the Ageless man. His features were carefully schooled, but he was a soldier first and An'thor an observant man.

He's afraid. An'thor waited for the man to speak, pale fingers picking at themselves while his gaze did not move from the ambassador.

Bren's eyes flicked to the conspicuously empty chair at the head of the table. "I heard a rumor, An'thor. A distressing one."

"And I've heard one as well, Brentemir, but I doubt you are here to discuss the new brothel opening on Jen Corner."

Bren scraped his hand through his hair. "I'm tired of dancing. Speak plainly."

"The time for that ended when I became general of Athrolan and you were the Military Commissioner of Mirik.

We're locked in this dance of kingdoms, and eventually the song will change."

Bren rolled his eyes at the flowery language. "You're a better warrior than poet."

"My legends won't write themselves, I fear."

"Tzatia's dead, isn't she?"

An'thor's fingers stilled. "That's a poor rumor to breathe life into, Barrackborn." He wanted to draw his sword on the younger man, to weep and confess all at once.

"It's a poor truth to keep from your own kingdom."

My kingdom. That is what Athrolan has become. If he had to burn to keep the city's flame lit, he would light the match with his own hands. "You came to ask if the rumor was true? If I'm hiding the queen's dead body from her own people? Denying them mourning and a new leader?" He shook his head. "She's ill. Her strength will leave soon. For now, though, she fights."

"Then you can tell her to renege her declaration about Alea's son." Bren's voice was hard, but it was with desperation, not sadness. "They deserve peace. They deserve freedom. There is still time to reinstate Daymir."

Certainty sunk its claws into An'thor's gut. "So there is a child."

"You know as well as I do that they disappeared. Who can say if they're even alive? But wherever they are, they deserve peace." Bren rose, clearly through with his demands. "I'll see you tomorrow. Perhaps then you'll have brought Her Majesty to her senses."

An'thor let the ambassador stalk from the room. His mind churned with Bren's careless words. It was only a matter of weeks before the truth of the queen's death wormed its way out of his careful plans. Now, however, there was hope. Brentemir had said "son." *He knows where they are and that she bore a child.* Somewhere, Tzatia had an heir. There was a time when he shared Bren's sentiments about Alea and Arman, but it was not now. Peace was a luxury heroes never found.

Raven would not give him the time. The fact that the secret lasted a month spoke to the commander's idealism and fear. *He wants this to work out.* No one wanted civil war. Not a man as nationalistic as Raven. An'thor heaved himself to his feet. Rumors were starting, and he would be damned if the truth escaped before he was ready.

He pulled on his cloak, though the balmy night did not call for warmth. He visited the queen's room each day, under the guise of tending the woman. The guards at her door rotated frequently. He was lucky that, from the outside, death seemed so similar to illness. *And that the queen isolated herself so much in the last year of her life.* He nodded to the guard. "Is the doctor in with her?"

"Yessir. He came an hour ago."

An'thor slipped into the foyer and carefully shut the door behind him.

The doctor sat at the desk by the door, a book propped on his knee. He glanced up. His face was lined and pale. His lips thinned at the sight of the general. "General Domariigo."

"Doctor." An'thor looked at the queen's bedroom door. "You've been well?"

"Well enough." He followed the Ageless man's gaze. "This is sick, you know. There are words for what you are, ones I won't utter in polite company."

"I've never been considered polite company." An'thor eased himself into the seat beside the man. "Ambassador Barrackborn told me he's heard the queen is dead."

The man blanched. "Are you accusing me?"

"Should I be?" An'thor's smile was bloodless. "I assume you love your wife enough to keep your mouth shut."

"I haven't breathed a word. I don't think it's any one man or woman who's let the truth slip, sir. The city's not blind. And there is the matter of the countess."

An'thor's eyes flicked to him. "You think she's given us up?"

"I couldn't say. And there is no 'us.'"

An'thor stood. "You may leave. We won't require your services until tomorrow. Thank you, Doctor." He waited until the man gathered his things and left before turning to the queen's chamber door. *Fates have mercy on me.*

The lock groaned as it turned. The door creaked inward, and he winced. The wave of sickly sweet rot buffeted him. He walked enough battlefields to control his roiling stomach, but his disgust at himself raged high.

The shriveled body on the bed no longer looked like Tzatia. It barely looked human. He slid the coverlet down, past the heaps of salt and sawdust packed around her body. She no longer rotted, her skin mostly leathered. The first week was the worst, before he thought to bring the salt to dry her. Unable to open the windows, for fear patrols would recognize the smell, he let the air stagnate between the stone walls. *At least the flies are gone.*

He smoothed her hair, covered her with fresh salt and a new, unstained sheet. "I'm trying to protect your wishes, I swear. I know I'll pay for this for the rest of my days, but please, wherever you are, forgive me." He pressed his lips to her brow. Her skin was stiff and acrid against his mouth.

"And there is the matter of the countess." An'thor's gut clenched. He smoothed the covers once more and stepped from the room. He refreshed the bowl of flowers and locked the door.

He did not bother to light his lamps. His hands found the bottle easily without light, and after draining a third, he donned the old clothes from the bottom of his trunk. The black breeches barely fit, and it took him a moment to fasten his jerkin over the paunch of alcohol. *Perhaps I ought to train with my officers more.* He pushed the thought aside and swung open his window. Spring mist shrouded the palace. The shadows of the guards were long, but he knew this particular window was rarely watched. It was why he chose it. He swung his leg out, then the other, dangling from his fingertips before letting himself drop. He hit the ground with a groan. *This must be why Bren chooses to rely on a sy network. We're too old.*

The houses of the noble district were ethereal in the backlit moisture. His feet traced the path to the tall manor belonging to the Count and Countess of Felden. He crouched at the rear gate and fumbled his lockicks out. It took a minute, many moments longer than it would have years ago, but he was in.

The small gardens were wilted and rain stained the whitewash to beige, though the front of the building gleamed white. Grass overgrew the stone path to the parlor's double doors. An'thor skirted the patio, counting windows. A lamp gleamed in the countess' study. He wedged the toes of his boots into the chipped mortar and hauled himself up. Waist-level with the window, he stopped. Countess Fiena was engrossed in a book. An'thor tapped at the glass.

Her eyes closed. When they opened, she was staring at him. She unlocked the window and stepped aside to allow him in. "General."

"Countess." He pulled himself over the window ledge and into the room. "Good evening."

She offered a chair opposite her own. The gesture was gracious, but she did not smile. "I wondered when you would come to kill me."

An'thor reared back. He had not realized it was his plan until he stepped into the garden, but somehow, she had known.

She must have seen the thought cross his face because her mouth quirked, and she said, "I'm not stupid. I've lived in this court my entire life—almost as long as you have, I would wager. I know when someone's days are counted. The moment I witnessed Tzatia breathe her last, I was as dead as she."

An'thor looked away. Despite all his paranoia and planning,this surprised him. "Why didn't you leave the city? You could be begging me, swearing you'll never tell. Why haven't you called the guards? Told your husband?"

"My husband is gone to our estates to meet with our son." She rose, moving to the window. The view from her study was of the city, just a sliver of one palace tower visible to the right. "I could beg or swear oaths. But I've already been questioned. That man, Peraan who is loyal to Daymir, he harasses me every day for information. Someone could blackmail me for the truth the way you've done to Doctor Jalmer—have you killed him, or am I the first?" She waved away his answer without turning to look. "Nevermind. Do you know what I learned, waiting on the queen?"

"I can imagine a lot."

"She was a phenomenal woman. Even weakened by war, she never broke. But what she taught me most was love. Not of family or men, for that I knew on my own, but the love of an idea, something intangible. When the gods were destroyed, Athrolan had already ceased its worship of them. Instead, Her Majesty taught me faith in Athrolan. You have your trust in the Dhoah' Laen. Commander Dorcal has his dedication to the Xain line." She swallowed audibly. "I have Athrolan."

An'thor's blood pounded. This was not how he planned it, if he truly planned it at all. The countess stood in the window, eyes harder than he bet his had ever been, and threw his faith in his face. "Fiena—"

"I'm not through, General. When I'm gone you will leave here, with these words ringing in your mind. It's not a condemnation, just a promise." She fixed him with her hazel eyes. "I'll die for this country, same as any of your poor soldiers. Not to keep your putrid secret, but because I know Tzatia would not want civil war. She believed in Athrolan more than anything. And she believed in The Dhoah' Laen's child. Her Majesty was old, but she was rarely wrong." She spread her arms out. "Stave off civil war for another few weeks. Bury her death with mine."

An'thor's hands shook. He stood. "I'll need you to write a note."

"Suicide? How poetic."

"Don't. Don't be like that. Cynical, harsh."

"No offense, but you don't know me." She went to the desk and drew out a plain sheet of parchment. "What do you wish me to say? I cannot bear to watch my queen pass, and I fear it will come soon?"

"Make it sound real, that's all." An'thor tilted his head, scanning the words as she wrote for treachery or code. If there was one, he could not find it. It was straightforward, the tone exhausted. His heart clenched.

"Satisfied?" She looked down when his eyes met hers. "As much as the city may think you're a traitor, a monster, I don't. I doubt you'll rest easy ever again." Her hand found his. "Get this over with."

He slid open the drawer of the desk, fingers feeling for her letter opener. The razor edge caught the chapped skin of his thumb. *Just as I suspected, a weapon hidden in plain sight.* He wondered if she saw the fear in the black depth of his gaze, the fear not mirrored in her own. "I pray I find half the strength you have."

Her lips quirked in the corner. "I think you will be disappointed."

He stepped close to her, shaking hand pushing the blade against her wrists. His heart hammered. Skin was more resisting than he remembered, and he stopped. Her face was smooth, even the lines from court life feather light in the face of death.

She met his gaze, expectant.

He bore down again. His grip faltered and he fell back. "I can't."

She grabbed his wrist, fingers hard, firmer than he would have imagined. She dragged his hand down, the letter opener sinking across her wrist once, twice. He grabbed her other arm and finished the job, his cheeks as wet as their hands. She staggered, hip crashing into her desk. The carpet turned from blue to burgundy.

An'thor guided her to the chair by the window. "Do you want me to stay? It'll be a few minutes."

Her breathing hitched. "No. Leave me. Let me die with my family's portraits around me. You are little more than a stranger."

He dallied another minute. "I'll remember this. Your family won't. Your kingdom won't, but I will. When the truth is finally known, when Athrolan is safe, I'll sing your praises. I'll sing them till the day I die."

"Always the poet." She flicked her hand, sending blood spurting down her skirt and across the arm of the chair. "Go." Her eyes, half-focused, roved up his face. "Love and luck go with you."

He swallowed the ball of lead in his throat and crawled from the window, pulling it shut behind him. A greased thread pulled the latch down from outside. He tucked the string away, eyes still fixed on the dying woman. *Go.* The last thing she saw should not be a shadow hulked in her window, but the scattered lights of the city she died to save.

He climbed down to the garden, locking the door behind himself. The streets were dark. Mist drifted, ghostlike, across the cobbles. He made it halfway across the district before the manor bells sounded the tragedy. The wall met his back, cold and hard. He slid down the stones, heedless of the gutter filth soaking his breeches. He had killed before. He would kill again. *Some deaths are harder than others.* He knew ghosts were only manifestations of guilt, but that did not stop them from haunting him. He dropped his head to his hands and wept.

Φ

The 25th Day of Lineme, 1272

Lanterns, hovering like starflies, rose in Keplan's mind. They flitted around the city, a hill of stacked earth huts. Keplan stepped through Ban's gates, laughing and calling greetings. Instead of greeting him in return, they stared, like Hi-taln. They pressed closer until he had to shoulder his way past. He could not stop his steps. Hands prodded him, grabbing his clothes until they dragged him down. Pain blinded him, white and burning. Acrid smells assaulted his nose — blood, a latrine, hot metal.

And then he was in darkness with only the sound of his breath. The space was silent. Something glimmered before him, a reflection of his own moon-pale face. There were differences though. The scars were deep, wet cuts again and his palms bloody. Salt and ink ground into the flesh under the abraded skin. It was far gorier than when he had received his tattoos.

"What is this?"

"Humans are terrible." Though his own lips did not move, those of his reflection did.

"Why are you showing me this?" Keplan's gut clenched in horror.

"You won't speak to me again." The words were quiet. His reflection's gaze was eerie and bright, almost colorless.

"How? You're a part of me."

"One of us has to die. They will kill you, and only I will remain."

His chest heaved, sweat cooling on his skin. His window was open, but he still felt trapped. The walls pressed in on him. He rushed through the door and down to the stables. Moly poked her head over the stall curiously, nudging him with her nose. She seemed more at home than she had in Ban. Keplan smoothed his hand over her flank, over the knots of her old Athrolani brand.

An Athrolani brand and a Mirikin blanket. Keplan's thoughts tore past the curiosity. A sharp breeze blew through the open door from the ocean. It carried the sharp smell of brine and smoke. His vision darkened, and images flickered across the backs of his eyelids. *Screams, crashing, the smell of ocean and fire. A woman's muttered words, answers in a deep, burning tone. And then he was suspended over a battle, incorporeal, as chaos reigned. It was a plain, or had been, but one side was covered in roiling black water, the other in towering white-hot flames. Again he heard the voices, louder in his mind than the sounds of death and fear.* The Dhoah' Faer, and the Earth Shaker, *he realized, as with each phrase the elements raged higher.*

Strong arms wrapped around him, rocking him. "Come back, 'Lan."

His eyes flew open, and he realized his throat was sore from shouting. He shook worse than before.

Firas held him gently, pulling away slightly as he came to. "Are you all right?"

They were still in the stable. Moly pawed at the corner of her stall, spooked by the noise. He nodded. "I'm fine."

Firas's brow rose. The usual jest and wry wit were gone. "You looked like you were having a fit."

"It was just a dream."

"You were asleep in the stables? I think not. I heard you run out here a minute ago."

"I wasn't asleep," he admitted before catching himself. He ran a hand over his face. "Never mind it. It's over now."

Firas seemed ready to say more, but his gaze fell to Keplan's exposed palms. "Keplan...." He took one hand in his, touching the tattoo carefully. When Keplan made a weak attempt to pull away, Firas's hand tightened gently. "Not everyone is going to hurt you, you know." He tilted his head. "One of my da's friends, who took care of my ma after the war, had nightmares. Sometimes he wasn't even asleep. When we see terrible things, our mind does that, as if it's trying to fix the memories, revisit them and somehow change what happened."

"I'm sorry I woke you."

"Nonsense. Let's get you back to bed. Dawn will come early." Firas helped him to his feet and followed him back upstairs. He waited as Keplan fumbled with his door. "I know Mirrel says I'm flighty, and never take a moment to be serious, but if you need to talk, honestly, I'm just upstairs."

Keplan smiled. The expression felt wrung out on his tired features. "Thank you."

Firas leaned in and pressed a kiss to Keplan's brow. "Feel better, 'Lan."

Keplan crawled back into bed, his sheets still warm from before. His body and mind were exhausted, but his thoughts refused to cease spinning.

Φ

The 30th Day of Lineme, 1272
The City of RoBal, Ban

Patrols doubled in beyond the Hall of the Purple Throne. It was evening when the floor shook with rushing feet. Rih flew to the window and shoved open the curtains. Women thronged around a wagon in the courtyard below, movements furtive. Rih's stomach knotted. The cart bore a wicker basket in the unmistakable oval shape of a coffin.

Please don't be Ki-elte. The woman was impatient and exuberant, but she was kind, and Rih appreciated their time together. They carried the coffin into the women's quarters, followed by the shaking driver.

A moment later Rih's door swung open. Ki-elte stood in the doorway. Summer sun tanned her face, and travel stained her robes. Her usually playful eyes were marred with shadows. "I'm glad you're awake. I'm sorry I was away so long."

"Has there been another accident?" She did not think much on the first time Ki-elte was called away, but the memory returned to her now. She repeated the question in writing.

The other woman's face was pale. "No, not really." She gestured to the ceiling. "The gongs rang for an assembly a few minutes ago. We're wanted in the women's hall."

Rih tucked slippers on her feet before following down the corridor. The women's quarters were built for privacy and contemplation, and so there were few large common areas. The exceptions were the baths and the low hall set into the basement of the building.

Like every room, silk draped the walls, cushions covered the floors, and even the table on the low dais in the back was rounded and richly patterned. The air was close, even for a summer night. Most of the seats in the front were filled.

Hundreds of footsteps shook the floor.

Ki-elte gripped Rih's hand. "I wish I could stay, but I have to speak." Her fingers clenched. "I'm sorry."

Rih watched her go, heart thundering, a thousand hooves on the battered ground of her chest. *Why is she apologizing to me?* Ki-elte ascended the dais and raised a hand. The crowd must have quieted, for the air stilled and her lips moved. At the distance, Rih barely made out a single word. A hand on her arm drew her attention to Hi-alan, two rows back. The piercer moved closer until she stood just beside Rih.

"I'll translate for you. She's talking about our negotiations with Mirik."

"Thank you." Even relief could not loosen the knot in her gut.

"Many of you know our role in the palace. Our role in the beds of our lords, our commanders. Some of us do not fight our war in the city. Many fight it in the distant small towns, in derelict army camps. And some fight it in foreign nations. Sa-at was one such warrior. She was traded out of the city and brought to Mirik. Hypocrites—they may not buy human flesh, but neither do they question how their exotic whores arrive.

"Sa-at reported to us, and we reported to the Imperial Inquisition. Four weeks ago her messages to us stopped. We were told of her death a week ago. It is not rare for us to be the first casualties. Around her wrist was a set of beads, symbolizing a single word: Hetmir." Hi-alan's fingers faltered as she spelled out the word. Tightness around her eyes told Rih the stumble was from emotion, not the guttural foreign title.

"Hetmir, a title assumed by the military leader of Mirik. And only during times of war. As of tonight, Ban is at war. Our sisters will march, to victory perhaps, but to their deaths. And in our way, we march with them. We will hold an appreciation for our sister Sa-at tomorrow at midnight. After, we go to battle." Hi-alan paused her translation to sign, "Ki-elte is asking us to recite the Woman's Code." She raised her arms, and around them the others did the same.

War. Rih's fingers trembled as they rent the words from her heart. "A woman has a single mind. She wakes for the Empire. She marches for the Empire. Her blood and heart and mind are Ban, breathing and alive. A woman has a single mind."

Φ

War barely changed the bustle of Ban. Poor still clamored for food, and stagnant water clogged with waste. The rich still lavished themselves with luxuries and gemstones. Dust rose higher beyond the walls each day, drummed from the earth by thousands of sandaled feet. Rih watched the red cloud drift across the tangle of Stytown. A gust of air told her the door had opened.

"You wanted to see me?" Ki-elte greeted Rih with shaking hands. Her expressive face was stoic.

"I did." Rih paused, her mission forgotten for a moment at the pain on Ki-elte's features. "You were close to Sa-at?"

The woman nodded, lapsing into voicing. She recognized many of Rih's signs now, but often forgot to use them herself. "When she lived here, we were lovers."

Rih looked down. "Then I grieve for you." She let the signs drift in the air between them for a moment. She pulled a chair out for the other woman and sat at her desk. It took a minute to shuffle through the scrolls and tablets before she found the right one. She handed it to Ki-elte without preamble.

"Fear," Ki-elte read.

Rih produced the larger tablet she used for conversation.

> *You asked me what commanded the Emperor. It is fear. I think I understand our role now, since Sa-at. We are invisible. We fight for Ban in a way the men cannot. We influence. We suggest.*

Ki-elte frowned. "Fear rules us all." Her hands knotted in her lap. It could have been a sign of weakness. The metal in her eyes, however, said it was determination.

> *But you are right. We are not allowed to be truly a part of this world, but neither are we spared its fate. War destroys so many plans, so many lives.*

Rih looked away. Ki-elte placed her anger on Mirik, and while she was not wrong, Rih did not wholly agree. *"Perhaps she has to, to survive this."* She straightened. "I meet with Mosil today, correct?"

Ki-elte made her repeat the two signs, then nodded. Her face brightened as she dug a broad, flat box from her clothes. "I brought you this."

Rih flashed her a smile and took the offered box. It was the plain wicker of a market ware, but the grasses were painted in bright stripes designating the shop was in a nicer district. Inside, a silk net lay on a bed of silk. It was a deep burgundy, shot through with white accents. The weights were cloudy sapphires chosen for their muted pink. Rih brushed the gift with careful fingers. As a soldier, she wore only what she was given, and the gifts to commemorate her induction day each year were few and practical. For years she turned her envy of courtesans' finery into scorn. "Thank you, this is beautiful!"

Ki-elte smiled, and her rare signing was perfect. "I'm glad you like it."

Tears blurred Rih's reflection too much to fasten it.

Ki-elte's gentle hands draped the net over Rih's shaved scalp. Two tiny bronze cuffs clipped to the top of her ears, holding the silk in place. By the time she finished, Rih's emotions calmed enough to see the handiwork. Though it did not match perfectly, the burgundy accented her purple outfit. *The color of Ban. The color of blood.* She squeezed Ki-elte's hand and thanked her again.

"We should go." Ki-elte reminded her.

Rih gathered her tablet and stylus and followed Ki-elte through the halls. The Purple Throne was subdued since Sa-at's death; even in the height of the day the bustle lacked its usual playfulness. Rih looked forward to her cousin's smile and the distraction of learning.

When the door opened, however, Mosil waited in the center of the room. In place of his usual casual robe, he wore loose breeches tucked into tall boots, a fitted shirt with buttons along the forearms, and a thick brocade jerkin. His hair was scraped back into an ugly horsetail. Sweat beaded his brow despite the open window.

"You look uncomfortable."

"Address me properly." Despite the curt words, his expression was gentle, and he gestured to his attire. "Pretend I am your future husband. This is your presentation at the Mirikin court, such that it is. We still hope for negotiations."

This is a test. She stopped at the edge of the dance floor and bowed her head. She understood now why Ki-elte had encouraged her to wear her new net. *This is my armor now.* She tucked her foot behind and bent into an Eastern curtsey.

She watched his spoken introduction then rose from her curtsey and signed her reply. *Will I be able to bring a translator with me?* Perhaps one of the women in her entourage would know enough signs to help.

When he extended his hand, she took it. When the time came would her hand tremble? Unlike during her lessons, his finger did not tap the rhythm against hers. She glanced at the musicians, counting as the drummer began the song. Her first step was uncertain, but Mosil's arm across her back tugged her left, and she fell into the movements. He made small talk, and though she only caught a few words, she saw he discussed the weather, the drapery, and the food they apparently consumed at their imaginary supper earlier. His smile was kind, if vacant. *I wish I could marry him. A man I know.* But baring impending war, she would marry the son of Mirik's Hetmir.

She almost collided with Mosil when he stopped. She blushed and gestured an apology.

He smiled and stepped away. "You did well," he signed. "A few steps out of place, but you will practice."

"How long until the negotiations are final?" *How long until what freedom I have is gone?* She followed him across the room to the tray of juice and fruit, watching his mouth curve down as he explained.

"It's difficult to say, Rih-elte. Negotiations are still underway, despite them declaring war. I wish politics were simple, but maybe then they would not intrigue me so. With luck, you will be married, and we will be at peace by the time the rains end."

"And what more do I have to learn?"

He glanced at Ki-elte but did not meet Rih's eyes. "What is left is not for me to teach. You will continue to meet with me, but only every fortnight. Ki-elte and the other mistresses will begin your tutelage in the carnal arts."

Rih choked on her juice, setting the cup aside before it shattered on the brown stone. *Of course. I am studying to be a wife.*

Ki-elte appeared at her elbow and motioned that they should leave. They returned to Rih's room, and Ki-ete ordered tea. If she spoke, Rih did not notice. Despite her usual restlessness, Rih was glad to be between four familiar walls again. She touched Ki-elte's hand to get her attention. "When does that teaching begin?"

Ki-elte's brows knit. Dullness fogged her eyes again. "Technically it already has. Everything we are, our understanding of our place in the world, and how we affect it, in turn, plays out as lovers. I fear a heavy heart is not appropriate for these lessons, but I will do my best."

Rih's stomach tightened. Giving her body to battle, to arrows or blades or to be trampled under the hooves of her own cavalry, as happened too often, did not frighten her. Sharing it with a man she knew nothing of, whose appetites were unknown at best, was worse than death. She hoped Ki-elte would reassure her. Now it looked like the woman shared her dread.

Tea arrived and Ki-elte prepared Rih a mug heavy with horse butter and spices. She drew Rih's tablet toward her.

> *To begin, we must be relaxed. Tea helps. Massage. Baths. If your husband is not interested in sharing such things, you do them for yourself. Have you lain with anyone before?*

Rih shrugged.

> *No man. Some of the soldiers, when we were in training, we would explore. It was more out of admiration for one another's bodies and urges than romance. Others preferred female lovers. Sex interests me very little, regardless of the partner.*

Ki-elte smiled. "Women are often different lovers from men. We make good teachers. Communication is the most important piece to lovemaking."

Rih winced at the words. Lover. Lovemaking. She doubted those were privileges she would enjoy. "Communication? I can neither understand Trade nor hear."

Ki-elte shook her head.

In this, you have the advantage. Our bodies speak volumes. The press of a hand, the tilt of a head, the nudge of a knee, these are all questions your husband's body will ask. Your body will answer. You will likely marry a boy. He's inexperienced. He may have developed tastes, but you will know more than his common companions. I cannot promise anything, but I can give you the tools to make it as bearable as I can.

Rih grimaced

I have heard about the horrors most women marry. Sex is like battle.

"In some ways yes." Ki-elte offered a faint smile.

I will teach you how to give him pleasure, but moreover, I will teach you control of your body – when and if you have children, and whether you are more likely to conceive a male or female child.

Her smile darkened. Determination slipped her into speech. "We will endeavor not to attack his field of battle, Rih, but instead, force him to fight on yours."

Φ

The 49th Day of Lineme, 1272

By Midsummer, Keplan could have told anyone the best places to buy sweetrolls, bacon, a flock of sheep or a barrel of fish. He knew which sailor had an affair with whose wife, what child was the bastard of the Duke of Pardelan, and the human-trading intent of certain merchants. Much like in Ban, his days took on a disinteresting repetition. He was certain Firas noticed, and perhaps Azimir as well.

It was mid-morning, and his chores were through. Summer was in its full, the sun bright and uncomfortably warm. He perched on the poles of the rickshaw, attempting to mend the hooks for the harness.

The *swish-bang* of the rear door was not yet as familiar to him as the wind through Hartland trees. "Morning, Firas."

The bartender's laugh was low. "You should join the air-tumblers with balance like that." He leaned on the stable door. "Tonight is Midsummer."

Keplan hummed in response, eyes narrowed on his task.

"There will be a festival with dancing."

Keplan finally looked up. He lamented over not having a normal childhood, a normal life. Now when one stepped up and asked, he almost refused. *What is wrong with me?* "Azimir asked as well." He sighed and climbed down from the rickshaw. "When you went dancing you wore a colorful shirt. Do I need something better than my usual?"

Firas's second laugh boomed. "Just don't smell like dung, and for fate's sake deal with your hair!" He returned to the kitchen, leaving Keplan to put a bewildered hand to his head.

Φ

When Azimir arrived just before dark, Keplan was glowering at the tolstovka on the bed. "In the woods, no one cared what my clothes or head looked like!" Keplan groused without preamble.

"That explains an awful lot," Azimir joked. "I rather think you haven't cared before now."

"This is different. And I was told I had to do something with my hair."

Azimir's laughter started as a snort. Soon he was howling, collapsing on Keplan's bed and the offending shirts.

Keplan turned his glare to Azimir. It was fine for a dignitary's son, who probably had new clothes for each hour of the day. He tugged the whitest shirt from underneath his still-chuckling friend and turned to change. Azimir's laughter died at the sight of the scars.

"I'm glad you came here," the younger boy began awkwardly. "After what happened. You're fine company if a bit odd."

Keplan finished buttoning the off-center breast of his shirt and fastened his belt. What did one say to that? He chose to smile. "Firas said to fix my hair," he reiterated.

"I should imagine. Most everyone wears theirs short now."

"I am not cutting it," Keplan stated. His room had a tiny copper mirror by the door, and he peered into it at the tangled mess of dark brown hair. He grasped at Azimir's favorite hero. "The Earth Shaker had long hair."

"He also shot fire from his hands. No one's going to tease you long when you can burn them to cinders."

Keplan ignored the comment and decided to leave his hair down and loose for once.

Firas met them outside the inn. The barkeep elbowed Keplan with a broad grin. "I hardly recognize you." He fell into step on Keplan's other side, arms swinging widely as they strode up the street. "Did you have celebrations at home?"

"My parents lit a fire on a few holidays. What about you, Azimir, do you have the same festivals in Mirik?" With the conversation safely off himself, Keplan focused on the thoughts racing through his head. They may have been uncomfortable, but details about those around him soothed his anxiety. *Knowing secrets gives me control.* It was the same reason he avoided telling Azimir or Firas anything more personal than his taste in ale. His mind grew louder the closer they drew to the crowd. Loudest of all were the small details trickling through Firas's firm hand on his shoulder.

The city ringed the marketplace with ropes and lanterns. Great metal barrels held cheery, crackling fires. Shadows hid emaciated dust-dealers and beggars. The disorder was different than during the day, and Keplan felt at ease. His father sung loudly and often, and made a small drum and flute to play, but Keplan never heard music like this before. Whistles accompanied various drums and cymbals. Once he thought he heard a Banis violin. Pockets of dancing sprang up, blending into each other and curving around stalls of food and wares.

He leaned across to ask Azimir over the undulating ruckus, how one knew the steps. "There doesn't seem to be any pattern." His words jerked to silent when Firas pulled him into a knot of stomping, twirling bodies. Keplan gripped the other man's hand, as much to keep from falling as to follow his path. Firas looked back, playful eyes glinting in the firelight. A thought, not Keplan's own, tumbled into his mind at the glance. "You want to kiss me?"

Firas's brows shot up, his voice pitching over the crowd. "I didn't think you were that bold."

"You were thinking it, not me!"

Firas frowned, and it was a moment before his smile returned. "I'll let you know." The music changed, and Keplan followed him back to where Azimir watched the festivities.

"Let's get some egg-breads." The noble's mind was, again, preoccupied with food.

"I'll find some if you wait here." Dancing and embarrassment still flushed Keplan's face, but navigating the maze of stall to collect food allowed him to order his thoughts. He returned with a full tray and an awkward grin. "Here we are."

Firas's face lit up and he gathered his portion into his hands. He leaned over to plant a quick kiss on Keplan's cheek. "Perhaps you were right."

Keplan busied himself with eating to hide his sudden blush. If Azimir noticed, or cared, he said nothing. The loaf in his hands was round, stuffed with eggs, onions, and mushrooms. "This is possibly the best thing I've eaten in my life."

Firas snorted. "Your standards are low."

"What did you discuss in my absence? How much better my hair looks than Azimir's?" *I'm apparently rubbish at flirting.*

"I think it might look even better than my own. But no, Azimir was ogling the women."

"I enjoy festivals much more now," Azimir defended. "I can appreciate the scenery."

Firas rolled his eyes and glanced over at Keplan. "So, is this sufficient to bribe you into staying here?"

Keplan stared at the crowd. It was a jesting question, but it had a more serious answer. The mass of dancing city folk was a great pulsing heart, lit with firelight. Swirling colors and winking jewels like stars shining through late evening clouds. *This could be home.* He allowed Firas to throw an arm around his shoulders as he grinned. "It might be."

Hours later, Keplan slumped against the back of a stall, holding a leather flask. "You're hopeless."

Azimir swayed gracelessly to the music beside him. Though Keplan did not dance again, his feet tapped along when Azimir spun with first one girl then another. Firas excused himself half an hour before, begging drunkenness and the press of responsibilities the next morning.

"What makes me humpless?"

"Hopeless, Azimir." Keplan giggled at the other boy's misunderstanding. At first, he disliked the bitter alcohol, but it seemed to improve the more he drank. "The girl with the dark curls, she has a fellow already. The navy captain with the thick brows."

Azimir groaned. "I thought she was giving me lover's eyes." He glanced over at Keplan. "So do you just notice more or is it some sort of...." He wiggled his fingers over his own head.

Alcohol loosened the hinges of Keplan's tongue. "I see secrets. Things you don't wish others to know. Whatever you think most, your history, it jumps into my head."

"Show me!"

"Pick someone." The game continued, Azimir choosing from the crowd. It was a fickle gift, if it was a gift at all, but he could read close to a third of the folk Azimir chose. He rattled off what sprung into his mind with eye contact. Dawn was closer than dusk when they meandered from the square. Azimir paused where they parted ways.

"What about me?"

"What do you mean?" Keplan suppressed a hiccup.

"What do you see when you look at me?"

Keplan glanced over. *I can't see much of anything. It's part of why I enjoy your company.* He pulled a grin onto his face as he lied, "You want to bed a city girl before you go home."

Φ

The 2nd Day of Aeme, 1272

Grit in the bottom of An'thoriend's mug added a certain authenticity to the topic at hand. Despite the rich robes of the council members, cheap candles lit the table, and the meal growing cold before them was meager. "This talk is fine," An'thor remarked, leaning back in his seat to the right of the empty throne, "but what of the civil unrest in the Slummer and Merchant Town? I would rather be in ill-graces than be hamstrung while paying my debts."

"Rabblerousers in the Thread or Slummer scarcely equal civil unrest, General, even with your dramatic touch," the senior consulate scoffed. The Athrolani Council was rarely called to meet in full, the two branches often functioning independently. Since word of the queen's failing health spread, the entire force of noble-representing consulates and commoner-elected House of Guilds had all but taken up residence in the meeting halls of the Ceir Athrolan's palace.

"Consulate Eron, please remain polite," An'thor asked, rubbing the bridge of his nose. "What's changed? Last I knew, you hoped to encourage trade."

"You're right." One man leaned forward, shipyard's insignia glinting on his breast. "However, few want to trade with an unstable kingdom. And there is the matter of a noble woman's suicide. If even the nobles are that concerned we do, indeed, have a problem."

Raven's brooding gaze rested on the paper before him as he toyed with a dry quill. He finally broke his usual silence. "The army is disbanded, sent to guard at home. The navy still barricades offshore, prepared for war between Ban and Mirik. Many of my navy men are still in port, however. I can send them into the city to bolster the guard."

"You bring a point," another consulate mentioned. "We are not at war, yet the general and the commander sit here as if there is a queen to flank and blood to shed."

An'thor's ring clacked on the table as he slammed his hand down. "Were Her Majesty not ill, she would be seated here to punish your insolence herself." The words echoed softly and settled over the tense conversation. "She should not be troubled by this. I, or her doctor, would be happy to convey your concerns to her, but she does not have the strength to sit state." His gaze swiveled to Raven. "Send aid to the guard, Commander. Our debts will wait until another day. Those of the Xain house arrive within the month. Until a decision is reached — and it will be, before Her Majesty passes into peace — Dorcal and I will remain." His use of the Commander's name made it clear they were united on the matter. *Despite his threat a month ago.*

With the meeting dismissed, the consulates of the House of Commons returned to the city. An'thor watched as the rest broke into their factions. When the door shut behind the last, his black eyes flicked to the commander. "Your men will not stop a revolution, Raven."

Raven fixed him with an exhausted stare. "Let it rest. You've made your point that Athrolan is weak. Let a lesser cousin take the throne and allow the queen some dignity. You've poisoned this. Between hiding her body, whatever you did to force the countess' hand — "

"I did nothing!" An'thor paced to the window. He drew a breath, then another. When he spoke again, his voice was too sad to be bitter. "I want to believe Tzatia knew best. I have to believe it."

"Her Majesty is what's best! Her blood, her line!" Raven's normally reserved features were rabid, then anger dissolved as his face sunk into his palms. "Fates, I wish she were still alive. She would fix this chaos."

"If she were still alive, we would have no chaos. I know you want me to tell them, but we need firmer ground to stand upon before we announce her death. Please, give me that time." An'thor paused, seeing the Commander's shaking hands. "You meant Eras." He frowned, staring out at the angry sky. "You think she would do differently than I? Goodness knows you and she agreed on precious little when it came to state matters."

"She was one of us, loyal to the queen."

"She was asai!"

"She was more Athrolani than you will ever be!"

An'thor had heard and said far crueler words, but the fatigue of ruling weakened him to breaking. "If you wish to watch our city fall simply because you are too stubborn to change, then you are a fool. My blood does not make me care for her any less." Slamming the door as he left was childish, so he let it click carefully into place, but his blood seethed.

Raven's pragmatic nature once balanced An'thor's idealism during their private meeting and during council. Now it opened chasms where there had only been lines. His feet found the worn path to the tombs without guidance, and he sank to the floor of the Vault of Heroes. His capped horns clicked against the stone of Eras' grave. Across the way, the white stone of the Royal Mausoleum glinted. He had not sat there since the night of the queen's death. Instead, he had an agreement with the stone sealing Eras away—he paid it in conversation, and it refrained from making him weep.

He had no such agreement with the blank stone that would mark Tzatia's grave. *When I admit she needs one.*

"Raven misses you," he told Eras. "He wishes I were in your place. He hasn't said as much, but he might soon." An'thor slid a hand along the floor absently. "All the blooded claimants are coming to the city. It's months away, and even if we announce it, I fear the city will consume itself. Already there are supporters—paid and volunteer alike—of each royal cousin, barking at street corners and in the square as if our capital is a damn village hall. Raven's close to begging Daymir to return." He rested a cheek on the cool stone. "He does not realize I already did. Daymir refused. Alea refused. Civil war is inevitable, but I fear Raven and I will fall on opposite sides."

CHAPTER TEN

The 4th Day of Aeme, 1272
The City of Ceir Athrolan

BREN SAT AT HIS desk, Reka across from him, when Azimir clattered up the stairs. The door banged open, and Bren glanced up with a wince. "If you had a fraction of your brother's tact, Azimir, it would be a miracle." His eyes brightened, however, when his son dumped a tray of honeyed meat haphazardly near the stacks of paper. "I dislike you spending this much time in the city alone, but if this is the result, I might turn a blind eye." He glanced up at Reka. "Begging your pardon."

She snorted and waved the comment away. "If I cared about my condition, I wouldn't be here." She offered an arm in greeting. "I don't believe we've met."

Azimir grinned and took her arm with youthful enthusiasm. "I'm Azimir A'hane of Mirik, second son of Ambassador Brentemir Barrackborn."

Reka's mouth twitched wryly. "I'd gathered. I'm Monareka Elang, a correspondent for your father."

"You're a spy!"

Reka glanced at Bren. "Well he's bright, I'll give you that."

"I doubt it was my doing." Bren flushed and looked down. He and Kemmer's arrangement with Reka was one he still danced around. As much as he wanted both his sons to know the woman who birthed them, Reka's wishes were just as valid. *Alleanthus discovered it for himself, but there's no need for me to ruin a good evening.* He pointed at the door. "Regardless of how bright you are, Azimir, we have state business. And I meant what I said about being in the city alone."

"I'm not alone, I'm with Keplan."

Bren's eyes narrowed. It was difficult to adjust to the threats that came with his station. The threats on his children, however, he took far more seriously. "And who is Keplan?"

"We met shortly after we arrived. I met him in the market when a guard accused him of picking my pockets."

Bren's brows shot up. "And I assume you didn't think he actually was."

"He really wasn't, honestly, Pa. He lives and works in one of the inns in the Slummer. The Wise Hare."

Bren's frown deepened. "I know the place." After a moment he waved the boy away. "Please use sense. And go practice in the training courts. You could stand to work on your upswing." He glowered at the honeyed meat. When his son was gone, Bren turned back to Reka.

Her thick black brow quirked. "Shall I look into this Keplan?"

"Please. This is the first I've heard of him, but I'd like to err with caution."

"I'll take care of it. In the meantime, keep your boy busy. Elsewhere. It could be a harmless friendship."

"Or a potential kidnapping."

Reka jerked her chin at the paperwork. "Pick this up in the morning? I find myself in need of a walk."

"Indeed."

Reka returned to her small room in the city only long enough to change into common clothes. A few practiced wraps of a *jahi* and a light cloak later, she passed for a Sunamen trader. Bren may have had soldier's roots, but he was naïve and Reka knew enough to never trust a man who befriended a noble's son.

She crossed the city in a winding route through busier areas. Her network of gossips and spies was irreplaceable, but she learned a lot from her own careful listening. She sighed with appreciation as she stepped up to the Wise Hare. Four years had passed since work last brought her to its bar, but the old inn had changed little.

She slid behind a small table and dissuaded any ill looks with a bright greeting to the bartender. Firelight filled the lively common room. Most faces she recognized as sailors, with a few traders tossed into the mixture. None were young enough to warrant suspicion. She was almost through with her meal and mug before she heard anything of interest.

A quiet figure entered through the rear door, brushing straw from a pair of breeches that looked both too loose and too short.

"How'd the errands go, Keplan?" The bartender slid a plate of food and drink to a seat at the corner of the bar.

Reka's curiosity piqued. Long hair told her he either did not know current fashions, or did not care. Hardship was evident in slumped shoulders. Scars on his cheeks spoke of time ill-spent in Ban. Her gaze fell to the gloves, still on despite both heat and being indoors. *I'd bet good money those hide a crimson palm.* He flashed a tired smile at whatever the bartender said and set about eating.

He cleaned his plate, motions precise, and turned to rest his gaze on her. Cold settled in Reka's gut. Azimir's friend may have been world-weary, but he was no more than a boy. Ice-chip eyes and awkward features echoed in her mind. His attention moved on as suddenly as it settled. After discarding his dishes, he whispered something to the bartender and disappeared upstairs.

Reka recognized the fearful nature. *Just because he's a victim doesn't mean he means no harm.* Unable to find the bartender, she left a silver coin and a handful of coppers on the counter and slipped back onto the street. She took a deep breath of the evening's cool air.

"What do you want with him?"

Her hand fell to her dagger's hilt. "I don't know what you mean."

The bartender leaned against the wall, tucked into the shadows of the alley. All mirth was gone from his narrowed green eyes. "You've visited us before, each time watching your fellow patrons. Usually one in particular. This time you were interested in our new boy."

Reka sighed. It was clearly too long since she last gathered information on her own. "He keeps the company of a friend's son. I was concerned his intentions were ill-willed."

The bartender laughed, though it was not a happy sound. "I wondered when milord's family would take notice of his slumming. Enough nobles lie about their birth for a night and spend time in places like this. I recognize the signs." His features sobered. "I don't know Keplan's full story, but the family need not worry. He's harmless."

Reka crossed her arms. There was no threat in the bartender's stance, but her nerves were wary. "Where is he from?"

The bartender shrugged. "The south somewhere. He speaks Trade as though born to it, but isn't accustomed to a city. He may be Athrolani, maybe not." His eyes hardened. "I haven't asked. It's his business." The accusation was sharp and hung in the air between them.

Reka had far outstayed her welcome. "Thank you for the food and your candor." She tucked her hands in her pockets and strode away. Her thoughts returned to the boy's face. The intensity in his eyes nagged at her. Somewhere, she had seen it before. Whatever it was, she lay it aside with her cloak upon returning to her room. Her report to Brentemir was quick and to the point.

> *-B,*
> *I visited the inn tonight and caught a glimpse of your son's new friend. He's about the same age, though appears to have lived enough for twice the years. Though skittish, I doubt he has any ill intent. The bartender was quick to defend him, and that speaks to his character.*

She paused, wondering what else to add. Her gaze paused on the portrait tucked into her writing kit. A much larger version hung in Brentemir's study depicting the Dhoah' Laen, her Rakos guard, Brentemir himself and the general and commander of Athrolan at the time. It was a contrived portrait, one that none shown ever sat for, but the likenesses were good. Upon her appointment as Bren's spy master, she received the much smaller copy, and one did not refuse a gift from the acting king simply because aesthetic tastes differed.

Her eyes narrowed on the painting. Lyne'alea stared back from the canvas. A few shades lighter and her eyes could have been the boy's in the bar. She tugged the painting into better light, eyes flicking from Alea's to her guard's. *Strong nose, dark hair. Sharp chin, cheekbones.*

"Deershit."

Keplan came from the south, far from people. Lyne'alea's son would be close to Azimir's age. "What are the odds you found your way here and befriended your own cousin?" Far stranger things happened. *Especially when your blood carried that much power.* Still, Lyne'alea could have passed for a striking Athrolani woman in her youth, and Arman's features were common enough in the south. She scratched another line before folding the letter neatly.

> *Perhaps you can ask to meet him.*
> *-R*

She did not add a postscript.

Φ

The 7th Day of Aeme, 1272

Steady tapping of summer rain woke Keplan just before dawn. Damp air gusting into his room brought the smell of soil and ocean. He reached up to fumble the shutters closed, but paused. Mist hid all but the closest buildings and muffled the normal city sounds. It reminded him of home, as if someone showed him their idea of what his childhood had been. He finally pulled the window to, leaving just a crack for fresh air. The closed space was all the more reason to begin work.

The stable was nearly clean when a knock sounded on the door frame.

"Were you planning on taking a trip to the market?"

He flashed a quick smile, vaguely disappointed to find it was Mirrel. "I hadn't thought yet. I could if you need something."

"Just the supplies for the week. The wagon would be easier. I'll make a list."

In another minute he was wrestling for the gelding's head as he backed the animal up to the rickshaw. Ragweed was used to the young man now, but nothing helped the horse's disposition. Keplan managed to get into the street with only two new welts from Ragweed's teeth. The market was less crowded, and Keplan silently thanked Mirrel for her timing as he moved along the stalls. Her formidable list set Keplan's stomach growling.

He turned back to the slums, but hauled Ragweed to a halt at the clatter of shod hooves in the mist. Riders approached from the west, heavy-boned mounts draped in yellow and brown. They were armed and armored, the figure at their center bearing a fur-lined cloak over his bare head. Keplan's eyes narrowed on the Athrolani insignia. He was so preoccupied, it took a moment to notice someone stopped beside him. Keplan opened his mouth to warn Azimir of Ragweed, but his words came too late. The younger boy cursed as he dodged the next attack. "You attract foul-tempered animals as well as people?" Even rubbing a stinging forearm, his smile was bright. He gestured to the disappearing recession. "What do you think of that, eh?"

"I think that is a lot of weapons for their mother city. Who are they?"

"Personal guards and soldiers of County Felden. The Countess recently passed." He switched topics with the usual grace. "Care for a ride?"

"Meet me at the Hare?"

Azimir grinned in response and took off back toward his manor. It was a matter of minutes before Keplan unloaded the wagon and returned the feral Ragweed to his stall. Azimir waited in the street with his own mount by the time Keplan groomed the temperamental beast and readied Moly for the ride. Despite his noble upbringing, Azimir took riding in the rain well, and Keplan was quick to remark on it.

"Fog comes in every morning over Mirik. It's as if we're the only land in the world until mid-morning," Azimir explained.

Keplan's eyes fell to the cob between Azimir's knees. The animal was a blood bay, with a mane most women would envy. The tack, too, was fine, but little helped Azimir's seat. "Are you sure you've ridden before, Azimir?"

The boy laughed brightly as they crossed the square. "My Ma says I've footsoldier's blood. Besides, look at your pony—you can't tell me you can do much better!"

Keplan snorted. Azimir's explanation always involved something his parents or brother told him. Keplan shifted his weight as they passed under the city gates, and Moly broke into a jaunty trot. If there was one thing he knew, it was riding. "Moly may be dignified in her years, but I grew up on her back."

"Where did you grow up?" Azimir asked. "I know you said the Hartland," he waved off Keplan's automatic response, "but I mean, did you ever visit cities?"

Keplan chewed his lip thoughtfully. "We lived a day's ride from Namus. My father visited often, but I only went occasionally."

"You're strange." Azimir held a hand up in defense, causing his horse to pause. "Fun, but bizarre."

Keplan's brows arched, but a grin tugged his mouth and he urged Moly up the slope. The landscape was enough like home to make him miss the smell of his mother's cooking drifting through the trees. The rain hissed on the grass.

"So, you had no friends?" Azimir had caught up.

"You and Firas are my first. I'm not certain about Firas, though. I knew better than to make friends in Ban." He winced at the thoughtless words and waited for Azimir's usual barrage of questions.

"They thought you were a Mirikin spy."

As grateful as Keplan was for the lack of judgment, the pity radiating from Azimir's face was worse. Plenty of people assumed, and probably most correctly, what caused his marks. Having someone know, for certain, made him vulnerable. *Secrets give them power.* "You said you were good at tracking," he began, not caring the subject change was obvious. "Do you hunt often?"

"My father has a close Border friend. I've only actually met her once, but she taught my father a lot. My mother is a skilled fighter as well."

Scars crisscrossed the eyes of the woman in Keplan's thoughts. Only one seemed to still function. "Your mother is partially blind? From the war?" The knowledge startled Keplan as much as the words surprised his friend.

Azimir's eyes narrowed on Keplan. "That's my father's Border friend. Our ma is Kemmer, Mirik's Military Commissioner and current Hetmir. Did you see her leaving the house?"

Keplan made a show of peering through the canopy to see how heavily the rain fell. "Something like that." He pushed back his hood and closed his eyes. The forest brought him peace. This was earthier than home and had a sandy smell about it, just as he could always smell the stone of the city. Forgetting himself, he stuck his tongue out to taste the rain as it rolled from the leaves above.

Azimir edged up behind him, and Keplan's hand darted out. He shook a sapling, dousing them both with rain.

"It got you too, idiot!" Azimir laughed, wriggling on his poor horse's back.

"I'm not a noble. It's quite fitting for me to be rain-soaked—I was raised by tree spirits." He angled his gaze at the vegetation around them. "Not strange white ones, like these, though."

Azimir laughed again. "Sometimes I can't tell when you're joking." He made a face when Keplan began to chew a strip of bark from one of the darker trees.

Keplan offered Azimir a piece. "It settles the stomach. My father makes beer from it."

Azimir declined but asked about the beer. He led the way further into the forest while Keplan explained the process. Their horses' hoofbeats changed from soft *whump-thumps* on the loam to *whack-skriss* as they climbed higher into the hills. The light rain from the morning turned to heavy blue clouds.

Azimir drew to a halt, nodding his chin to the bare hilltop ahead. A plain stone stood amid blackened trunks. It was white, stained from two decades of rain. It had been left uncarved, its rough sides smoothed by erosion. "Have you seen the Rakos' tomb?"

The small hairs on Keplan's arms rose as gooseflesh peppered his skin. "The Rakos is dead?"

Azimir shrugged. "There are a few different versions of the story. It's not a tomb for him, exactly. It is titled 'The Tomb of Madness.' General Domariigo said when the Dhoah' Laen joined the worlds again, she thought the Earth Shaker was dead. She camped here, and in the middle of the night, a thunderstorm raged, and the Rakos came to her. With one touch she erased his madness from the war." Azimir shrugged. "No one comes up here much anymore."

Sweat bloomed on Keplan's palms. *Blood boiling through stone veins, dust and dried gore cloying his throat. Insanity and power sloughing from his skin, sinking back into his veins.* He shuddered, stomach clenching. Moly tossed her head and backed downhill until they were once again outside the ring of scorched trees. The scent of woodsmoke drifted between the blackened trunks. "I envy him."

"Envy the general?" Azimir's voice seemed to echo from a league away.

Keplan shook his head, as much to rattle his thoughts back into place as to answer. "What I wouldn't give to bury madness."

Azimir's dark eyes widened, and he gripped his reins with white knuckles. "Your secret-seeing."

Keplan pressed his brow to Moly's wet mane. "I came here looking for answers. All I have is a name from years ago, and too many voices that don't belong between my ears. So yes," he drew a ragged breath, chest still yawning in the wake of a fraction of the Earth Shaker's power. "I envy the Earth Shaker's madness, washed away in a storm."

Azimir looked at him for a very long time, silent. Then he shrugged deeper into his cloak and turned away. "I think our cook will be starting supper, and I'm getting cold."

Keplan counted the retreating hoofbeats, hands knotted in Moly's mane. He was not sure what made him toss his trust at Azimir with an awkward confession. Whatever it was, he regretted every word.

"Well, are you coming? I thought you could meet my father." Azimir waited at the head of the trail, face puzzled.

Relief exploded in Keplan's chest. He tried to hide it, but by the time he drew abreast of Azimir, he was grinning.

The manor houses clustered on the highest tier of the city, built neatly against the barracks at the city's southern gate. Stone walls separated each house, small turrets flying various pennants. Azimir drew up outside the gate of a narrow manor with a small garden in the rear. Sounds of stablehands and horses drifted across the empty courtyard from the stable along the right wall. Azimir's face brightened as he dismounted and led them inside. It was strange to hand Moly over, and Keplan made sure to thank the young boy who took her reins.

"My pa is back." Azimir nodded to the gleaming chestnut mare that turned to eye them with interest. "That's his Dawn."

Keplan reached a hand out to the animal with a broad smile. The horse was beautiful and clearly well cared for. "A lovely name for a lovely girl," he said softly as he scratched her poll.

Azimir snorted. "Her full name is Blood of Dawn, and she's a powerful warhorse. Sweet here, but vicious in battle."

Keplan's brows rose, but he gave her one more pat before following his friend to the private courtyard in the back of the manor. He expected the same opulence of the nobles in Ban. Instead, the finery was understated, the colors simple. Green and vermillion featured prominently, but muted. The boys threaded their way through a potted garden and up to a large wooden double door, one side of which was open. Azimir tossed his cloak and riding gloves onto a rack at the door. Keplan did the same, though he kept his gloves on.

A windowed room down the hall offered a small buffet of fruit and bread, upon which Azimir descended with alarming excitement. Keplan had a mouthful of pear when a face peered into the room.

The man was several years older than they, but had the same dark skin and black hair as Azimir. "Azi, did you just return?" As Azimir nodded, the newcomer caught sight of Keplan and stepped inside. "You must be my brother's city friend." He held out an arm. "I'm Alleanthus A'Hane of Mirik."

Keplan took the arm gingerly. "Keplan Wardyn."

Alleanthus turned back to his brother. "Da's busy. A missive just arrived from our mother. He wants you here for supper, though he will not join you. I'm off to meet with our clerks." He returned to the doorway. "Well met, Keplan." He left as quickly as he arrived, and Keplan stared after him.

"The nobles here are different from what I expected."

Azimir spoke around a mouthful of fruit-decorated bread. "You thought we would be pretentious?"

"In Ban anyone inferior is like furniture. Or worse."

Azimir made a derisive noise. "My father never shook free of his humble roots. I'm told we show his influence more than we ought. Athrolani nobles are more traditional." He scraped more jam onto a slice of bread and gestured to the stairs. "Come meet him."

"Didn't your brother say he was busy?" Keplan noted as he followed Azimir up the curved stairway in the front of the foyer.

"I think he will like you. Besides, he asked to meet you. He dislikes me spending time with people he doesn't know well." Azimir knocked on the closed wooden door at the top of the stairs and opened it before an answer came.

Keplan trailed behind, eyes wide. The study was plain and dark, with a large desk behind which sat Mirik's Ambassador. His thin lips pursed in a frown as he surveyed a thick document.

"Not now, Azimir. The breakwater took on some damage in that storm last week. This could slow trade to nearly half, and with the war...." He trailed off and scratched his head before continuing. "Ask Al if it's something important." He glanced up then, flashing a quick smile at his son and Keplan. "Is this the boy you met?" His eyes dropped back down to his work.

"Yes. Keplan, this is my father, Ambassador Brentemir Barrackborn of Mirik."

"Keplan Wardyn, my lord." Keplan bowed unsteadily. "Forgive me, I don't know the proper way to greet someone of your status."

Brentemir looked up, frowning at the introduction. "And where did you say you were from? I understand you were not raised in the city."

"He didn't, Da, and he's not a criminal."

"It's all right, Azimir," Keplan muttered. The questions made his skin crawl. "I'm from the south, the Hartland."

The ambassador's gaze swiveled to Keplan's face then fell to the boy's fidgeting hands. "Thank you for humoring me. I hope you and Azimir enjoy the evening." It was an obvious dismissal, albeit polite, and Azimir tugged Keplan away, calling a brief goodbye to his father. "He's been scatter-minded lately. There's a lot of busy talk about Ban."

Keplan glanced back as the door shut. Brentemir stared through the rain-streaked window seemingly lost in thought.

Φ

Keplan woke on the floor of his bedroom, back aching and a hen's egg on the back of his head. "Damn," he hissed, probing at the offending lump.

"Do you always run about in your sleep?" Firas's voice was gentle. He stood in the doorway, eyes still bleary. Gooseflesh dotted his bare chest and shoulders.

"There's not enough time in the day to get things done." Keplan's voice was so soft, Firas almost did not catch the joke.

He grinned finally and padded over to Keplan's prone form to tug the blankets from under him. It took a second to remake the bed, though Firas left the sheets untucked. Keplan wondered if it was out laziness or distraction.

The women in Athrolan were strong and curved, and his body responded to them often enough. Firas was different. His build tended toward stocky and he moved with careless ease. Keplan realized the bartender had spoken. "What?"

"I asked if you wanted to talk. Is it often? You can't tell me you don't remember them." He settled on the end of the bed, elbows propped on his thighs. A short dark curl fell across his forehead, but he made no move to brush it away.

Keplan pulled himself to his feet and slumped onto the bed. "I remember them. It's not every night, but more often than sometimes." He glanced over. Firas was not running. Keplan touched one curl with his long finger before pressing his brow to Firas's.

"Can I touch you?"

Keplan nodded, nerves singing under his skin. Firas's hands brushed shoulders, skimmed forearms, smoothed the small of his back. Featherlight but assured.

Keplan mimicked the gesture, his movements hesitant. He leaned back, blanketing his body with Firas's. Heat followed the scrape of Firas's beard against Keplan's neck, and the younger man shuddered. The bartender may not have had curves, but Keplan's body did not seem to care. He stopped Firas's hand as it moved further down. "Just this, please."

He felt the other man smile against his mouth. "Of course. I'm patient." He brushed Keplan's hair back carefully and pulled him closer. "This won't make you forget, 'Lan."

Sensation and the breath between them silenced Keplan's thoughts. *With one touch she erased his madness from the war.* He raised his chin and kissed the other man. "You do not know that."

It was not screaming, or fire, or pain that woke Keplan the next morning, but sunlight. The sheets beside him were still warm. He sat up with a yawn, running a hand through tangled hair. A love-bite marked his chest beside his scar. Keplan did not know what he expected, or whether Firas was just another piece of denial in his chest. He only knew that his sleep had been dreamless.

Φ

Reka had just hung up her cloak when rapid pounding shook her door. She sighed and slid back the leather flap covering the hole in the wood.

"Reka, it's me. Please just open up."

She jerked the door open. "Was I right about the queen?"

"What?" Brentemir blinked. "No. Perhaps. May I come in?"

She gestured for him to make himself at home. The single room was sparse, made for little more than sleeping. The kettle chuttered over the fire, and Reka nudged the coals with the poker before stripping off her wet clothes and hanging them on a rack by the fire.

She glanced back to see Bren was staring at his hands. Usually, her lack of modesty triggered a reminder from him that he was, in fact, married. *As if I'm interested. There are far too many emotions there for my taste.* She tugged on a dry shirt and breeches and set out two mugs. "Alright. Tell me."

"She was in my life for all of a year and then gone as quickly as she came."

Reka rubbed the knots of scars on her nose. "If you want to reminisce, I'd rather not do it at this cursed hour."

Bren looked up. "You're angry." His expression bordered on bewildered, and Reka wondered when he last slept. "I was waiting across the way since this afternoon."

She heaved a sigh. "When will you act like a noble?"

He looked back at the portrait. "I think Keplan—Azimir's new friend—is their son."

"Do you?" Reka leaned back. "He's a wretch and troubled by eight kinds of darkness, but I think he's just a boy."

"I met him. I was distracted, focused on the war and problems at home, and I did not look at him fully at first. His eyes are my father's, and he has the nose we are all gifted with. But his mouth and jaw could be Arman's exactly."

"And you're not seeing these things because you just found out they have a son? I saw him," she reiterated, "and he could have been any Athrolani mongrel." Bren winced at her words. Whether it was her chosen term or disbelief that offended him, she wasn't certain.

"His surname is Wardyn."

"I know. You had me follow him for three days."

"He comes from the Hartland."

She fingered the handle to her mug. "All right. Let's assume—for the sake of your desperation—you're right. The Dhoah' Laen's son has returned to Ceir Athrolan. What will you do? You claim him as nephew and An'thoriend will grab him faster than you can declare war."

"If he refuses the throne, then Athrolan will be at war—it might even if he didn't."

She glanced at the writing kit tucked into her desk. Brentemir finally realized what she knew for days. "If anyone is their son, it's him, Bren. But you're wrong to drag him into this. What if he refuses to be your child-champion and end your war before it begins? When we discussed the queen's choice we assumed their child would arrive well before the queen's death, on a foaming warhorse, lighning in one hand, fire in the other. This boy is poor and haunted and possibly mad. You claim him, you rob him of his future just as surely as Alea and your blood robbed you of yours."

Φ

The 8th Day of Aeme, 1272

Had Keplan been given to whistling, the rafters of the Hare would have rung. The sun seemed warmer on his skin and the day brighter. When Firas shot him a smile across the common room, he returned it tenfold. He sat, cross-legged, mending a table leg. A particularly vigorous whack from the mallet sent pegs skittering across the floor. One bounced off the highly polished boot of the man standing in the doorway.

Keplan's eyes met those of Mirik's Ambassador. "Fates." He scrambled to his feet and bowed. "Would you like to sit?" His eyes fell on the un-mended leg. "Though perhaps not here."

Brentemir held up a hand. "I am not here officially."

Is there any other way for you to be? Keplan's pulse thrummed. "Is Azimir all right?"

"Quite. He doesn't know I'm here. Perhaps we could speak somewhere privately."

Keplan led the way, opening the door wide and allowing the ambassador through first. The space seemed much smaller with the tall man in its center. Keplan did not know where to stand. He leaned against the wall, only to straighten when Brentemir politely accepted the offer of a glass of water. "It was not so long ago I frequented this tavern. Seems like lifetimes, though." Brentemir was transfixed by the glass in his hands.

"You've come to ask me to leave your son alone." Keplan was frankly surprised it took this long for the man to stop his son's slumming.

"Not at all." On less fatigued features, Bren's expression would look surprised. "No offense, but such a request would not warrant a personal house call." He gestured to the narrow chair. "May I?"

"Of course." Keplan continued to stand and crossed his arms over his chest.

"Will you tell me about your parents?"

What is he getting at? "Not much to tell. They came to the forest a few years before I was born. I'm seventeen now. They built their homestead with their own hands and rarely left."

"And their names? Wardyn like yourself?"

"My father's is. Arman Wardyn. And my ma is Alea. I don't know what her surname was before they married." He frowned. "Or whether they married at all, actually."

Brentemir seemed to make a study of Keplan's boots. He was the picture of patience but for the white knuckles of his hands gripping the glass. After a moment he drew out a canvas. It was in the style of a lover's portrait—intimate, discrete. Discoloration at the edges showed where a frame usually rested. "May I show you something?"

Keplan did not move to take the picture, forcing the ambassador to rise and reach across the distance between them. The young man waited until Brentemir sat again before looking down. He frowned. It was one he knew well. It captured a moment of joy on the road. A young woman was mid-step in a fire-side dance. She wore traveling clothes and her black hair hung loose. The man she danced with was serious, but his eyes burned even through the dried paint and canvas.

Keplan tilted his head at the image. "Where did you get this?"

"I thought you would recognize them better this way."

Keplan shook his head. "No, where did you get the painting? My parents have its twin in our house. They said it was from years ago, before the war."

"Not before the war, exactly. The night before the battle of Clai'miirn. By the time we all met, the war raged for over a decade."

Keplan glanced up. "You knew my parents?"

"We fought together for a time. Though they went by different names than they do now." Bren's face was casual, schooled into tense neutrality. "They went south after the war, and I received no word, not a letter, not a sign. I grieved for your mother as if she were dead. I began to think she was."

"Was she your lover before my da?" Keplan did not really want to know the answer.

Brentemir winced. "Certainly not. She was my sister. Your father, my friend."

Disbelief and anger reared in his head, drowning the ambassador's words. *But your sister is the Dhoah' Laen.* It was impossible to marry the fierce image with his unassuming parents, but the proof was burned into his mind. They were not hiding from the horrors of war, but the horrors of themselves. *They weren't protecting me.* "They were protecting themselves."

Bren straightened. "What do you mean?"

"The Dhoah' Laen and the Earth Shaker left this city, left Athrolan, to protect themselves, didn't they?" Everything he knew of himself crumbled in the face of truth. His mind filled with the inhuman reflection from his dream. *"One of us will die."* "Your sister, her guard — where did they go?"

"I wasn't certain until recently. They built a homestead in the wilderness, a day's ride away from a town called Namal, I believe."

"Namus." It was a curse hissed through a trembling jaw. Mania coursed through his body, spurred by denial. "My parents are peasants. They live in the Hartland in a house they built with their own hands and leave only a few times a year to trade for supplies in Namus." Keplan's eyes flicked up. Rage thundered through him, and something darker rose in his blood, in his mind. Something that, until then, had no name. "I can't say how often she thinks of you, or whether she healed, but I can tell you she was happy. By running, by keeping their identity a secret from even me, they were protecting themselves."

Bren's neutral expression melted into surprise, into something close to horror. "You didn't know." It was not a question, but a statement, nailing every speculation into place. Bren did not wait for an answer. "I thought I'd come here, and you'd be grateful to have found family again, that you were keeping their secret for them. I thought you would be happy. All this time and you didn't know." He put his head in his hands. "If it's not because of your mother's promise to Her Majesty, then why are you here?"

"I came here for peace." A dam broke. Denial may have mentally blinded him, but now a flood of information tumbled into his head. "How can you sit here, a king in my barren apartment, hoping I'll end a war you've only just begun? You're a symbol of everything I could have had if they chose to raise me here. And I'm just a madman." His voice rumbled. He lifted his apron over his head and folded it, then placed it on the desk. His heart hammered, as if a single misstep would send the pieces of his psyche clattering to the rough hardwood. "When I return, you'd best be gone."

He crossed the city quickly, steps fueled with as much panic and confusion as anger. Early hours deterred all but the most dogged of city folk. Dew still sparkled on the worn, thyme-covered steps to the cemetery. Just beneath the white Xain mausoleum stood the Heroes Vault. Dried flowers crunched underfoot. Months had passed since anyone left offerings in memorial or gratitude. Mosaics ringed the black granite tower, scenes most of the known world could recite. *The Gods' War.*

He thought of the reverence and fear surrounding his parents. Heat roiled in his veins. The shell holding his emotions in check shattered. Ban would never have touched him. *I would have grown up with Azimir, with education and friends and safety.* His pal smacked against the cool tiles, against the tidy pattern of their faces.

The Rakos's body was plated with stone, his joints cracked and bleeding magma. His yellow eyes glared through Keplan. Breath caught in Keplan's throat. Familiar features flickered under the ferocity. Through the thunder in the titan's chest, he heard the voice that instructed him how to draw a bow and build a fire.

Keplan snarled. He would give anything for it to be a mistake, for his mind to be playing tricks on him. For once he prayed for madness. Dark stone bit into his fingers. "What did you promise the queen?" *The Dhoah' Laen's eyes blazed, striking sunbursts from her armor. The rush of power dragged a scream from her throat. Ageless, ceaseless, and the scent of salt.*

"I cleaned horse shite!" His scream broke, booming against the stones. "I was tortured and forced to eat from waste piles when I could have been raised here!" His hands hammered the stone depiction of silver eyes and golden hair. Riches did not matter, nor had he dreamt of being a prince. But he could have had peace. *They will kill you, and only I will remain.*

"Unless you want to be arrested for crimes against an official monument, I suggest you lower your voice." Threat laced the calm words. A milk-pale man leaned on a headstone, fully black eyes narrowed. Morning light glinted off the iron capping his chipped horns.

Keplan's eyes bounced from the horns to the signet on his tunic. *The general grieved alone, grieved for a queen that no one knew was already dead.* "You're the general. You keep the city from ruin. Barely."

The implied insult was ignored. "And you are a madman screeching in a cemetery. Don't bother trying to destroy that thing — it'll stand long after you rot."

Distraction dragged the panic from his limbs, leaving exhaustion in its wake. Keplan staggered, catching himself before turning back to the city.

"Who promised Her Majesty something?" The general's eyes narrowed. "I believe that's what you said. Your smacking fists made it difficult to hear."

Keplan froze. "General Domariigo. An'thoriend Domariigo. An'thor." The words clattered from his mouth like pebbles before a landslide. "'Instead, she named your child, should you have one. We need you. Ceir Athrolan needs you. Just once more.'"

"So, they did receive the letter."

"It's the reason I'm here. One of them."

An'thor extended his hand. "You said you wished you had learned, wished you had respect. You came here for knowledge. Come inside. Just come talk with me."

Keplan glanced to the cliffs, to the city behind the general. His instincts screamed that whatever the general offered, he did not want. "Perhaps another time."

"I could have you arrested."

"And I could tell the world that the queen has been dead for over a month." He stepped down from the monument and nodded to the stunned general. "Good evening." The destruction inside his heart yawned beneath him, pitching him into darkness.

Only I will remain.

Φ

The 10th Day of Aeme, 1272

Bordom made Rih grateful her shaved head prevented her from ripping her own hair out. Despite her morning stretches and practicing her dance steps, her muscles sang for movement. *And pacing really only does so much.* Every scroll she re-read. Every dance step was memorized. Every sexual nuance understood. *Or at least as much as I can stomach.* She wanted conversation. She wanted exercise. Loneliness clawed at her chest. When she was restless in the barracks she would practice her atlatl or bathe.

Her gaze fell to the tub tucked in the alcove by her window seat. Ki-elte mentioned there was a bathing hall, and, though never invited, Rih assumed she was allowed. She gathered her key and ducked out the door. The halls were empty at mid-morning, but a few carved signs steered her toward the baths.

Rih slipped into the room, offering a tentative smile to the woman at the foyer. She sat on a dais surrounded by silk curtains. The shelves behind her held the folded outfits and sandals of those already inside. Rih traded silks for a towel and ducked behind the row of screens. Lilies wafted on the thick air. Red and purple glass softened the lantern light filling the low room. The floors were tiled, like the bath in the barracks, but purple and gold designs patterned these. She sighed at the warmth under her bare feet. Three tubs descended into the floor, one steaming, the others still. While the barracks offered a razor and oil for sore muscles, the Hall had rooms for stretching and grooming. One row of alcoves held masseuses.

A long breath pulled tension from her heart. *I might be the chattel in an international negotiation, but perhaps it's worth it to spend a day here.* It was not, and she knew it, but for a moment she would pretend. She set aside her towel and slipped into the heated water. Minerals from the spring lent a tang to the water, and she licked the earthy taste from her lips after dunking her head.

A woman several years older paddled up to Rih. Her grin flashed the polished ruby replacing one dogtooth. "Hello?" The sign was uncertain and exaggerated, but unmistakable.

Laughter bubbled from Rih's chest. She straightened and repeated the sign. "How did you know?" She could count on her hands the number of women in the army who knew her signs. The language was far more common where her mother was raised, where close to a quarter of the male nobles were also deaf. She was lucky enough to have lived her first few years there. The capital, however, was different.

"Ki-elte told me about you. My brother was also born without hearing or speach." She bit her lip, searching Rih's face for understanding. "You can read lips, yes?"

"Yes, though it's not always easy." Knowing this woman had family like Rih made it easier to be honest. Reading lips was exhausting, but explaining was sometimes more effort than it was worth.

"I am Hamin." She spoke the name and allowed Rih to correct the hand sign for two of the letters.

"I'm Rih."

"Would you like some tea?" She brushed a finger past her mouth mimicking the path of a smile, then made a gesture as if she stirred spices into the tea.

"I'd love some, thank you!"

Hamin waved over one of the young girls who worked as an attendant. When she was done speaking, she looked back to Rih. "Do you mind company?"

"Please." Rih moved aside to give Hamin room on the tiled bench beside her. "I talk to few people."

"You are preparing for marriage?"

"I am, to the son of Mirik's Hetmir. Alleanthus?"

Hamin frowned. "You must mean Azimir. He's the younger son. Alleanthus was to be wed to Ambassador Jien's sister, but the engagement fell through in favor of another, to the daughter of an Athrolani noble."

"Azimir?" She did not know much about their second son, only that he was younger than she.

Hamin shrugged. "He's a boy, apparently hotheaded like his father. They're beautiful to look at though, both of them. Tan and fit, not sickly pale, like soured milk, the way half the east is."

Rih smiled at the description. It suited the few Easterners she had seen. "How do you know so much about Mirik? Have you visited?"

Hamin's face grew serious. "My sister served for a time for the ambassador, and she told me all the stories when she came back. She is the one that passed recently, Sa-at."

Rih's chest ached at the thought. She remembered comrades dying in battle. She could only imagine losing a true sibling. "I am so sorry"

When the tea arrived, Hamin's eyes were overbright, but she switched easily to talking about the drinks.

Rih took the hint and set about preparing her tea. The tray fit neatly over the edge of the bath and held the usual pot of spiced butter and cups of thick tea. Necessary to maintain energy on marches, the rich tea was a luxury in the Hall. She took a long slow sip and closed her eyes. When she opened them, Hi-alan had joined them. Her iron-gray hair was long enough to curl at the top.

"Your ears are healing well."

"Thank you, it's good to see you again." She gestured for Hi-alan to help herself to some tea before settling back into the water. Her muscles loosened, limbs settling. Peace eased through her nerves. Hamin and Hi-alan fell into a voiced conversation about a mutual friend, as far as she could see. Leather covering the tub's rounded edge pillowed her head. She smiled and let her eyes close. It was enough to have friends near. Rih drifted somewhere between dreams and waking for a moment. Water sloshed, startling Rih back to wakefulness. The other two women turned as Ki-elte rushed into the room. Her face was ashen. "I'm sorry to interrupt." She knelt, offering Rih a towel. "I need you to get dressed. Ambassador Ebal is calling for you." Shaking hand's made Ki-elte's rudimentary signs difficult to understand. "Quickly."

Rih frowned and hauled herself from the water. She dried too quickly, and the silk of her kalas clung to her damp skin. She ran a hand over the prickles on her scalp. "I should shave."

"No time." Ki-elte handed her a net as they wove through the halls.

Rih fastened it as they went. She was not sure if it was her teacher's urgency, or something more, but the halls seemed more crowded than usual. There were fewer smiles.

Now they did not meet in the opulence of the Lapis Room or the vast dance hall. Instead, Rih followed Ki-elte across the courtyard to the Dignitary Wing. An inlay of Mirik and the Athrolani coast decorated the heavy screen across the door.

Ki-elte barely finished knocking when Mosil slid the screen back. Wrinkles creased his clothes. Shadows clung like smoke to the undersides of his eyes. "Rih-elte, thank you for meeting with me." He gestured to their seats with an absent wave of his hand. "There has been a change in our plans."

Rih's heart was a bird trapped in the cage of her ribs. "What happened?"

"War. War happened. Rih, we are mighty, but Mirik's navy is their pride, and rightfully so. I do not fear our victory, only the cost it will require."

"We cannot negotiate?"

"Write it, please," he snapped. "I cannot think and translate too."

Rih stopped herself from pointing out thinking and translating were exactly what his role as ambassador entailed. She ordered all expression from her face and wrote the question on her tablet.

"Negotiations are tense. We're debating whether this war will become violent or just a show of power, with the only deaths those of messengers and spies."

And our women.

Muscles worked in his jaw, but his face was otherwise unreadable. He stalked to the window. She could not see his mouth, and Ki-elte's hands stumbled in her attempt to catch up with translating. "You're naïve, you're idealistic. Mirik is our enemy, and our hope at fixing this by throwing a faulty wife at their son is gone. I don't blame them. It was an insult. His Eminence was wrong in thinking they would see it differently."

Pain sparked in the heart of her anger, and though she wanted to look away, cut the cruel words off with the finality of closing her eyes, she needed to know.

"You will not marry Mirik's second son. You will be lucky if you marry outside Ban at all. I am meeting with His

Eminence in a week to discuss our course with Athrolan now that we're at war with their ally. I cannot be bothered with matchmaking for you."

Rih's gaze moved to him when Ki-elte's hands stilled. Fury burned in her gut. "Faulty? Naïve? Idealistic?" Her fingers hardened around the signs.

Mosil rubbed the bridge of his nose, more tired than angry it seemed, now, and pointed at the desk. "Please, I asked you to write."

All Rih's carefully curated patience snapped. If her ribs could open and free the thundering wings of her angry heart, she would have cracked them herself. Clay shattered beneath when her hand smacked the tablet. She surged to her feet. "No! For once in your life, do your job and listen!"

His eyes widened before her violent signs, but for the first time, he did not turn to look at Ki-elte as she translated.

"I am not faulty, not any more than you, who clearly cannot think past yourself. I am not naïve. I've killed, I've seen my sisters fall in battle and at the hands of our own people, valued less than the horses our officers ride." She gathered her bag, leaving the tablet, with its accusation glaring on the desk.

"Wishing for freedom? For respect? Only someone who has never wanted for either would think that was idealistic." She slid open the door, but paused in the doorway. "Write if you find anything to teach me I don't already know."

She stalked from the room, hoping Ki-elte followed, hoping her cousin would not, hoping that guards would not arrive at her door in a minute to haul her away for her impudence.

By the time she reached the Purple Throne, she was running. She burst into her room, adrenaline hot in her limbs. The door shut, and she felt the tap as the lock slid into place. She pressed her head to the wood, hands splayed on the frame. *What did I just do?* Whatever path she might have had, the one she stared down now was darker. The wood under her brow shook with a knock, but her body was frozen. If they wanted to take her away, they would have to drag her. The lock shifted again. She caught herself on the doorframe as the door slid from under her.

Ki-elte was alone in the hall. "Are you alright?"

Rih collapsed on the other woman, hard arms gripping the softness of shoulders that never threw a dart. After a moment she pulled away. "I don't know." She backed into her room. "Will he call the guards on me?"

Ki-elte lifted a shoulder in a shrug. "I hope not." Her eyes narrowed on something out the window only she could see. "I think he sees the sense in your words. You might have shown him you make a better wife than he thought." Her mouth twisted. "But I hope he does not think too hard on what you said. We all have those thoughts, Rih, but they are for us, and us alone."

Rih turned away. Her heart was no longer thunder, was no longer a bird begging to break her chest apart. It fluttered, uneven, as panic faded to exhaustion. She dropped her hand to the other tablet, to the single word written across the wax. The Emperor was not the only one ruled by fear.

CHAPTER ELEVEN

The 12th Day of Aeme, 1272
The Feld be Baran

WARM AIR TUGGED A smile onto Alea's face, and she drew up at the hill's crest. She loosened her shirt front and folded up her sleeves. Green grasses rolled away on all sides , dotted with persistent white and blue wildflowers. A cluster of brown mounds on the eastern horizon marked a village.

"Enjoying the view?" Arman's voice was low, his face more serious than hers. His horse shifted its weight, as uneasy as its rider.

"I was thinking this was the first time we really traveled in good weather. Every other time, winter was either just beginning or just ending. It's beautiful."

Arman smiled. impish light filled his sidelong gaze. "I'll race you to that rock over there, the outcropping that looks like the Commander's awful haircut."

Alea nudged her horse into a gallop. Arman thundered down the hill a pace behind. Dirt spattered the roadside as they passed, and Alea let out a whoop. Her heart hammered as the air whipped her braid into disarray. Arman drove his horse up the embankment, cutting off the turn in the road. Her eyes narrowed, cheeks stinging from her horse's mane. She leapt a narrow stream and wheeled in front of Arman as he tried to rejoin the road. They arrived at the outcropping simultaneously, breath gasping with laughter and excitement.

"A draw." Alea's eyes were bright. After twenty years of solitude her veins missed adrenaline.

"Nonsense, I would have won had you not cut me off." Arman nudged his horse closer to hers and leaned out of the saddle to kiss her. "But I do love how competition looks on you."

She kissed him back before loping down the road again, trailing dust and laughter behind her.

The village emerged after another few hours of riding. Windows glinted with reflected sunset and newly lit lanterns. Several streets paralleling the main road and a low wall ringed the largest buildings. Alea nodded at a brightly painted sign to the left. "How does the Jumping Pebble sound?"

Arman snorted. "Like someone drank too much before they named it." Stablehands waited for their horses in the narrow courtyard and Arman unbuckled their packs. Alea watched as the boys joked back and forth on their way to the stables. They were young, barely thirteen, and moved with easy confidence. *What life would Keplan have had in a place like this?*

"Alea?"

She glanced over to where Arman waited on the stoop. "Sorry." She jogged up the steps.

He followed her gaze, expression sobering. "Every boy is going to remind us of him, I think. Until we hold him again." Rolicking music and the smell of bread and honey rolled through the door when he opened it. "We'll find him, love." He shouldered through the crowd, rough hand clasping hers. The bar was battered but ran the width of the common room.

Alea caught the innkeeper's eye and leaned over the bar to talk above the noise. "We need a room for the night."

"That'll be a silver if you want board with it."

"Please." Alea slid the coin across the table. It may have been a long time since she saw the inside of a tavern, but the price seemed steep. "You've plenty of business."

"Best inn in the province," the man boasted. "Supper's rabbit pies and honey." He handed her a key and turned away. Alea glanced back. The press of noise was a balm to her frantic mind. Most seats were full, but many were locals, come for the drink and conversation, but not stay for the night. "I'll bring our packs up — can you find a table?"

Arman nodded and wove toward a quieter corner.

Winding, narrow stairs curled up to the uneven floor of the second story. Wood smoke and ale brought a smile to Alea's lips. *Add a layer of moss, and this could be Vielrona.* Their small room was tucked between the roofs of the inn and the stable beside. A grimy window overlooked weathered tiles, a sliver of the Felds visible beyond the walls. Unpacking their few belongings was pointless for a single evening, but Alea took her time changing and rebraiding her hair. Gray strands outnumbered the black now; frown lines and gray lent better anonymity than isolation ever had. *We could be anyone.*

The music hummed under her skin, and the heat and smoke were dizzying. Arman perched on a stool by a tall table in the corner. She flicked the skirt of the only dress she brought in an attempt to remove the wrinkles and grabbed two mugs of ale. Arman's gaze wandered over the musicians in the corner. She slid his mug across the table with a warm smile. "I haven't seen you here before."

He took a deep gulp of ale before mirroring her smile with one of his own. "I'm just traveling through. You?"

"On my way north. Mind if I share your table?"

He bit back a laugh and shoved the other chair toward her with one mud-stained boot.

She sat, dipping one shoulder as she leaned on the table. "Maybe after you finish that ale, there, we could share a dance?"

"I'm afraid I'm not very good."

"Ah, surely you're just being humble. Give me a turn and I'll decide for myself." Mirth war with apprehension on his face, the latter slowly washed away with alcohol. Under the dim light of the common room, he was just a southern man, gray from a hard life, lined from long days. Boyish beauty was now quiet strength. She wondered absently what he saw when he looked across the table, across the years.

He knocked back the last swig of ale and shoved himself to his feet. "All right, missy, you get one chance at dancing with me. Up you get."

Φ

The 13th day of Aeme, 1272
The City of Ceir Athrolan

It was dark when the letter arrived. Rain peppered the glass, but the clouds seemed content to do little more than spit. Bren leaned his forehead on the window, The streets were busy for a gloomy day. *The whole kingdom is uneasy.* His eyes flicked to the palace. Reka was rarely wrong, but palaces gossiped, and a queen's death seemed too big a secret to keep. *Even for An'thor.*

A soft knock heralded his steward. "A letter, sir."

"From home?"

"No, sir. It's addressed to you by name, but they've gotten the title wrong. They call you the Military Commissioner." The man glanced at the envelope. "It's from a place called Namus?"

Bren crossed the room in two strides, almost tearing the letter in his haste to open the envelope. "Thank you, that will be all for now." Old travel stains and fresh rain stained the parchment. His hands shook as he turned it over.

> *Wardyn Homestead*
> *Namus Township*
> *Pardelan Province of Athrolan*

He sank into the armchair by his window. The handwriting was not Alea's thin elegant lines, but the solid and crisp hand he recognized from his time in Mirik before the war. *Arman.* It was not what he wanted, exactly, but it was better than silence.

> *Bren,*
>
> *I hope this finds you well. I cannot imagine what has passed in the last twenty years — twenty, can you believe it? Sometimes it feels like yesterday. I hope you found peace and happiness. We have. We both have. It seems foolish to write after decades of silence, but I have little choice. Something is changing. The world is not the blissful end we hoped. Alea has dreams, and I feel churning in the earth.*
>
> *Moreover, our son is gone.*
>
> *He is young, seventeen. We kept our power a secret, hoped he would live a normal life, one of simplicity and peace. One we only dreamt of. I see you shaking your head at our folly. Weeks ago he disappeared into the woods bearing a bow and some sparsely packed saddle-bags. He found a letter from An'thoriend. An'thor may be a hero, but he did not*

become one for his kindness. He means to make him the heir.

I realize this letter is scattered and makes little sense, but I am trusting you to keep our secret from the world, keep our son safe from a kingdom that would rip his future away. Find Keplan. Find him and bring him home. I do not care if he learns every story ever told about us. Just bring him back safely.

My thanks, and Alea's,
Arman

Bren's chest ached, and his throat burned. After so many years all he wanted was news. Now it came briefly as small talk and the request of a favor. Still, Alea had not written. Even if Keplan managed to live in anonymity, it was likely civil war would shatter the city about their ears before he decided to return home. Bren reread the letter, flipping it over, searching for anything else that might help.

He grimaced as another knock interrupted his thoughts. "What is it, now?"

"Sir, General Domariigo is here to see you. He says it's urgent. About the queen."

Bren's brows rose. Perhaps the man had not been lying about the woman's death. "Show him in." He leaned against his desk and dropped the letter behind him. His arms were firmly crossed when the general stepped in.

"Quite the summer we're having. This rain does not bode well for our crops." The Ageless man glanced out the window. "I suppose Mirik is used to this sort of weather."

"Rather. Why are you here?"

An'thor's lined face was unreadable, black eyes distant. "I met someone yesterday, a new friend of yours. He goes by Keplan, I believe. What was his last name again?" An'thor tapped thin lips with a battered finger. "Ah, yes," his gaze snapped to Bren's, "Wardyn."

"Toar, An'thoriend, cut the dramatics." His jaw tightened. "What did you do to him?"

"Nothing. I found him having a fit in the cemetery yesterday evening. He was pounding on the mosaic of your sister and her guard, apparently quite peeved he could have had a normal life. Frankly, I think he might be disturbed."

Bren shoved himself off the desk. "You saw his scars, didn't you? If you think he's disturbed, perhaps you should let him be."

An'thor shook his head. "There's something about his eyes. They see too much."

Bren threw a hand in the air. "Did you expect a normal child from their blood?"

"I expected a powerful answer to my every prayer." When Bren scoffed, An'thor slammed his fist on the table. "Gossip is all over the streets. I have people claiming I'm poisoning the queen. Colonel Hamacad is calling his men to the city and others bolster each fort. All the lords have drawn their personal troops home. This man, Peraan, rouses dissent in the lower city. He wants Daymir back, and he's not alone. Raven as much as proclaimed loyalty to him as well."

"And what of it?" Brentemir's skin crawled in the face of An'thor's obsession. He knew why Arman could not trust the man.

"You need to contact him."

"Peraan?"

"Their son, idiot," An'thor snarled. "Bring him to the manor, write him a letter, fates, sing under his window for all I care."

"And what happens when I return to Mirik?"

"I'll show him the declaration and hold a welcoming ceremony. He'll be Heir Apparent within the year."

"And his entire life will be forfeit. No."

Dim light made his unyielding eyes blacker than ever, and Brentemir understood why the Ageless were so often likened to predators. An'thor's hand found the discarded envelope and turned it over. He skimmed the sender's address and offered Bren a tight-lipped smile. "You claim him, Barrackborn, or I will."

Φ

Northern Clai Province, Athrolan

Even in late summer, mist rose from the river at dusk. Lovers would think it romantic. Peraan Goen of Littie's Green used it for cover. His forty-seven years showed in stiff legs and hard eyes. Night etched his features in blue. It was a good place—the center of the river emptying the Iron Sea. The rowboat bobbed on its mooring, but the slap of waves was quiet enough for Peraan to hear approaching oars.

"Ho," he called. "Does your ship fly the flag of Athrolan?"

"Aye, that of her king." The skiff drew close, and faint moonlight showed it had come from Meren. The viscount himself was seated in the aft, his emblem covered by his cowl. "May I come aboard, Master Goen?"

"Indeed, Lord Eier." Peraan took hold of the other boat, steadying his own as the lord stepped over the side. The skiff pulled away to moor further down river. Peraan turned back to his guest. "I'm glad to see you well. I trust your work is moving along?"

Eier fixed the man with an expressionless stare. "I haven't stayed in popularity for so long, even as my patron fell, without some pragmatism. You speak of Daymir's claim and yet make no move to send word to him about all that is done in his name."

"I think it wise to have strength before we show him our desires."

"Of what strength do you speak?"

"You are not the only lord with whom I meet. I have my own network. Others call their men back. It's no secret the country is wounded and howling. With your men, we would have a force to rival the army. Once you sign fealty to Daymir, we could move. Commander Dorcal, even, shows signs of supporting us."

Eier looked away. Though of equal years, he was in better form than his companion. "What do you offer?"

"A way to correspond with the true king without drawing suspicion. I still have contact with all his guardsmen."

"And what about the other rumor? I trust you have heard it."

"You mean the boy?"

Eier turned back, his eyes dark. "I mean the Dhoah' Laen's son, Peraan. I find it difficult to believe Ambassador Barrackborn to allow anyone else to wander about with his son so readily. The general is reportedly interested in him as well. The poor man clings to the idea that ancient powers could save us. I think we both know better." He raised a hand to signal his boat.

"I have seen him myself. He bears the marks of torture and distrusts others. I think there is something ill about him. Not evil, but broken beyond repair. I swear to you, he bears no inhuman blood."

Eier swung himself over the edge and onto his skiff. "Peraan, you forget many say Athrolan, too, is broken. Be careful."

Φ

The 15th day of Aeme, 1272
The City of Ceir Athrolan

Bren never found a place he loved as much as Mirik's cliffs. The manor in Ceir Athrolan was decorated almost identically to his private rooms at home, but it was not enough to keep homesickness at bay.

Azimir burst into the room with his usual careless assurance, tapping a belated knock on the door frame. "Have you heard from Keplan yet? Is An'thoriend coming? I wanted to ask him about his revolver."

Bren sighed. "Keplan did not respond, and I don't know if it's a refusal. General Domariigo will not be attending as I'd rather not frighten Keplan off." Distaste for difficult conversations was unchanged in his transformation from soldier to ambassador. "I'm having Keplan to supper with you and Alleanthus. Alone."

"He should meet the general—"

"They already met, and I imagine your friend would not like to repeat the experience." He gestured to one of the armchairs by the window. "Sit, and for Toar's sake, listen for a moment." He sat on the edge of his desk and crossed his arms. It was as much to hide the shaking as to lend authority. "Do you remember when I met Keplan?"

"You interrogated him."

Bren squeezed his eyes shut. "I questioned him only after I heard his last name. It's one I haven't heard in a long time. I barely slept that night. Keplan looked familiar to me. I met with Captain Elang and she confirmed my suspicions, as did Keplan himself."

"You saw him?"

"Azimir, I asked you to listen. Before he went by Arrowlash, Arman's surname was Wardyn. When my sister rode off into the wilderness years ago, she did indeed take the Rakos with her. And now their son returned to Athrolan."

Azimir was silent for a breath, then a grin blossomed across his face. "Will he come to live with us in Mirik? Have you told him yet?"

"I thought he already knew who his parents were. I was wrong. He's scarcely an orphan whom we need to take in. He has a life here. This meal is, in part, to learn more about him. First, I need to ask you something." He fixed his son with a level stare. "You spend a lot of time with him. Is there anything different about him? Different from a normal seventeen-year-old?"

Azimir looked down, his open face showing an internal battle.

"If you know something, you are honor-bound to tell me. No one expects you to keep secrets from family." Uncertainty warred with hope on his son's face, giving away as much as his mouth tried no to.

"Anyone could see he's different." Azimir glanced up, jaw set with a stubbornness Bren recognized from the mirror. "But he's family now too." He rose. "Is that all? Could I go fetch him now?"

Bren waved at the door. "Fine. He'll take better to you than he would to me anyway." He watched Azimir leap down the stairs three at a time. Children were a beautiful trial. He could see himself young again. *But now I realize pigheaded and obnoxious I must have been.*

Φ

Bells tolled evening. Keplan paced his room. Now the thoughts kept at bay by work sprang to the forefront again.

Rage still echoed in his veins, but it was distant. Everything he learned about his blood seemed like a lie, until he looked at the madness mapped within his mind. *And now the ambassador wants to have dinner.* It was late enough he could feign illness, but part of him balked still at refusing a nobleman. The decision was made for him when Azimir arrived with the last bells before nightfall.

The younger boy edged in after Keplan refused to answer his knock. Reservation shadowed his features, and he shifted from foot to foot as he stood by the open door. He cleared his throat. "Da told me who you were. That we're cousins."

"Shut the door."

Azimir did so, then leaned against the wood. "You could have told me."

Keplan raked his hands through his hair, hauling it back into a horsetail. "I didn't know." He hated being questioned, but it was worse only having half the answers. "When your father told me, I was in no mood to see anyone. Besides, you might have thought me angling for power."

Azimir snorted. "You can barely handle a crowd, let alone standing before one." He jerked his head at the door. "Will you at least come to supper?"

Keplan stared, unseeing, out the window. *I wanted to know why I'm mad.* "I suppose it would be rude to refuse the ambassador himself."

"Rather." Azimir's bright face still held a frown. "He asked if you had any of their power. If you were different from normal folk."

Keplan paused in lacing his jerkin, eyes flicking to Azimir's in the small mirror. "It's not a power. I can't shoot lightning from my hands or channel the sun. I can't even control whose secrets I see most of the time." Hissing rushed through his ears. "What did you say?"

"I said you were the one to ask. I wouldn't break confidence, especially since you're family now." Defiance lit his eyes at the words. "C'mon, we'll be late."

Keplan glanced around his room. In the wake of his world crumbling, he was a ship without a rudder or sails. With no way to steer himself, drifting after Azimir was as good as anything. Firas and Mirel's voices drifted from the kitchen, but the common room was empty. Before Keplan thought up careful answers to every question he might be asked, the manor eates loomed above them. The absence of Azimir's usual boisterous nature did nothing to help Keplan's anxiety. Wan laughter bubbled up, finally when he mentally likened the manor's white stone to a tomb.

"What is it?" Azimir allowed Keplan to walk through the gate first.

"This is a dinner, and I'm acting like it's an execution."

Azimir's grin was nervous, but there all the same. "You aren't much for state, eh?"

"Hardly." Keplan followed him into the foyer. Scents of peppered meat and wine drifted from an open door, and the ambassador's booming laugh echoed in the tiled hall. Conversation died when Azimir stepped in. "I brought him."

Keplan paused outside the door, slowing his breath in an attempt to steady the hammering in his chest. *Only I will remain.* The refrain wound through every thought now. This was not Ban. An ambassador requested his presence—practically begged for it. The dark part of him, the glowering half lurking in the dark, grinned. *They should beg.* Keplan rushed through the doorway before another thought surfaced.

"Good evening." He bowed to before taking a seat, wishing the only chair as anywhere but directly across from the ambassador. "Thank you for having me."

Steaming water sat in a bowl before him. After shooting a glance at Azimir, he tugged off his gloves and dunked his hands into his own bowl. He dried them swiftly and tucked them under the table. Awkward silence weighed on the room until Keplan looked up. Brentemir watched him, eyes thoughtful, and Alleanthus's gaze held open curiosity. Azimir stared at his plate.

Alleanthus offered a smile. "I imagine this is odd for you. And pretty miserable. We're a family of soldiers, and we don't do pomp well either. Would you feel better if you knew more about us?"

"Please." Keplan thought his cheeks might crack from disuse when he smiled. "I felt like I was walking to my doom the entire way here."

Brentemir choked on his drink and shot a dismayed look at his older son. "I told you I thought I frightened him off."

"That's because you always sound like you're delivering desperate or bad news." Platters arrived and Alleanthus leaned back. "I was born in Mirik, shortly after the war. Our Ma was a general then, and Pa, Hetmir. The city was in disarray still, I was raised by carpenters as much as warriors. Now I study state affairs so become an ambassador like Pa." His thumb jerked to the south. "Perhaps in Berr. I could stand to see more ships." Azimir added his own anecdotes, some of which Keplan already heard.

It was odd, eating around a table talking to men who grew up with servants, with manors. *With each other.* Keplan had not wanted a sibling until he met Azimir. Now yearning for family was a bright ache in his chest. *I should write them.*

"I remember your father played music — do you at all?" It was the first time Bren ventured a question.

Keplan picked at his shirt. His stomach was gloriously full and his eyes heavy. Alleanthus was quick-witted, but quieter than his brother, and put him at ease. "I have no skill with music—I can't carry a tune either."

Mead or memory misted Brentemir's eyes, and he looked down at the chalice in his blocky hands. "Your mother was a terrible singer. She loved it, but thank Toar Athrolan has no dogs, because she would have set them howling."

Warmth twisted in his gut. "We have a trader from Ban who used to stay with us when I was little. He traveled with a dog and my ma would sit on a stump outside with her and they'd cry at the moon." He met Brentemir's eyes. They knew two sides of the same woman—Bren the fierce, violent warrior, Keplan the quiet, wild mother. He might have missed home, missed his parents, but Bren had been without his sister for twenty years. *He tore the countryside apart searching for her, and she never spoke his name.* "Ma has a large garden—all our food is grown there. They taught me to hunt, to cook, they taught me everything. Though I realize now my history lessons have some large gaps."

Bren leaned forward. "When is your birthday?"

"Snowmelt. I left shortly afterward. I have questions I didn't think they could answer," he explained. The questions still made him vulnerable, but kindness and food and the sense of family steadied his nerves a fraction.

"What did they say of your time here, or in Ban? Did you tell them you found us?" Bren asked.

Keplan flexed his hands under the table. "I rode away in the night and have yet to write to them. I couldn't, in Ban. Now I don't know what I would say." He glanced up, hope a warm bloom in the pit of his stomach. "Perhaps you could tell them?"

"Me? Fates." Brentemir stared, incredulous. "They've had no word from you in months? Keplan, you ought to let them know you're alive."

"Some letters are more difficult to write than others," Alleanthus interjected.

"I just realized my world was a lie." Keplan picked at his nails. "Surely you understand the feeling."

Azimir's hand flew to his mouth as if this was nothing more than banter among bar friends, but the ambassador's jaw tightened. The words silenced conversation for a moment, and Keplan mentally kicked himself.

"I'm sorry, that was rude."

Bren sat back. "No, I see your point. I speak as a parent, and I know how I'd feel should Azimir wander off, silent for months."

The footman halted Bren's next words. "Ambassador, sir, General Domariigo is here to see you. Shall I show him in?"

"Toar." Bren surged to his feet. "Excuse me." Though he stepped into the hall, anger carried his words through the half-open door. "Dammit, An'thor, you told me to act, so let me!"

"Is the boy—"

Alleanthus snapped the door shut, but panic already burned through Keplan's limbs. Bren's words sucked the air from the room. Tugging his gloves over his palms, he made for the hall. "I'm sorry, Azimir, Alleanthus. Thank you for the visit, it was lovely."

He shut the door carefully behind him and turned to meet the general's glaring black eyes. "General." He turned to the ambassador. "Forgive me, I find myself ill." Measured steps brought him to the safety of the stables. Once he and Moly slipped through the gate he nudged her into a lope.

Curiosity did not bring Brentemir to his door. It was plotting and whatever sick race he had with An'thor.

Firas was almost asleep when Keplan pounded on his door. The bartender peered into the dark hallway. "'Lan? I scarcely see you for days, then you beg at my door?"

"I need to talk." Keplan realized he was a hand taller than the other man. *We were almost at eye level when I first arrived.* "So much is changing."

His coy smile faded. "Come in, then."

"I don't know where to turn. I'm tired of running. I'm a damned coward, but fates, I'm so tired from running I don't have the strength to stand." Keplan slumped onto the bed head sinking to his gloved hands.

"Would it help to tell me what you're running from?" Firas's voice was quiet, so soft it drifted in the breath between them. "Why was the Mirikin ambassador here?" Firas brushed his hand over Keplan's gloves. "Does it have to do with these?"

"I'm not a spy for Mirik, if that's what you mean. He knew my parents during the Gods' War." His heart hammered for him to explain everything, each thought he had no right to know, all the history his parents never told him. "My parents ran from the war, and it seems now I'm running too. I'm pulled in so many ways and I scarcely know why."

Firas brushed Keplan's hair away, untying the horsetail with steady hands. "Is it something to do with the way you know things?"

Keplan moved away, eyes wide.

"Don't give me those big blue eyes of yours. You think I'd believe Mirrel told you about Pa's wagon? And you knew I wanted to kiss you during the festival. You see people better than you ought."

"I think it does have something to do with that. With who my parents were. I don't know who I am anymore." He had not even spoken it aloud to himself. "I'm so tired."

Firas's gentle hand ran down the bumps of Keplan's spine. "Tomorrow you can stand. Tomorrow you won't run anymore. But tonight, between these walls, you can rest. You keep me from drinking too much and tease Mirrel, and sometimes she even laughs. You work in the stables during the day and share my bed at night. Tonight, everything else is gone. The whole world can fit right here," he tugged Keplan's glove off and held their hands a hair's breadth apart.

Keplan pulled off his shirt with aching arms. Gooseflesh rippled over his abruptly uncovered skin, interrupted by smooth, pink scar tissue. "I know I said I was tired, but I don't want to sleep tonight."

Firas blew out the candle on his bedside. "I didn't plan on sleep." Even in darkness, Keplan heard the smile in the other man's voice.

The 16th day of Aeme, 1272
The City of RoBal, Ban

ADRENALINE STILL RACED THROUGH Rih's veins at every new visitor. No threats or retaliation arrived for her dangerous words to Mosil. It was as if he forgot her entirely. The rains would come soon, the dust and burnt brown of the grasses replaced by the sweet smell of new growth and moisture.

Rih checked the hoops in her ears, but stilled when she caught sight of her hand. Brown fingers tapered to short the nails marked with a pale crescent at the base. *These aren't mine.* Her calluses were all but gone, shadows left where hard skin once lay across the pad of her palm.

Greif flooded through her.

Ki-elte found her perched on her bed, hands loose in her lap as if detached at the wrist. Rih jumped when the woman touched her shoulder. She waved away Ki-elte's hasty gesture of apology and signed, "I must have lost track of time." Her back ached from stillness. Her neck was stiff, and her feet tingled with compressed nerves. It was evening, the sun almost faded from the sky.

"Are you—" Ki-elte faltered for the proper sign then shrugged and spoke aloud. "Troubled?"

Rih glanced at her desk. It was covered in scrolls and tablets of notes, most on etiquette and customs of Mirik. She half-expected them to bear a layer of dust. "We had aurpose in the army. Even if there was no war, there were skirmishes, raids from the Vales or bandits. If there were no raids, we trained, kept our muscles fresh, because there will always be war."

Ki-elte's smile was faint. "You are restless?" Her signs were smoother, but her vocabulary was a fraction of Rih's own.

"I feel lost." Rih began to write instead. She did not have the energy to explain herself half a dozen times.

> *I do not recognize myself. In the army, we were a piece of a mighty whole, a fraction of Ban. I can't remember when I was my own self. Now, I find I have interests outside of war, outside of weapons, outside of my lessons here. It is a strange feeling, meeting myself for the first time.*

Ki-elte sat back, expression thoughtful. "And what do you think?"

"Of what?"

"Of this person you are becoming, or have always been, but did not know?" Ki-elte voiced.

> *You spoke of how we are invisible, the unseen warriors and politicians of Ban. Yet I feel trapped in this room. I wish I could do something useful.*

Ki-elte shook her head. "We have a training hall, down below, but only a few dozen of us use it, and I'm afraid we don't have any teachers. It is more to help us in our other duties."

Rih's brow quirked. "I fail to see how throwing darts would help anyone be a better lover."

Ki-elte's chest hitched in a laugh. "Grace and stamina are hallmarks of a good lover."

Rih shook her head. "Throwing darts will not help me in this war, not anymore at least." She watched Ki-elte struggle to find the right sign. Rih grabbed her hand to interrupt. "I found some women who know my language. And you've been learning."

"I heard." Ki-elte smiled.

"If I asked, could you call several of the women together? A small group, no more than you'd have for a social gathering." Her heart pounded, unsteady but certain.

"Anyone in particular?" Dread shadowed the c in Ki-elte's eyes.

"Hamin and Hi-alan." She paused. This was the gamble, the dice that could end her life, end the faint plan uncurling in her heart before it ever bloomed.

> *You once asked me what ruled His Eminence. I responded with fear. Fear that we will see him as less than a god. Fear that we will see him as a man. Fear that we will be like Sa-at and realize we are more angry than we are afraid.*

She met Ki-elte's gaze. "Find me women who agree."

The other woman's eyes widened, but not with horror. "Would this evening be too soon?"

Rih's stomach flipped. Her limbs hummed with energy again, but now it was the flame of determination igniting her nerves. "It would be perfect. Thank you." She scarcely paid attention as Ki-elte began her lesson on herbal teas that would increase arousal or relaxation. After a moment she realized Ki-elte had stopped speaking. "What?"

The other woman's dark eyes rolled and she giggled. "If you are going to create a network of support and not be caught, Rih, you have to play the part. And these things I teach you, while not as exciting, I'm sure, are going to be vital for your life as a wife."

The long sentences were lost on Rih. When Ki-elte repeated herself, Rih insisted, "I was paying attention!" She pointed to the teas in turn as she listed off their properties. "Sleep, relaxation, stimulation, arousal, contraception—"

Ki-elte's waved hand interrupted her. "You've switched the last two around."

Embarrassment dampened Rih's excitement. "I'm sorry." She tapped the top of the box marked with a bog onion. "Contraception? How does this work?"

"Of course you'd be more intrigued by that." Ki-elte sat back and wrote the description.

> *It makes your body inhospitable to growing life. It makes you queasy in the mornings sometimes, but not terribly so. Other mixtures will cause miscarriage, but you have to be more discreet with those. I know your argument—a prison without bars is a prison still. An opulent palace can be a prison as terrifying as a dark cell. I know. Trust me, Rih, I do know.*

When Rih looked away, Ki-elte took her hand, drawing her gaze back to her face. "I wasn't always a tutor. Things happened that I would never wish on another. I think you see learning the rules to this mighty game as surrender."

Rih's cheeks flamed. Her chest and throat tightened. She knew nothing of Ki-elte's life. It was so easy to think soldiers were the only ones who saw death and war, who saw suffering. Silks could hide many things leather armor could not. "I know it's not the truth, but it's how my heart feels."

Ki-elte's hand covered hers for a moment before rising into a sign. "How can you break the rules if you don't know them as well as those who wrote them?" She tapped the teas again and switched back to speech. "If you memorize these and where they're from—by smell and look, not just their container — I'll let you leave early. In the meantime, I have your message to relay."

Rih nodded in agreement. When her tutor slipped out, she drew the first box toward her. *Chamomile. Harvested from the west and dried. Used to calm.* She was close to memorizing the second box's properties when Ki-elte burst back into the room.

"It's time."

Rih glanced out the window. Though the sun itself dipped below the horizon, warm gold still washed the cloudless sky. "I'm not through with the teas."

"Now you take your duties seriously. They're dried. They made it all the way from RoKetta. I promise they can wait a little longer." Her head tilted back in a laugh. "Most of our duties begin with nightfall."

Rih's eyes narrowed. "I thought chai was from the hills."

Ki-elte's smile broadened and an eyebrow quirked. "Good catch," she signed. Her warm hand wrapped around Rih's, and she tugged the other woman to her feet.

Rih felt the tremble in her teacher's body, the tension in her hand, watched the line of her shoulders bunch higher from nerves. She tugged her to a halt. "You're scared. I am too." She held her arms out in an offer for an embrace.

Ki-elte's expression softened, and she stepped into Rih's arms for a moment before pulling away. Her fingers curled and flicked in the first sign she had learned. "Thank you."

"They're waiting, come on!" Rih brushed past her and jogged down the stairs before she realized Ki-elte did not say where they were meeting. When she looked back, her teacher pointed to the bathing hall.

Rih wove through the foyer and into the main bath house. A woman in full robes — albeit lighter ones for the heat—raised a hand in greeting and raised the curtain to the largest exercise room. Rih froze when she ducked inside. She expected half a dozen women. Perhaps ten at the most. The dark gazes of twenty-seven women turned on her. A few she knew by name, several others by sight. Over half she had never seen. She offered a faint smile. Uncertainty replaced the excitement distracting her all afternoon was replaced with uncertainty. She never spoke to so many people at once. Watched them speak, surely, but never were so many eyes fixed on her hands, learning her words.

Rih settled herself onto a cushion at the front of the room. The women were restless, and she saw matching anxiety in many faces. The few words she caught on their lips were nervous. She raised her hand and Ki-elte called the crowd to order before settling into her own seat.

Rih found Hamin in the crowd. "Will you translate, please?" When the other woman nodded, Rih began to sign. "You are here because we are soldiers, and we are at war. We are the spies and politicians no one sees. You've known it better and longer than I. Just like with the army, though, we are the front lines. Women are the first to be called to action and the first to die. That will never change if we don't work as one." She waited while Hamin finished translating. Her soldier's eyes picked out distrust, women who seemed the kind of nervous that begat betrayal.

Rih leaned forward, pinning the uncertain women with her gaze. "I know what being invisible means. It's a prison, like these bodies we did not choose, but invisibility can break these bars. We already communicate silently—the colors we wear, our piercings." A surge of excitement filled her gut again. "I am here to broaden your vocabulary."

Hamin turned to them. "A few of us are fluent. Others know basic words and simple conversation. We can help you when you are confused."

"Are there questions?" Rih asked. "I know how easy it is to fall behind when communication fails."

A sea of head-shakes answered her. "Then let's start simply." She signed a polite greeting, fingers adding details and flourishes to the fairly universal raised hand and motioned for the others to mimic her. One by one they tried the sentence themselves. When most had the gist, she continued, Hamin translating. "When we first learn to read, those of us who are able, what do we learn?"

One woman raised a hand and replied, "The Woman's Code."

"Then let's start there ourselves." She fell into the memorized series of flicks and curls, letting the rhythm of her arms add cadence. It was her way of singing. "A woman has a single mind. She wakes for the Empire. She rides for the Empire. Her blood and heart and mind are Ban, breathing and alive. A woman has a single mind."

Rih's heart fluttered at the sight of two dozen women all gesturing back, all replying in her language. Most were clumsy, or signed in the wrong order, and it was more mimicry than fluency, but that was just a matter of time and practice. They went through the Code several more times, pausing for her or the others to clarify the nuances.

After an hour yawns punctuated the signs she and waved for them to stop. "It's late, and I'm sure you are all just as tired as I am. I hope you will return next week at the same time to learn more. And remember to practice!" She pointed to the women already fluent. "If you have questions or cannot come to my lessons, these women will help, too." She stepped down from the dais, nerves weakening her knees for a moment. She offered her hand, palm up, to the nearest woman. "Thank you for coming."

The woman repeated the goodbye with a smile and pressed her palm to Rih's. The former soldier moved down the line of her new students, thanking each in turn. Ki-elte joined her at the door when she was through, watching as they filed out. Without colored silks and sharp eyes the room was darker.

"You did well." Ki-elte clearly tried to avoid voicing. "I think this is a good thing. Learning is important. And community."

"I'm glad." Rih grabbed Ki-elte's hand. The other woman's pulse throbbed under her hard fingers. "I realized something about the person I am."

Ki-elte's smile broadened. "That you like her?"

"That I would want to be her when I was small." She was suddenly glad she did not have to speak through tears. "I'm proud of her."

Φ

The 17th day of Aeme, 1272
The City of Ceir Athrolan

Keplan woke alone. His mind was clear and his body sore. He rolled deeper into sheets that were not his. Sunlight struck his eyes, and he sighed. Days began despite how little rest he might have found the night before. He was checking his buttons in the mirror when his gaze fell to his hands.

Stop running.

A choice was laid at his parents' feet—join the war or let the world die. The clarity of that choice was enviable. Quests to save to world rarely happened. Instead, a multitude of dark paths twisted ahead. He could run, stay in Ceir Athrolan as a bar-boy and Firas's occasional lover. *Or I could make sense of the power my parents gave me.* Footsteps sounded in the hall and he peered out, hoping for Firas.

Mirrel's eyes narrowed on him. "I knew he was bedding you."

Keplan matched her glare. "Is he downstairs?"

"No, I left the bar unattended, so the patrons could rob us."

"Thank you." Keplan ignored her sarcasm and trotted down the stairs. He was fairly certain the patrons were honest folk, if a bit rough. Firas was serving breakfast to the few who stayed the night. Keplan found his usual seat in the corner, blushing when Firas shot him a coy wink.

"You're not usually one for breakfast."

"I was wondering if there was a library. I find I'll be in Athrolan for longer than I thought."

"You serious?" At Keplan's nod, Firas frowned. "The palace has one, but I doubt you'd be allowed in. There's a block of buildings down by the Guilds, though, along the docks. The Scholars' Hall. Scribes go there to work and learn. News barkers too. You certain you don't want something to eat?"

Keplan surprised Firas with a wink of his own as he ducked out the door. "Maybe I'll come back for supper."

Dust and the caustically sweet smell of cooking ink hung over the Scholars' Hall. Arrogance pinched the faces of many scattered about the rooms. Luckily, he passed without much notice, save for foul looks. The unfinished floor and walls cast everything from the tomes to the scribes in yellow. After several ill-received wrong turns, he found the library in the rear of the building.

Political and historical tests filled most of the shelves, peppered with philosophical works and sheaves of scribes' records. It was everything Keplan had been hoping to find. Replacing the knowledge his parents kept from him would take years, but he must begin somewhere. He settled on a sunlit window sill and laid a stack of older tomes beside him.

A Soldier's Account was riddled with narcissism, and *Gods and Men* seemed more intent on damning any but the human players in the war. It had been months since he read a book, but he did not remember the few his parents owned being so dry. A year ago he would assumed it was due to his mother's taste in poetry. *It's easier to keep the truth from someone when there are no histories on their shelves.* Frustrated, Keplan opened *Time of Faded Sun,* and found a world that worshiped his mother as a god, and feared the earth his father crossed.

The bells began at noon. Shouting followed, ringing from one tower, then another. Hooves snapped against the stone as guards flooded the docks. Fear exploded in Keplan's gut, twisting in a knot too tight to even be sick. It reminded him of Ban. Somewhere a horn sounded. Scribes traded bewildered looks as they flooded out the door, barkers grabbed wax tablets to record what they could. Keplan followed the press of people, shouldering his way through the door and into the street. People crowded the docks and square. Each time he caught someone's eye, his panic borrowed steam from theirs.

A gray charger thundered down the street from the palace, parting the crowd like waves before a prow. *An'thoriend.* Keplan ducked into the shadow of the Hall, but the general only had eyes for the bulky man by the docks.

"You fucking traitor!" The horned man flung himself from his horse's back. Fury twisted his pale face.

He batted An'thor away as the general tried to haul him from his perch on a piling. The emblem on his chest was Anthrolani, but Keplan did not recognize the black uniform. Other seemed to, however. Scribes fell back from the fight, faces white. In the harbor, sailors swarmed their ships. Black canvas cascaded from every naval mast. *Black uniforms? Black sails?*

Several paces away a barker clambered onto a crate. "Commander Dorcal brought news from the palace! Queen Tzatia is dead!" The words pierced the chaos like an arrow through fat. Keplan's heart faltered. *This is my home.* The only home he still clung to despite everything. Now war loomed over Ceir Athrolan's sun-bleached dome. Others ran to street corners to pass the news. Shouts rose across the city, and someone began to wail. Cannons fired in the harbor, bells booming from every tower. Cobbles shook with pounding boots.

Keplan could not move. His eyes found the general's across the churning crowd. Their blackness yawned, a void beneath Keplan's pitching heart.

Inheriting the Greatest Burden

CHAPTER THIRTEEN

The 24th Day of Aeme, 1272
Marl Black, Glasden Province of Athrolan

AFTER TWENTY YEARS DAYMIR Blackhouse was used to the cold of the mountains. He still detested it. Exile for a noble was far better than for a common man, but the sweeping desolate hills surrounding the Xain manor—now known as Manor Black—were still a prison. Turning his horse's head toward home, his eyes narrowed on an approaching visitor. Mail and supplies brought company, but it was infrequent. *Anything to keep my mind from scattering even further to the winds.* The last visit brought a begging letter from An'thoriend.

Perhaps this time the news would be better.

Rocks clattered as he raced down the slope, weaving between evenly planted apple trees. Sixty years weighed only on his mind, rather than his bones. He arrived with enough time to drink a tall glass of water and be seated calmly in his study when the soldier stepped in.

"Captain Hylier," Daymir greeted with a smile. "I'm glad to see you."

"Master Blackhouse." The man bowed his head. Despite his soldier's uniform, he adopted the casual stance of a comrade. Pale hair and blue eyes spoke of southern blood, but he was raised in the Xain manor.

"You're two weeks late."

Hylier frowned. "Four weeks early, actually."

"I must have lost track of the days." *Again.* Daymir looked away to hide his embarrassment and gestured to the table between them. "Do you want something other than water?"

"No, thank you. I'll get something later for supper. I have news." Hylier's usually easy smile was absent. Doffing his hat, a nervous hand flattened the short cropped hair.

Daymir's heart sank. "Her Majesty?"

Hylier nodded. "Commander Dorcal announced her passing just a few days ago. She left this world on the 42nd of Llueme."

The exile stared at the place his signet ring once rested. The tan lines were long faded, but he still missed the weight. "That was months ago. Why am I just hearing of it now?"

"Because none of us knew until the commander told us. Ceir Athrolan is in an uproar." Pale eyes softened. "I'm sorry. That's really not what you want to hear right now. She was at peace, and with her attendant, Countess Fiena." He looked down. "Sadly, the countess took her own life not long ago."

A sigh slipped through Daymir's tight throat. "They were fast friends." He glanced up from his hands. "How long will you be here?"

"I'm set to return tomorrow. I thought it would be best coming from a familiar face."

"It is." It was not. *It's never easy to hear the woman who raised you, mentored you, disowned you, died without goodbye.*

His eyes flicked up. "I need news. Not just what the scribes wish me to know."

"You want the barkers, the gossip. You want the truth."

"I want to know how close to war Athrolan comes."

Hylier bowed his head. "Of course. For now, I'll leave you to your thoughts. We can discuss details in the morning."

Daymir's voice stopped him in the study's doorway. "Thank you. We may have been estranged, but she was still family. You, at least, never forgot."

Φ

The 25th Day of Aeme, 1272
The City of Ceir Athrolan

Keplan's mind plummeted back into his body, and he lurched out of bed. His chest heaved, and his throat burned.

"Are you all right?" Firas's voice battered its way through the screams piercing Keplan's mind.

Keplan drew a breath. The screaming stopped. The air was still and close. "Just a dream."

Firas placed a hand on his shoulder. "From what happened to you before you came here?"

Keplan glanced back at him. Firas was an escape, a tiny world free from worry. That peace would shatter if he knew the truth. "I'll be all right." He glanced at the window. "How do you sleep with that closed? It's cloying in here."

"You don't like the smell of our passion from last night?"

Keplan made a face. "It's not that. I just can't breathe."

Firas sobered. "I closed it because of the smoke."

"Smoke?"

"You were resting, and I didn't want to wake you. Someone torched a warehouse."

Keplan glanced at the window again. "I was safe here. And now we're on the brink of civil war." He caught sight of Firas's sudden grin. "What?"

"You said 'we' like you're Athrolani."

"I'm not anything else, really." He sighed softly. "I haven't seen war."

"You're a bit young for that." Firas shrugged. "I haven't either. I was born of it. My da died in it, protecting the Dhoah' Laen."

Keplan froze. "He was her guard?"

"Well, not like the Rakos. Da ran with him for a time. Drinking buddies while she was off learning how to kill the gods."

"Did you ever see them? Afterward, I mean?"

"Not the Rakos. Mirrel saw the Dhoah' Laen. You could ask her about it."

Keplan snorted. "I'd most likely get slapped. We've had a few moments that weren't openly hostile, but that ended when she realized we spent nights together."

Firas's low laugh rolled through the dark room. "I only properly bedded you a week ago. It was all whispers and chaste kisses in the dark before that."

Keplan blanched. "Fates, she doesn't know that. I hope. I'd rather she not know any of it." He glanced back at the window. "Why was a warehouse burning?"

"I think we're all afraid of what will happen if An'thoriend can't produce his promised heir. Trade will plummet. Even Mirik can't be expected to help us with their own war brewing. One thing to be said about the Dhoah' Laen—she brought us together like no one else."

Keplan looked away. *Brentemir wants to use me for the same reason. Whatever inexplicable trait that made her a cavalcade of power has only made me see things that aren't mine to see.* "Do you think Athrolan will survive?"

"I think whatever happens she won't look the same afterward." He tugged Keplan's arm. "I love talking to you, 'Lan, but I also love sleep. I promise the city won't burn down around us in the night."

Keplan tucked himself against the other man's back, threading an arm around his waist. Now, even with the window shut, all he could smell was smoke.

Φ

The 26th Day of Aeme, 1272
Western Glasden Province, Athrolan

The road changed as they moved north. Soft brown soil turned packed gray dirt and rocks. Sweeping hills rose from the Borderland, too steep for trees. Here the wind was a funeral dirge. Perched atop the next hill was a weathered, crooked signpost at a fork in the road. Alea drew up and peered at the sign. Ugly black paint marred the carved wood. "Blackhouse?" She glanced back at Arman. "What is this?"

"It looks like politics to me, honestly. I think 'Blackhouse' is the surname given to exiled nobles. Perhaps it means Daymir." His eyes scanned the horizon. In the distance, a cluster of buildings clustered on the crest of a small mountain's root. A gray line of scree switchbacking up the sullen green of the slope served as the only road. Unlike the towns in the heart of the kingdom, this had walls. High ones. "There've been few traders on the road the past few weeks. A tinker yesterday and that was it."

"It feels like last time."

"It feels like winter," Arman suggested. He jerked his chin at the road leading from the mountain village. "That looks like a messenger." The rider moved swiftly along the road, helm glinting over the black of a tabard and the horse's trappings. Arman glanced at Alea, wordlessly agreeing to wait for the courier to pass. It took a minute for the rider to reach them. When she did, she barely slowed enough to hail them. "The queen!" she called when she was still several horse-lengths away. Her voice rasped, and shadows marked her eyes. "Her Majesty Tzatia is dead!"

Alea stared, moving aside as the woman thundered past, carrying the grim news south. Her eyes flicked to Arman. "No heir, and a dead queen."

Arman looked back to the crude word marring the sign. "It's not the winter, then, making roads deserted. It's war." He leaned an arm on his pommel. "Alea, what is this? We've avoided all the wayhouses and towns for the last week. If Keplan's written we wouldn't know, and there's no way to say which way he rode."

"I know what it looks like," she bit back. Worry for her son was a fathomless gulf in her chest, but the best way to protect him was down this new, dark path.

"It looks like running, Alea."

Her lips thinned. "I don't know where to begin. I can't just ask if anyone has seen a mad old woman. We'd be introduced to every grandmother between here and Berr."

"We need news, if for no other reason than to know the state of the kingdom we're traipsing across. What did you do during the last war?"

"Hoped I didn't die." She shrugged.

Arman rolled his eyes. "I meant besides the human bits you couldn't really help."

"This is different. That war revolved around me and you and the gods. We were the keystone in those battles."

"I love you, but that's nonsense. That war was about the world crumbling around all of us. Hundreds of battles were fought before either of us even drew breath. This war is the same—everything crashing down, orchestrated by the few who can escape the chaos." He sat back. "So—what did you do?"

She glanced up, finally. "I fought. I learned, I planned, I gathered allies. Mostly I fought."

"So fight. This is our kingdom. Well, at least more so than any other. Our son is somewhere out in this world, and our best chance at finding him is ensuring he isn't lost in the mess of the impending civil war."

"I have an idea, one I've been thinking over for days. You won't like it." Just as she knew the madwoman was the key to whatever was left of their power, she knew Daymir was the key to saving Keplan.

"I've liked plenty of your plans. Once I knew about them, of course."

Her brow arched in skepticism. "You've liked exactly one of my plans."

"I've liked all the ones that didn't include death and war and fire and lightning and madness and gods."

She allowed a faint smile to cross her mouth. "Those were most of my plans."

Arman snorted. "Well, our powers are gone, and the gods are dead. What is left to dislike about this one?"

"We need information. We need sanctuary and passage wherever we go next. One man can offer all those things." Her gaze swiveled to the vandalized road sign. "I want to go to Manor Black."

Φ

The 27th Day of Aeme, 1272
The City of Ceir Athrolan

"This should be different." An'thor's words sank in the silence of the Xain mausoleum. The half dozen personal guards on duty said nothing. There was nothing to say, truly, in the face of everything he had done. The queen's body lay in state on the marble slab in the center of the tomb. Behind her, past the graves of her father and daughter, the wall stood open, a black maw waiting for bones.

An'thor tugged the torch from the brazier and dipped it into the network of oil-filled troughs carved in the slab. The flames caught, clawing their way across the stone and onto the oiled shroud covering Tzatia's form. An'thor knelt and pressed his brow to the stone, headless of the heat raging over his head, the flames close to the capped stumps of his horns. If he had his druthers, he would pitch himself on the flames beside her. The shroud caught with a roar and the fire devoured hair and mummified flesh.

Bile threatened to crawl up his throat, but he clenched his teeth. It was not the smell or the sight. He had seen worse, done worse himself. *She's gone.* Mourning in secret was agony. But now he could not escape her death. Black hung from every rampart; a stone effigy would replace her body.

An hour passed before the queen was a pile of charred bones cupped in the hammered metal tray set into the slab. Decades of soot stained its bone handles. An'thor staggered to his feet. His knees ached, and his legs burned from crouching, immobilized with grief.

If it were not a time of war, Tzatia's commander, heir, and the Council heads would help him bear her body. Instead, he was joined only by his own few guards and Lord Henack of the House of Commons.

Hot metal groaned when they levered it from the stone and crossed the mausoleum. Bitter, sharp smoke wafted across An'thor's face. He lowered the front of the metal tray to the hole under her effigy. Blackened bones slid from the metal with a rattle and an inglorious puff of dust. Her name and title, the places and times of her birth and death graced the heavy stone lowered into place over the hole.

"General, sir there's visitors coming from the south. They fly the colors of Pardelan and Tetran."

An'thor squeezed his eyes shut. He hoped the war between Mirik and Ban would prevent travel, but the potential heirs to the throne were more dedicated than he thought. *Unlike Daymir, of late.* As it was, camps already crowded outside the gates as people waited to be let into the city proper.

"Sir, the men at the south gate want to know if they should allow them through," the guard repeated.

"Prepare another tent in the detainment camp for the Duke and Lady. And post a guard. I'm not letting nobles in, ally or otherwise until I know the details." An'thor brushed ashes from his suede tunic. Like every piece of clothing, it was black and gray. At least he had not needed a new wardrobe for National Mourning.

The small south gate wedged between the palace and the barracks, more often used for the military's comings and goings than anyone of state. Smaller meant easily controlled, however, and An'thor seized every inch of control he could. The streets were mostly deserted, but not quiet. Soldiers on street corners barked orders to those still out. An'thor glanced at the sky. Curfew would be called soon, and while safety was important, he did not want the army wasting slim resources on simple city folk late from their shops. When he reached the gate, the bells sounded the hour, loud and brassy, too demanding to sound joyous. "I'm here to see the Duke and his sister. Are their quarters ready?"

The soldier guarding a gap in the camp's makeshift fence relaxed from attention. "In a moment, yes, sir. They're at the edge, under the windows of the east barrack wing. You may escort them yourself if you wish."

"I'll let the captain handle that honor." He smiled at the sarcastic quirk to her brow at his choice of words. "I ought to survey the camp as it is. Thank you." He edged through the narrow opening. The tents were large ones used for infirmaries or groups of squires on training missions. Now lesser merchants and those unable to justify entering the city packed between the canvas walls. He counted at least a hundred cots, maybe more, not including the mess tents and those taking advantage of the literal captive customer base. What started as temporary delays now looked closer to a prison camp.

An'thor found the nicer, officer's tent tucked in the lee of the city walls. He nodded to the guard stationed outside the backlit canvas.

"General An'thoriend Domariigo of Neneviir and Claimiirn to see Duke Tzavanir of Ceir Pardelan and Lady Gella of Tetran and RoBal."

"Show him in."

An'thor ducked through the tent flap. A young man dressed in travel-stained finery paced along the rear of the tent. A woman, his double save for the long hair, stood in the center, a baby feeding in her arms. Their retinue gathered in separate tents outside.

"Sir Tzavanir, I'm glad you made the journey safely. And you, Gella, you must have had a long ride from Ban. How were the roads?"

"I know exactly what this is, general—" the Duke began.

"The journey was fine, if a bit long. My body tells me it grows longer each time I make it, but our carriage driver says it hasn't changed in length." Gella flashed him a smile. "Please forgive my brother. This entire unfolding of events took us by surprise. Even you, I'm sure." Her smile faded, and she shifted the baby from her breast to her shoulder. "But I agree this was not the welcome either of us expected."

"Of course." An'thor's stomach churned, heart sinking low enough to take root between his boots. "Of course. I understand. This may seem inhospitable, but it is for your safety. We cannot risk the only two heirs in a war-torn city. You should be comfortable here until we can fix this mess with the commander. I already have plans for negotiation."

"My sister has a babe in arms, and you consider this prison camp safe?"

Ah, there's the accusation I anticipated. "Tzavanir, this is not a prison camp. It's a refuge. You will have a cadre of my own personal guards at all times, and should you need to speak with me, you can contact me directly through them." He backed toward the tent door. "We will speak shortly, I am sure. For now, I will let you settle in and rest." It was a coward's retreat, and they all knew it, but An'thor could not bring himself to care. He needed to meet with Keplan, just long enough to shove a crown on the boy's head and put an end to the uncertainty.

After decades among them, An'thor's love for humanity was tinged with a father's disappointment, and an outsiders contempt. Tzatia's human heirs could not save them now. It was up to a boy in the slums, mad and lost, and brimming with power.

Φ

The 30th Day of Aeme, 1272
The City of Ceir Athrolan

Summer's end turned Athrolan gold. The hills flamed into yellow and orange, and the stone glowed in the still-warm sunlight. Crops ripened in the apron of fields to the west.

Keplan's afternoons were spent in the Scholars' Hall, and crisp nights were warmed by Firas's body.

It should have been peaceful.

More fires broke out. Storefronts that withstood the last three wars were shattered and robbed. Even the impending harvest was not enough to distract the city from Tzatia's death. Firas rolled away, muttering to himself in sleep and taking most of the blankets with him. Keplan let him have them. Even with the window open, he felt trapped. The darkness in the tiny attic was too similar to his cell. There were a few hours before their duties downstairs began, but Keplan could not rest. He pushed himself up and padded across the floor, collecting his clothes as he went.

He was halfway to the docks when he realized the Scholars' Hall was undoubtedly locked for the evening. *I want answers.* Research often seemed to tangle his thoughts further. There was nothing groundbreaking, no sudden epiphany. Until he learned he was too old, he entertained training to become a consulate.

The streets were no longer cheery in the evening, and Keplan missed the noise. His feet turned him toward the Thread. In the colors and chaos, he was sure to find something, even if it was only distraction. He heard the district before he saw the glow of lanterns. Another two turns and he broke into the bubble of sound and color. Wares were much more expensive, and he shoved his hands into his pockets to avoid the desire to brush them over the shiny metal and rich cloth. He paused at a stall displaying curved blades. Some were simple, clearly practical. Others had only a raw tang for a hilt, ready to be worked to a buyer's specific needs. He lingered a moment too long.

"You interested in a blade?" The Banis smith's smile was broad. "We've got a variety, including some Anthrolani styles."

Keplan held up a gloved hand. "Forgive me, I'm afraid I can't afford such quality. I was just admiring. My father was a bladesmith." He winced at the revealing words.

"Ah, anyone I would know?"

Someone everyone would know, but not for his skill at the forge. "I doubt so. He worked far to the south, in a small city. I think he would have liked your work." He nodded a quick goodbye and stepped back into the crowd. Distraction made him careless, and he was not ready to claim the blood pumping in his veins. He lost himself in the flicking facts from the people he brushed past and the shouts of news from Ban, Mirik, Sunam, and countless other nations. The barkers were not all foreign, it seemed. A small crowd clustered around one brandishing an Athrolani poster.

Keplan's eyes narrowed on the man's grim face. It was the same barker from the market, a man dressed more finely than his battered box stool implied. The drawing depicted a dark-haired man imprisoned, the Ageless general holding the keys.

"Daymir's claim is rightful, Athrolani bred and born, even the queen's own declaration to support him! She only cast him aside when the horned beast arrived! He seduced her with his evil words until she knew no better. And when she disinherited her only heir, he poisoned her!"

Keplan heard little about the exiled heir, though the tomes accused him of moving funds about. *Most of the city wants you, Daymir, so why are you hiding?* Gossip would steer him in no useful direction, and he was due back at the bar. He heaved a sigh and shouldered his way back toward the slums.

"You're late." Mirel barked at him, tossing his apron over. Firas rolled his eyes behind her back. Exhaustion lined his face, despite his nap following their afternoon tryst.

Keplan shot an apology over his shoulder and set to work. The doors banged all night, despite the curfew, but the conversation a bitter rumble different from its usual levity. Between running mugs of ale for Firas and wiping tables between patrons, there was no time to rest. Sweat dripped down his back despite the chill creeping into the night air. He paused for a moment in the kitchen, leaning on the wall to catch his breath.

"You set, 'Lan?" Firas poked his head through the door.

"Yeah. It's just loud out there. So many people. Every single one angry." He shuddered at the insidious thoughts.

"I know. Hard times drive everyone to drink. It's a boon to us, but makes more work than we can rightly keep up with." He turned to shout a response to a patron before glancing back at Keplan. "Take a minute outside, then come back. I need you too badly to let you off for the night, though."

Keplan flashed him a faint smile. "Thanks." He shoved off the wall and slipped out into the courtyard. The walls seemed to encroach on him, and he jogged through the alley and out into the street. Cold freshened the stagnant city air.

"War makes things feel a bit close, eh?" The low voice grated from the shadows as if the words themselves bounced over the cobbles.

"War?" He peered into the darkness between the buildings across the street.

"You smell it. The grief on your face says as much. Same with the fatigue in your shoulders." A woman stepped into the street. She dressed like a ranger, in leather and layers, but it was black, not brown.

A spy, then. He recognized her from the corner of the Wise Hare weeks ago. "What do you want?" Facts trickled into his mind. *Azimir's mother. No, he's barely met her.* That was a puzzle for fiddling.

"A word, if you please, Wardyn." She shifted, her cloak slipping away from her hip and showing the set of various blades, all of which looked well used.

"You're threatening me. It won't work."

"I'm making you listen."

"You work from Brentemir." Keplan leaned on the wall. "The ambassador asked you to drag me across the ocean?" Keplan guessed.

"I'm not here for Brentemir. I'm here for all of us."

"Noble." Keplan looked away.

Reka offered a sheaf of paper to him. "Brentemir would be furious if he knew what I'm doing. Athrolan is Mirik's greatest ally. If we go to war without her, against a force as ancient and great as the Banis, we will be sent back in the very shackles we seek to break. Athrolan falling to civil war would jeopardize trade, our access to the southern lands, not to mention our business with the kingdom itself. You are a wise man, if barely out of boyhood. I trust you'll understand the duty and its necessity."

"The duty of what?" Keplan unfolded the parchment. Reka did not respond. He skimmed the words. It was formal speech, something he disliked but understood. Limp, crumpled ribbons hung from old wax. The first was a declaration of inheritance, naming Daymir heir after the death of Tzatia's daughter. The second was a more recent declaration, written just before the war. It proclaimed Daymir a thief from the crown and stripped him of various titles and honors. "I've heard what happened to Daymir. I don't understand why it's relevant now."

"The next one, Wardyn."

Keplan tucked the older documents away and peered at the most recent. It was another declaration of inheritance of the crown, drawn up years before. The queen's signature was almost illegible, but the words above were written by a scribe.

> *It is to be known that in the absence of a living direct descendant of Queen Tzatia of Ceir Athrolan and the Xain House, and in the event of the former heir, now known as Daymir Blackhouse, being exiled from the kingdom during the Gods' War, that a new heir has been chosen. The child of our closest Ally Dhoah' Lyne'alea and the Earth Shaker Aud'narman Arrowlash, known to have been born in the south, has been named by Her Majesty as her rightful and honored heir. Upon the arrival of the child and his or her coming of age, it shall be declared that he will ascend to the throne to rule after Her Majesty passes into peace.*

There was more, but the letters blurred before Keplan's eyes. There were a dozen seals on the paper—the queen's, the general's, various lords and a slew of clerks. *This is official.* Blood raged in his ears, drowning out the sounds of the city below, the hissing of the waves against the stone. He was cold. Now, more than ever, he needed Daymir to claim the throne.

"So, this unnamed thing the general mentioned in his letter was the Crown of Athrolan." He pressed his forehead against the stone wall. "Why do you all think a peasant boy from the forest will serve better than an exiled man? Better than a contested distant cousin? Is my parents' blood so powerful?"

"I imagine so."

"Domariigo's a madman."

"But he's not wrong." Reka pushed off the wall and gathered the documents. "If I were you, I would sleep on this. And then do what you know you ought. Good evening, Wardyn." She disappeared up the street.

Screaming filled his head, surging through his mind like thunder. He crumpled by the stairs.

"'Lan, I need you in the front!" Firas burst through the door, glancing down at the heap of his lover in the street. "Fates, you look ill."

Keplan could not look the man in the eye. Truth might tumble from his mouth. "No. I'm set. Just tired is all." He dragged himself up with Firas's offered hand. "I'll get to work." He wove into the crowd before Firas could ask more. Heat and conversation were overwhelming, but for once Keplan welcomed the cacophony in his head.

Later, he sat in the darkness of his room. Boards closed his window, shattered by vandals days before. The small space was stifling without airflow. His hands shook, and his mind skipped to the next thought before finishing the last.

Papers glared at him from the desk top. Most contained notes on what he had read in the scribes' hall. The parchment under his poised pen, however, was blank.

He began letters to his parents a dozen times, but never wrote further than "I'm sorry." He hoped this letter would be easier. *What does one say when they're asking a man to rule a kingdom?* He was certain many wrote to Daymir, people with far more influence than he. It did not matter. Before, Daymir's refusal to take the throne threatened Keplan's sanctuary. Now it threatened his future. Brentemir added the figures and discovered Keplan's heritage. It was only a matter of time before others did the same.

He had not written a word. He could not claim to be anyone important; the lie would be obvious. If he explained who his parents were, it would seem too far-fetched to be the truth.

Finally, he scratched out a few lines. He would not accuse or presume to offer advice. He would convince the man war was inevitable, and Daymir himself was the only man who could save them.

If that failed, he would beg, and hope to fate the man answered.

Φ

The 32nd Day of Aeme, 1272
City of RoBal, Ban

Rising wind brought the smell of burning grasses. Soon, rain would pound the flames into ash. Changing seasons filled Rih's body with energy. She paced her room. With her lessons on hold for the war, she had more time than ever, and nothing to do but read. There were only so many times a woman could bathe, and while she enjoyed teaching signs, teaching did not help her relax.

Luxurious robes and tunics gave her power, but now the silk was cloying, like smoke clogging the breath of her skin. The clothes pooled on the floor, and she stood naked, trembling with nerves, before the windows. Tucked in the dark of her room, she was certain few could see her. *I don't care. They don't know who I am.* Even she did not recognize herself any longer. She missed the strength in her limbs, the understanding with her body that she would ask and it would obey.

At least in the army there was always work. Always something to practice, to mend, to learn. Her gaze fell to the soldier's training gear folded, forgotten, in the basket on her shelf. Rih only walked past the training hall on her way to the baths, but she trusted it would be close to empty in the afternoon. Most of the women were with their clients or resting for the night ahead.

She broke into a flurry of motion, heart deciding before her mind. Training clothes were on in a moment, soft fingers remembering tasks from harder days. After a wrong turn she found the small training hall, narrower and more dimly lit than those in the barracks. *At least the weapons are serviceable,* she noted, pacing down the modest rack of atlatls, spears, and crossbows.

Lanky arms made her best at the spear, and atlatls were most challenging. Her fingers brushed the grip of a mid-length one. It lacked the rich patina from years of use, but it was still supple and strong. Her grip tightened around the leather-wrapped wood, eyes lidding for a moment. Waves of wind across the prairie. Smoke and sun-cooked grass. Powerful hooves under her the few times she was allowed to ride. *That was freedom. For a moment, a single moment, that was freedom.* She wondered if she would be punished for impersonating a soldier if she left the Hall this way, acted with purpose and fled the city, fled Ban altogether. *Where would I go?*

Shaking the treasonous thoughts away and let a dart fly. Running from the frontlines of battle was not an option, even when she swore they faced Toar himself. She had a job to do. It might be one she hated, it might break her heart, but these were simply new tactics, a foreign battlefield.

War was war, and she would not run.

Her second dart landed closer to the target's center, but still outside the wounding area. *I'm out of practice.* A breeze eddied across the room, drifting through the packed straw on the floor. She glanced over at the door.

Hamin leaned on the half-open screen, wearing a shorter, loose kalas clearly designed for movement. Linen wrapped her hands for combat and she was unarmed. "I haven't seen you here before. What's on your mind?"

"I feel soft." Rih shrugged, not sure if the other woman would understand. Hamin fell into a ready stance, then spun into a slow, graceful dance of blows and blocks. Rih's third dart zipped through the air, thudding into the target a few hands from her first two. It took another half hour before her muscles remembered the motions. She jogged back from fetching her darts and turned to see Hamin watching with narrowed eyes.

"You're good," she noted. "I was once the markswoman of the 103rd March."

"You were a soldier?" Rih's smile widened. "I didn't know."

"Several of us were. It's not common, but you aren't the first. I learned languages well, so they made me a companion for visiting dignitaries." Flurried blocks interrupted her signs, but after a moment she continued, "I didn't keep up with practice once I was here."

"I don't blame you—I didn't either. I just felt restless. I'll have little cause to practice once I'm married, unless I'm lucky enough to wed a Valen man," she joked. The matriarchal Vales were something of a legend among the Banis foot soldiers.

Hamin's face sobered. "You'd be more lucky to see a Valen raid than the inside of their bed chambers. They wouldn't accept a bride from Ban any more than Mirik will, it seems." Her hands stilled, and she watched Rih toss another two darts. Each was closer to the target's center.

Hamin held her hand out for the atlatl. "May I try?"

Rih handed the weapon over, eager to see a markswoman throw. Hamin settled the concave end of the dart on the spur. Her movements were unconscious, graceful in their certainty. She drew her arm back and brought it forward, the power in her shoulders sending the dart hurtling through the air. It split Rih's with a puff of shattered wood. She handed the weapon back so she could sign again. "I don't blame you for wishing to be married to Vale."

"It would be easier if they didn't hate us so."

"It's not hatred." Hamin's brows curled together. "It's enlightenment." Her head tilted at something unheard and her shoulders sagged in a sigh. "I'd best go. I just stop by here between visitors. Steadies my thoughts." She waved and slipped from the room.

Rih's heart thundered again, the same as when she stared down her cousin with all the fury she had never shown. *Enlightenment? If we are cousins, then how did things change so much?* Neither books nor Ki-elte would help. Questions led to trouble. It was the first rule of interrogation they learned in the army: find the source.

Replacing her atlatl and darts, she jogged back to her room. She did not bother to change before unrolling a blank scroll on her desk. It was one of the only times she used the pull by the door to summon a serving woman.

"What can I do?"

Rih wrote a quick line on her tablet.

I need to speak to Instructor Il-fald of the army. Tell her Rih-elte needs her advice.

"If you need a guard, we would be happy to send one."

"This is a personal call."

The woman bobbed her head in deference and slipped away.

Il-fald arrived with the darkness. Rih did not realize how much she missed the smell of leather until her nose was buried in the muscle of her former mentor's shoulder. She pulled away so she could sign, "I've missed you so much."

"You planning on sneaking back to our ranks?" Il-fald gestured to the training clothes.

"No, I was tossing darts and got distracted by some thoughts." She noticed, then, that the trainer's own clothing looked haphazardly arranged. "I'm sorry I interrupted your rest."

Il-fald's lined face broke into a rare smile. "I wouldn't say I was resting. She was pulled away by her own distractions, anyway." As usual she voiced and signed simultaneously. Her smile grew sad. "I miss having you at practice. You lent a certain humor that is lacking."

"You called me cynical," Rih countered.

Il-fald laughed. "Well, it wasn't unfounded. Have you learned much?"

"I did, but war slowed my lessons. I'm too still. And it seems my cynicism isn't as appreciated here as it was in the army."

"You said you wanted advice—is it about that?"

Rih looked down. *Why did I feel the urge to ask Il-fald to visit?* It seemed dire at the time, and now she felt dramatic, foolish, almost. "Part of it was loneliness," she hazarded, "and curiosity. My friend Hamin and I were discussing the likelihood of a marriage to one of their men. I knew you encountered them more than once and I wanted to know more. There's so little in the histories."

It was Il-fald's turn to look away. She ran a finger along the scar on her face. It began as a delicate line over her nose then widened across her cheek and ended at the missing tip of her ear. The Valen history with Ban was either erased or never written. Often the only accounts came from the few Banis women who survived meeting them in battle.

She was motionless for so long, Rih wondered if she would say another word. "They are ruled by a Queen." Il-fald's eyes remained fixed on the desk, the only movement her fingers and lips. "Unlike Athrolan's, though, she is a warrior. Their women are their warriors, like us, but they are also generals, strategists. Men stay at home and mind the children and farms. It's small wonder His Eminence hates them."

"I envy them," Rih interjected. "Hamin said they didn't hate us, rather they were enlightened." Fire hummed along her nerves and she clenched her fists before continuing. "I want to meet them." The words were signed before they were fully formed in her mind. *What good would meeting them do?* Teaching others her language, seeking advice from those who had overthrown their master—she saw what, together, those pieces made, and it was terrifying. *And liberating.* She glanced up, realizing Il-fald was signing while she thought. "I'm sorry?"

"Of course. I just said I am angry too. I promise you, I did not willingly give my body and soul to war, but this is our world. I see what you're doing, even if you don't realize it." Il-fald paused, eyes searching Rih's face. Her expression softened. "I think you just realized it too. But you must know a single woman cannot change something so ingrained."

"But she can be the catalyst." Now that she knew the secret lying in her heart, calm washed over her. "We are not the only women to be angry. I have a roomful of women willing to learn an entire language in order to speak freely. And like you said—the Vales are enlightened. We were once the same people. And now we're not. They changed their path. I can change ours." She pulled a scroll from her desk drawer. "What's her name? This Queen?"

"Majilah Ag of Vale."

It took a minute before Rih knew how to begin, and ten more before she had something worth penning. In the end, she chose simplicity. She leaned over the desk and reread her words.

> *Your Majesty Majilah Ag, Queen of Vale,*
> *You do not know me, but I am told our people*
> *were once the same. I am a daughter of His Eminence,*

*the Emperor of Ban. I write because I have been sent
from our army to learn to be a wife. I've learned more
about the world, about our place in it as women, in the
last few months than I ever did as a soldier.*

*And I want it to change. I want to know how you
broke from us and took back your power. I hope you can
help.*

In confidence,
-Rih-elte

It was not perfect, but it was a beginning. *Everything I
do now depends on beginnings. Everything started somewhere.*
She needed to know where that place was. She rolled the
parchment into a tiny scroll case and laid it on the table
between them. Il-fald's expression was wary, but she made
no move to leave. "You have informants, people who spy —
on us as well as for us," Rih guessed.

"It's part of my job to know who to trust. The baniol
might not think I'm capable, but I'm far from stupid."

"Could you to get this across the border to Vale?"

"Is it treason?" Il-fald pointedly did not read Rih's
words.

"It's questions. It's hope." Rih shrugged. "Would it
matter?"

Il-fald did not answer, but tucked the scroll away in her
clothes. "Rih, this could kill you. Doesn't that scare you
enough to stop?"

Rih's gaze bore into Il-fald's "If the gods still walked,
they themselves could not stop me."

CHAPTER FOURTEEN

The 41st Day of Aeme, 1272
Marl Black, Glasden Province of Athrolan

IT TOOK A SECOND knock for Daymir to realize Hylier stood in the doorway. "I worried I'd find you cold when you didn't answer. Do you want me to come back later?"

"I was lost in thought." Daymir glanced over with a wan smile. After a moment before he remembered why Hylier was there. "I would rather not wait another few weeks for the mail. I trust the weather has not been too bad?"

"Not yet, though there are rumors of the first winter storm."

"I was displeased to hear the servants discussing snow yesterday." Daymir gestured to the chair across from him. "Please, sit. Tell me the news. I've seen a lot of traffic on the roads lately. Many swords."

Hylier sat with a heavy sigh. "Athrolan is in trouble. Everyone sees it, none acknowledge it, really. Each has a different idea about how to fix the problem." He handed Daymir several letters. "There are some new ones in there."

Though it was Hylier's job to keep Daymir from creating a revolution, his practice of reading the exile's mail stopped after An'thoriend's letter. Daymir knew he now straddled the chasm between exile and prodigal. "Reports, more reports, letter from that supporter, Peraan. Letters from cousins." Daymir put them all aside for later, peering at the last two. Neither bore a sender's address on the outside of the envelope. The dates were two weeks apart and the hand was the same. "Did you read these?"

"I'm not supposed to anymore."

"Doesn't mean you don't." Daymir slit open the older envelope and tugged the letter out. "Any idea?"

Hylier shrugged. "Shall I call for dinner while you read?"

Daymir's nod was distracted. Curious words scrawled across the page engrossed him. He turned so the light struck the page better.

> *Daymir Blackhouse,*
>
> *I assume you get news from the city, whether by legitimate means or otherwise. You saw the Gods' War, and I assume you can imagine what the city looks like now. There are barkers on every corner that hold posters defaming Domariigo or you. Just as many cry for support. I am not someone you know, just someone with questions.*
>
> *My first: What happened just before the Gods' War and how can we prevent Athrolan tearing herself apart? I promise you, she will.*
>
> *Write to me at the Courier's Hall,*
> *Lan Guardsen*

It was not a familiar name. Something underlay the frank tone.

Hylier thumped into the chair opposite him with a sigh. "You look troubled."

"This letter's odd. The man—boy, perhaps, since he doesn't recall the Gods' War—writes only to ask me a question. Here, read it yourself." Daymir tossed it over and opened the next.

> *Daymir Blackhouse,*
>
> *It occurs to me that mail to your estate might be slow. It also occurs you may not reply at all. War is nearing. How can a city save herself when her allies are caught in their own chaos? That is not my second question to you. Instead, it is this: which conflict is threatens us more — Mirik's war with Ban, or our own with our brothers?*
>
> *Lan Guardsen*

Hylier put the first letter aside. "I don't recognize the name, though the surname is common enough. He's to the point. Perhaps he's recording a history. What do you think?"

Daymir handed it to Hylier wordlessly and waited as the other man scanned it. "Or perhaps the name is false and he is a political figure."

"You're paranoid." The food arrived, and the guard made room on the table between them. "You think he's truly an ally?" He took a large bite of the bread and meat, allowing Daymir to consider his question.

"I have no motives for the throne, thusly cannot have allies. But I will answer him."

"You're that lonely?" Hylier's brows snapped up.

Daymir's smile was sharp. "I'm that curious."

Φ

The 44th Day of Aeme, 1272
The City of Ceir Athrolan

Rain splattered against the glass. To An'thor's eyes, it was the spray of Athrolan's blood. Pale hands clenched on the stone window sill. He listened as Raven poured a drink from the general's well-stocked cabinet. "Why are you here?"

"Because you invited me for a drink."

"Don't be coy."

"I'm here because I hope you've seen sense. I'm willing to listen, willing to come to some agreement."

An'thor glanced over his shoulder, eyes narrowed. "You've never been willing to compromise in your life."

Raven stared at the drink in his hand. "For her, I would be."

An'thor wondered absently if Raven spoke of the queen or Athrolan. *Or Eras.* "So, what do you propose? I pay for your secret whores, and you'll allow Keplan to be king?"

Raven's growl was low. "I am trying to be an adult, Domariigo."

An'thor turned to lean on his desk. "And I'm trying to do what is best for our kingdom. Daymir is not a young man. His letters tell me his clarity is not what it once was. If he ascends, we have maybe fifteen years before we need another heir. The two cousins who are eligible have little training—"

"And you've trapped them in a prison camp while you stall negotiations."

An'thor sighed. "Gella has no interest in the throne, and her brother is next to useless. Keplan is young. He's who Tzatia wanted for king, and he is powerful. He's a symbol, Raven—one we need. Our ally is at war, and if you and I can't come to an accord, we will have larger issues on the table."

"Daymir will buy us the time to make this choice properly."

"We had twenty years, and we're still ready to throw each other into the storm."

Raven looked past An'thor to the portrait behind the desk. It portrayed the queen in her thirties. Eras stood at one hand, An'thoriend at the other. The commander's eyes were fixed on the former general. "She would hate us for this. She always loved Athrolan so much. She loved the queen and the city and every piece of this kingdom."

"Eras had allegiances higher than the queen, Raven, and you know it." An'thor rapped his knuckles against the rough wood of his desk. "Both she and the queen are dead, and it's left up to us. What is your compromise?"

"Allow Daymir into the city to speak with us."

"And what will you do in return?"

"I won't crown him the minute he steps through the palace gates."

An'thor rolled his eyes. "You don't have that power."

"With enough of the House of Nobles, I do. And you are a fool if you think they won't choose him over a power-addled pauper." Raven knocked back his drink. "Decide, Domariigo. You have five days. After that, you'll have no choice."

Φ

The 46th Day of Aeme, 1272
Marl Black, Glasden Province of Athrolan

Bitter wind buffeted the manor, whipping the mourning flags. Daymir sank deeper into his chair. Vaulted ceilings were beautiful but hardly homey. Even with a roaring fire, it was cold. He brushed dry fingers down the page of his book. Despite reading the words half a dozen times without comprehending them. Solitude may have become him in his youth, but now it chafed. Even for the mountains, a squall in Aeme was unexpected.

He slapped the book on the table and stalked to the window. Outside the world was white. Ice glittered in the churning sky. Fog swallowed everything beyond the head of the road. *If this isn't a metaphor for Athrolan's current state, I don't know what is.* Glass rattled under a blast of wind. Movement caught his eye as he retreated to the fire. A shadow moved through the whipping wind. It was faint, but approached up the road. Daymir's eyes narrowed. His servants sheltered in the town below, and he doubted he would see any before the storm retreated. Last winter he went an entire month without news.

Fifteen minutes passed before the shadow reached his courtyard. By then it formed the shape of two riders. He threw on his cloak, lacing it tightly before he yanked the door open. Snow spilled into the foyer. The riders dismounted, and the shorter of the two raised a hand in response to his.

"The stable's unlocked!" His battle-voice pierced the wind, and the visitors led their mounts inside. Unlocking the door between the manor and its stables, he headed to the kitchen, shedding his cloak as he did.

Pots of gravy and sweet sauce hung over the fire to heat, and Daymir collected bread and cold meat on a platter. Boots stomping snow from their tread interrupted his preparation of tea.

The hall was quiet as his visitors set aside packs and outdoor attire. Daymir stepped out of the kitchen as one rider rounded the corner. He froze. "Fates."

Alea's eyes still sent ice sliding down his spine. Lines mapped the history of her expressions, but her face was as striking as their last meeting twenty years before. "Good evening to you, too." She offered a tired smile. "Arman will be in once the horses are settled. We both thought it best if I greeted you alone."

"Indeed." *The Dhoah' Laen is in stocking feet in my foyer.* "Where have you been? An'thoriend would have a fit if he knew you were here. Fates, I might have a fit once I recover from the shock." He stopped himself from rambling further and resorted to simply staring.

Her dark brows arched as she waited for him to fall quiet. "I'll gladly answer everything. Might we stay a night, maybe two?"

"Of course. You're likely to be trapped here with this weather, though."

"We made it here. I'm confident we'll make it out."

The door to the stables shut softly, and Daymir heard a deep sigh as boots were shucked off. "Alea?"

"We're in the hall," she answered without taking her eyes from Daymir's. The kettle began to squeal.

"I've completely forgotten my manners. I set out some food and tea. It's not a feast, but it'll do until morning."

Alea followed him into the kitchen, and when he turned Arman stood in the doorway as well. The Rakos's ferocity was now an ember under steady might. His uncertainty was gone. Arman offered him an arm, which Daymir took.

"You grew older." Daymir raised a hand in defense of the obvious comment. "I know, we all did. I just never expected you to turn gray. Or, perhaps, I never thought I'd see it."

"We're as much human as we are anything else." Alea smiled. "Besides, now no one can say they thought the Dhoah' Laen would be older."

Daymir snorted. "Perhaps." He took the pots from their hooks and nestled them into their places on the platter. "As much as I was raised a noble and should make small talk well into the evening, I find I can't help but ask why you're here."

Arman looked down. "We started riding months ago. It seems we missed much being out of the world. We need to be caught up."

"So it's not for my witty company." Daymir shoved off from the counter with a sigh. "Well, let me bring these into my study, and I'll set a fire. There's a room at the top of the stairs, beside the black hall table. It should be warm enough. We can talk once you've settled your things there."

Quiet steps muted their conversation as they climbed up to the room. His shaking hands rattled the teapot. He did not know whether the tremors were from fear or excitement. He sat in a chair, then rose to stand by the door, and finally decided to wait by the fire. *No visitors for weeks and then the queen passes followed by a visit from the most powerful creatures in the world.* His mind tripped over the thought. Memories were dim more often of late, even erasing them entirely on occasion. He was happy that, at least for the evening, his mind was clear.

"You've got a lovely place here," Arman's voice rumbled from the doorway. He moved through the stacks of books, glancing at their titles.

"Yes. For a prison, it's quite lovely." Daymir looked down. It would not do to alienate his guests, however unexpected. "Sorry. I've been a bit restless."

Arman's brows rose. "I'm surprised you haven't returned to the city."

Daymir's gaze inched over the other man's face. He had no idea what Arman knew of Athrolan's current affairs. "Exiled is exiled. Perhaps news should wait until Dhoah' Lyne'alea joins us?"

"Perhaps." Arman's mouth curled with tempered mirth. "It's been a while since we answered to those titles.

I'm not sure which is more uncomfortable, the fact that we forgot them so easily or that they still fit." He gestured to the seat. "May I? The way houses were full, and we've slept on benches more than beds."

"Of course." Daymir took a seat across from him. "The roads are busy?"

"Until we came farther north. The closer we get to the capital the few travelers we've seen." Alea breezed in. "This looks lovely, thank you." She collapsed into the third chair with a sigh. "You're taking this in stride. I'd almost believe you expected us."

"I've had my share of oddities lately. Before we dive into dark news, might I ask where you've been for the past twenty years?"

"Nineteen years and four months." Alea's voice was just above a whisper. Her eyes fixed on her untouched plate. "I've counted too, you know. I missed this world as much as I avoided it. I missed Bren, missed An'thoriend, even you at times."

Arman glanced at her. "Alea."

"I know. It was our choice. My choice. Doesn't mean it wasn't difficult."

"You've avoided contact, even with Bren?" Daymir leaned back with a sigh. "I correspond more, and I've been in actual exile." He twirled his cup thoughtfully. Alea knocked him off center, ripped his balance away. "Perhaps you ought to tell me what you do know, lest I assume and make an idiot of myself," his eyes flicked up to Alea's, "again."

Her smile was tired, but genuine, and after a moment she laughed. "Well, we've heard rumors of war—both between Mirik and Ban and civil unrest within Athrolan herself. Various nobles bolster their cities with personal guards. We've heard many shouting support for you from their windows. And support for another, a person An'thor promised."

"Do you know who it is, or are you hoping the rumors are wrong?"

"We knew An'thor's intentions, your aunt's intentions, if we ever had a child." Arman sighed, rubbing a rough hand over his weary features. "We had a son, and he's gone, after reading An'thor's pleading letter."

Daymir watched their expressions, eyes narrowed. "You came here to beg me to take the throne?"

Arman shrugged. "We came here to talk."

"No," Alea interrupted. "We wanted to look for our son, and I needed answers."

"Answers?"

Alea shoved herself out of the chair and wandered to the window. Outside the storm raged. "Something's coming, Daymir. Something more terrible than the gods, older, darker than what I faced. And I think I might have caused it. I need your help."

"How could I, possibly?"

"I keep having dreams, and this mad old woman tells me I'm poisoning the world. When I can make sense of it, she mentions a city in Berr. We need to go there."

"What's it called?"

"I don't know. It's in the mountains, tucked up above a plain."

"What's there?" A puzzle might keep his mind sharp for a little while longer.

"I don't know, but it's where the poison starts. In my vision, it's the place where something poisons the world. Where the blood turns black."

"Alea," Arman began, but Daymir cut him off.

"I think I have something. But why don't we let it rest for the evening?" He saw the mania in her eyes, the exhaustion in Arman's shoulders. "Tell me about your son."

Φ

Blood washed over the mountains, purple-red waves breaking on rocky slopes. The flow pulsed from a gaping hole where Ceir Athrolan once stood. Instead of ragged earth, a bleeding, tunneling wound, swollen flesh where bermed earth and towers should stand. Trickling blood stained the ocean black.

"You did this. You killed the gods, but you created something else, something mightier still, and now it strangles the world."

Alea sat up with a gasp. A sickly sweet metallic scent hung heavy over the bed. *Blood.* She scrambled free from the sheets. The privy's washbasin was full, and she dunked her face into the perfumed water. Still, the cloying sweetness clung in her nose. Raking back her hair, she peered in the mirror. The stress of the past month made her face closer to the woman in her visions than the Alea she once knew. "What do you want from me?"

Her reflection remained silent. She tugged on a dressing robe and left Arman sleeping. Below, a light told her someone else was awake. The library was warm, still, the hearth the only light in the room. Daymir slumped in a chair, a stack of books beside him. The one on his lap seemed full of outdated maps.

"Mind if I join?"

His eyes flicked up. "Not at all. Storm have you up?"

Alea shrugged and slid into the chair opposite. "Something like that."

Daymir's head tilted, and she was abruptly reminded of the calculating attitude he had been known for in court. "What of your power? Do you still wield it?"

"Only echoes."

He hummed thoughtfully and turned to look at the orange flames. "So, it passed to Keplan."

It was her turn to regard him carefully. "I didn't say that."

"Power like yours doesn't just fade." He ran a hand down the page of the book before him. "I'm surprised you never saw anything odd in him."

Alea sighed. "Arman would tell you we did him a disservice, raising him away from other children and without the knowledge of what monstrous things crouched in his bloodline."

"You disagree?"

"Children are complicated. It's so easy to forget they're human. Like parents, they are so often a symbol of something simpler in your mind. And then they surprise you, and you're forced to remember they're not an extension of yourself. I wanted a normal life. I wanted peace. I wanted simplicity and happiness. We've earned it, I think. But Keplan hasn't walked the paths that made him want those things." She narrowed her eyes. "What kept you up?"

He drew out the book of maps. "I was studying Ban's former borders."

"Ban?"

"Mirik is at war with them." He flipped to the front of the book. "The oldest I have of Berr is from 982."

Alea peered over his shoulder. "There." Her chapped finger tapped the parchment. "Except there isn't a lake in my dreams. But that's where it is."

"Tut Kunis." He frowned. "I know that name." He handed her the book and rose, muttering titles as he wove between the stacks of books. "*The Making of an Empire, Fall of Leaves, When Snow Falls in Summer.* Ah, here. *Matricide: The Death of Balance in the War Against the Laen.*"

"That sounds like something I'd rather not read."

Daymir snorted, flipping through the pages. "Here. A list of every Laen citadel and their guard cities. Look at the fourth from the bottom."

She tucked her hair behind her ear and bent over the book, tilting the page toward the firelight. "Citadel Lymorda. Guarded by Tut Kunis in the Orn de Galin in Berr, above the Ocean's Child."

Daymir measured the distance in finger-widths. "It'll take you three weeks if you ride hard. I can give you horses and food."

Alea turned away, scrubbing her face with her hands. "Am I truly doing this, again?"

"Saving the world?"

She shook her head, palms still pressed to her eyes. "It never feels that way, not to me, not inside my thoughts. It feels like I'm leaving peace in favor of war." She moved to the window. "There's something over in that city, maybe something left by the Laen, or even the gods. And in my gut, I know that this puzzle holds the answer to Keplan." She rolled her head on her neck. The world rushed around her, twisting, changing as they took each step. She did not like the sensation. "I think we'll leave tomorrow, at dawn."

"You can't stay longer? I could claim I want you both to wait out the storm, but truthfully you're the first new face I've seen in a long time." Air shrieked against the manor, punctuating his words.

"I wouldn't worry about the storm." Dreary weather followed them from the Hartland. "Something tells me it'll be gone when we are."

"Well, pack warmly. I'm sure I have things that will fit you. It'll be cold as this, colder."

She shook her head. "You spend enough time with my power, you wouldn't feel it. Besides, the Northlands were worse."

Daymir joined her at the window. "I didn't know you'd been."

"Just before the battle. And I intend to go again." She heaved a sigh. "Well, perhaps not as far, but a ways in. I'm happy to be on the road again."

"I'm sorry. You came here hoping for answers and found a pathetic exile who can't remember his mother's name half the time." He looked down at his hands. "Fates, how did we get here? This old, this jaded?"

"Speak for yourself." Darkness in her eyes shadowed Alea's small smile. "Hearing you speak, your careful, powerful words, it feels like yesterday."

"Since Athrolan?"

"Since I threw you from my room after you asked me to marry you." She glanced sidelong at him, imagining the dozen different paths her life would have taken. *Would I still have had a child? Would they have been Keplan?* "You were right—we would have made a powerful match. But we're far too similar for anything more romantic."

"It would have been a mess. I know that now. It's hard to see something so close sometimes." He reached over and took her hand.

After a moment Alea squeezed his fingers but did not answer. Her gaze was fixed on the iron sky and the cluster of thunderheads marching north.

Φ

The 49th Day of Aeme, 1272
The City of Ceir Athrolan

The kitchen smelled like home. Spices from breakfast breads and supper meats hung in the air. Keplan propped the pantry door open with a loose cobblestone and set about tidying. Mirrel eyed him from the stove but said nothing. It spoke volumes that she allowed him near her organized realm at all. He smiled and wiped dust from the shelves. The ground shuddered under him.

"Did you drop something?" Mirel snapped.

"You felt that?" He half expected it to have been in his mind. A second tremor shook flour dust from the rafters. Wood splintered in the distance. His eyes met Mirrel's, met the narrowed expression that so many mistook for anger.

It was fear. "I remember that sound. That's an attack."

Keplan shook his head. "We're not at war, Mirrel. I'll go look. Perhaps the aqueduct needs repair." The third cannon hit as he crossed the common room. Decades-old wood flew into slivers. The foundation shattered. Stone dust exploded around them. Rafters rent. Timber screamed and twisted under the impact. Buzzing filled his spinning head. Warmth trickled down his back and face. His vision pulsed between focus and blurry shapes. Mirrel was speaking, screaming, but he barely heard the words through the echoing in his ears. She was trapped, a fallen rafter blocking the kitchen door. Smoking coals spilled across the dry floor.

Her voice clattered into his mind. "The barrel outside!"

"What?"

"The rain barrel, you idiot! Get water before this place burns!"

Keplan's legs churned him to his feet, and he staggered through the rear door. Smoke already curled from the narrow window between the kitchen and their tiny courtyard. A bucket sat beside the rain barrel. His weak fingers trembled as he passed it through the window, dumping half the contents over his own head. Steam billowed from the window now, the hissing distant to his blown ears. "More?"

"No, I've gotten it."

"Can you climb through here?"

There was a pause, then scrambling feet on wood more accustomed to flour. Mirrel's head popped over the window sill. "I think I can manage. Grab a stool for my feet, would you?"

He did as she asked, glancing between her careful escape and the upper storey. "Where's Firas?"

Mirrel dropped down beside him, brushing the dusty hair from her face. Her eyes were bright. "You, sit. Here on the stoop. Away from anything that might fall on you. Keep your eyes and ears open. I'll be right back."

She disappeared into the inn and Keplan turned to the stable. "Moly?" He ducked through the door, wincing as something pulled at his back with the movement. The horses spooked, but fine, and the beams above looked undamaged. Navigating through new debris in the alleyway, he emerged in the street. The house opposite the inn was gone, a hollowed trench where the third cannon passed. Cannon fire still sounded across the city, puffs of dust rising into the clear sky. There were no Banis flags in the harbor, as Keplan expected. The Mirikin ships had yet to return.

The warships were Athrolani.

The pennants were the Commander's. Keplan's knees became water. He hit the cobbles hard.

A warm, rough hand brushed his hair back. Firas caught his gaze, peering into his face with worry. "Are you all right?"

"It's shock, Firas." Mirrel stood at the edge of what was once their neighbor's house. She drew a shuddering breath, then another, firmer one before she knelt by Keplan. Her hands were gentle on his cheek as she turned his face first one way then the other. "Close your eyes for me. Open." Her eyes narrowed on his. "You're all right." Her fingers found a stinging, sticky patch of scalp. "Just a gash. It'll mend." She sat back on her heels. "Shirt off."

He blinked at her. "What?"

"'Lan, love, you're covered in blood. We've got to get you patched." Firas offered him a smile, but the expression was weak. "What happened?"

"The third blow. I was by the door." Ringing in his ears lessened to an annoying whine. His thoughts still swam through honey. Mirrel snapped her fingers at him, but there was no contempt in her expression. "Keplan, shirt please."

He pulled it off, wincing at the stinging ache under his shoulder at the movement. Sudden exposure focused his thoughts further and he saw Mirel's gaze skim his scars. She turned him to look at his back. "This will be uncomfortable. Breathe in while I count to three."

Keplan did as she asked, scanning the building crowd and the soldiers racing through the upper city. Smoke and stone dust thickened the air filling his lungs. Mirrel reached two. Pain exploded across his back. Muscles seized, and his vision turned white. Hot liquid dribbled down his side and pooled underneath him. He glanced down, blinking his eyes clear again. Dark blood spread on the cobbles. It was more than he expected. He looked up at Firas. The older man's face was sickly white. "What happened?"

"A piece of our rafters found its way into the muscles of your shoulder blade." Firas seemed unable to look away from the blood. "Mirrel is a cold-hearted monster who never shies at injuries."

"If you saw your own blood every few weeks, you'd be cold-hearted too." Mirrel's fingers prodded the swollen flesh around the wound. "I got it all, I think." She rose, finally looking at the chaos roiling around them.

Keplan took Firas's offered hand and rose with a groan. Fading adrenaline left his body aching in strange places, injuries making themselves known. Turquoise flooded the road between the palace and the barracks. *This is my home.* Athrolan had been safe. Keplan's gut clenched.

The ground shook again, but not from cannon fire. Screaming metal pierced the smoky air. The towering white pillars spanning the harbor shuddered, and massive gates inched across the water. The rusted portcullis was taller than any city tower. Spikes several paces long fell outwards as the gate closed the harbor's entrance. *That will gut any ship brave enough to ram them.*

Athrolani battleships stretched to the horizon. Her army massed on the hills. *If they lay siege to either end of their own city, Athrolan will starve within a month.* Keplan's thoughts were quiet, for once, and his heart empty.

Φ

The 2nd Day of Lumord, 1272
The City of RoBal, Ban

Dust hung heavily under the layer of smoke. Rih tucked a fold of her scarf over her head and nose to keep the worst of it out. Still, though, it was pervasive. Since her time as a soldier, she had not navigated the streets alone. Hard cobbles bit through the thin soles of her sandals. Wagons trundled down roads usually reserved for foot traffic. Horses pawed new furrows in the packed dirt of the barrack courtyard as Rih slipped through the gate. Rough hands yanked her back against the wall to allow a march through. She pressed a hand to the letter folded inside her wrap. It was still there. The woman who pulled her out of harm's way waved a dramatic hand before Rih's face.

Rih frowned at the rude gesture. "What?"

Recognition filled the soldier's eyes, followed by scorn as she took in Rih's attire. "Oh, you're the simple one. I thought they traded you off?"

Rih swallowed bitterness with the hard words she wanted to use. A few months ago that scorn was hers, too. "I'm looking for Il-fald." She held up her tablet with the woman's name carved across the wax.

The soldier jerked her head at the barracks. "She's watching the formations."

Rih jogged up the stairs, forcing her expression into something between concern and determination. She could not risk looking fearful. She could not risk anyone questioning her. *Not with this letter on me.* A ladder at the end of the hall led to the ramparts. Rih hurried up it, shielding her eyes from the glare of the sallow sun. The dust was worst here without the shield of the city buildings or walls. Il-fald stood on the walkway, hands braced against the earthen wall. Black paint helped her eyes with the glare. Rih faltered, catching sight of the fresh green tattoos staining her newly shaved head. Il-fald always inspired her. Now she intimidated.

The older woman glanced over, and the lines of her face rearranged into a smile. "Rih. I'm glad to see you again. Do you bring news?"

Rih returned the smile, the expression deepening at the double-meaning. "I do." Her gaze lingered on the green designs on Il-fald's scalp. "I see you have been promoted."

"I am now in charge of the drill." Her fingers brushed the oil preventing the tattoo from forming scabs. It was a stylized horse's hoofprint with an atlatl crossing it.

Rih suppressed a shudder. The symbol reminded her of a skull crushed under a warhorse's hoof. "I need you to read this." She withdrew the letter and handed it to Il-fald. "It is vague, but I'm still fearful." Her former instructor's expression faded to neutrality as she scanned the letter's contents.

> *R-*
>
> *I was delighted to receive your letter. Your questions are good ones, but complex. I hope to answer them in person during my next visit to RoBal. I'll find you.*
>
> *-M*

Il-fald rolled the letter wordlessly and returned it to Rih. Her dark brows furrowed over the black smear of paint. "I didn't expect this."

"I wanted friendship, answers. I did not expect a meeting."

Il-fald hunched over the wall. "Why don't you speak with your tutor—Ki-elte? She seems like she would be a good source of support for you during this time of change."

Rih noted the change in demeanor and glanced over her shoulder. Another officer approached, male by the long lock of black hair braided at his neck. "We are friends, perhaps, but I worry I cannot trust her this far. These questions are difficult."

Il-fald switched to signing. "I cannot un-read that letter, Rih. You have my confidence, but be careful. You need women outside the army to help you. More than you need me."

"Ki-elte is willing to play at subterfuge, but I think this is too close to treason for her to stomach."

"This is treason."

The ground trembled, and Rih turned. It was rare a sound was loud enough to register for her. The sensation came again, and she caught sight of the woman at the tower just above the ramparts. Her barrel chest expanded, and she pressed her lips to the brass mouth of the massive horn. It was washed with copper, a tiny moon to the massive golden sun of the palace gong above the squalor of the city.

The plain below was not the rolling gold of the rainy season, the lush grasses carved with the black curves of the river. Instead, the undulating land was stamped to dust. Vegetation no longer hid the huts of the poor smattering the muddy banks of the Ninaket. She saw the prairie during the dry season before. That is not what made Rih's heart lurch its way between her teeth. She clenched her jaw to keep it from escaping.

There was no horizon. The mass of marching soldiers bled into the dusty distance. Bodies blurred into the sullen sky. "Il-fald, what is this?"

"War. You haven't seen it before. You've seen battles. You've seen death and the edges of what might become war. But this is its heart." Her shoulders heaved in a sigh and she voiced, "We're marching soon."

The older woman's mouth tightened around the words. Rih could not remember a time the woman was uncertain. Or scared. She remembered the earth vibrating through her boots, quaking under the might of thousands and thousands of feet, under the call to arms. She wished to grab Il-fald's hand, to have the grip of an atlatl in her palm. Instead, her fingers wrapped the rail before her.

"I cannot help but think how many won't return, their names forgotten, ground into the dirt with their bones and blood." Il-fald's hands were low, shaking as they signed. "Promise me you'll change it."

"I can't say it will look different at first. We'll still die. We'll still bleed, but this time our bones will make a bridge for us to cross. He has spent enough time winning wars with our bodies, throwing us into rape made legal by marriage, into battle made heroic by his cavalry. I'm tired of being tinder for his hateful fire." She clenched a fist. "If I'm going to burn, I will make it an inferno."

CHAPTER FIFTEEN

The 5th Day of Lumord, 1272
The City of Ceir Athrolan

AN'THOR'S HEAD ACHED, AND his back cramped from crouching over the council table. "I want every soldier we can spare to surround the nobles. Send word to each headman in the provinces and counties still loyal to us. I want our militia raised. Athrolan's military is coming here, and the towns and cities will have to fend for themselves."

"Sir, do you honestly think that's wise? Our neighbors are close to war."

"And we're already at war, Colonel." An'thor scrubbed a trembling hand over his face. He wanted a drink. He hated the weakness flooding his limbs every sober moment. "Squire, if you please?"

The boy bowed out of the room. An'thor remained silent until the boy returned with a thick glass brimming with wine. An'thor grimaced as the sweetness slid across his tongue. *It'd be ill form to knock back wraith in this company, I suppose.* He took another, smaller swallow and turned his attention back to the maps. Calm was returning already. "What are Dorcal's positions?"

"The Commander—"

"Dorcal, dammit! He's a traitor, and that's the only title he deserves." An'thor bit back the rest of his vitriol. He took another breath, another gulp, and wet his lips. "Forgive me. I hoped my camaraderie with Dorcal would prevent this disaster."

"We all did, sir. Many of us have kin in the navy."

An'thor looked down. Facing family across the battlefield was something he hoped never to feel again. "Let's begin with his ships. He's got the north and east fleets out there—" An'thor bit back a curse as another runner appeared in the doorway. "What is it now?"

"The warehouses are burning, sir. The Thread is unraveling, if you pardon the pun." When An'thor did not smile at the weak joke, the boy barreled on. "The nobles are squirreled in their manors, each with their personal guard. Any who spoke of support for Daymir are gone, left in the night."

An'thor moved to the window. Smoke clogged the air, and soldiers swarmed through the barracks below. "Do not allow anyone else in or out of the city, save our own troops. The gates are closed as of this moment. Instate a curfew— two hours after sundown. Anyone out later will be detained. As for Raven—any ships arriving with his supplies are to be burned on sight."

Φ

Keplan ran a cloth over the counter, smoothing his hand after it to assure the sticky ale was indeed gone. The door banged open behind him. "Hey, Firas. We ought to make better use of this time while Mirrel's out."

"What?"

Keplan whirled, blood flushing his cheeks. A blond soldier stood just inside the door, long coat still wrapped around his shoulders. "Forgive me, I thought you were someone else."

The man's smile was quick and genuine. "I noticed. I'm sorry to disappoint." He jerked a chin at the empty, damaged common room. "I don't suppose you're open?"

"Not until afternoon, I'm afraid, unless you need a room."

"I've let a room in the Lily and Ahonsa." He slid onto a stool. "I'm actually looking for someone."

Keplan leaned on the bar. "They have a name or face I'd recognize?"

"Not sure about the face. I'm looking for a Lan Guardsen."

Keplan's heart leapt then clattered to a halt somewhere between his boots. "Who's asking for him?"

The soldier laughed, an easy sound, and patted his short hair. "No need to get your hairs up. I asked at Courier's Hall, and they said the letters were sent by a boy of your looks. Asked a bit more and they said you also delivered mail from the Wise Hare."

"And you've come to what, warn me? Threaten me?"

"You're quick to distrust. Though any man who doesn't use his own name must be running from something. Daymir's curious about you."

"Curious?" Keplan was too preoccupied with keeping his nerves in check to search Hylier's face for secrets.

"Aye. Said to give you this." He slid a thick letter across the counter.

"He could have sent it to me."

"And he thinks he has. He's a good friend, and I wanted some information for my own concerns. If you need to reply, I'd deliver it for you. Easier, with the city closed. Why the false name?"

Keplan shrugged. "I doubted the former heir would write a kitchen boy in the slums."

"I doubt most kitchen boys in the slums would write to him with the same articulation." He tilted his head. "You're clever. You claim to be an ally, claim to want answers, but never say why. You're a right puzzle. Who are you, really?"

Firas burst through the back door with a dramatic sigh. "Honestly, if one more urchin weaves me some tale about their poor baby sibling needing sup, I might just break down and try begging myself. It's far more lucrative than owning any inn." His brows arched at the sight of the man at the bar. "Keplan, really, I'm gone an hour, and you invite strange men in off the street?" The way the bartender's gaze lingered on the stranger's shoulders and forearms, however, told Keplan that, given the choice, Firas might have invited him in himself.

"Sorry, Firas. Master...." He glanced at the soldier.

"Hylier. Captain, actually," the officer offered with a broad smile.

"Captain Hylier was just leaving."

Hylier glanced between the two men before rising. "Right. Sorry to have imposed." He paused at the door and glanced back. "I hope you'll consider writing again. Good day."

Firas watched him go, gaze appreciative. "You have good taste, 'Lan."

"I wasn't flirting with him," Keplan protested.

The door shut. Firas's face hardened, and he turned to Keplan. "I know that." His eyes were dark. "I've welcomed you into this inn, into our family. Fuck, I welcomed you into my bed. I've comforted you when the world seemed on your shoulders and tupped you could sleep. I never once demanded where you came from or why you were running. Not once!" His quiet words rumbled into thunder, and he brought his fist down on the counter.

Keplan stepped back a pace. The captain's questions weaseled into his chest and lay there, a coal smoldering on the rug. Firas was the one person he opened himself to, and the sharp words burned. "I don't know why you're angry."

"Of course you don't. You're like a child sometimes. You see so much of the world you think everyone else about you is an idiot. You've had people asking after you. The ambassador's spy, with the scars on her eyes, came more than once, and I've seen others follow you home from the market. And now a captain?" He sank his head in his hands. "Oh, that life were as simple as you think it is for us. But you bring trouble after you, you bring it here."

"I didn't bring trouble, Firas. I'm a pauper's son from the woods."

"How does a pauper's son bear the marks of torture? How does a pauper's son befriend the child of the Mirikin Hetmir?" His voice lowered, and he looked down at the letter, forgotten, on the countertop. "How does a pauper's son write to Daymir Blackhouse? I can't read the words, Keplan, but I know that seal." He turned away. "Go upstairs, go walk the markets. For all I care, stowaway on a smuggler's ship. Just take your trouble with you."

Keplan waited a moment, but the man did not look at him or say another word. The floorboards turned to water and he was drowning. Tucking the letter into his shirt, he stumbled to the door. It did not matter which street he took or where he headed. He only wanted air and silence.

Chills already filled the void left by the other man's skin. Another cannon boomed across the harbor, and he winced. The battle might have started as a pointed dialogue between the navy and army, but with civilians caught between them, it turned deadly. The bodies pulled from rubble ranged from a few dozen to a few hundred, depending on who counted. *Civil war.*

His hands paused on the letter from Daymir. Even now his fingers faltered over the unbroken seal. Knowing the truth about why he was wanted in Athrolan changed things. *Daymir and I are equals, technically.* He paused in a pool of lantern light and pried the wax free. Richness was evident in the weight and smoothness of the plain parchment.

> *Lan,*
>
> *I admit I'm curious about your interest in me. Not your stated concerns, but the root of it. I see the same warning flags in Athrolan as you. As isolated as I am, I see forces moving in the valley below Marl Black. I see them bristling with weapons, wearing provincial colors boldly. But when they stop in town, their faces are scared, not proud.*
>
> *I've received many letters from supporters, but none as candid as yourself. Some are commoners. Others are officers and lords. I fear the numbers are equal on either side. When we went to war against the gods it was easier. We had a queen. We had allies. We had the figurehead of two titanic creatures. We have none of those things. You ask why I refuse the crown? The answer lies there.*
>
> *My advice to you is this — do not turn to history. We never listen, and now is not a time to start. Look to the future. Ambassador Barrackborn did this when he reformed the Mirikin government as Hetmir. I'm not proposing reform — Athrolan is too large for that, and her government too complex, if unstable. Mirik's was nonexistent.*
>
> *Let me pose a question to you in turn: which do you think would benefit Athrolan more — a mythical*

heir of the aforementioned creatures or an old exile of older blood? Let us pretend both were present and willing.

I look forward to your response.
-Blackhouse

Daymir's personal hand was clear, flourishes marking only the first letters of the paragraph and his signature. Anger burned in Keplan's chest. The man was born for royalty, trained for the throne. *So where are you when we need you? You're Athrolan's damned heir, and you've let her destroy herself, let her rot, slavering at her own limbs.* He caught sight of the manors on the highest tier of the city, and his thoughts tripped to an abrupt halt. Scarred eyes and the low voice of Mirik's Spy Master loomed in his memory: *"...do what you know you ought."* Daymir was not the only one shirking duty.

Keplan looked again at the letter. He should write the nobleman, explain everything, confess to his blood, explain why he was unfit to be a monarch. The exile was clearly curious, enough to talk to a stranger. Keplan raked a hand through his hair. It would take months to convince the man of his birth, however, and Athrolan did not have months.

Athrolan did not have days.

What if we met? Adrenaline pooled in his stomach. Hylier's words returned to Keplan then. He did not need to earn Daymir's trust. Hylier already had it. He glanced up at the guards on the street corner ahead. Curfew would be in an hour. Soldiers were either tired from their watch or too busy to be bothered with a bar boy.

The Lily and Ahonsa was set in the heart of the Silver Apron. More expensive than the Slummer, it was a section of the city he rarely visited. Now it was a breeding ground for rebellion. He took his hands from his pockets and began to jog. If he was lucky, Hylier would not have left. He turned a corner, backtracked along a narrow road overgrown with leaning houses. The street twisted around an older smithy and spilled into a square. A building rose across the empty space. Pillars and arches told him it once was something official. Now it bore a sign with a white flower and a tattered green ribbon.

Keplan crossed the square and slipped through the door. Like every alehouse the past few weeks, it was both crowded and hushed. It was an unsettling combination. He slid onto a stool at the bar along two of the inn's walls. The bartender jerked a nod at him, taking two orders on her way to where he sat.

"What'll it be, sir?"

Keplan grimaced at the honorific. "I'm looking for Hylier."

She frowned. "He's out, but he'll be back within an hour if you want to wait and have a drink."

Keplan slid a coin across the bartop. "Fire-ale please, miss." Anonymity gave him confidence, and he turned to watch the musicians. He could not recognize a good tune if it spent the night with him, but the other patrons seemed pleased. The bartender delivered his drink, and he took several gulps without tasting the acrid flavor. It burned down his throat, a flame nestled between his ribs. His fingertips tingled when the glass was empty. Alcohol brought numbness, silence, but it was the silence of stunned ears, not peace. *Still, it's better than the cacophony.*

The barmaid delivered another without a word. When she was gone, a man stood in her wake. Hylier's hair looked greasier, though it was no more than a few hours since they met last. "You change your tune quickly, Guardsen."

Keplan grunted and pointed at the chair opposite him. "Sit, will you? I'm not used to looking up at people."

The soldier folded his cloak over the back of the chair and settled himself. His eyes did not waver. Keplan noted they were almost as blue as his own, albeit warmer.

"Where are you from?"

Hylier frowned. "I grew up on one of the Xain estates. It's how I met Daymir. Why do you ask?"

"Your eyes. Blue. Not the usual gray and brown of Athrolan. Your hair, too."

Hylier ran a hand across his scalp with a mocking look of horror. "My hair's turned blue?"

Keplan's lip curled at the bad joke. "Never mind. You said I could find you if I wanted to speak to Blackhouse. Said it'd be quicker, with the city under siege."

"Aye, mail's all but stopped. The only correspondence is military. I could get a letter through for you, though, if you convinced me it was urgent."

Keplan looked down at his half-empty glass. He barely convinced himself this idea was a good one, let alone whether it would work. The door banged open, wind blowing dead leaves and a cloaked stranger into the room.

The barmaid waved her dishrag. "Peraan, good to see you. I worried you were trapped outside when the city locked down."

"City this big, it's hard to watch every part of the walls all the time." He tossed her a bloodshot wink and asked after the business as he sat. Keplan's eyes narrowed on the thin beard, the deep-set eyes. *Arthritis from working the docks for years. He and his brother lost their parents in Capital Siege during the Gods' War.* More than that he wasn not sure. His gaze fell to the stack of posters the man dropped on the bar. They were propaganda, the familiar caricatures of An'thor and Daymir locked in a dramatic battle. *He's the barker who wants Daymir on the throne.*

Hylier followed Keplan's gaze, then rolled his eyes. "There's one on every corner. Barkers claiming one thing or another. Probably the same rhetoric about this mythical heir the general spews."

The man—Peraan, apparently—heard Hylier's comment and turned in his seat, raising a glass to them in solidarity. "This officer clearly knows the truth. Domariigo poisons the city, turns the people against us."

Keplan braced his elbows against the bar. As much as he disliked the general, he distrusted the bleary expression in the barker's eyes more. "What lies does he tell?"

Peraan's brows shot up. "What hole have you been living in?"

"A dark one. I arrived in the city just a few days before the gates closed," he lied, ignoring Hylier mouthing in silent confusion beside him. "It's hard to tell rumor from fact during a war."

Peraan's smile widened, no doubt seeing a new follower. "He's got this heir, right? Supposed child of the Dhoah' Laen and the Rakos."

The barmaid shuddered. "He was a piece of work, the Rakos was, let me tell you. Tried to take me to bed and burnt my sheets. I think he fancied I looked like his woman."

Keplan blanched. Those were stories he would rather not know. "And no one knows whether the boy exists?"

"Well, the general seems convinced, and the Mirikin Ambassador has been secretive enough lately. No doubt he has aims to take Athrolan over if she grows too weak." His thick lips pursed. "But the heir left us to rot, waiting to pick our bones when we're dead. A coward, running from duty like their parents." Peraan tilted his head. "You said 'boy'—you know something I don't?"

Heat bloomed in Keplan's gut. He wasn't angry, at least, not in the conventional sense. Anger was a flash as fat hit the fry pan. This was a caldera exploding. He hated lies. He hated questions. His gaze snapped to the barmaid. "If I took you to bed, I'd burn the evidence, too."

Her face tightened. "That's your last mug, boy."

"Fine. I'd rather not drink with idiots." He shook Hylier's firm hand off his shoulder.

It was Peraan's turn to glare at him. "Do you have a problem?"

"You're my problem, and people like you. Spitting lies like they're rote."

Peraan scoffed. "I think you ought to step outside."

Keplan knocked back the last of his drink and staggered to his feet. The alcohol burned truth into his tongue. "My parents weren't running from duty. They were protecting themselves. And you could call me a lot of things, but I'll be damned if I'm a coward."

The woman shouldered her way from behind the bar and grabbed Keplan by the back of his collar. "Out. Now."

The room whirled before Keplan's eyes. The mug in his hand shattered on the edge of the bar. He glowered down at the woman, mouth twisted in a grimace, broken glass held out. Blood thickened the air. Stinging in his palm told him the glass had cut through his glove.

Her eyes widened, and she let him go. "Fates. Those eyes."

His snarl curled further. "Thank you for your hospitality." He kept his eyes down as he swept from the common room. Once the door slammed behind him, he slumped against the wall. His body trembled in the wake of confrontation.

"Alright, I'll listen." Hylier stood just outside the ring of light from the tavern's lantern. "You were a passing curiosity before. Now you've got me properly intrigued."

Keplan's head cracked against the stone as he twisted to look at the soldier. "I'm tired of war. I've not even lived through one, and I'm tired of it. I need to talk to Blackhouse. I've got information that will convince him to take the throne."

Hylier's eyes remained fixed on Keplan's, but the boy sensed every inch was being memorized, every word recorded. "That information have something to do with what you said in there? They'll chalk it up to drunken rambling if you're lucky. But that anger looked like it has been brewing a while, and I know you weren't drunk." He watched Keplan weave himself upright. "At least, not that drunk."

Keplan shoved off the wall. "Say you believe me, now you know why they can't rely on this mystical heir to show up. Blackhouse has to take the throne. He knows you, trusts you, and you're a soldier—you can come and go as you please even with the city under siege. Get me to him."

Hylier glanced at the sky, then scanned the walls nearest them. "Watch will change in two hours. I'll send a bird to him. By the time he receives it, you'll be on the road. There's a small town; he'll know it and he'll meet you there a day after you arrive, two at the most."

"You're not coming with me?"

Hylier grinned. "As far as anyone's concerned, for the next week, you're Captain Hylier."

Φ

The 7th Day of Lumord, 1272
The City of RoBal, Ban

Shuddering gates shook the Hall as they opened, interrupting Rih's study of eastern eating customs. Despite the dust, she left her window open, sunlight filtering through the loose weave of a robe she hung over the wooden latticework. She pushed aside the cloth and peered down into the courtyard. It was late, and most of the visitors who could afford a carriage used tunnels from the lower levels of the palace instead. It was a cart, not a carriage, and the passengers filing from the benches wore chains, not jewels. Rih's hands trembled. All were female.

Most women who worked in the Hall were younger daughters sent so as not to burden families with no hope of wedding upward in the noble hierarchy. Some were common women, others who had few relatives chose the life themselves. *And some are slaves.* It wasn't common in a concubine house as prestigious as the Hall, but it happened. The soldier escorting them jerked a rope, and the women fell into line, entering through the rear door. Rih turned away, unable to watch any further.

She had no sooner returned to her study when Hi-alan appeared at the door. "Rih, a summons came for you."

"Is Ki-elte alright?" Her heart hammered, remembering when the news of Sa-at's death arrived.

"She's with a visitor right now." Hi-alan handed Rih a thin parchment. "This is from one of our sister halls, down in Stytown."

Rih skimmed the summons. It was a single line:

> *Requesting the presence of Rih-elte to discuss training logistics.*
> -M

The initial stilled her heart. *She's here.* "How do I get there?"

"There are wagons and carts, but if you're good at maps, it's not difficult. I'd walk you myself, but I have something to tend to."

Rih's lips thinned. "The new women?"

Hi-alan looked down. "I'm angry too. But change won't happen in a day, and it will not succeed without planning." She sought to meet Rih's gaze, her eyes warm. "Your outlook and methods are new. Your spirit is new. But you are not the first woman to have these thoughts. Many of us did as well. Many even succeeded for a time. But this isn't a place that fosters such things."

"I would think it was exactly the place that did." She knew what Hi-alan meant, knew she was not the first, knew she stood on the backs of a thousand women before her, just as a thousand women would stand on hers. *I'll just see to it that I stand tall enough for them to climb these prison walls.* She changed her wrap to her favorite sapphire blue. It was darker than the usual fashions, but it was evening, and even in the driest part of the season, nights were cool. "Can you pass on the invitation to learn with us?"

"I will. I'll even teach them a few words if they're willing." Hi-alan's expression was closed.

Defeat in the piercer's eyes burned determination into Rih's bones. "Where is this other Hall?"

"In the center, off of Ivory Circle. The sign is plain black. It's called the Tower of Jet. They can't even name something without being obsessed with their own phalluses."

Rih grinned and settled her net over her scalp, grateful she was bored enough to shave her head that morning. "I know the place. Wish me luck, then."

"It's just a meeting—they probably wish to make you a trainer if you can't be married."

Rih could not keep her smile from widening. "What is it you said? 'My methods and spirit are new?'" Before Hi-alan could ask, she ducked from the room. "Good evening."

The city was a different animal in the dark. Even with war looming, energy was high, a taut wire waiting to be plucked into the first stanzas of music. Colors were bold and bright now, replacing the pastels and whites of day. The brick street from the Hall ran north along the tall wall circling the palace itself. This close, she could only see the top tiers of the mounded structure. The road continued, but Rih turned right, down a broad street through the noble and merchant houses of the Rises. It was one of the only times she did not look out of place. As a soldier, she ran messages between the barracks and merchants requiring an official guard. Now she could have been any one of the wives or lesser courtesans in the district.

She slipped past a cluster of market stalls when she caught sight of the signing. A middle-aged woman leaned on the counter of her stall, mouth moving leagues a second as she discussed her daughter's upcoming wedding to someone named Kirka. Her hands, however, told another story. "She's close to war, there, close to the ocean where the Mirikin will attack. I must be sure she has allies, people who will help her come home if he's a monster, or when war erupts."

The other woman responded, but her back was to Rih and the signs hidden.

Rih faltered. Already people used her language to speak openly. She looked away, allowing the women their privacy, and hurried further down the road. She smelled Stytown before she saw the ugly, hulking walls. Human waste and the pervasive smell of rotting food hung low over the rickety, towering buildings. Lumps of hardened clay replaced the fired red bricks and the cleaned gutters. Rolling her shoulders back, she dropped her careful steps. A soldier's stride was impossible with skirts, but she raised her chin and walked as if she expected the crowd to part before her. In Stytown, it paid not to look weak, and for Ban, demure was weakness.

So was asking for directions. A looming guard tower marked the southern of the two central squares. She had only been stationed there a year, but it was enough to taste bitterness in the back of her throat at the thought.

Stytown was less of a city district and more a work camp gone feral. Most inhabitants were not allowed to pass through the towering walls. Those who did were only visiting for some seedy purpose, or to find someone disillusioned enough to trade poor freedom for indentured servitude in a place with less squalor. *Or to start a rebellion.* She winced, afraid to even think the words. A rebellion was not what she wanted. She wanted liberty. *And how do I expect to get freedom?*

The winding street dumped into the square. The two squares around the twin guard towers were the only cleared space, the dead area around a section of poisoned crops. *Except here the crops are people.* Those unaware, or desperate enough, to stumble close were rarely seen again, and if they were, they were not the same people. Rih had been stationed in Stytown long enough to know why they feared the towers.

In Ivory Circle, she found the Tower of Jet. The black monstrosity was dwarfed only by the guard tower opposite it. She slipped through the door unbothered and followed the widest hallway to a low, open foyer. It was not as fine as the Hall of the Purple Throne, but it was clean and lit with the usual soft lantern light.

The woman on the dais glanced up. "May I help you?"

Rih wrote her name and explained her presence was requested by a visitor. After a second she added a line about her lack of hearing and ability to lip-read.

The woman read it, then looked more thoroughly at Rih. "I'm Delan. My mother learns signs from you." Her smile was bright, and Rih realized she could not have been more than sixteen. "She says it's a good way to keep our minds sharp."

Rih nodded, not knowing what else to say. All learning kept the mind sharp, and she wondered if their mother felt that way, or if she was laying groundwork for a later conversation.

"You'll meet your friends down the stairs at the end of that hall, and it'll be the fourth room on your right." The girl gestured down the hall behind her.

Rih offered a wave of thanks and followed the directions. The stairs were narrow, the walls decorated with silks and pieces of velvet. While the colors above were deep blue and bright purple, like the Hall, down here the decor lived up to the Tower's name. Black silk, black velvet, scorched-black clay walls. If the bowels of a monster were picked out in luxury, she imagined they would look like the basement of the Tower of Jet.

Plain candles lit the lantern outside the fourth door on the right. She knocked. The door slid open to reveal a tall woman, dressed as a warrior. "Yes?"

Rih held up the tablet again. She wished she had a translator, but she did not trust anyone other than herself with this meeting.

"Come in, then."

Rih slipped inside. The small room was crowded with an entourage of a dozen women. Each wore armor; decorated beads denoted their rank. A large cushioned chair served as a throne. The guard turned back, frowning, and Rih realized she must have missed something spoken.

"This is Her Majesty Majilah Ag, Queen of the Vales," the guard repeated, this time for Rih's benefit. "Your Majesty, this is Rih-elte."

The queen was as tall as any Banis, with the same brown skin. Her black hair was long, though and kept back in a series of intricate tiny braids.

Majilah rose, hand outstretched like a soldier, not a queen. "I am pleased to meet you."

And I you. Thank you for meeting me.

"Is it all right if I speak, or would you prefer I write as well?"

Speaking is fine, though I find it much easier to read if it is more than just a phrase or two.

The queen gestured for tea, and waited for it to be prepared to her liking. She was compact, her body hard the way a soldier's would be. Majilah looked up and caught Rih's stare. She smiled, hazel eyes flashing. "I see you are a soldier too."

I am a bride. Once I was a soldier.

"There is no 'once' when one is a warrior. I see it still in you. In your walk. In your heart." Her eyes flicked to Rih's, dark and intense. "In your request to meet me."

Rih lifted a shoulder, but her gaze did not waver.

I was curious.

Majilah leaned forward to write her response.

If you were solely curious, my dear, then you would have been disappointed at the dearth of my people in histories and moved on. One does not invite the enemy of the Emperor to tea out of curiosity.

I did not invite you.

Rih corrected her with a faint grin. She liked Majilah.

The queen's brow quirked. "Didn't you?" Her eyes closed for a moment as she took a slow sip of tea. "I miss this. We have the spices, but our butter has little flavor, made without the rich palace grain. What did you wish to know?" She switched subjects as if she drew another breath, and it took Rih a moment to catch up.

Now the woman was before her, the task seemed insurmountable.

How did you become queen? Why do we hate you so? And why do you hate us — though my teacher told me it isn't hatred. I wish for freedom like you have, and I wish it for my sisters, too, and the slaves we keep.

"That's a large wish." Majilah leaned forward to elaborate.

Your teacher is right: we do not hate you. Pity, perhaps. Scorn sometimes if you refer to the upper echelon of society. But not hate. Hate means we fear, and that would imply you have power over us.

Rih frowned, trying to marry the image Majilah painted with all her indoctrination.

Our army is ten times yours. Three times the military of most other nations, save perhaps the Berrin navy. We have power over you. How did you manage to wrest power from them and escape? I read we were one people once. Not cousins, but brothers and sisters.

"So why have you never invaded us? You cannot say we have no resources — we have the rainforest. We have almost as many mines as Ban. So why are we untouched?" Her arched brow punctuated her next question. "What does a dog do with a snake?"

Rih sat back. *What commands the emperor?*

She avoids it. Leaves it lie. Barks, perhaps.

"Your emperor's propaganda against us? Barking. He does not dare to bite." She took another sip of her tea and continued her explanation in writing.

We didn't wrest power from anyone. They took it from us. Two centuries ago we had an empress. They never tell you that, do that? There were poor. There were rich. I am never going to say it was perfect. But it was better. She had a general who wished to be her consort. Some tales say they were lovers, others they never met. Regardless, she refused him. He did not take it well. You have seen a child throw a tantrum, yes?

It was much the same, except this was a man, with wealth and influence at his disposal. Like a tantrum, she ignored him. Our female generals began to die, were killed more often in battle, were poisoned while spying. By the time we realized it was him, it was too late. RoBal was once a broad and beautiful city, but the coup toppled it, and in its place was built this hulking mountain, built on our bodies, our bones. The women who could, escaped. Some with their families, some from them. They are my foremothers.

Rih's heart faltered. She heard the walls of RoBal were built over the bodies of their enemies. Now she wondered how literal that was. *It wasn't built on the bones of our enemies, but the bones of our mothers and grandmothers.*

And what of your men?

"They are strong, and often taller. So, we leave them home where they can build and protect." She shrugged. "It simply makes sense that way." Majilah leaned forward and touched Rih's hand. "I feel for you. I do. But no one will give you freedom, not in Ban. Just as they took it from us, you must take it back."

Rih's blood raced, the bird of her heart trembling against the cage of her ribs again. It was no longer a fledgling thing, all bones and no feathers. She took in the the warriors around her, the strength in their faces. Finally, she met Majilah's bright eyes.

I have a network of women, those who speak my language and who teach others. They share my same wish. I will take it. I'll take back the freedom of every woman in this empire.

Would you like to help us?

Majilah's grin was wolfish. "You said yourself you have an army ten times mine."

Yes, and they will help, but not all of that army is mine. You and your women would be a great ally.

Majilah beckoned her clerk over. "Draft an alliance, please. We will sign it now and not risk it traversing the city. I have two more days to conduct business. I visit once a year, but I fear war will keep me away for longer." When the scroll was written and decorated with seals, Majilah pressed her hand into ink then onto the broad, blank bottom of the parchment. She handed both it and the pot of ink to Rih.

Rih patted her palm with a damp rag then pressed her hand to the sheet of dye and onto the space beside the queen's handprint. She held it there, noticing the ridges and whorls that denoted callouses. Her head pounded with the weight of those handprints, with the rush of rebellion in her veins. The meeting itself lasted less than an hour, and yet her world changed. There was no returning. *I could be married off and never return, but this is in my heart now. I can't forget this.*

The guard leaned forward to whisper in the queen's ear. Majilah nodded and rolled the declaration into a plain scroll case before handing it back. "You'd best be getting back, Rih-elte. I have a few more things to attend to before the night is over." Calculations filled Majilah's gaze. "Who will sit on the throne when you're done?"

I assumed one of our male allies, someone within the Emperor's blood, but perhaps without his cruelty.

"Would you take a bit of advice?" When Rih nodded, the queen leaned forward, a prairie cat ready to pounce. "Dream bigger."

Rih wiped their conversation from the tablet before tucking it and the scroll case away. "Thank you."

Though the queen did not know the language, her response made it clear she understood. "Good luck. You will need it."

The words hung in Rih's mind for her return walk. It was close to evening, the streets crowded with a different sort of business.

Hi-alan ran into her at the woman's entrance to the Hall. Exhaustion hung on the piercer's eyes. "I have a message for you."

"Another? From whom?"

Hi-alan switched to signing. "The women I was tending, they're from the east. A town on the border that apparently was harboring alleged Mirikin spies."

Rih snorted. The definition of who was a spy depended more on the emperor's convenience and less upon actual evidence. "What of it?"

"One of them brought a message from a soldier stationed there, Jih-alan. Said she knows you."

"We were in the same patrol." Rih held out her hand, but Hi-alan offered her nothing. "It wasn't written?"

"No. 'We are on the frontlines of battle, and the women are tired of being fodder. Women here wish for liberty, women with allies and family across the border in Athrolan. We await your orders to us, and to them.'"

"Orders? I'm not their captain."

"No. You're their general. It appears your rebellion begins, whether you start it or not."

Rih's head spun, and she fell back against the corridor wall. "I can't command women to their deaths, to fight for me when I am holed up here in this cushioned, silk-wrapped existence."

"His Eminence does. They'll die anyway. They will fall before Mirikin blades regardless of who makes the order. You could help give them hope."

Dream bigger. "How do I get a message back?"

"She said the 213 March joins them in three weeks. You should talk to Il-fald."

"I'll think about it."

"You have allies. More than you realize. And more than women. I have close friends, men, who know we struggle, who hate to see the station we're relegated to. I'd trust them with this. I'd trust them with my life, with your life. We need people in higher positions, political ones, and ones of noble power."

Rih scoffed. "If they are so sympathetic to our cause, why haven't they used their power to help us?"

Hi-alan scowled at her. "Rih-elte, you don't know what they've done. You don't see it because no one is supposed to. I know men who have smuggled hundreds of women to better cities—and yes, there are better cities, better Halls than this, even within RoBal herself. Don't you go thinking you blaze a trail. There are highways you would never know exist."

Rih looked down. Hi-alan was right. "I'm sorry. If you vouch for them, I welcome their help, but please use utmost discretion. We can't afford to misplace our trust."

The older woman squeezed her hand. "You won't regret it. And talk to Il-fald."

Rih pushed off from the wall. For the first time in weeks, she sat in her room, without a lantern, and watched the light fade from the walls. The last, red rays crossed the tablet discarded beside her desk. It still had "fear" inscribed, her reminder of its power over her. She had the network. She had the language. Only details and allies remained. Allies who would do more than lie. Allies willing to commit treason. *Allies willing to die.* Her gaze rose to the sky, teeth bared in a grin. A single thumb stroke smudged the word away.

Φ

The 10th Day of Lumord, 1272
The City of Ceir Athrolan

Trash and bodies tangled in the streets. An'thor shifted on Theriim's back. Years passed since he wore armor. The few pounds he gained in the past decade chafed under the metal even through his leather jerkin. "Raven's a damn fool, starting a war when everyone's become old and fat," he growled.

Each district dissolved into factions, and violence rose on the edges. Deaths ranged from political assassination to desperate murder. Raven knew half of An'thor's moves ahead, those loyal to Daymir relaying information to the navy through birds and lanterns.

Burning war-oil filled the air over the Silver Apron, wind tugging it down to the warehouses through which he now rode. Excepting military personnel, the streets here were closed. Many merchants fled at the announcement of the queen's death. Now the vacant buildings held makeshift infirmaries and morgues. Rot was cloying even in the chill of autumn.

An'thor drew up outside the largest of the converted buildings and dismounted. Wool and silk from his layered headwrap kept out the worst of the stench. "This is a nightmare."

"Yessir, it is." An exhausted captain leaned against the building, her stance a mockery of attention. Like everyone, her face bore shadows of hunger. The harvest had been meager, and already a quarter of the city's stores for winter were gone. Most of what remained was set aside for planting in spring. Soon they would choose between starving this winter or the next. The captain jerked her head in the direction of the dead mounded inside. "We pulled three more from the rubble on the Merchant Tier."

"Any living?"

"None, sir. And there are rumors of a riot brewing down on Mossing Square."

"They have every right to riot." He heaved a sigh, mind pausing on Keplan. The boy was a burning distraction from the failures piling in his wake.

"General!" A squire skittered down the street, tripping over rubble from the harbor walls. He slid to a halt, bracing himself on his knees to catch his breath before remembering to salute. "Sir, the soldiers on the walls report the Commander is launching another assault on the harbor."

"Then tell them to answer it!" An'thor snarled. "I didn't order them there to sit with weapons up their arses." He wished for Nenev cannons.

"Sir, they said you'd say that. We're out of fire-arrows. Commander Dorcal took the last of the fire-goo. And the shipment from the south hasn't come in yet."

"Lord Eier's deliveries arrive every month. And it's war-oil, idiot—you'll be a gallant someday if you survive long enough. Learn the terms."

The squire seemed too tired to care about the castigation. "Lord Eier supported Dorcal, sir."

An'thor's eyes tightened in fury. This was not how he pictured ending his days, holed up in the city he loved most as he helped tear it apart. He jerked Theriim's head around and headed toward the palace.

The boy trotted after the warhorse's exhausted steps. "What are your orders, sir?"

"Fuck them all."

CHAPTER SIXTEEN

The 12th Day of Lumord, 1272
Marl Orna, Clai Province, Athrolan

THE AIR WAS SOFTER in the forest. Wind that shrieked through the city hummed between tree trunks. Even with winter glowering on the horizon, the weather retained summer's playfulness. Keplan followed the curve of the river, crossing via the ferry by noon. A few days brought him out of the trees and onto the rocky steppes that made up most of Athrolan's landscape. The mountains curved from the massive peaks near Fort Stone to the desolate hills behind Claimiirn.

Despite the nature of his time in Ban, the rolling prairie spoke to him. Barren fields here echoed with the same watchful emptiness. Now it made his hackles rise. Keplan smoothed the light jacket under his cloak with nervous fingers. Hylier did his job well—though his clothes were a bit long on the shorter Keplan, he was slim enough for them to fit. Dark gray and white, however, seemed too bright in the brown monochrome of the Feld de Barran.

Dusk cast the town ahead in yellow, a topaz set in the tarnished brown of the fields. He rode easily the last few days, giving Daymir time to receive the letter and set out on his own road north. How the man would escape from his mansion-prison was beyond Keplan, but Hylier had faith. If the soldier's math was correct, Daymir would arrive the next evening.

Exhausted and road-worn, Keplan reeked of horse. His borrowed mount may have been a well-bred pacer, but she still smelled like an animal. This far south, the town's gates were still open, at least until nightfall. He urged the horse faster, trotting down the hill to the gatehouse. Being a commoner might lend anonymity, but being a soldier gave him passage. When he raised a gloved hand, his cloak fell away from the captain's insignia on his breast. "Sir, I'm looking for The Hillock."

The gatekeeper hopped down from his post and peered at him. "You people never bring good news." His smile was rueful, and he jerked his head toward one of the only three-storey buildings. "The inn's up there, at the high side of town."

"Thank you." Keplan tossed the man a coin and headed across the town. Most of the streets boasted pairs of soldiers, more than a town that size warranted. Keplan shook himself. *The capital city is under siege; what did I expect?* The inn was large, made of timber and mud. He left his mount at the stable and ducked inside. Between Firas and Azimir, Keplan saw the common rooms of several taverns in Athrolan. Windows let in the sunset behind the hills, but there was only a single, narrow bar. A man with a face as gray as the mountains was the only patron. His head rested on the weathered wood, chest rising with an ease only drink would bring.

Keplan blinked away the sun-stains on his vision and raised a hand to the barkeep. "Afternoon."

"Captain." The tone was measured. "Welcome to Marl Orna."

"Thank you. I'm looking for a room for a night, maybe two."

The barkeep dug through a drawer behind the bar for a minute before fishing out a heavy key. "Food as well?"

"Please." He watched as the man tallied up his charge. It was strange to be treated with deference. A dark inner part of his heart reveled in it.

"It'll be ten, half now, half before you've gone." His mouth twitched in apology. "Travel's not as safe, so things are expensive. Time was I didn't even need a guard." He jerked a thumb in the direction of the soldiers standing in the courtyard. "Where you ride from?"

Keplan handed him the coin. "Ceir Athrolan."

The man's bushy brows arched. "Fates. No wonder you look like death. No offense, Captain."

"None taken." Keplan did not have to fake the sorrow in his eyes. "It is death there. Most of the city folk try to go on like normal, but it's not pretty. I have hope there's a lamp at the end of this dark, dank tunnel, though."

"I'll believe in hope when it does me good." He shoved off the counter with a sigh. "Supper is when you want it. If you wish to eat in your room, just ring, I'll send it up."

Keplan nodded his thanks and headed toward the stairs. At the landing he paused. "Master Barkeep, I'm expecting someone. I'm Hylier. He'll ask when he arrives."

"Very good, Captain."

Keplan found his room at the end of the hall and locked the door behind him. Perhaps it was the open air of the fields; perhaps it was the clarity focus brought, but his mind was quieter.

The room was a few paces larger than his bedroom in the Wise Hare, and the window faced the mountains to the east. It was a reminder of why he came so far. He upended his pack on the bed before stripping. The tub was a barrel sawn in half, and the water arrived just above room temperature.

It had been a long time since he was alone with his thoughts. As much as he kept his own council, Firas wormed into Keplan's heart. Even Mirrel, with her unexpected moments of kindness, had grown on him.

He scooped water onto his face to banish the thoughts with cold. Instead, he saw a face looming from the surface. The eyes were manic and blue, sunken cheeks marred with knotted purple scars. Trembling fingers traced the planes of his own face. The only thing missing was the battered black and steel crown.

His tattooed hands clenched, and he ducked under the water, eyes opening to look at the warped room beyond the surface. By tomorrow his future as an Athrolani commoner would be secure. *Even if it means relinquishing my parents, becoming a clerk or historian.* Tomorrow, Daymir would accept the throne, and Keplan would be free.

Φ

The 12th Day of Lumord, 1272
Marl Orna, Clai Province, Athrolan

Daymir's eyes narrowed on the road into Marl Orna. Only once in the last decade had he slipped from Manor Black, navigating the wood-walled tunnel between his root cellar and the house of Currow's widow. Currow was loyal, not to the Xain house, but to the man he served for the last fifty years of his life. As he drew up outside the gate, Daymir was grateful, again, for his steward.

"Who goes?" The gatekeeper peered into the dusk.

Daymir pushed his hood back from his gray hair. "Dam Ornsen." His former aliases were too well known, dragged through the mud of gossip when he was exiled. This one, though, was older still, almost unused since he was crowned heir decades ago.

"And your business?"

"Meeting an old friend who brings me news from home. My brother's unwell."

The man's face softened, and he stepped aside. "Sick's been going about, seems. World's not what it once was."

"You're right about that." Daymir offered him a wave and nudged his horse up the road toward the inn. The Hillock had changed since he last saw it—larger stables to make way for the popular stagecoaches, another storey perched atop the structure, expensive glass in the windows.

How much had Ceir Athrolan changed?

He left his horse with the stablehand and slipped through the rear door of the common room. Like all inns during war, it was swaddled in an uneasy, honest darkness.

The barkeep filled a mug with ale and slid it down to an in-stupored man before jerking a nod at Daymir. "Evening. Room for the night?"

Daymir shook his head. "I'm meeting someone, actually. He should have arrived yesterday, perhaps the day before. A Captain Hylier?"

"Ah. Quiet fellow. He's there, in the booth by the fire."

Daymir followed the man's gesture. Indeed, he could see the lanky gray-breeched leg jutting from under the table. The shoulders under the jacket were thin, and he never thought of Hylier as a quiet man, but civil war changed a person.

"What can I bring you?"

"Privacy." Daymir crossed the room and slid onto the other bench. Unless they started shouting, they were out of earshot. His gaze shifted to the man opposite him. Adrenaline sparked in his limbs. His tablemate was a boy, all man's height, but without the muscle to make his movements graceful. In place of cropped blonde hair was a length of brown tangles. "You are not Hylier."

"Just as your name is not whatever you said to get yourself through the gate." Wide eyes were colorless in the dim light. He extended a gloved hand. Like his feet and nose, it was too large for the rest of him. "I'm Lan Guardsen."

Daymir found his nobleman's ability to keep thoughts from his face suffered from disuse. "You're not what I expected." He examined the boy, who seemed tolerant of him doing so, if uncomfortable. The pale eyes darted from Daymir to the table then back again. Shadows on his cheeks could have been scars, could have been dirt. He pictured a middle-aged man with wit and steady eyes. Instead, Lan fidgeted, the kind of nervous more becoming of an addict. His eyes held manic intelligence that made Daymir's skin crawl. "I hoped to correspond with you again, but I did not expect a personal call. You wear Hylier's uniform. Tell me: 'what overcomes a black oath?'"

"'The red oath, for blood stains deeper than ink.'" The answer to the safe-phrase seemed awkward in the boy's mouth, but it was correct.

Daymir leaned back. "So, he found you?"

"Apparently it wasn't as difficult as I hoped. I asked to meet with you. He agreed my reason was important enough to warrant hauling you out of your luxurious prison. Perhaps we could discuss more over a meal."

Daymir's brows rose. Even stripped of his titles, the manor staff and townsfolk treated him with respect, albeit without honorifics. This boy seemed to either not care about such things, or not know any better. *You're only "master" now, and who knows his upbringing.* "You've got quite the set, meeting under false pretenses then asking for hospitality."

"I was led to believe you were curious about me."

Daymir snorted, but waved the barkeep over. When they had ordered, he turned back to Lan. "So you've come to discuss the war? The capital? My refusal of the throne?"

"All, hopefully." He frowned. "I'm most interested in your last point, there."

"I'd like to know whom I'm speaking to. I see no scholar's robes or medallions of mastery about your shoulders."

"I did not say I was a scholar."

"No, you didn't." His gaze lingered on the nervous hands, the old style of the boy's long hair.

Lan waved away the topic. "About this Peraan: how many of his rumors are true? About the support for your claim and about the general."

Daymir allowed the subject change, but noted it. "I'm told in the long run, most are true. Have you met the man?"

"Peraan? A few times, in passing. He doesn't take to me."

Daymir wondered if anyone did. "So, you beg me to take the throne, but you don't come from Peraan." The arrival of ale and a steaming mound of bread and meat interrupted Daymir's further speculation. When the barkeep retreated, Daymir continued, "If Hylier found you, I assume you received my latest letter."

"It's what urged me to meet with you in person." His expression darkened, and Daymir saw the boy under the thick façade. "Do you have any idea how bad it is there?"

"I heard there was civil unrest. Heard Commander Dorcal and General Domariigo are locking horns — if you'll excuse the expression — over who will claim the throne."

Lan lurched forward, his lip curled in a feral snarl. "It's not unrest, Blackhouse. It's war. Dorcal set a blockade of battleships across the harbor. Domariigo burns any ship sending reinforcements or supplies, just as Dorcal destroys any trade ships attempting to supply the city. I steer my cart around bodies on my way to and from the market. The House of Nobles' loyalty is split, and so whatever supplies the city could receive are divided. Cannonfire destroys buildings, lives every day. I pulled a chunk of beam from my back a week ago. It's a disaster."

Daymir frowned. Something nagged at the back of his mind, slipping through the weakening fingers of his memory. "You speak as if you're familiar with them. The general and commander, that is."

"No. I just have little respect."

"You aren't old enough to be that disillusioned."

He shrugged. "You wanted to ask me about my letters?"

Daymir drew the letters out of his coat and smoothed the paper before him. He made a show of peering at the words. "It strikes me odd that a common boy—forgive my assumption that you are, indeed, common—takes interest in who sits on the throne. Your actions, too, are odd. You write to me, ride here unannounced. But whatever you told Hylier, it was enough for him to give you the uniform off his very back. Perhaps you should include me in the secret."

"The throne is you blood. Your training, your experience makes you perfect. The queen exiled you—so? You're proud, but I don't think you're so petty as to let your kingdom fall to ruin over a false claim of treason." He tilted his head. "I'll tell you why I want you to wear the crown if you tell me why you refuse to. Don't say you know there's another heir, don't give me the tired line that Athrolan needs change. I'm offering you a trade—truth for truth."

Daymir's saw, now, his too-large eyes were blue, luminous ice glinting through bloodshot lace. His skin crawled, remembering another set of eyes, silver and black lace. The memories were so clear today. *And yet, a week ago I went the whole day forgetting how to lace my own shirt.* Dichotomy riddled the past year—days of confusion, and days of clarity made bittersweet by their increasing rarity. Now he sat across from a boy whose anonymity barely cloaked his mercurial character.

The exile played the cards of political intrigue enough to recognize the two ways this game could go. His common sense told him to keep his cards to himself, but the deeper burn of instinct told him it was time to fold. *Common sense and pride have not served me well of late.* "Do you know the stories of my grandfather? The king before Her Majesty Tzatia?"

Lan shrugged. "He was a fair ruler. He reign was peaceful. There's little about his later years, but I'm told he was still alive when Tzatia took the throne."

Daymir winced at the lack of honorifics, the brusque treatment of his late aunt's name. "Do you know why that is?" When the boy shook his head, Daymir looked down. "He lost his mind. Not in the bloody, maniac way some argue King Azirik of Mirik did, or the fragile paranoia of Her Majesty Tzatia. He literally lost it, left pieces of it along the way until he could not remember his station, his family, or even how to eat." He took a bite of the meat between them and wiped the grease from his fingers. "It's a madness that, it seems, is hereditary."

Lan's dark brows curled together, and his attention seemed suddenly fixed on his gloves. Whatever the boy expected, Daymir could see his response was not it. "And it cannot simply be because you've been isolated for too long?"

Frustration sparked through Daymir's hands, his fist rapping on the table top. "Dammit, boy, you think I don't wish that? I forgot I was exiled for two whole days. They found me wandering the hills south of Marl Black. I had to claim I was drunk just to save my dignity."

"Then I'm sorry. Losing your mind is a terrible thing." Something in Lan's tone made Daymir wonder what part of his own mind the boy no longer controlled.

"You have my truth, ugly as it is. Give me yours."

Lan stared at the table. "I am going to answer your letter's question with one of my own. What would destroy Athrolan faster: an heir of old blood slowly losing what makes him worthy of the crown, or a boy?" Lan's gaze slid across the table top, up Daymir's jacket, and stopped at the older man's eyes. "A boy whose parents never told him why he sees things that aren't his to see, hears thoughts he should not be privy to. Power is hereditary too, and is a kind of madness."

Daymir drew a breath. Lan's eyes did not waver now. The exile wondered if the boy even blinked. "I did not think Athrolan's throne would be decided over drinks in a country alehouse. Perhaps we ought to start again." He offered his arm. "Daymir Blackhouse, former treasurer and exiled heir of Athrolan."

Lan's mouth quirked, and something dark ignited behind his eyes. "Keplan Wardyn, son of the Dhoah' Laen Lyne'alea and Earth Shaker Aud'narman."

"And heir apparent to Athrolan's throne."

"Yes."

Daymir stared. Rumors hinted, but the floor still lurched under his feet. Weeks ago the Dhoah' Laen herself strolled through his door. Now her child sat across from him with the same intensity. *What are those odds?* He wondered if the boy knew his parents visited, but tucked it away for later. "You think you'll make more of a mess than I?"

"I'm untrained. I was never given a chance at proper teaching or knowing my heritage."

"You sound like a petulant child."

"And you are an incredible coward."

"Some of your father's teeth, I see."

"Not really." Keplan glared at a scuff mark on the floor. His gloved hands trembled on the table.

Daymir did not see destruction if Keplan took the throne. It was possible, surely, but Tzatia did not rule alone. Neither would the next monarch. There were advisors, officers, and the Council. Athrolan would not look the same, of that he was certain, but she sorely needed change.

"So, is this it? Civil war will decide what happens to her?"

"If it were easy, Wardyn, then we would not be here." Daymir gestured to the bar. "I need a drink. I've made my choice. You've got to make yours."

Φ

Keplan stared at the food, forgotten, before him. Across the room, Daymir ordered something and settled onto a stool. His conversation with another patron was low and meaningless.

Keplan's gut clenched in panic. The fickle ability to read others told him only enough to know Daymir did not lie. He expected to be awed by the heir, expected the older man's promise to take the throne. *An hour's conversation, no more.* Instead, he sat alone, trying to crush the insidious thought that Daymir was right. Keplan would make a better king. *Perhaps it wasn't he who needed convincing, but me.*

Another ache bloomed, but this one hunkered between his ribs. *I would miss Firas. And Mirrel.* He did not want to miss anyone. He did not want responsibility, the distance that meant never learning the particular sounds of someone's steps on the stairs. Loneliness clenched his heart. He thought of never seeing Firas's smile or watching Mirrel roll her eyes. Never listening to a third of Azimir's prattled words as they navigated the city streets. *Even if I give up my name, my heritage, the throne, I might never see those things again.* Civil war ripped happiness from the world in a way other wars only dreamed.

But he could end the war. He could assure Firas and Mirrel and Azimir stayed safe, stayed how he remembered. *I can't face them again. Not as their lover or friend or cousin. Instead they'll see these scars, these burning ideas, the son of the Dhoah' Laen, son of an Earth Shaker.*

I'll face them as a king.

His heart hammered loud enough for all Marl Orna to hear, he was sure. If he wanted the Commander on his side, he needed to arrive with Daymir in tow. *Give them what they want — both heirs.*

He crossed the room in four strides, as if he could outrun the voice that screamed he was making a mistake. He stopped at Daymir's elbow, his gloved hand resting beside the exile's drink.

Daymir turned to look at him, dark eyes unreadable beyond faint curiosity.

"Come to Athrolan. Meet with them, and with me. If you support me before Dorcal, he'll have no choice. Unless he's far less stable than we hope, it might just work." He glanced at Daymir. His stomach writhed from the noise in his mind and the shadow in the older man's eyes.

Daymir frowned. "I am an exile."

"I formally invite you, as," Keplan's voice faltered, "as Heir Apparent. Stay in the capital as Regent for a year, or advisor, or something, until I've learned enough to not destroy the kingdom. Your estate is lovely, but minds like ours do better in chaos." His skin hummed with the urge to move, and he flexed his hands. "I'm going to pack my things. I'll leave in an hour, at dawn. I can't do this without you. If you're willing to help, meet me outside." He retreated upstairs.

Dread stilled the quake of adrenaline. If he stayed the Wise Hare's bar-boy he and Firas would be as doomed as he was in his Banis cell. Keplan heard the hitch in his own voice at the title he would claim soon, the growl that accompanied "chaos."

His parents' power was his. The weight of their choices, their unfinished business, pinched his shoulders. *They don't ever tell you how much it scares us. How much we give up.* He swept the room a last time and found his cloak hanging by the door. Dawn swallowed moonlight as it crept up the sky.

His borrowed horse waited, head bobbing with anticipation. Keplan helped ready the animal, flashing the sleepy stable boy a smile with his thanks. Daymir's beautiful bay stood, unbothered, in his stall.

Come on, Blackhouse.

Rumbling boots heralded another patrol, and he looked away as they passed. It would take a single breath to scare him from his goal now, and he could not afford it.

Athrolan could not afford it.

I haven't earned the right to run yet. Keplan smoothed the horse's fur under the padded leather while he waited a minute, then another. In the courtyard, the sky was more gray than purple. He glanced back at the inn, mostly dark, not yet touched by morning. The disillusionment in Daymir's eyes, the fatigue, terrified him. Even if the man accompanied him, he could not stand in the former heir's shadow or the shadow of his parents. He drew a breath, reveling in the bite of cold air, and mounted up.

The inn door swung open. Daymir emerged, dressed in traveling clothes and bearing an old pack. He caught Keplan's eye with a smile. "I had to send word to my manservant." His eyes narrowed on Keplan. "You thought I wasn't coming."

"A bit, yes."

The exile snorted. "I don't miss the duty, but that house feels like a prison more each year. And you were right about our minds." The stableboy appeared holding the reins of the gelding and Daymir swung into the saddle. "You realize you implied your reign will be chaos."

Keplan's smile was sudden, and his heartbeat thundered just a bit slower. "Aren't they all?"

Φ

The 15th Day of Lumord, 1272
The City of Ceir Athrolan, Athrolan

Marching and shouted orders replaced the usual cacophony of the city. Spitting clouds blotted any warmth from the mid-morning sun. Keplan drew up on the crest of the hill. The grassy expanse between them and the city swarmed with troops. The detainment camp looked closer to a village.

"This looks like my nightmares." Daymir shifted his seat. "I assume we'll wait until morning?"

"We've little time, and besides — they've been expecting my parents' child to ride in on a flaming horse or some nonsense." He glanced over. Honestly, he would vomit if he stewed in anticipation any longer. "Do you disagree?"

"No, I'm just impressed with your...gumption."

"That sounds like a disease, not a compliment."

"More than one thing might be true, Keplan." Daymir frowned at the city. "Are we declaring who I am?"

"We'll deal with it if they recognize you. Otherwise, you're just my guest." Keplan nudged his horse into a trot and straightened his shoulders. Whatever Daymir labeled "gumption," Keplan knew was closer to impatience. Political dances already exhausted him. Silence filled the last minutes of their journey.

"Halt!" A soldier trotted up to meet them on the road. "The city is closed. You'll have to take your business elsewhere."

Keplan raised a hand to silence her. *I'll need to get used to being imperious.* "No need, Captain." He flashed his rank.

"I wasn't aware. You're free to go."

Keplan stuck to the damp shadows of the dark street. Firas's words, Mirel's promise, Peraan's threats, all rattled around his mind, the tinny tapping of distant war drums. Running from his past was fine, if the only person his cowardice destroyed was him. Now he was newborn, naked and squalling in the cold streets after the warmth and naivete of his months in the Wise Hare.

Torches bloomed against the stained white walls of the palace, and the guard tripled around the gates. *How, again, did I plan for this to work?* They stopped outside the walls, and he fumbled Daymir's letter from his pocket.

"You're breaking curfew!"

He shielded his eyes from the rain and shouted up, "I bring a message to General Domariigo. It's urgent."

The guard raise a hand and after a moment the speaking-door in the gate flapped open to allow the man to get a better look at Keplan. "Who's it from?"

"See for yourself." Keplan held up the back of the waxed envelope with its heavy black seal.

"I'll take it from here, Captain."

"I was told to deliver it to him personally." Keplan shrugged. "Could you tell him we've come? Say it's Keplan Wardyn." He stepped back from the gate, forcing himself to look unconcerned at both the treatment and the rain. Daymir simply stared up at the walls, hung with sodden, mourning black. Everything rode on the next hour. The palace doors opened, slammed. Rain sluiced from the walls, from the dome, forming tiny cascades through the gutters along the street. He supposed rain was the world's weeping and, like tears, came at transitions.

"Captain Wardyn?" The door opened in the gate, and the guard ushered him in. "General Domariigo asked to see you right away. Sorry about the wait."

"Not a problem, sir. It's good you're thorough." He caught the polite condescension in his voice and bit back other words. *Save it for when I know the way I leave An'thor's room.*

No bells sounded their arrival, no banners waved. Instead, the wet clap of hooves echoed against the walls, and the fresh tang of salt clung to the dew-drenched stone. The wind tumbled from the hills inland, sweeping the cloying smoke out to sea.

He glanced back at Daymir's quiet scoff. "What?"

"You'll have to get used to being known. The moment you're declared, you'll never go unrecognized again."

"You seem to be doing all right." Keplan snapped. He dismounted and followed the steward inside.

His thoughts stalled as he entered the inner courtyard. Gravel crunched under their boots. A birch pergola stretched the length of the entryway, the gray wood stained black from years of water. Scenes of the city's golden days inlaid the doors themselves. Above him, the dome loomed, a milky, glaring eye. The inner halls spoke of the same heritage—old and opulent, and long since faded. An entire wing to the north was boarded off. *What did my parents feel, riding into this city, heralded by parades, banners, bells? Did they ever grow used to it?*

"My mirror tells me the years took their toll." He scratched at the full beard left travel-long. "Besides, I'm exiled. People don't see what they don't expect."

"Perhaps we can use that to our advantage." They were ushered into a foyer and left alone. Fur and iron decorations told him it belonged to the general. Keplan paced to the window, twitching the curtains back. "If it wasn't too late, now would be when I rode for the fields."

Daymir hummed thoughtfully. "Smuggling the former heir into the city, staying long enough so he's not executed then escaping into anonymity? Not the worst plan I've heard."

Keplan's heart faltered, and he looked over at the older man. "I'd do it. In a heartbeat, I'd do it. I'd hand over the throne and the crown and this entire mess." He watched Daymir's calculating expression and the steel in his shoulders. *But I'm wondering if I should.*

"I'm not offering." Daymir's tone echoed the dust on the mantle. He moved to the window, hands clasped behind his back.

Keplan watched the man assemble his court facade, a warrior with armor unused during years of peace. How long before he had his own mask, before that mask was so familiar he forgot the face beneath it? He scraped his sopping hair back from his face. It would not do to look like a drowned gutter dog.

"May I offer you some advice?"

"That's why I brought you," Keplan reminded him.

"For the next days, months, years even, you'll need enough confidence in yourself to outweigh the uncertainty of the entire kingdom." Daymir glanced at him sidelong. "It doesn't have to be real, just convincing."

The door opened, and Keplan straightened, lacing his fingers. Perhaps he already wore a mask.

"The general will see you, this way." The guard opened another door and gestured for him to enter. Keplan stepped in alone and shut the door. Despite the fire in the expansive hearth, the study was deserted, stark. The few decorations showed the man's heritage and love for Athrolan.

"I didn't believe it was you at first." Domariigo's voice was ice cracking in bitter cold. He leaned on the darkened doorway to the rest of his chambers. By his easy stance, Keplan realized he stood there all along.

"Good evening."

"You avoid me for weeks, then show up to drip puddles on my carpet at midnight and all you offer is 'good evening'?"

Keplan smiled. "You don't have any carpets, Domariigo, and we're at war. I doubt you'd sleep as it is."

"You're late. A little later and we'd have burnt the place down. You brought a message from Daymir?"

"I had to get through the gates, didn't I?" He held up the letter. "It's from Blackhouse, but it's addressed to me, not you." He tucked the letter back into his cloak and straightened his shoulders. "I don't want the crown, you know. But I want war less. I'm here to accept."

An'thor's black eyes raked the boy's face with curiosity—Arman's jaw, Alea's nose, Azirik's eyes. "As much as I badgered Barrackborn, I was starting to disbelieve."

Keplan pointed to the chairs by the fire. "Might we talk?"

An'thor's chin jerked in an exhausted nod. "I'll call for some tea." He drew a bottle from his desk. "Unless you want something stronger?"

"Tea is fine." Keplan watched the general move about the room, lighting lamps and calling for tea. When he stopped and perched on the edge of his desk, Keplan held out his arm. "I won't pretend to like you, and you seemed uninterested in overcoming that."

"Perhaps." An'thor's tired mouth twitched. "I've supported you from the beginning, but others will need convincing. How do you plan to do that?"

"I need help—not just with that, with everything. I don't know what I'm doing. I don't know what it means to be noble or be a king. You heard from my own mouth about all I know is how to clean stalls. I'm mad as they come, but you're just as mad for supporting me. You've been ruling this city for months. I'll need a teacher."

"I don't think any would call what I've done 'ruling.'"

"Clearly. I wasn't speaking about you. Blackhouse will teach me."

"The fates themselves couldn't force that man to set foot in this," An'thor dismissed. "And I doubt he'd agree to teach you."

"Not the fates, just me." Adrenaline waned from Keplan's body and his hands trembled. Buzzing thoughts from the palace wormed into his head. Even the general's thoughts were a low, wordless murmur. He shook the sounds away and jerked open the door. "Ask him yourself, Domariigo."

The general's albic brows arched, and he peered against the brighter foyer light as the exile entered. An'thor's faint smile did not chase the exhaustion from his eyes. "Daymir." He moved across the room and offered his arm.

"An'thoriend." Daymir took the arm, but his gaze roved to the mess of soldiers visible outside the window and the chaos in the lower tiers of the city. "I can't say I like what you've done with the place."

An'thor's smile faded. "Perhaps if we'd had help, it wouldn't have come to this." He trudged back to the credenza beside the hearth and fished out a bottle. The glasses were the only thing in the room not covered in dust. "You've changed not a bit, I see. Still as much of an arse."

"Could we not do this right now?" Keplan drew a ragged breath. "Small wonder we war amongst ourselves, with Domariigo too drunk to hold his tongue and everyone else too tired of listening to it." He forced each word around the urge to vomit. "I'll walk out and let you ride this kingdom straight to doom."

An'thor looked like he wanted to correct the boy, but kept his thoughts to himself. "What do you intend to do, then?"

Keplan stared at the general. "I don't know the first thing about being king. I don't know what I'm doing. I barely know the details of Athrolan's government." He sank into the chair by the hearth. "A kingdom the size of Athrolan, she doesn't have one sole heir. There are lines, carefully tracked by clerks and historians. Daymir surely has cousins."

"I had a sister," Daymir offered. "She was next, after me. She's dead. There was my father's cousin's son and daughter Jaytian and Dirma, and their children. The first fell ill four years ago. The second was lost in childbirth. Truthfully, House Xain has been plagued by accidents and tragedy." Keplan watched the man's gaze flick to the general. "Much like the family of the Count of Felden, of late."

Keplan frowned. There was something there, an accusation, an admittance. He was not sure. It was a problem for tomorrow, someday when war no longer slavered at his future. "And those children, the cousin's grandchildren, they're unfit? Too young?"

Daymir faltered, but the general barreled on without noticing.

"Dirma's son, Tzavanir, is fit. He is Duke of Pardelan and nineteen. Jaytian's daughter, Gella married an ambassador from the Vales. Fit and of age is not the issue, Keplan. The queen declared an heir. One who is present." Daymir reminded. "Those alternates were in case no heir was chosen or found. Besides, they seem to have gone missing."

An'thor sighed. "They are currently housed with their entourage and every other visitor to the city since we locked the gates," An'thor looked away, "in the camps outside the walls. We could not risk them becoming the figureheads of further coup, intentionally or otherwise."

"Fates, Peraan's ramblings about your plot against the Xain house were true," Keplan remarked.

An'thor whirled. "If your parents hadn't shirked their duty, I wouldn't have had to plot, and plan, or play general and king and assassin to get you to this throne. Sometimes heroes make the greatest cowards." Glass rattled as he poured himself another. "But here you are. Let's forget how you got here and focus on wedging a crown on your reluctant head."

Momentum hurtled Keplan ahead, and each time he glanced back he saw the way closing behind him. As much as he dreaded what was to come, it was no mistake. Not yet, at least. *Perhaps I'm saving all those for when tens of thousands of people depend upon me.*

Daymir was an ally, but not a friend. An'thor's empathy barely glimmered through the tangle of duty and alcohol. Keplan expected loneliness. He had not expected it to bother him. He wanted Firas, wanted the escape and the warmth of the other man's bed. The ground seemed to collapse under his boots.

"Well, Wardyn?"

Keplan turned, realizing An'thor had been speaking for a minute. "I'm sorry." He shook himself back to attention. "I was somewhere else. What did you ask?"

"I asked if you wanted to meet Dorcal today."

He shrugged. "We don't even know what the Council will say. We can't call the Council without alerting the whole city. Whatever it is, we'll need the whole plan before we take a step." He looked at Daymir. "At least I can boast you as an advisor." Grinning felt false, but he tried at humor anyway. "Perhaps you'll remember the taste of power and take this hideous duty off my hands."

An'thor's eyes narrowed. "Whatever your reason for avoiding the throne, would this assuage it?"

"I would agree, yes." The former heir turned to Keplan. "I don't know if you'll be a good king, but I know you'll have a better chance than I do."

"What do we do about Dorcal? The Council?" Keplan looked between them. "Is there a vote?"

"This is a monarchy, not the damn town hall."

"Oh, stuff it, Domariigo." Daymir stalked across the room and poured himself a drink. "This stopped being a proper monarchy when you hid my aunt's body from her people."

Keplan pressed his brow against the cold glass of the window. Smoke drifted over the harbor from the latest attacks. If it would stop the death, the violence, he would march into the streets. "So, call a Council and announce my presence, announce my idea. If disputed, an heir needs backing by seven provinces, correct?"

"Or twenty lesser lords," An'thor added.

"How many provinces favor you? Us?" *Me.*

"Five and the Head of the House of Commons. Raven's got six and the Head of the House of Nobles."

"If I petitioned the council to see reason, I could win enough of them to gain favor. Then we convince Dorcal to stand down. He seems difficult."

"You have no idea." An'thor spat the words, and made as if to pour himself another drink. At Daymir's glare, however, he stopped.

"From what I've heard, he's a formal man. Adheres to tradition. His reasoning for his current course was wanting a blooded heir, I assume?"

"All true. He's also a superstitious and racist bastard," Daymir offered.

"So, my heritage was an issue." Keplan sighed. This was worse than he thought. *Give up while you're still free, still uncrowned. Let Athrolan follow the steps of Mirik and do away with the throne all-together.* "He's a warrior, though. He responds to strength?"

"He hated your mother most of all. He responds to whatever counts as right in his thick skull." An'thor ran a hand through his age-yellowed hair, black gaze following Keplan's pacing. "What are you thinking?"

"Other than diving off the harbor gates?" He swallowed hard. "If I gain favor, Blackhouse will request an audience with him. I'll go along. It would prove I was clever enough, strong enough to get backing."

"I cannot decide if you're a genius or a madman." Daymir's tone was dry but honest.

"Most geniuses are mad." Keplan's stomach interrupted his words, and he winced. Breakfast seemed years ago, and fatigue shortened his temper. It did not bode well for negotiations. "It's almost nightfall. Might we call the Council after supper? I doubt I'll gain any support by gnawing the foot of the closest councilor."

An'thor finally grinned. He tugged at the bell beside the door and issued orders to the servingman stationed outside before turning back. "We'll meet them in two hours."

Daymir rose "May I borrow your privy, An'thoriend? Marl Black has lower grooming standards than the palace."

"Of course." An'thor watched the man retreat into the private rooms beyond the study. His face was unreadable as ever. "I can't say I trust him, but I'm not sure I trust you either. You're both just better than war."

"Best come up with some better lines before you present me to the Council." Keplan picked at his hands, flesh peeling enough to bleed. The small mirror by the door helped him scrape his hair into further order. There was no question he had traveled for a week. "I ought to clean up too. I won't bother with a bath, because I might see sense and try and drown myself."

An'thor laughed. "I might not even blame you. I'll call for water and a clean set of clothes." He paused by the door. "I know you're scared. I know this doesn't feel real, yet. But you managed the impossible, bringing Daymir here. Remember that."

Keplan shook his head. "You just went about it wrong. I knew nothing less than both heirs would stop the war. The Council is welcome to fight over us, but they will damn well do it with words, not swords."

CHAPTER SEVENTEEN

The 16th Day of Lumord, 1272
The City of Ceir Athrolan, Athrolan

PERAAN CHECKED THE LOCKS on his door a third time before navigating the winding stairs of the Lily and Ahonsa. It had seen far richer days, but war made people drink. Moreover, this particular establishment was an unofficial headquarters of Daymir's, and by extension Commander Dorcal's, supporters in the city proper.

Peraan waved to the bartender. "I'll be out for the evening if anyone comes for me." He moved to the door, slinging his cloak over his shoulders. A group of armed men sat by the door. Though they played a round of blood-hand, the darting glances and arrangement of their seats said they were there to keep the peace. The pot in the middle held only a few rounds-worth of coin, and their mugs were still partially full.

Peraan nodded to the bearded one among them. "Jakim, I'll be back late. Keep an eye for that boy, will you? I don't want him back."

He ducked into the street, eyes roving from the alley beyond to where the side street spilled onto High Arch. Curfew and cannon fire cut Athrolan's usual bustle.

Peraan followed the arc of the side street. Keeping to the shadows was easy with every third lamp destroyed by cannonballs or riots. Another third were drained to create makeshift war-oil for the answering volleys.

He knew many of the militia and which roads were patrolled by his supporters. He raked a chapped hand over his face. War was exhausting. He was a boy when the Gods' War ended. Raising Daymir to the throne would hopefully not involve more bloodshed. *But we are men, and what can we do, but murder each other?* Glinting steel of army shields flashed ahead and he turned down a side street.

It took another half hour to reach the palace. Torches blazed, four dozen dying suns in the face of the yawning night of war. He skirted the wall, grateful for the decorative trees lining the stained white stone. He swung over the edge of the bridge to the gate and dropped. The gardens were quiet. Gravel crunched, mimicry of the city crumbling before Dorcal's volleys.

He upended the thick envelope from his cloak over his hand. Lilac pressed flat between the folded parchment. Only a time marked the parchment. A stand of lilacs encircled a bench beside the memorials' entrance. The trees bore only withered leaves, the ground cleaned of their brown, fallen flowers. He wondered, absently, when the bloom in his hand was collected.

"I thought you'd leave me waiting forever."

Peraan rolled his eyes at the saccharine tone. "Never, my dear." He caught the hand of the woman tucked against one of the twisted trees.

She let him keep a hold, but dropped the simpering act. "I don't have much time. They're calling us for extra shifts."

He held up his hand. "I shouldn't know any more about you." Poorly hemmed skirts aside, her bearing said she was a soldier. Her information told him which company. More details would be dangerous, and self-preservation extended to his network. *It has to operate with another man at the helm.*

She snorted. "Right. That why you gave me the false name, 'Vanabren'?" She exaggerated the name.

He extricated his hand from hers. Keeping up the pretense of romance if they were seen grew difficult the more they interacted. *Let them think we're quarreling.* "You wanted to meet tonight, so it must be important. Unless now you're dragging me out past curfew for conversation."

She made a face. "You're too old for me. And yes, it's important."

Peraan touched the gray at his temples with a wince before drawing out his thin notebook. "Go on."

"A boy entered the city this afternoon, from the east. He dressed as a captain. He went to the palace and demanded to see the general. Said he had a letter from Blackhouse. They wouldn't let him in until he said to give the general his name." She watched, disinterested, as Peraan jotted down her words, then continued, "A minute later they bowed him into the palace."

Peraan kept his breath level, but his mind churned. "Do you think Domariigo saw sense and sent for the true king?"

She snorted. "I'm not sure the man had any sense to begin with."

Peraan heaved a sigh. She was right, and he knew it. "What name did the boy give?"

Her expression settled between alert and conniving and Peraan remembered why he only trusted her with his brother's name and not his own. "That's why I thought you'd want to know. Keplan Wardyn."

Peraan frowned. "That supposed to mean something to me?"

She hiked up skirts she clearly had no use for and headed back toward the palace. "You'll catch on, Vanabren."

He watched her go without comment. No information she gave yet proved false, but he trusted her about as far as his arthritic shoulders would carry her. Enough of the Royal Guard was disillusioned with the general that they would accept Daymir. He tugged his cloak closer and took off along the wall.

Ruined buildings and battered streets made his bones ache more than the night's chill. Soot and blood smeared Athrolan's gray cobbles. Trash and debris clogged the gutters. Though poor folk and the Slummer suffered most, war's teeth were long enough to sink into the merchants and clerks of the Silver Apron.

Fine houses were dark, small gardens overgrown and untended. Fountains ran dry. Smoke filled the streets even there, and Peraan tugged his scarf over his nose as he descended to the warehouses. Decay and sweat joined the acrid stench of creosote. Patrols lessened; other than the dead, there was little left to loot. Peraan paused beside the skeleton of a glassblower's stall and let out a low, trilling whistle. Behind him, the beams of the warehouse creaked. A muffled thump heralded his second informant.

"Peraan." The man's voice could have been further creaking floorboards.

"Luben." Peraan fixed the half-Berrin man with a glare. "You were supposed to arrive weeks ago."

"Didn't expect the city to lay siege to herself, now did I? Vinegar still burns my nose from the barrel I smuggled myself in."

Peraan shrugged. "If you were here on time, you wouldn't have had to. Besides, vinegar is an improvement. All your people smell like fish."

Luben sighed at the racism. "You're lucky the cause needs you. What do you have for me?"

"Something's stirring in the palace, I'll need to learn more. In the meantime, a man lives down by the docks, an old hand named Sar Salt-tongue. Fates know what name he was born to. He informs Domariigo on the Commander's movements and network here. Kill him."

"I didn't join you to kill the homeless."

"This is war, Luben. Or didn't you notice the bodies you walked over to get here? You bring any news from the east?"

"Daymir disappeared. My cousin in Marl Black sent word. The true king arrived in Marl Orna alone, and left with a scarred young man dressed as a soldier."

Peraan frowned. *Seems to be a rash of boys with scars.* "Any word where he's headed?"

"West. Treason, him leaving Marl Black. Whatever his reason, it's a good one." The man sighed. "Ready for this business to be over. Nothing good comes from a blasphemous heir. Nothing. My brother, still in Berr, far to the north, he tells me a new god's coming, and all that cling to the titanic forces of the past will come to see their err."

Peraan frowned. "Your cousin a madman?"

"No more than any other prophet."

He shuddered. Religion made him queasy. "Regardless of blasphemy, Luben, we will see this through. I don't suppose your cousin caught the name of this boy with the scars?"

"No. You think you know him?"

"Just information, that's all." Peraan shoved off from the wall. He needed to know more about Domariigo's visitor before he started passing information. "Take care of Salt-tongue, and I'll see you in a week's time. Same place." He waited for the man to disappear into the wreckage by the docks before turning home.

It was only later, in the dim light of the Lily and Ahonsa's hearth, that he drew out his notebook. He read over the information again, rolling it in his mind like he rolled spiced whiskey around his mouth.

When Nikola poured him another mug, she handed him a letter. "This came for you. Looks like it's from your old friend in the palace."

"I've not heard from him in years. Figured he died." He tucked it into his pocket to read in the privacy of his room. "Nikola," he stopped her as she turned away. "What does the name 'Keplan Wardyn' mean to you?"

"Nothing, really. Wardyn is common in the south, but it was the surname of the Earth Shaker."

"That was Arrowlash."

"Not when he first came. Aud'narman Wardyn. He's come up twice too much lately." She frowned. "Why do you ask?"

"Just adding to the puzzle." He looked back to his book, eyes narrowed on the name. *"until he said to give the general his name."* Whiskey no longer burned his throat. Ice in his gut told him the general's inhuman heir had already arrived.

Φ

"Tell me again why I'm doing this." Keplan swore when his hand caught in the decorative tie of his horse-tail.

"To save the kingdom," An'thor spoke as if to a child.

Keplan frowned at the mirror. "Fuck the kingdom."

"Wardyn."

"Right. Saving the kingdom. Easy." He straightened. The gray outfit turned his skin sallow and his eyes overbright. It did not fit. "I look terrible."

"You look like a symbol of youth and hope."

"I look ill, Domariigo." He clasped his gloved hands before him to hide their shaking.

The room beyond hummed with conversation, a mutter to the chaos in Keplan's thoughts. "I can't do this, An'thor. I wasn't lying when I said I might be sick all over the nearest councilor."

"Which is why I made you eat something."

Keplan rolled his eyes. He never felt more powerless. *Secrets give me power.* Beyond that door lay a dozen people with more secrets and power than most in the kingdom, Keplan would bet. He looked over at An'thor. "Let them ignore me. Let them work out their issues at the idea. Then introduce me."

An'thor rolled his black eyes. "You do love the dramatic entrance, don't you?"

Though he did not particularly care about An'thor's opinion of him, the observation was not wrong. Between his isolated childhood and the weeks of torture and invisibility in Ban, he was ready to turn the tables. *It's time someone listened.* "People expect heroes to arrive in a blaze from the sky. The least I can do is deliver some good lines. Besides, I want to observe them for a bit."

An'thor eyed him before tucking his tunic tighter around his thick middle and facing the door. He nodded to the squire.

"Sir An'thoriend Domariigo of Neneviir and Claimiirn, General of Athrolan's Army." The squire glanced, panicked at Keplan, but he shook his head and slipped into the room.

Three council men ranged about the table. War did away with formality, it seemed. Keplan scanned the room from the doorway, steadying his heartbeats by sheer force of will. Hair looked hastily done, and their eyes sank in shadow. Their squires clustered in the rear of the room playing what looked like a version of tiles. An'thor took his seat near the head of the table with a sigh.

The table was long and broad, with seating for the full Council—the House of Nobles and House of Guilds alike. Each chair bore a lacquered emblem of its user's position. The monarch's chair stood at the head of the table, flanked by the general's and commander's on the right and the two Head Councilors' on the left. Drapes hung between each window were the faded turquoise and black of mourning.

The other two Councilors presumably under An'thoriend's influence, entered a moment later, squires and personal clerks in tow. Keplan used the distraction to cross the room and stand by one of the wide windows. He eyed the latch on the casement. Perhaps, if he was careful, no one would notice him pitching himself out of it. *And then they'd have to crown Daymir.* He caught An'thor's level gaze. The man raised two fingers and tapped his brow, his chin and his collar in a subtle salute. Keplan drew a breath, then nodded a second time. *I did the impossible. I brought Daymir here. Alone. And now I have both his support and Domariigo's.*

The other half of the Consulates arrived en masse, eyes wary. Keplan noted they were accompanied by guards. Neither side looked pleased.

An'thor rose, cutting the mutters and speculation short. His black gaze slid from one Consulate to the next. When he made a silent visual circuit of them, he began. "Thank you for your prompt arrival, though my request gave little notice. Rarely do all of us agree, and our values are not something to take lightly. Indeed, that variation lends Athrolan her greatest strength. But this war has gone on long enough. There is a solution, but it requires cooperation and trust. This kingdom needs a king. Both Dorcal and I have reached out to Master Blackhouse without luck. The man has no interest in taking up the throne, and frankly, I can't blame him. We exiled him. But he was not the only man named the heir."

A noble rose. "We understand the situation with Blackhouse is complicated, but he is not the only blooded descendant of Xain."

Pardelan province's representative, a tall woman bearing a nose like a hawk's beak rolled her eyes. "He's imprisoned the only ones left living just outside our walls, Jantian."

"General, sir, Commander Dorcal will not surrender," another noble promised. "Your search for this mythic heir needs to end if we hope for peace."

Keplan's eyes roved from speaker to speaker, filtering through their ranks and names and opinions as quickly as he could. Some were prideful, others desperate, and, like An'thor, idealism and hope still filled another two. He filed what he could away for later consideration. One thing, however, lingered: every Consulate was exhausted and terrified of their kingdom's future — or at least their part of it.

"There's talk of madness, sir." A gray-haired man dressed in green interjected.

"Not to mention drunkenness —"

An'thor's fist slammed on the table. "Drunkenness — ?"

"Enough." Keplan flexed his gloved hands and rose from his perch. Startled silence fell. A moment passed before the council traced the low, firm voice. He moved to the head of the table and rested a hand on An'thor's shoulder. "Your logic got us as far as it will. Let the legends do the rest."

Murmurs rose. He remained silent as An'thor returned to the seat to the right of the monarch's chair. It was not the introduction he hoped, but he would make it work. *I have to.*

Terror rooted in his bones, a chill that steadied his gut out of sheer necessity. Slipping into the role of every Banis noble, every legend his father told him made it easier. "Bickering gets us nowhere. Athrolan tore herself apart these last months. I've seen a fraction of the war all of you lived through, and it's already exhausting. While you ripped this kingdom to pieces, I went to Blackhouse. You follow Daymir?" *Demand respect*, he reminded himself. "Good. Because he follows me."

This earned a narrow glare from the Duchess of Pardelan. "And you are?"

"Ah." He rested both hands on the tabletop and inclined his head a fraction. "I'm Keplan Wardyn, son of Dhoah' Laen Lyne'alea and Earth Shaker Aud'narman Arrowlash, Heir Apparent for the throne of Athrolan." He let surprise burble and die before rattling off their fears. "You don't know me, save my heritage. I'm young. There is no proof of my blood. I'm not noble, or even Athrolani, save by birthplace. But I have something no other claimant does. I have the support of both General Domariigo and Master Blackhouse himself." He hoped his faint smile looked kind and not manic. "Not to mention a writ in the queen's own hand declaring my right to the throne."

"Master Wardyn, we don't have—"

"Proof that Master Blackhouse actually supports me?" Keplan glanced at the door. "Squire, please invite Daymir in. You'll find him waiting in the foyer."

Daymir stepped into the room before the words left Keplan's mouth. The exile's white hair was trimmed to the nape of his neck and combed back. A small tuft under his lips was all that remained of his messy beard. Black clothes fit, but were a decade out of style. He nodded to An'thor before moving to Keplan's left hand and bowing. "Thank you for having me." The clear words were pitched to sound friendly, as if meant for Keplan's ears only.

He's a master at this game. "Of course." Keplan's gaze swiveled to the Council.

Daymir gestured to the seat. "If I may?" At Keplan's nod, he sat and directed his sharp gaze at the others. "Half of you promised to follow my wishes for the kingdom. You wrote your support to me and followed Commander Dorcal's attempt at revolution in my name. Yet here I am telling you to put your names behind this man.

"Your concerns were mine too, at first. He is young. He is inexperienced. He is not Xain blood," Daymir repeated. "And I don't care. He is driven and inspired. He is wise beyond most men twice his age. He does not have Tzatia's blood, but that of the most powerful creatures this world has known, and Her Majesty's own seal on his claim to the throne. It takes more than heart to rule a kingdom, and I have agreed at Master Wardyn's request—no, his insistence—to act as Chief Advisor to the Crown for a year's time. This will allow him to benefit from my experience and understanding of government, and you to grow the same trust in him."

A black-haired man with Tetran's sigil ignored Keplan and Daymir both, dark eyes narrowing on An'thoriend. "General, have you well and truly lost your mind? This boy is a child. He looks starved, scarred, and I doubt those arms could lift a sword."

An'thor turned on the marquess with a snarl. "I am trying to end this war, you piss-stained—"

"Did Tzatia raise a blade?" Keplan interrupted. "No, she had an army. Did Tzatia make every choice alone? No, she had us behind her. Did she choose to lead? No, it was chosen for her."

"What do you want? Coin for your acting? You are an overgrown shepherd. You ought to attend your flock before they get out of hand and destroy the countryside!"

"The way your civil war threatened to?" An'thor's face twisted into an ugly sneer.

"It was as much your war as ours, General!"

"I'd rather run into the woods." Keplan rose from his chair, pleased that the room settled into stillness. "I'd rather stay a bar-hand in the slums. It's easier. But your inability to end this war on your own forced my hand. You don't have to like me. My parents didn't have the time to earn Her Majesty's trust, but she followed them anyway.

"I know it won't be easy. I know I need you. But I'm not just the lesser of a poor choice. My parents raised me as a commoner so I'm new to state, but I'm clever, and learn faster than you could imagine. Mirik thrived under a soldier Hetmir. Let's see how far Athrolan climbs with a pauper king." He paused for a moment. "I will leave you to discuss this among yourselves. Cannon fire should be enough of a time limit."

An'thor and Daymir rose, the councilors hastily doing the same. Keplan kept his steps unhurried, as he left the hall and returned to the general's study. He sank into the chair by the window. Seconds, decades seemed to have passed in the span of the meeting. Already his back ached with the weight. The view of the harbor was so different from his room in the Hare. In place of cascading small Slummer houses perched atop the ordered navy barracks and offices, he was treated to the glittering Silver Apron and smoky ruins of warehouses. Midnight swallowed the expanse of graves and memorials.

"They'll be at it a while, you know." Daymir shut the door softly, face a neutral mask. "I can call for a meal."

Keplan frowned. "I don't think I could eat right now."

"By tomorrow afternoon you will probably be king. You need sustain yourself on more than stirring speeches. Even during the horrible, uncertain times."

Keplan hummed in response. He did not really care about supper, or breakfast, or whatever meal this was. He only cared how a shaggy pony fared without him, and what a Slummer bartender thought at that moment. *It's been a week.*

An'thor arrived with food and the ubiquitous glass of alcohol. Even considering his translucent skin, he looked wan. "State affairs are more tedious than I remember."

"State affairs haven't included four heirs and a civil war in many generations, general." Daymir watched the Ageless man pile meat and sliced potatoes onto a plate. "Remember to save some of that for His Majesty here. Can't have the boy starving to death before —"

"Don't," Keplan murmured.

Daymir handed a plate to the young man. "Don't what?"

"Call me that. Not yet. Not until you have to, and then, please, only in public. I've got less than a day before I sacrifice my life to this kingdom. Afford me some freedom until then."

They fell silent, only the sound of eating echoing in the small room. Bells clanged out the hour before dawn and An'thor rose. "I'd best see they don't wrest the kingdom from my hands now that they're all in one room. I'll call you both when we've decided."

Keplan rested his head in his hands. Buzzing conversation filled his mind from the Council Hall. Outbursts punctuated the unclear words. *I can't think about that, can't listen in until they've decided.* Instead, he focused on the thrum of his pulse and the bells counting down to the moment his future would be sworn to the crown or to war.

Thunderheads smudged the golden coin of the rising sun, changing faded blue sky to the vermillion of fresh wounds and the burgundy of bruises.

Keplan tugged his glove from his right hand and raised the palm. It was the same color as the clouds.

"What does it mean? That tattoo."

Keplan glanced back at Daymir. He could not find the energy to replace the glove. Instead, he removed the left as well. He spread his fingers, displaying the contrary marks. "They were given to me in Ban. The first, the red one, proclaims me an enemy of the empire. The second pardons me."

"I thought gloves were a quirk, some tic you inherited from your parents. Fates know they were odd at times. Or perhaps fear of touch, after what you suffered."

"I wear them to avoid the questions. Scars on my face will fade, perhaps not fully, but with time. These won't. They remind me what humans are capable of, what war does."

"When you say those things, I know you'll make a better king than I."

Keplan snorted, but the steward's arrival halted whatever retort he could devise.

"The council's finished." The man's expression was the careful mask of a servant, and unreadable. "They request your presence."

Keplan straightened his robes. "And?"

"Don't grill the staff, Keplan." Daymir moved past him and into the corridor.

The steward caught Keplan's eye as the young man followed the former heir. "I've spent a lifetime serving people, and they are still an enigma. If it were solely my choice, I would have crowned you at 'pauper king.'"

Keplan grinned down at his shirt as he adjusted it. "It wasn't the worst speech, was it?"

"No, sir."

"Thank you." Jogging to catch up to Daymir at the door to the Council hall, he half expected the palace floor to buck him from its flagging. He returned to the head of the table in silence. An'thor would not meet his gaze, black eyes fixed on some point out the window. Relief swathed the room. *Whatever it is, they've decided.* "You've chosen?"

"We have." The Head of the House of Nobles rose, folding her hands. "We would like to address the factors that led to our thinking. As leaders of our provinces, we have many concerns. You are young. You are inexperienced. You are not Athrolani. You are not of the Xain house."

Keplan's stomach fell. He did not want the crown, but their decision meant further war. Deeper, an unnamed part of him already wrapped bony hands around the Crown. He forced himself to listen.

"But there is a greater concern. One we all share, and that is for our future, our families, our people. We see you, too, have that concern." She gestured to him and to Daymir, a step behind. "Would you agree to sign a Regency order? It would ease this transition."

The floor stilled under Keplan's feet. "Whom did you have in mind?"

"Master Blackhouse. If he agrees."

Keplan looked to Daymir.

The man's expression softened, and he dipped his head. "If you wish it, I would agree."

Keplan turned back to the councilors and swallowed his heart back into its proper place between his ribs. *Short of them forcing Daymir into the role, this is the best of all possible choices.* "I accept." His voice was faint in his ears. He cleared his throat. "I accept your terms."

The Consulates stepped back from their chairs and knelt in a ripple, tapping chest, lips, and brow with their fists. The Head of the House of Nobles looked up. For a moment, Keplan thought he saw tears in her eyes. "You have our support."

Elation and terror exploded in his chest. Tears clogged his throat. *Do not weep.* Instead, he tucked his shaking arms behind him and bowed low. "I am honored." He straightened and turned to the clerk poised at the table's corner. "Draw up the necessary paperwork and have it brought to Master Blackhouse and myself as soon as possible." He turned to An'thor, still kneeling on the tiles. "My first command to you, General—call for a ceasefire and request Commander Dorcal's cooperation. Tell him the council wishes to negotiate tomorrow at dawn."

To a one they looked more exhausted than relieved. *That makes all of us then.* After an awkward nod, he slipped into the hall. It was odd not to be dismissed, and instead, be the first to sweep from the room. An'thor caught up at his door. Keplan sank onto a bench, head in hands. No one spoke until the locks clicked into place behind the new Regent.

"Are you all right?" Clinking of glass as An'thor poured wraith punctuated Daymir's low voice.

"I don't feel sick anymore." Keplan's words rasped and he leaned against the wall, as much for support as for conversation. "Tell me I didn't just make the largest mistake of my life."

"You didn't. It might have changed the entire course of your life, but as someone who made those same choices— the hard ones, the ones easier left to others, I promise you, it's the right one." Alcohol misted An'thor's gaze, but Keplan ignored its probable influence.

"You think you never made a wrong decision in your life?" Daymir scoffed.

"I didn't say that." An'thor bit back.

"So, what now?" Keplan attempted to redirect the conversation.

"Do you think you could sleep?"

"Maybe out of necessity." In truth, he wanted nothing more than to bury himself in blankets for a month. But voices and memories not his own chattered against the barricade of his mind. Sleep only brought nightmares and little rest.

"You could kip on the cot in my study. The next few days will not be easy," An'thor offered.

"I'd think they would give him his own quarters. Being the Heir — King — and all."

An'thor shook his head. "It'll take a day to ready chambers in the guests' wing. The royal wings are currently under repair."

"As they scrub rot from the walls?"

Another bickering match was the last thing Keplan wanted to hear. "The room can wait. I have to get Moly and some things from the Hare, and I don't feel like sleep yet anyway. We can meet in the morning for the ride to the harbor." He tugged his cloak on and edged out the door before they could argue. A guard fell into step behind him at the palace gate. After Keplan's second glance, the soldier smiled. "Hylier," Keplan greeted.

"Orders from the general and His Highness the Regent. You'll get your own guard soon enough, Your Majesty."

Keplan winced at the term. "And can I dismiss you?"

"That wouldn't be advised in the streets."

"Very well. Just until I arrive at the Hare."

"Of course, Your Majesty." The honorific was a heavy yoke around Keplan's neck. "I'll wait outside."

"I might be a while."

Hylier shrugged. "I've done longer shifts."

Keplan's steps were quick through the streets, but he forced himself not to run. There was enough chaos without him causing more. Gossip and news echoed from the winding rows of houses and storefronts. Keplan did not need to meet anyone's eyes to know their thoughts:

"...and thank the fates that the curfew's been lifted..."

"...but still the matter of the prison camp..."

"...I hear Blackhouse is back in the city..."

"...another heir, something about a farm boy...?"

He clenched his jaw and turned down the street to the Slummer.

Φ

Moly's acceptance, particularly in the face of tears, was something Keplan would never take for granted. She pushed her head against his tunic, muttering in her horse language, checking for injuries. He offered the apple he stole from the palace. "I'm so sorry. I did not know I was leaving until I was already out the gates, truly. I would have taken you if I could."

He ran a hand down her flank. Someone groomed her, and her already respectable girth had grown. "Mirrel always makes you fat."

"Apologies are easier to animals." The quiet voice cut through the cozy smell of the stable.

Keplan whirled.

"You left a letter." Mirrel's lips pursed.

Keplan looked down. "I know. I'm sorry." He tried to look behind her without making it obvious.

"Why ought I let you see him? It's not like him to get emotional."

"It wasn't a lovers' quarrel. He didn't like the attention I brought."

Mirrel's brows lowered, but for once it seemed out of worry more than anger. "I noticed too. More than once I've shooed people off. And now there's a guard out front."

His heart tightened. *She protected me.* The hardest woman he ever met, and she protected him. "I cannot thank you enough for that."

She lifted a shoulder. "Just come back. Between the lack of help and Firas pining, I don't have enough hands to do everything."

"I wish I could. I came back to collect my things and say goodbye, actually."

"You're leaving?" She paused in her feeding of Ragweed and turned to face him properly.

"You two are my home. Athrolan is my home, and I can't just stand by when I could stop a war."

Something dawned on her face, but it was not surprise. "The ceasefire. We heard the heir arrived, but I never thought—" She closed her eyes, and when she opened them again, they were bright. "Of course, it's you. When I realized you knew things you ought not, I wondered. I just never thought it would come to this."

"I'm so sorry for everything I caused you both, just being here. I don't understand why you let me in, but thank you." He swallowed past the seemingly permanent lump in his throat. "Why did you?"

"You worked hard and had no one else. Besides," she lifted her chin, "our da died protecting your ma, and I'll be damned if I don't carry on that duty." She rested her hand on the door latch and was suddenly back to being the business woman he knew. "I expect this is the last we'll discuss it."

"It is. I just need to find a way to explain it to Firas."

"I don't envy you, but do it kindly. I'm the one who gathers the pieces when you're through."

The door slammed behind her, and Keplan wondered if he was better running. Breaking someone's heart was more terrifying than any throne. *Besides, I'm breaking two.*

"A minute, you salt-head!" Mirrel's bellow to a patron cut through his thoughts as he edged up to Firas's attic bedroom. He was raising his hands to knock when the door flew open. A single greasy candle backlit the bartender. Hard arms wrapped Keplan's shoulders in warmth. "I recognized your footsteps."

"I wanted to come back sooner, but everything—I'm so sorry," Keplan began, but the other man's mouth was on his, and he forgot why he was there, forgot why he ever left. Keplan's smile faded when the man pulled away. Firas's eyes were bleary and bloodshot.

"Everything?"

Keplan winced. Saying it aloud to Daymir or An'thor was one thing. To Firas it was impossible. "I left a letter but.... Did you find someone to read it to you?"

Firas slumped on the bed. "I didn't know how sensitive its contents were. You could read it to me now, but I have something to say first." He turned so they faced each other fully. "I don't want you to leave. I'm sorry I said that, I'm sorry I distrusted you." He raked at his hair. "I thought I cared about who you were, before, but I mostly just care who you are now."

"Don't." Keplan's heart clenched. "Don't go down that path. I was a warm bed at night, help when the inn's busy. Don't make it more complicated than either of us want." It was a lie. Firas was more than a friend; he was solace, but solace was one luxury a king did not have.

Firas flung his hands up in exasperation. "Fates, 'Lan, I'm not talking love, I'm talking decency. I'm the first to admit I don't want to settle with one man. Doesn't mean I can't care about the one I spend time with." He held out his hand. "Whoever you are, whatever you did, it doesn't change the man I've come to know."

"You were right."

Firas peered into his eyes but moved back at whatever he saw in them.

"'A pauper's son.' I didn't mean to bring trouble, didn't know it followed me until I got here. And I lost the will to outrun it. I thought I could drown myself in work, in you, but I can't."

Sadness smoothed desperation from Firas's face. "The night you left, I told Mirrel everything, told her I knew you were a bastard of someone or a noble running. I might be daft, but Mirrel's not. She's got a bigger pair of stones than any man I've met. But the thing about older sisters is, they're never wrong. Said she knew who you were and she didn't care." He sighed, the sound catching in his throat. "And I suppose I don't either."

Keplan could not force words past all the lives he could never live. He cleared his throat, then tried again, "I think I should read you that letter now." Sooty prints and what might have been tears stained the letter. It looked how Keplan felt.

> *"Firas,*
>
> *I know this is abrupt, and for that I'm sorry. The city is crumbling around us, and while I was not born here, it's my home. You and Mirrel, you're home to me. And I would be a poor friend, a poor lover, if I didn't do everything in my power to protect you, to protect this way of life I love so much.*
>
> *I would rather stay here. But that would be selfish, and I can't watch you die when the walls crumble.*

I hope you can forgive me.
I don't know if I can.
-K"

Keplan's stomach churned from too much adrenaline and too little sleep. He forced himself to look at Firas.

The bartender's eyes narrowed on some unseen speck on the floor. "Where did you go?"

"I went to Marl Orna, a town halfway between here and Marl Black."

Firas's jaw moved in thought. "But you came back."

"To explain things." Keplan frowned. "You thought I wouldn't?"

Firas shrugged. "In my family, when people ride off, they don't often return."

Keplan chewed on his lip. "I can't stay. I want to, but I can't hide here while your entire world falls apart at the seams."

"So your letter says. Doesn't explain why it's up to you. One man can't stop a civil war." Firas laced one muscled leg through Keplan's long ones.

Keplan wondered if the gesture was to anchor him to this world. He wished it would work. "The heir of a kingdom can. You thought I was a bastard. I'm not sure whether my parents ever married, but I'm fairly certain it doesn't matter when they're not human. The queen declared me the heir, not knowing who my parents' child would become, not knowing if I even existed. That takes a lot of faith. I'm not a man of faith, or legends, or greatness, but I can end this war. To protect you. To save Athrolan. I went to Daymir Blackhouse and begged him to take the Crown instead of me, but he refused, so I asked for his support. There can't be a war if the two of us agree."

"And he gave it? That's why the cannons stopped?"

"The general, the Council, they agreed at noon."

"You'll be gone. You'll be king."

"Just across the city," Keplan corrected.

"Lan, when you're in a palace, and I'm in the slums, 'across the city' is the same as gone." Firas's face was shadowed. "I don't know what to say. Part of me wishes you'd stay selfish. I'm not a one-man lover, but, fates, I could have been for you. I wouldn't mind war if I had you."

"Don't be dramatic. That's my territory." Keplan wove his fingers through the bartender's hair. "I have a few hours before I'm expected back." *Before I'm no longer a commoner. Before I'm no longer Lan.* "Do you think I can spend them with you?"

Φ

The Eastern Border of Athrolan

Arman crouched before the pile of tinder. New, deeper lines accented his frown. Cold gnawed his fingers and toes, a persistent predator. The wood got wetter by the moment. He reached out, willing fire into his palm. Nothing caught. Not even a line of smoke rose from the pile. He inched closer and tried again. Twisting roots of magma and fire were choked, the lava slowing, cooling into a sullen quagmire of not-quite-rock. Even with the silence and peace of the forest, his mind skittered over the earth's surface, unable, or unwilling, to puncture the crust. The only reaction was the pervasive scent of burnt bone and sodden creosote.

Alea trudged over the rise, arms full of rain-darkened twigs. "Fates, what is that smell?"

"The fire won't light."

"Tinderbox probably just got wet. Use your power." She dumped the wood beside their campfire and slumped down beside it. "I'm tired of rain as much as you. Can't seem to keep anything dry. Truly, what is that smell?"

"It's me, alright?" he snapped. "It's my power. I can't light the fire. I've tried, even with the tinderbox which, for the books, was dry as bone." He flexed his hands, chapped and cold for the first time in two decades. "Alea, I think I'm sick. Like, inside, in my mind, in my power. I can't access it like I used to, can't pull it from the earth. It's as if my connection to it atrophied." He swallowed hard. "Your dreams say anything about that?"

She sank to her knees beside him, colorless eyes searching his. The concern made his heart ache, but the fear was worse, a knife to his gut that said she did not have an answer. "Arman, I'm so sorry." She pressed her lips to his brow, and he heard the hitch of her breath. "You're cold."

"I know." The usual furnace burning in his chest, thundering between the ribs of his mind, guttered. "I'm scared."

"How did you overcome your fear during the war?"

"Which fear? War brings several."

"Any of them. Fear that you were going to die. That we might lose. Fear that I would die?"

"That last one I never overcame, Alea. I knew we could lose, at first, but when you returned from Le'yne so little could stop you. And when I saw you on the cliffs at Calimiirn, I realized there was no way we would lose. Die, perhaps, but not lose. When I learned I would die—granted that wasn't what I saw, but I was so certain that it still counts—it was trust. I surrendered to you, to your draw on me, to your power over me, to your faith we would win."

"You make me sound like this unfathomable being."

"You've never seen yourself from my perspective." He offered a smile. Complexities, carefully established roles defined their relationship. Sometimes he wished they could change, they could meet as they were now, without the weight of who they were before. He clenched his fist, willing his mind deeper into his power. Striations, glowing golden stains, marked the inner walls of his mind, high-water marks from when his power overflowed his magical body. Now the golden fire sloshed deep in the stagnant depths of his heart. "Alea, do you think we were supposed to?"

"Supposed to what, love?"

"Live."

She looked away. "I remember when I was in Le'yne. There was this tome. It must be somewhere in Mirik now if it ever made it out. But it was from when they predicted events — tapped into the power of the world and felt the ebb and flow like the tide. It predicted us."

"Doesn't mean it's right, doesn't mean we were meant to live into our middle years." Arman watched the lines of her face change, echo her fears. "You told me we were going to win, and whatever came afterward would be beautiful." He squeezed her hand. "Maybe we're just aging. Hold on to that faith." Something told him whatever was coming, they could not stop it.

Perhaps they were not meant to.

Φ

The City of Ceir Athrolan, Athrolan

News of the ceasefire spread through the city. The night was clear. Knots of soldiers on the walls and in squares stood down. It was not peace, but it was no longer war. An'thor propped his chin on his hand. "This feels too easy."

Daymir glanced up from his place beside An'thor's hearth. "Probably because you're not the one doing it. You're not Keplan, ill-prepared but determined to do the proper thing. You're not me, forced into a role I've avoided for the past decade. Walk in our boots a spell and see if you still think it's easy."

An'thor turned back to the window. "Why did you?"

Daymir sighed and laid his book aside. It was clear the general's mind was too busy to allow quiet. "Why did I what?"

"Avoid it. You spent your entire childhood — well, once Her Majesty's daughter passed — learning how to be a king. You forsook your dream of becoming a gallant to study finance and strategy. You were the best heir any monarch could ask for. When she exiled you, it broke your heart. Broke the kingdom's too, in a way." He fished a bottle of dark gray liquid from his desk. "And yet now that it could be yours, you've done your damnedest to avoid the throne."

"Can you get through one day without drinking? One conversation, even?" Daymir waved off An'thor's response before the words escaped the man's pale lips. "I'm not avoiding the question. Just observing. And that looks like gutter water."

"You're passing judgment, Blackhouse, and I'd like to remind you that, while I might not be able to do them sober, I didn't abandon my responsibilities."

"I didn't want it. Ever. When Princess Tzatte died, I was old enough to know I was next in line, to know it would be my duty, whether I wished it so or not." He fixed the general with a pointed stare. "What have I been known for?"

"Other than the unfortunate incident of treason, perhaps your determination? Cleverness?"

"I'm a perfectionist, general. I did not want the job, but I'd be damned if I didn't do my very best. What broke my heart was not that I lost the throne, it was that my aunt — more of a mother to me, truly — did not trust me. Losing her trust, my standing, the reputation and respect I had earned, it destroyed me."

"You could take it back now."

"I want it even less now, and honestly, Keplan will be better than I. Perhaps not at first, but he will." Sadness tinged with desperation tugged at the lines around his eyes.

An'thor could not bring himself to chase the truth. "You sound certain." Alcohol's slur softened the sharp words, but only just.

"For someone who sent the city to war over him, you sound awfully uncertain," Daymir retorted.

"You left me little choice, Daymir. He's the only thing that could stop this."

"The only person, Domariigo. He's a man, not a thing. And I thought the only person would be you or Dorcal, considering you started it in the first place."

An'thor slumped into the chair at his desk. "Forget I ever asked. I wish I hadn't."

"I told you he has the heart for it. I wasn't speaking thoughtlessly. He loves this city. It might have started as comfort and the place his lover sleeps, but it's become home. He speaks as if born here. And you ought to know what lasts in legends longest. It isn't tired duty or perfectionism."

An'thor pulled on his fur-lined coat. "I ought to see the Xain cousins on their way home. Camp was dismantled this morning." If Daymir responded, he did not hear. His head buzzed with despair and the drink drowning it. He wanted to believe a scrawny boy with scars and a battered heart filled with love could save their kingdom. Deep down, there was a part of him that did. A larger part, the part that drank, that cursed every morning he woke instead of died, told him that the war was not over.

Φ

The 17th Day of Lumord, 1272

Keplan slipped from Firas's bed without waking the other man. His room was as he left it. He folded his borrowed clothes and wiped the street grime from Firas's father's boots. Save for a handful of papers and a few collected knickknacks, which he shoved into his pack, the room was the same as when he first arrived. He ran a hand over the already smooth coverlet, checked the boards on the window. By some tiny mercy, the hall was deserted. He listened for Mirrel preparing breakfast, but the common room below was silent. Keplan's boots were heavier than ever as he crept into the cool morning. Fog cloaked the city, the clanging of the harbor bells with each swell somehow distant through the swaddling cloud.

Hylier waited in the stable and greeted him with a deep nod. "Where to, Your Majesty?"

"I need some time. Can you follow Moly?"

The guard glanced at the pony. "As long as she's better tempered than that yellow monster." He jerked his chin at Ragweed.

Keplan's laugh was fake in the early air. He took the long way through the city, passing through every district. War marred them all, buildings battered and no amount of sleep could remedy the fatigue on the residents' faces. Pre-dawn light turned the white stone ghostly, and Moly's hooves were muffled as they ascended. The palace was invisible through the fog, hidden until he paused in the street. The gates were shut, but the small door opened for him at his raised hand.

"Good morning, Your Majesty."

Keplan glanced at the guard, but there was no judgment in her eyes. "Good morning, Captain."

The steward appeared in the doorway as Keplan dismounted and handed the reins over. "Your chambers will be ready shortly, Your Majesty. And General Domariigo asked that I remind you to see him."

"Thank you." He paused. "I'm afraid I don't know your name."

"Master Valadai, Sire."

"Thank you, Master Valadai." Keplan rubbed the bridge of his nose and went to find An'thor. Light glimmering under the door told him the general had either been up since the night before or risen in the dark, early hours. He suspected it was the former. The door jerked open after a single knock.

An'thor's face was haggard, but his eyes bright. "Wardyn, glad to see you made it back. I was beginning to worry."

"Best get used to that. Worrying after me, I mean. I'm told people are supposed to worry about a king." He offered a smile he did not feel. "Any word from Dorcal? And have you eaten yet? I'm starved."

"Nothing yet. I just ordered mine, but they always send too much." The general's eyes lingered on Keplan's throat. "Did you rest a bit, at least?"

Keplan peered in the mirror. A love-bite marked the side of his neck along his collar. "Dammit."

"It's cold enough to warrant a scarf." An'thor did not meet his eyes for a moment. "I trust that was goodbye?"

Keplan raked a hand through his hair. "I suppose it has to be. I'm not an idiot. I know noble-commoner love stories are the plots of tragedies."

"I think one commoner is enough to grace the palace halls for now. I'm not doubting your discretion, but you will be watched more than most monarchs." The general finally looked him in the eye. "Let's keep the drama and scandal to a minimum, shall we?"

Keplan did not want to think about it. "Where's Blackhouse?"

"You need to start using titles. He'll be along shortly to go over the declarations. I'm told they found you a room."

Keplan hummed in response. He did not really care about new rooms or decorated writs. He wanted to be sure the commander agreed. He wanted to be certain civil war was through. "What did you do with the heirs in the prison camps?"

"Detainment, please. You make me sound like a savage."

Keplan looked up, ice-chip eyes boring into the black pits in An'thor's face. He smelled the tang of blood, felt the chill of night, heard the rasp of whispers. "Aren't you?"

An'thor's hand stilled its tracing of the desk's edge. "I don't know what you mean."

Keplan allowed himself a faint smile. "You'll learn it's very hard to lie to me. Most folk, if they think they've tricked me, it's because I allow them." He shrugged. "I'll figure it out, but it's nothing to waste my energy on today."

"Figure what out?" Daymir asked as he entered.

"Why our dear general smells of blood." Keplan offered a quick wave.

The new regent snorted and dropped a stack of papers on the desk. "You're probably mistaking the mixture of liquors coming off his breath."

Keplan laughed, but he felt the itch of An'thor's eyes on his back. *You've not shown all your hand, and there are many cards yet in this deck.* He shuffled through the parchment Daymir brought. The original declaration of Keplan's inheritance sat at the top. Below it were writs declaring Keplan and Daymir's new titles. "Do I just sign these? Like I'm buying a horse?"

"And seal them, with your signet," Daymir added.

"Which he doesn't have, Daymir," An'thor reminded. "The boy doesn't have a house or rank or anything really. Aside, of course, from His Majesty the King." The general sighed. "We'll deal with that later. The name and the Consulate's seals are the most important at this juncture." An'thor dipped a quill and handed it to Keplan. Metal scratching parchment was the only sound for several moments.

Ink's sheen became a matte black as it dried. Valadai's rasping voice interrupted the rushing in Keplan's ears. "Your Majesty, Commander Dorcal sent his response."

Keplan turned with a frown. "And?"

A soldier stepped around the steward and held his hand out to the young man. "We found this shot into the wood of the harbor barricade." Crumpled in his hand was a length of tattered, white fabric. It appeared to have once been a sailor's left sleeve. The wider edge was purple with blood.

Φ

Raven slumped against the rail of his ship. Everywhere he smelled the sea, the stench of unwashed sailor, the bitter tang of doom. He wanted to believe An'thor saw sense. He knew the general for too many years to actually think it was possible. He was as idealistic as the commander was stubborn. His battleship dwarfed the approaching craft, but the latter did not bear scars and stains from the last weeks. The boy in the bow raised his flags. *Come aboard.*

He shoved himself upright, head too heavy to lift. Pitching his weary voice over the snap of rigging and groaning wood grew harder every day. "Lower rowboat!" Raven tugged his helm on and gestured for two of his sailors to join him. They swung over the rail into a rowboat.

The mariner in the fore scraped her salt-caked hair into a horsetail. "How could Master Blackhouse get into the city without the general knowing, sir?"

"I don't think he could, Tzane. This looks like the outcome we wished for, but my gut tells me a piece is missing."

"They were blasting us a day ago. You don't call for ceasefire at dawn an hour after a fire-volley unless something changes." The Commander's squire was clever — sometimes too clever — but young.

"The smallest things can end war."

"And start one." Tzane shrugged into her cloak, brown eyes fixed on the small ship as they drew up alongside. There was the expected cluster of clerks and no small number of guards. Daymir himself stood by the cabin's door. He waited for Raven to straighten his stained clothes.

"Welcome, Commander Dorcal. It's been a long time."

Raven bowed. "Longer for some, I'd imagine. I'm glad to see you well."

"Thank you for meeting with me on such short notice."

"How'd you get into the city?"

Daymir's gaze moved past the commander, and Raven followed it. The two Head Consulates stood in the cluster of clerks both dressed in full state robes. "I was invited."

Raven's brows lifted. "I'm surprised the general came to his senses." *Or it's a trap and you've walked to your death.* It was more likely than he cared to admit. That an act of war during ceasefire was treasonous did nothing to calm his nerves. He had no doubt An'thoriend committed more war crimes than legends told.

"Please, join us."

Raven followed them into the cabin. It was brightly lit. The obvious difference between his battered clothing and their own was not lost on him. *He's making a statement.* The clerks and Head Consulates ranged about the desk. Daymir perched on the edge before gesturing to the chair before him.

"I can stand, thank you."

"Suit yourself." He held up a paper. "Do you know what this is?"

"It's a letter. Judging by the seals, one I sent to you declaring my side of the disagreement."

"It's war, Commander, call it by its proper name." Daymir stared at the paper, though his eyes were still, not actually reading the words. "A line here says: 'I swear to uphold your wishes for the crown, uphold the wishes of the true king.'"

"It's true, my lord." Something settled in Raven's gut. Every instinct told him this was not the peace he wanted.

"You swear to uphold my wishes for the kingdom, for the Crown and accept the king's command?" Daymir's eyes bore into his, darker than Raven ever remembered them.

"What is your command?" Raven hated the falter of his voice.

"Stand down." The voice was not Daymir's but another, much younger one. It rattled from behind the gathered officials. A boy waved aside the clerks. His clothes and long brown hair were older styles. His blue eyes were manic. He lifted his chin but did not stand. "Commander Dorcal. I don't believe we've met." He made no move to offer a hand. "My name is Keplan Wardyn. I'm told you knew my parents, even traveled with them for a time." The set of his face, the ice-chip glint in his eyes, spoke of something sickening in his blood. "My mother ripped the blood from her enemies, and my father opened the earth beneath their feet. Surely you remember."

Raven's stomach writhed. The boy before him was not human. *Run. Run while you can.*

"I see you understand me." Keplan jerked his chin at Daymir. "You requested Blackhouse's presence in the city weeks ago. You realize doing so is a direct violation of a royal decree. You would be an accomplice of treason. I doubt I have to explain the punishment."

"He's here now, without my urging. He, too, would suffer the fate of a traitor." He loathed the weakness falling from his mouth.

Daymir glanced at the commander, eyes narrowed. "You change your song rather swiftly, sir."

Keplan dismissed the impending argument. "Master Blackhouse was invited expressly by the Heir Apparent of Athrolan. His titles, the ones he still wished for, have been reinstated. Added to them, Regent of the Crown for a year's time. I repeat," all mockery disappeared from the boy's face, "stand down."

The commander faltered, dark eyes scanning the men before him. "What will become of me?"

"House arrest for the time being," Daymir explained. "Further orders will come."

Raven was a man of might, of battle. And he knew when he was beaten. Keplan's expression was stone in the face of Raven's frustration. He glanced at his two subordinates and gestured at the ground. "Lay down arms. Shipman Tzane, send word to the fleet." His raised hands shuddered and he dropped to his knees. "I surrender."

CHAPTER EIGHTEEN

The 17th Day of Lumord, 1272
The City of Mirik

"A BIRD'S COME FROM Athrolan." Alleanthus shoved the door shut with his boot as he peered at the letter.

Bren glanced up curiously. "From Keplan?" He and Kemmer often shared her larger study. Their desks faced each other, separated only by a low bookcase.

"If it'll distract me from writing this missive, I welcome it." Kemmer rubbed her eyes. "I'll go mad if I have to explain how to start a war one more time."

Alleanthus expression tightened. "It's for Father, actually."

Bren frowned when Alleanthus met his curious gaze. "What is it?"

Kemmer glanced up, brows curling together as she echoed his question.

Bren recognized the plain seal as Reka's and grabbed the parchment from his son's hands. She never sent word by letter unless it was urgent. Word of mouth was far safer.

The words were a dozen leaded blows to his gut. "It's from Monareka. Keplan's King of Athrolan. Or will be." He met his wife's eyes across the desks.

"Bren, I am so sorry."

"I'll go. I have to. Not just as ambassador, but as family. Fates know he won't tell his parents." Bren scraped his fingers through his gray hair. He hated the relief he felt that Keplan was safe from being used as a tool of war, but he hated his disappointment more.

"You could write if you want," Kemmer offered.

"I don't want." He rose. "Where's Azimir? We're leaving on the next ship."

"You're taking him with you?" Kemmer frowned, putting aside her work for the first time all afternoon.

He glanced up at her. "I remember suddenly being in charge of a nation. What I needed most was a friend."

Her eyes softened. "Come say goodbye, please, before you leave."

He ignored Alleanthus's grimace when he bent and kissed her. "Always." He shoved his son's shoulder as he passed. "Soon you'll have a wife, and I will make the faces at your ridiculousness." The mirth fell from his features as he strode from the study. As much as he jested with his family and claimed to understand, the soldier's ideals in him burned at An'thor's plan, and Keplan had stumbled into it. He took the stairs quickly, though not several at a time as he once could. Distraction made him rude, and he shouldered into Azimir's room after pounding the door once. "Azi, get your things."

His son scrambled from his bed, naked despite the early evening hour. "Da! What'd you want? And can't you knock?"

"I did."

"And wait until I answer?"

Bren's gaze swiveled to the privy door, behind which came a muffled giggle. "Toar. Get whomever that is out and pack your things."

Azimir bundled the sheets around his waist and dodged about the room collecting his clothes and a green gown Bren assumed belonged to the resident of the privy. "Why?"

"Keplan's made a terrible mistake."

Azimir frowned and turned. "What did he do? Why am I packing?"

Bren stepped from the room, calling over his shoulder as he shut the door. "You can ask him yourself. We're going to Athrolan."

Φ

The 19th Day of Lumord, 1272
The City of Ceir Athrolan, Athrolan

Keplan watched night fall away. Darkness slid down the city's pale walls like rain sluicing from the hills. The palace rumbled into wakefulness, servants beginning the rounds of tidying halls and chambers. Across the palace he presumed the Council Hall was being prepared. Sheaves of paper filled the scribes' desks. Perhaps the monarch's chair finally warranted polishing. Double guards flanked the commander's rooms. Keplan drew a deep breath of the tiny corner of peace he found. The glass ceiling of the palace greenhouse afforded him a clear view of the mid-morning sky. The birds housed there were awake as long as he, it seemed. It was not the earth and trees of home, but the scent of wet earth and growth calmed his mind.

Bells tolled, and he forced himself to rise. He was among the first to arrive the day before. Today he would be the last. He rolled his shoulders and patted down the long coat. Mirik's tunic-and-breeches became popular among Athrolan's nobles in the last two years, but Keplan suspected he balked tradition enough for one week. *Besides, thousands of buttons make me look less like a starved common boy.*

He nodded to the guards he passed at each doorway. Nerves surged in his gut each time they responded with "Good morning, Your Majesty."

A young woman in the mourning black of the household staff greeted him at the door to the Council Hall before swinging open the door. "His Majesty the King."

Keplan breezed in, forcing his steps to be assured. "Good morning, consulates." He took his seat without preamble and gestured for them to do the same. "I trust you are as eager as I to begin discussions for the future." He folded his hands. "I would like to address, first, the current status of our divided military. Most notably, what to do with Commander Dorcal."

"'Do with' him? Surely you intend to strip his titles," An'thor suggested.

Keplan's brows rose. "I was hoping to hear each of the consulate's concerns."

"He sees reason, I believe. He was afraid—as many of us were," a countess argued. She addressed Daymir, her gaze unwilling to rest on Keplan for longer than a moment at a time. "He is a good man, one who always put Athrolan at the forefront of his concerns."

"Who are you implying didn't?" An'thor asked.

Keplan caught the sharp bite of alcohol and concealed his sigh. The general was as much a concern as the commander, but one that would keep. "One of the admirals would take his place, I assume."

"Unless you want to give the position to a little friend who's never seen aw a boat." The biting tone came from Delle.

Keplan did not bother to hide his laugh. "Yes, I see the metaphor, Duchess. While I'm at it, perhaps I'll do away with all of you and find new lords and ladies to surround myself with friends instead of enemies." His tone turned somber. "Considering I appear to be the only one taking my role seriously here, it might do Athrolan some good."

Silence followed his words and he gestured to the room. "Now, if we could continue without barbed comments, I would appreciate your thoughts on appointing a new commander."

"There is something to consider, Your Majesty." The Head of Guilds leaned forward. "Athrolan has relied on the trade of her wool and ore for generations, but with Mirik's navy growing, and Berrin exploration increasing, we might be pressed to find new commodities. Even in war, trade is lifeblood. Perhaps Commander Dorcal would be more suited to something in that sector."

Keplan hummed in response. The idea had merit. The room buzzed with opinions, and through the veil of fear, he caught a glimmer in their voices.

Hope.

After the last Consulate spoke, he rested the embroidered sleeves of his jacket on the table, gloved hands clasped before him. "I see we are working toward the common goal of Athrolan's safety. Dorcal's fear is a pebble perched on the mountain of his stupidity, forgotten until it begins a landslide."

Keplan shook his head. "I don't intend to have a Commander who starts civil war rooted in fear. That said, he is a valuable strategist, and I do not wish to exile the man, for he, too, has Athrolan deepest in his heart. I wish to have him under house arrest until the end of the year. We need to be certain he will not try to raise a new rebellion. After that time we will address his new role. In the meantime, I wish those officers supporting him also be removed from their stations and arrested similarly. Their subordinates will take their places for now. Any naval order will come directly from myself or Blackhouse." He looked to Daymir. "Do you agree?"

"I do, Sire. Perhaps we could address the next few months of your reign. A monarch goes on Progress his first year."

"Progress?" A snort rose from the table, but he could not pinpoint its source.

"A monarch travels the kingdom to meet subjects, see how the land fares. It boosts economy, morale, so forth." The Head of Nobles offered. "Something to look forward to, for the common folk. When your parents arrive to aid you, they would go too."

Buzzing filled Keplan's mind, and his mouth tasted of blood. "If you wanted them as monarchs, you will be disappointed. The regency ends in a year. If I went on Progress then, when I am fully King, would that be acceptable?"

"Yes, sire, however, we still must announce you, officially. We were on the brink of war. Half the time I don't believe we're through with it, and I imagine the cities to the south feel the same." The Viscount from Ceir Bodian rubbed a hand over his face.

"Many question the validity of your claim. They will need as much convincing as we did."

Keplan shook his head. "I understand this world in a way many do not. Perhaps that is what General Domariigo saw, and His Highness Regent as well. Each person has different doubts for different reasons, and thus I will address each as they come. We're to have the coronation in a few days. Use that as our declaration. You want something the city, the nation can see?" He gestured to the smoking, tattered city outside the window. "Lift the curfew. Remove the blockade. Send news that our war is over and announce the coronation. Other missives will follow with details, but I promise no one cares about those. Phrase it as happy news."

Admiral Fess frowned at him. "And is it? Happy, I mean?"

"I don't know what you see outside your windows, up late at night, unable to sleep. I don't know what you see in the rolling hills to the south or the vast forest between here and Ban. But I see sorrow. I see a kingdom that forgot what she was. And I see how far we could go if given half a chance and a little bit of hope." Keplan forced his hands into stillness. "War is over. A new king has come. In the legends, that is always happy. And, as it's been mentioned, I am born of legends." *Even if I don't feel it. Even if legends aren't ever as real as we wish.*

He turned to the Head of Nobles. "Lord Tevon, send writs to each of the cities and townships, along with invitations to the coronation. Most will be unable to make it in time, but please stress recovering from the past year is most important. General, open the gates and drop the watch down to single on the walls, double on the palace. Someone let the navy come home to berth. I think it is about time we let the city breathe. Tomorrow we continue our work. I look forward to hearing your suggestions." He nodded to them and strode from the room.

Daymir caught him in the hall, his quiet words drowned by the swell of voices in Keplan's wave. "That was perhaps the shortest first Council of a king's reign."

Keplan winced. *Did I forget something?* "It took the entire morning. You can't stay in there and keep them from plotting to murder me?"

"They won't murder you. Besides, An'thor is your ally as much as I am. This next month will be hard, for the

Council and for you." He offered a smile. "I suggest you take advantage of whatever moments you have to yourself."

Keplan laughed and turned to find Valadai by the door. "Master Valadai, are my chambers ready?"

"Yes, Your Majesty. Would you like me to show you to them?"

No, I'd rather burn them to the ground and go back to bed in the Hare. "Please."

The palace's halls radiated from the dome of the central ballroom and throne room. The first floor, at level with the courtyard and entrance, held staterooms, libraries, training rooms. The lower storey, built into the ground on the level of the gardens and stables, consisted of higher officers' quarters, and those of the squires and pages. Valadai led Keplan to the third floor, where nobles', consulates', and highest officers' chambers were. *And those of the royal family and one stable boy.* The royal chambers themselves took up an entire corner of the palace, still boarded up by An'thor's orders. Keplan was led to the western wing. A set of guards stood outside the plain door and bowed when they appeared.

"I hope the rooms are to your satisfaction. Let us know if there is anything else you'll need, Your Majesty."

Keplan barely heard the man through the rushing in his veins. He turned the key waiting in the lock, slipping it into his coat as he stepped through the door. The first room was a foyer, decorated with portraits of nobles Keplan did not recognize. *What's wrong with a proper mountain landscape?* The first of the two doors led to a parlor boasting a tall window and several chairs and couches. Keplan doubted he could fill the room with all his friends and allies combined. The second room off the foyer was smaller, a rich study equipped with a broad desk and more shelves than Keplan knew what to do with. Here, at least, artwork was limited to a portrait of the late queen and a seascape.

Through the study lay his bedroom. The canopied bed crouched against the wall opposite a bank of windows. When he pulled back the velvet curtains, he realized two of the windows were doors to a narrow, planted balcony. Noon sun cast the barracks and Noble Quarter in white and gray. Warm autumn air muted the noise of the palace. Save for the distant clacking of training, even the city was quiet. His fingers combed the stiff vegetation of a potted rosemary. Here was his solace.

The deep bell atop the palace tower clanged, another joining it, and another, and another. Every clock tower in every square and circle of each district exploded into sound. Brassy fanfare announced a monarch returned from battle. Keplan braced himself on the balcony's wall, hands gripping the worn stone. Already the burble of speculation of the streets beyond trickled into his mind. *Let them gossip. Let them make a thousand stories.* Along the horizon, the ships' sails unfurled, billowed into fat bellies to carry them home. Patrols returned from along the hills, weapons cupped under relaxed arms. For the first time in weeks, the gates opened.

Perhaps it was in his mind, but somewhere, he thought he heard a cheer.

When wind had whipped most of the warmth from his body, he traded his fine coat for another, more simple linen one. His tiny garden may have brought peace, but he still took the longest route to Daymir's room.

"You have yet to run away," Daymir remarked when Keplan entered.

"I can't tell if you sound disappointed." He took the seat across from the regent. One leg bounced, and his hand tapdanced over the chair's arm. "Blackhouse, it takes years to learn to rule a kingdom. I have wisdom others don't and the weight of two terrible bloodlines, and I won't be on my own for another year. But all these people doubting my abilities — what if they're right? What happens then?"

"Then Athrolan falls into chaos."

"So, what was the point of An'thor finding me at all?"

"Because it might not." Daymir stared into the fire. "You're clever, you're powerful, and you have a good, honest heart. I've got to believe you'll succeed."

Keplan looked away. *Clever, certainly, and powerful, perhaps someday. But honest?* "How can I fit a decade of learning into a few months?"

"Even with the general and myself helping you, and all the consulates, you will need to focus, to hone your mind. Your priorities must shift to allow Athrolan to be at the top of the list."

"I know."

"I'll see about that." Daymir flipped open a canvas-bound notebook. "You and I will meet twice a week. We will find tutors for the subjects in which I am not proficient — dancing, music, history and such. Every two weeks begins with an audience. Do you know what that is?"

"When the cityfolk come to discuss issues?"

"Basically. You will hear them, as will the House of Commons and House of Nobles. Both are made up of a score of Consulates, some of whom advise you, and the Heads. The next day you meet with each House separately, and then the day after that you meet with the Council together, to come to decisions on the matters brought before you. Most can be decided during the audience and without any involvement on your part — the guards and District Masters take care of most small things before the complaints even reach the palace."

Keplan rested his head in his hands. "Fates, this is complicated."

Daymir chuckled, though the sound was far from humorous. "The other days you will take lessons in History, Government, Economics, and Politics."

"Will I learn a weapon?"

"Not unless you wish to on your own time."

Keplan massaged the dyed skin under his gloves. "Perhaps eventually."

"Have you any skill with one?"

"Bow, yes. For hunting."

"Then practice archery at your own will." Daymir's eyes paused on what looked like a letter. "Ambassador Barrackborn arrived this morning with his younger son. He's not pleased."

"I never thought he would be." Keplan looked away. "I did not know Mirik was so close."

"An ambassador's ship is swift, and I suspect the general sent his letter first."

"I'm certain the Ambassador has an extensive network that helps him acquire information." Keplan remembered the alleyway where he met the spy master. *I'll need my own network soon enough.* "Is that all?"

Daymir sighed. "One more thing—have you spoken to your parents?"

Guilt churnned in his chest. *What could I say? How do I explain the events of the past months?* "No, not lately. I know I ought to, but I simply don't know where to begin. And the longer it goes the more difficult the words are."

Daymir looked at his hands. "I don't have children, but I know they would be looking for you, hoping to find you, protect you."

Keplan caught an echo, something flashing across the regent's eyes. "Did they write to you?"

"No, but I think you will find they understand the inibility to write difficult letters." Daymir cleared his throat. "I'll see you tomorrow morning, before the meeting?"

Keplan nodded and rose.

"Speaking of your friends from before, and," Daymir did not meet his eyes, "the bar in the slums and the proprietors there."

"What of it?" Keplan was not aware Daymir knew of Firas.

"It'll need to end."

Keplan's chest tightened. "It already has. Don't worry." He turned back from the door. "I may not have been raised a noble, Blackhouse, but I'm quite familiar with loneliness." Keplan slipped from the regent's chambers without further farewell. He was already recognized on sight, and a guard fell in behind him. The time would come, he was certain, that every step would be followed by attendants and clerks and guards. He shuddered and buttoned the front of his coat before stepping into the chill of the road to the ambassador's manor. It would only grow harder to talk to them, and if he had an afternoon free of duty, it ought to be used for apologies.

Azimir thundered down the stairs when the footman announced Keplan's arrival. "I wondered when you'd come visit." He spared a glance for Keplan's clothes. "Since when do you like traditional fashion? Mirrel paying you more?"

Keplan laughed. The fact that Azimir thought palace finery could be bought with a bar boy's highest wage told him much about the boy's understanding of money. "Not exactly." He turned back to the steward. "Would you tell Ambassador Barrackborn I'm here and would like to talk at his earliest convenience?"

The steward bowed himself down the hall, Azimir watching him go. "What do you need to talk to Pa about?"

Keplan nodded to the parlor. "Mind if we sit down? I've had a long few days."

"I imagine. I'm surprised at the cease-fire. Part of me wondered if it would go on forever. If this was the new war, stacked atop ours with Ban." He led the way into the room and collapsed into a chair. He tossed Keplan a pear and chose an apple for himself. "Why are you here?"

Keplan turned the fruit in his hands, suddenly without appetite. Azimir didn't know. Brentemir had not told him. For whatever cruel series of reasons, he forced Keplan to tell him himself. *How do you even keep that a secret?*

"We're only here for a week, I heard. You should come back to Mirik with us when we go, though. I'm sure my father will let you."

"I don't think I can." He looked down.

"Of course, the Hare. But surely Firas could spare a day or evening."

The words stung more than Keplan liked, and he paced along the table. "I can't go to Mirik because I have duties here, now, new ones—"

"Keplan?" Brentemir's voice boomed through the foyer, and for a moment Keplan could not tell if it was in anger or fear. The creased brow and finger-tangled hair said it was the latter.

Keplan straightened his shoulders and raised a gloved hand. "Ambassador." He forced his tone to be level. *This is good practice.*

Brentemir's expression changed from confusion to sorrow. His shoulders sagged, and he dipped his head. "Your Majesty."

"What?" Azimir whirled to look at Keplan. "What does he mean? What new duties?"

"I wish it could be different, but my dreams are less important than the safety of a kingdom." He looked over at

Azimir. "The queen named my mother's child heir. And I've accepted."

"We were gone just a few weeks. How did all this come to pass?" the ambassador asked.

Azimir waved his father's question away. "But this means you'll stay in the city, right? And we can see each other more often?"

"He'll have a lot of new tasks, planning balls, heading councils, waging wars."

Keplan winced at the bitterness. "Or avoiding them," he corrected. "I didn't give up so much, only to descend into war again." Later he would think on what that meant for Athrolan's relationship with Ban or her alliance with Mirik. Now he just needed to solidify the tentative peace his presence brought. "I might have, at first, but I cannot focus on that now." Keplan looked down at the forgotten fruit in his hand, letting Brentemir process the last few moments in the silence that followed his words.

"Can you give us a minute, Azimir?" Brentemir's frown softened. "We can talk over drinks, as a family. We're still family."

Keplan wondered who Brentemir was trying to convince. "Alright." The silence continued upstairs, interrupted only by the clink of glasses while Bren poured them both a glass of liquor.

Keplan took a wary sniff before tasting. It was acrid and bitter, but grounded his senses. He moved to stare out the window.

Bren leaned on the sill beside him. "I remember my few moments of peace after I chose to take up Mirik during the Gods' War. Am I intruding on yours?"

Keplan glanced at him, shrugged and looked back at the sky. "No. Sometimes the quietest times for me are when someone talks. There are so many voices in my head, I can't even hear my own if I'm alone."

"I've got a fair few in my head too — my father's. Alea's. My captain when I was younger. Kemmer's." His gaze slid over to Keplan and then back to the city. "I know, that's not what you meant. Whatever you feel and hear is vastly different. The thing is, Keplan, that's the case for everyone. No one in this world feels what I do. About some things, perhaps, but we are, none of us, the same. It might be the one thing we all share." He ran a slow hand through his hair, fingers a ponderous echo of the excitement he once had. "How did you get here?" He waved a hand between them. "Standing here beside me about to be King."

"Honestly, I just kept making hard choices. Some didn't even feel like choices, but I guess I could have always run."

"And Blackhouse truly won't take up the throne?"

"He'll be Regent for a year."

"Even still, I'd expect him to retreat to his manor again or take the throne. He's not the man to half-finish a job."

"He has good reasons."

Brentemir's eyes narrowed. "Good enough to thrust an inexperienced boy onto a throne he doesn't want?"

"Shadows follow everyone, Barrackborn. If you want to know more, you can ask him yourself. Besides," Keplan glanced over, letting his carefully maintained façade of earnest kindness fall, "I'm not just any boy, am I?" He felt the burn in his skin, the ice in his veins hinting at his parents' powers.

Brentemir sighed in response. "Then I have some advice for you. Before I took Mirik over, I still wanted to be a soldier, but it killed me watching her fall to ruin. Tzatia herself rebuked me — before the whole Council, to my horror — and said I could not have the glory and power of a king with the responsibility of a soldier." He poured himself another glass and topped off Keplan's. "Stop being the boy. Stop being whatever mess An'thor wants you to be. You're stuck on the edge of so many things—the throne, manhood, sanity, empowerment. Stop waiting. Leap from that edge, and let yourself fly."

Keplan forced speech past the sudden lump in his throat. Brentemir understood more than he expected. The idealism was different, but he forgot the man walked in these same boots twenty years before. "Feels like falling right now."

"And it will. Sometimes I still feel that way. But then you'll look back and realize you haven't smashed on the rocks below."

Keplan nodded. "Thank you."

"The worst part was learning to compromise," Bren confided, peering at some distant point past the horizon. Perhaps it was Mirik.

"The worst part is leaving a life and people I love." Keplan finished off his drink. He was aware of the weight of Brentemir's gaze. "I'm afraid I'm giving up sanity. Being with Firas brings peace I haven't felt in a long while."

"The bartender?"

Keplan glanced over. "Yes."

"I had someone like that during the war. I understand."

"Your Spy Master."

Brentemir's frown was sudden. "Who told you that?"

Keplan shrugged. *Let him think I just heard rumors.* "You had to give up that relationship, though?"

Bren ran a hand over his face with a sigh. "Not because of appearances. She wasn't interested in anything more, and frankly Kemmer was entrancing."

"Right." Keplan rolled his neck. He was not particularly comfortable hearing the details of the ambassador's love affairs. "I was told to end things between us. I've already said goodbye." The words felt strange in his mouth. "I understand, of course, and know the reasons. Doesn't make it easier."

"No, it doesn't." Brentemir drew a shuddering breath. "I don't agree with your choice, but I made the same one. Perhaps that's why it's so hard. But if you need anything in the way of advice, I have a lot of years as uncle to make up for."

For once Keplan's smile felt like a proper one. "I'm sure I'll make use of it."

Brentemir nodded to the lower storey. "Perhaps you ought to talk to your cousin a bit. He's confused, I think."

"Perhaps you should have told him," Keplan countered before finishing his drink and setting the glass aside. "I know this isn't what you wanted."

A shadow flitted across the ambassador's face. "I'm sorry, too."

Keplan pulled the door to and turned. Azimir stood at the top of the stairs. His dark face was hard with bridled hurt. "Did you know, when you befriended me?" Azimir asked.

Keplan's fingers tightened on the banister. This did not sound like a conversation he was interested in having.

Azimir blundered on. "You said I looked interesting when we first met. Me, out of an entire city? I'm flattered, but there are far more interesting people. You said you kept my company because you knew nothing about me. You, who reads secrets like a farmer reads the weather. It's simply not possible." Azimir's voice was low and would have been angry, were it not for the vulnerability. "I want to be your friend because you're funny, if odd. I don't have many friends in the city who aren't over-bred nobles. But I can't understand why you want to be mine. Unless it was because you knew who you were, and you wanted access to the general, to the commander — "

"Azimir, let him be." Brentemir's voice was firm, fatigue replaced with compassion. He stood in the study door, cloak in hand. "I promise he had no idea. I saw the betrayal on his face when he discovered it."

Keplan raised a hand, stopping the rest of the ambassador's words. "I am friends with you because you didn't care where I came from or why I have scars. You are filled with hope that I can't find. You remind me I'm just seventeen, and sometimes I forget that." *And because I wanted Ban to burn.* He offered Azimir his hand. "Besides, now we're family."

Azimir shook it, but his expression remained reserved. Their goodbyes were brief. The evening closed around Keplan as he slipped out. He wished he could be honest with Azimir, but as much as they were cousins, Azimir was not ready for the truth. Keplan's answer was a pleasant thought, and for a while, he would let even himself believe the lie.

Φ

The 20th Day of Lumord, 1272
The City of Ceir Athrolan, Athrolan

Bright colors writhed together, mourning blacks and grays doffed for brilliance, and yet the faces bore the lines and exhaustion from war and uncertainty. The bells were silent. The streets were full, the palace brimmed with guests. An'thor paced another round of the palace before returning to Keplan's room. He nodded at the guards flanking the door. "It's almost time." He stepped through the foyer and into Keplan's chambers. Two serving men offered various adornments while a tailor finished the hem of his breeches.

She glanced up at the young man. "I'll be just a moment, Your Majesty. You seem to have grown since we took your measures."

An'thor met Keplan's panicked eyes and waved the servants away. "When you're through, Miss, I need a word in private with His Majesty."

She glanced at Keplan, who nodded. His face was sallow and his lips thin. He stared at some invisible point on the wall until the woman rose and curtsied her way out.

"You look like you're going to vomit."

"I've already done so twice, and I doubt there's anything left in me." He took a tottering step from the dressing stool.

An'thor caught the man's arm and pressed him into a seat before calling for bread and wine. He sat on the edge of the desk.

Keplan's bloodshot eyes roved up to An'thor's black ones. "The words I'm supposed to say, they sound stupid. The promises I'm supposed to make sound hollow."

An'thor shrugged. "And they will be. But starting tomorrow, you will make them not hollow, not stupid. Today just worry about saying them." The bread and wine arrived, and An'thor tore a piece free. "Eat this. Small bite, then a sip. You need food in your gut if you don't want to faint in front of all your new subjects. What are you going to promise?"

"I don't know." Keplan winced as An'thor smeared faint pink makeup on his cheeks.

An'thor stepped back, eyeing his handiwork. "At least you don't look dead." He levered Keplan to his feet. "Whatever you say, mean it. You've told us many pretty things. You stormed in here with ideas and fire and desperation. Don't lose it yet."

"I'm trying. Without burning out, that is."

The general watched Keplan peer into the mirror, remembering a different coronation, a terrified, young woman.

"Now you're the one who looks ill," the boy remarked. The reflection of his colorless eyes met An'thor's. "Regretting your support already?"

An'thor snorted at the wry comment and made a shooing motion. "Take a moment alone, breathe. We'll fetch you shortly."

"You're not afraid I'll escape out the window?"

"Your father did that frequently, but I think the threat of civil war is enough." An'thor backed out of the room, catching Valadai on his way past the foyer. "Quarter of an hour?"

"Yes, general. And the guards?"

"Full guard on the palace, double on the throne room. Entourage has double for the ride into the city." They had gone over the plans four times in the past twenty-four hours, but nothing relieved the knot in his gut. Seven people awaited him outside Keplan's chambers. Fess winked, new Commander's badge glinting over her left breast. "Almost."

He grinned back and took up his place beside her. Keplan would walk behind them, followed by the Heads of the Houses of Nobles and Commons. The whole was surrounded by four guards. *And I hope to the buried gods four's enough.* He already silently gave thanks that coronation finery allowed the carrying of weapons for those within the royal entourage. Fess alone bristled with blades and armor, mail showing through the splits in her sarafan.

The palace shook with the sound of bells. Valadai rapped on the door. "Your Majesty, it's time." He paused, then knocked again.

Keplan burst through the door a moment later. His hair was no longer in a horsetail, but tidy. "Sorry, I'm alright." He slid into place, and An'thor glanced back.

"You have no need to apologize, Your Majesty. Athrolan turns on your clock now." He watched the boy square his shoulders and drop the wide-eyed, nervous expression.

An'thor's chest tightened as they started down the corridor. He watched half a dozen monarchs rise and fall, and Tzatia's reign was the second to break his heart. Now Keplan, young, inspired, and scared, echoed in the halls of those memories.

Φ

Hundreds of strangers turned as the ballroom doors opened. Noise and the warmth of too many people spilled out, thoughts eddying around Keplan's feet. The wine dulled the details, but snippets tangled and tripped his nervous mind.

The fanfare was bold and somber. Mourning ended with the coronation, and the crowd was brilliant blue, purple, and crisp white.

He fought the urge to check whether his embroidered tolstovka still hung straight under his fur-trimmed coat. The throne was a spot of white stone at the end of the aisle, a stone pillar just to the left held the declaration. The usual mutters of the crowd were drowned by horns, and he hoped they covered the thunder of his heart.

Too young...

Poisoned by the general....

No music was loud enough to muffle their thoughts. He tried to pull an appropriate mix of reverence and confidence onto his face. *Don't trip.* He ascended the dais,

Daymir a step behind. When he turned, the thoughts crashed against him, and he clenched his hand on the stone.

If only His Highness Blackhouse would take over....

Inhuman spawn....

So, begins Athrolan's new golden age....

He searched the crowd for whoever thought the last. The woman stood at the edge of the aisle where the folding walls of the throne room usually crossed. She offered him a smile, which he returned. Knots in his hunched shoulders loosened.

"Your Majesty," Daymir whispered.

The Head of the House of Commons knelt, opening a heavily jeweled box. The ring within was silver, newly polished, with the jagged tower wrought over of the flat face of the aquamarine. "With this ring you accept your duties as Sovereign of Athrolan, to rule with the lives and dreams of every Athrolani held over your own."

Keplan slid the ring onto his left index finger, then raised his hand. "I accept."

"General, sir." Whispering behind him cut through the reverence.

Keplan glanced back. The master of the palace guard spoke swiftly into An'thor's ear.

Keplan did not catch all the words, but "assassination" and "apprehend" were two. His heart crawled higher in his throat, and the ring bit into his fist. He caught An'thor's eyes. Soldiers' boots thudded in the hall.

An'thor shook his head slightly and jerked his chin at the crowd.

Keplan stepped up the final stair to the throne. Had he been given more time—years like Daymir, perhaps—he would have sat before the stone seat for hours before this, contemplating his future. Instead, this was his first glimpse. It was cold. Fingermarks wore into the arms. Daymir appeared from the left and took a ring from the box the head of the House of Nobles offered. He regarded it for a moment before facing Keplan. "I swear to act as Regent to Your Majesty, to guide and advise until a year's time." His voice rasped with emotion, but his raised left hand was steady. Two guards delivered a chest to the Headmen, and Daymir lifted the crown from the fur mound within.

Thank goodness I'm sitting, elsewise I'd probably faint. Blood rushing in his ears covered Daymir's footsteps and whatever traditional phrase the regent intoned as he held the rough silver over Keplan's loose hair. Keplan wondered if they weighted the crown with lead. It dragged on his skull. Daymir's hands dropped, and he stepped back, falling to his knee. "Long live the King."

Keplan drew a breath, grateful he was expected to sit for a moment. He wondered if it became a tradition after too many monarchs fainted from the nerves of coronation. When the crowd stilled, he raised his hand, heavy with the signet ring. "I swear to prepare myself for every onslaught, every challenge Athrolan will face. I swear she will not face it alone. The weight of the Crown is a heavy one, but precious to me—"

Sharp cracks echoed from the hall, followed by shouts. Keplan rose, ignoring An'thor's hissed command to stay in his seat. *I'm not running, Domariigo; stop your fussing.* He pitched his voice over the concerned mutters. "Athrolan is invaluable to me. From the moment I accepted this duty to stop the war, to keep Athrolan safe, to keep my people from harm." His throat tightened. "I love Athrolan more than I've loved anything, and I swear she will not face these uncertain times alone."

His eyes fixed on the heavy brocade of Athrolan's flag, and knelt, the bow of a peasant before liege. Fabric rustled, swords and jewels clinked as the crowd knelt. The movement swept the hall, flowing into the palace halls. "From this day forth I swear to serve Athrolan, for she is the true sovereign here."

His chest heaved, and his cheeks were abruptly wet but he was smiling. He rose, knees shaking. Daymir gestured to the aisle with a bow.

They fell in around him, escorting him from the room. This time the fanfare sounded brighter, the pace hurried. The moment the doors swung shut behind them, An'thor whirled to Valadai. "Get His Majesty to his chambers. The ride to the city will have to wait until this mess is cleaned up."

"What happened?" Keplan turned to catch An'thor's eye. Guards clogged the hallway, most with weapons drawn. Commander Fess pulled one guard aside, her voice too low to hear. "What was it?"

"An attempt, but not on your life. That's all I can tell you now." An'thor pointed down the hall. "Go rest. I'll be by in an hour to ride to the city, or I'll send a messenger if we need to postpone further."

Keplan jerked his arm from Daymir's hold. "I'm not bowing to rebels my first day."

"Your Majesty, it's not safe—"

"Horseshite, if the attempt wasn't on me, then there's no reason to wait." The scent of leather and canvas, tar and ocean barreled through his mind when he met An'thor's eyes. "Dorcal? Why would they attack their own figurehead?"

Fess raked a hand through her shorn hair. "Your Majesty, there are still two sides to this, even if they no longer war. It was one of your supporters, actually." When An'thor glared at her, she shrugged. "My brother is in the Guard. News travels."

Keplan found it hard to draw breath. Of course, one of his own supporters was capable of murder. His thoughts fell on An'thor and the scent of blood lingering around his hands. *More than one, I'd wager.* He sighed. "Very well, I could use something to eat, and I ought to find my hat."

"All waiting for you, Your Majesty." Daymir offered him a smile. "Court affairs are always late anyway. You can't get that many people organized on time."

Keplan saw the sense and wondered how many of these conversations he would have, being convinced of reasoning, waiting, acting. *"The worst part for me was learning to compromise."* He returned to his chambers, followed by Daymir and his personal guard. The food was welcome, his nerves loosening their hold on his gut for the first time in days. There was more, worse to come, he was sure, but for a moment he could relax.

He left Daymir and his guards in the parlor in favor of the quiet bedroom. His gaze traced the arching line of the aqueduct cutting between the palace and the barracks. Perhaps it was his mood, but the air was clear, the city bright. Black mourning banners were exchanged for brilliant blue or turquoise or white. *I know so little. What possessed me?* A soft knock interrupted his musings.

"The steward tells me fifteen minutes. Guards should have cleared up by then." Daymir's gaze was distant.

"Are you all right?"

"I'm anxious for Her Majesty to meet you. She'll like you, I think."

Lead thudded into Keplan's gut. "Blackhouse, I—"

"Blackhouse? Who is...?" Daymir blinked, then shook his head. "Of course. Forgive me, I was lost in my memory. A different state ride."

"Of course," Keplan echoed. *Please keep your head, just for a few months longer.* Somehow his feet carried him through the doors and into the hall lined with scribes, with servants, with every member of palace staff who managed to slip away from their duties long enough to catch a glimpse of the strange boy suddenly crowned King. A horse waited in the courtyard beside An'thor's gray charger and the various mounts of the Council and two dozen mounted guards. Keplan rested against the horse's flank under the guise of adjusting his reins while the world spun.

An'thor paused beside him. "Breathe, Wardyn."

"Right." A shuddering breath cleared his head. "Through the square and down to the docks?"

"Yes. We'll pause there, and you'll wave, smile. You'll look for all the world like a collected, clever young man." An'thor's thin lips twisted into a wry grin.

"I thought you said my best trait was honesty." Keplan's chuckle was weak, but sincere. He hauled himself into the saddle. "Where's Moly?"

"In her stall in the stables. You can't honestly expect us to let you ride through the city on a scruffy draft pony. This fellow's my re-mount." An'thor shook his head. "You need to look the part, Your Majesty." He jerked his head at the courtyard gates. "On your signal."

Keplan rolled his shoulders back. He found he was smiling and nudged his borrowed horse into a brisk walk. The weather held, despite the clouds. Bells joined the crowd's shouts, and for a moment even the thoughts were quiet. An'thor and Fess's faces were stone, eyes scanning for movement. There were more guards surrounding him than the usual Coronation Ride, but he let himself believe it was due to civil war.

Flowers and rotted fruit were tossed into their path in equal numbers. He remembered the phrase his mother murmured every morning: *Today everything begins.* Not when the crown settled on his head, or the signet ring slipped over his knuckle. Or even that moment in the bar when he watched Daymir admit to his impending madness. *Today, and every day after.* The wind rose, tugging his hair into disarray. He reached to tidy it, then gave up with a rueful grin.

Instead, he waved. "Good morning, Athrolan!"

Φ

The 22nd Day of Lumord, 1272
The City of RoBal, Ban

Maps replaced scrolls of dance patterns. Tea boxes and stylus jars weighed their edges. Rih scanned the parchment, a falcon seeking prey. Brown marked all countries, save for Ban, which was outlined in bright green. Vale was a dark afterthought far to the south, bordering the forest there, tucked between the foothills of the mountains and the older forest the Easterners called the Hartland. It was a military map, unwaxed to allow for additions. She rummaged through a basket until she found a quill and made a tick mark beside Ban for every ten thousand soldiers. She did the same for the Vales, and Mirik.

After a moment's thought, she marked Athrolan. Given their recent civil unrest and close bond with Mirik, their alliance with Ban was uncertain. *Information is important, even if we don't yet know how.* The only rumors of the newly crowned king claimed he was coddled by their general and a former heir regent. She marked the number of officers in Ban. There were more soldiers, of course, but not every woman would rise to the cause, and officers had far more wealth and resources. The Vales added another fifteen thousand. Mirik, while not an ally, could serve as a distraction. *For both our cause and the Emperor's, though. Every woman who dies for him is another woman who cannot join me.*

Ki-elte's hand tapped Ban. When Rih looked up, she smiled. "Planning an invasion?"

Panic burned along Rih's arms. She was not ready to share this with Ki-elte, to tell any one person how far this plan had already gone. *The rebellion has begun, even without my command of it.* It was a wild thing, released from her heart and thundering free. "I'm justing thinking over some news."

"War makes generals of us all. Or we'd think so. We all think we know the officers' careers better than they." Her head tilted as she signed, "What rank were you?"

"The lowest. I couldn't do many tasks they needed for higher ranks, due to my lack of hearing and their lack of accommodation. I proved valuable in other ways, but I suppose they weren't important enough to warrant a promotion."

"Depending on who you marry, you might outrank them all."

Rih shrugged. It bothered her for years, but that passed. Now she simply saw them as allies. "I need to meet with Il-fald, actually, soon."

"I could come if you needed translation."

Rih smiled but shook her head. "She knows my signs. Besides, it's nothing important." She caught Ki-elte's look of disappointment. "If you don't have a visitor this evening, perhaps we could meet and practice then. I have missed our more regular conversations over tea."

Ki-elte's lips quirked. "Why do I feel as if you're the teacher now?"

"Everyone learns from each other. We just take turns." Rih paused. "Thank you, for teaching me so much, for helping me when everything seemed so bleak."

"Thank you for breathing energy back into me." She squeezed Rih's hand and rose. "I'll leave you to your war. Tonight, though, no war, just conversation."

Rih laughed. "Agreed." She began to wrap her robe over her face, but stopped. Blues and purples were her favorite, but inspired calm and peace. *I want to inspire peace, but not yet.* When she emerged from the Hall, purple draped her red kalas, and a pale orange silk covered her head and face from dust.

Though the sun waited until noon to bare her teeth, heat rippled off the baked clay of the buildings, pulsing against her upturned face. In a few weeks, the dry season would end in a deluge. Rih smelled the barracks before she saw them: leather oil for armor, sawdust on the training courts, smoke from one of the city's only metal forges. Rih rounded the corner and jogged up the hill. It was a familiar route, but her thighs burned after disuse. The courtyard churned with activity, and Rih kept to the lee of the wall before slipping up the stairs. Il-fald's office curtain was pushed aside. Rih glanced at the lamp on the desk, lit despite the mid-morning hour. There was a common saying in the army: "War-horns only wake the gods, for no soldier sleeps before battle."

Rih knocked on the doorframe and peered inside.

Yellow sunlight silhouetted Il-fald in the single, narrow window. After a moment she turned. Her gaze was still distant, as if she returned to the room from a thousand leagues or a hundred years. Her expression brightened when she caught sight of her visitor.

"Rih!" The woman's hard arms wrapped around her.

Rih felt the rumble of more words and pulled away with a smile. "What was that? I couldn't see."

Il-fald offered a rueful grin and signed, "I'm sorry. I've been worried." She nodded at the doorway. "Want to pull the curtain? I have an hour before we run drills."

Rih shook her head. "Not here. The meditation rooms."

Il-fald's open expression faded. "Of course." She gestured for Rih to lead the way. The dozen small rooms in the basement were intended for a single person. In the wake of the Gods' War, they were place for introspection rather than actual religious meditation. At mid-morning they were deserted. The room Rih chose was lit only by a smoldering brazier in the center. A censer hung above. The gray-haired woman lit incense and settled into the traditional crouch of meditation.

Rih assumed the same stance, after a brief tussle with her skirts. She caught the mirth crinkling Il-fald's eyes. "I'm still not used to these."

Il-fald's smile bloomed. "Why are you here?"

Rih pulled out her tablet. Il-fald may know many signs, but this was not a time to risk miscommunication. The danger of misreading lips was large enough.

> *I met her. And I need your help. Rather, the help*
> *of any woman you trust. There is a message I need sent*
> *to the frontlines. I'm told a march is headed there soon.*
> *War is beginning.*

The alliance was tucked into a crack in the wood of her desk and nothing was worth the risk of carrying it with her.

"Was she sympathetic? War began a long time ago, ever since Mirik's upheaval." Il-fald often spoke aloud as well as signed.

Rih pressed two fingers to her lips to silence the older woman. She wrote another line and handed her the tablet.

> *She was. I don't speak of our war with Mirik,*
> *though I think that has a part to play. If the gods still*
> *walked, I would say it was their will. And for all his*
> *parading, His Eminence is not a god. Who wins wars?*

Il-fald's writing was careful, the letters simple.

The larger army, or so we are taught to believe. Though I believe it is the smarter one. Or the one that comes as a surprise.

Rih penned the next line, surprised to see her hands were steady.

And how many soldiers do we have compared to officers?

The training master rocked back on her heels. Her dark eyes fixed on the censer, brows twisting as she put together the meaning of the younger woman's words. Her shaking fingers were clumsy as she signed, "Treason."

Rih shrugged. "We have the larger army. Many may not realize it, but we also have strategists, politicians, spies. We have spies in every man's bed, politicians in every court and brothel of our allies. We have strategists on every street." Her grin bloomed brighter. "And when I'm married off, we will have one more."

Il-fald's head tilted in question.

"I marry Mirik's lord or any other, I'll be out from under the watchful eye of the Emperor. No one listens to us or cares for women's work, women's talk."

The instructor grabbed the wax tablet back.

We can't pass this along, not without being caught, Rih. Why do you think we've never rebelled before? There have been attempts, and I've led the soldiers to cull those insurrections. I'm sure there were many I don't know about too.

Rih shook her head.

Look at my hands. It took you months to learn enough to understand me. More to know enough to respond. We have that time. Time to spread the word to every corner of the empire.

"Rih, this is foolish." At least, now, Il-fald only signed, her lips sealed in a thin, nervous line. There are dozens of men, hundreds in RoBal alone, who speak your signs as well as you."

She cut off Il-fald's sign as she tried to repeat that it was treason. "What are we taught, first and foremost?"

"The Woman's Code."

Rih wrote out the lines, underlining the nation's name.

A woman has a single mind. She wakes for the Empire. She rides for the Empire. Her blood and heart and mind are Ban, breathing and alive. A woman has a single mind.

Her finger tapped the underlined word. "Ban is not our home. We are our home. Each other. We will use phrases they don't know, new signs, and others that mean more to us than to them." She held Il-fald's gaze. "If you won't, I'll find someone else. Think about it." The incense between them was nothing more than ash. She left without another word.

The sun glared from the bleached sky, baleful and sallow. Rih's heart burned brilliant in her chest, crimson as the silk wrapping her skin. She had an hour before Ki-elte returned. She swept her desk clear, save for the maps and her stylus. Then she pried the alliance document from the desk's leg and set it on the map. Usually, she ordered tea, but the energy in her veins begged for an outlet.

Her unused hearth lit quickly, and she slid the shallow black skillet over the flames. A palm-sized ball of thick yellow mare's butter softened there, joined by spicy ginger, sweet honey, sharp pepper, and the bite of coarse, pink salt.

Flat bread and chopped mango arrived a few minutes before Ki-elte, and when her tutor slid the panel aside, she was met with Rih's calm smile.

"I hope you weren't waiting long!"

Rih laughed and shook her head. "Please, sit. I regret to say I lied, though."

Ki-elte voiced a few lines, but the angle and her distraction made it impossible for Rih to see. Her tutor scooped a lump of the mixture into her mug and poured the deep brown tea over it. When she set it aside, Rih asked her to repeat herself. "Oh, I was wondering what the special occasion was, since we usually just order our meals. How did you lie?" She added a few signs to emphasize her voiced words, but it was still uncommon for her to use signs alone.

"I promised not to talk about war." Rih paused to stir her tea. "But I need you to send a message."

"To whom?"

"Every woman you know who is loyal first to her sisters, her daughters, her mother, her friends. We'll create a safe gesture, one we make with hello, when we buy our bread, when we greet our neighbor. Those we trust."

Ki-elte's eyes widened. She set aside her mug and signed, "Rih, this sounds like—"

"Read this." Rih slid the alliance across the desk. She watched anger dissolve into disbelief, into fear.

The other woman's hands shook when she laid the scroll aside. Her gaze settled on Rih's dark eyes.

"This has already begun. I'm sending word to the front lines already. This is real. And I trust you."

The last words melted the daze from the tutor's expression. Something ignited behind the honey of her irises. "Start with those who sign? What if there's a woman who we trust who doesn't know your language."

"We already speak in other languages, a dozen, a hundred, maybe. The language of color, of piercings. Symbols over stores selling herbs, horses, meat, those are languages. We start there, and they can learn enough to get by until they are able to have a private conversation. I'm not saying it will be easy."

Ki-elte's usually expressive face closed, though whether out of determination or fear, Rih did not know. "It'll take some teaching, we can work on that. We need a way to know each other on sight."

Rih's pulse caught Ki-elte's unwavering energy. It would be dangerous to have these conversations, and more dangerous still if they were had before the wrong people. "Colored sashes?"

"It would be too easy to mistrust due to fashion. You said the language of piercings. A type of ring or gem?"

"What about no gem? A simple band." Rih fiddled with the metal of her own rings.

Ki-elte whirled to stare at the door. Her face paled.

Rih grabbed her hand. "What is it?"

"I heard the floor outside creak."

Rih tossed a robe over her desk to hide what she could of the map, then shoved the door open. The hall was dark after the gleam of evening light in her room. A figure blocked the top of the stairwell. "Hello?" A tilt of her head added a question to the sign. If they spoke, she could not hear.

Ki-elte joined her at the door. Rih felt the tremor of the other woman's heartbeat against her shoulder, and the hum of words.

Il-fald staggered into the light. Tears and dirt stained her face. "I'm finished with this life, Rih." Quivering lips almost erased her words.

Rih caught the older woman up in her arms. It was a different embrace than the one they shared just hours ago. Her hand held the back of her head, memories of calluses catching on the newly shorn skin. She pulled away and beckoned her in. "We have tea." Rih prepared a third mug and pressed it into Il-fald's hands. "Why did you leave?"

"I heard someone speaking, and I lost my nerve. Today tried me. I'm not sure why, for it's the same as every other day."

Ki-elte glanced between the two of them. "I could come back another time."

"Stay," Rih insisted. "As long as Il-fald is comfortable."

Il-fald nodded, gaze falling to the mug in her hands.

"You met with someone? Your hair wasn't shaved when we visited earlier."

"I met with the baniol of the Third Arc. About a riding I trained." Her hands were bruised, one wrist swollen, but she managed to sign.

"What happened?"

"The usual—blame for the death of a hundred women who were never ready for actual battle. But this time," she shrugged, "perhaps it was because of our talk, or perhaps I simply had enough. They attacked a caravan with suspicious passengers. Suspected Vale spies. The March was slaughtered." She refused to meet Rih's eyes now. "He said it was my fault as their trainer, that they weren't ready for battle."

"That's rat piss." Rih's hands shook out the curse. "Majilah was here to meet me. And take care of a dozen other things, too, perhaps, but I have a piece of that blame, and the others she met, but not you."

"No, you don't. And neither do they. The Vales defended themselves. Baniol Evem is to blame and no one else." Her lined mouth curled into the echo of a smile. "And that's exactly what I told him."

Rih's stomach clenched. She knew how an officer would remind a subordinate who owned them. Her hand covered Il-fald's for a moment. "What can we do?"

"The tea is good." Il-fald rolled her shoulders and straightened. "And maybe you could tell me the message you wanted me to send."

"Are you sure?"

Il-fald's gray eyes burned into hers. "We're going to die anyway. They punish us, take the cost of our thoughts out on our flesh whether we think them or not."

"He's decided our fate for generations, decided when we live, where and how we die," Ki-elte spat, hastily repeating her vitriol in signs for Rih.

"Our turn." Rih's fingers tightened around both women's hands for a second, long enough to forge solidarity. Then, with Il-fald helping Ki-elte understand more complex signs, she continued, "Ki-elte will spread the word to talk to those we trust, teach them our signs. Those who are sympathetic will wear a plain gold hoop in their ear. No gem, nothing. I don't know what soldiers could wear instead, but we'll think on it. I need you to share that, concisely, to the reinforcements headed northeast. I want them to relay whom among them cannot be trusted. Names. Those who oppose us need to be placed at the forefront of the battles with Mirik. Those who prove their value should be on the roads, the better to pass news."

"You will take the troublesome and put them in a position to be killed?" Ki-elte's cheeks lost their pink for a moment.

"For now, all I want is the movement of information."

"Teaching signs will take some time," Il-fald reminded. "But we can frame it to be about secrecy in the war against

Mirik. If we're lucky, the fog of that war will disguise our own."

"Many already know signs. Enough to get by. And when you tell them, you will show them their first word." Ki-elte's grin brightened.

"And what will it be?" Il-fald asked. Her face was lined with pain, but her eyes shone with clarity.

Rih raised her clenched fist between her breasts, her hand curling up and out as it opened, as if she released a bird from the cage of her heart. "Liberty."

THE SHADOW OF MADNESS

CHAPTER NINETEEN

The 25th Day of Lumord, 1272
The Town of Tut Kunis, Berr

ALEA NEVER KNEW THERE were so many shades of colorless. The land was gray, from the steel of the sky to the iron of the mountainside, to the smoke rising from the cluster of buildings. Even the smallest was built of rough-hewn granite. The road leading up was bare rock, moss and grass clustered along the roadside and the pitiful river were a soft dove.

"Fates, can anything be more dreary?"

"I think it's beautiful."

Arman's scoff stilled in his throat, and he looked over "I suppose you would. But, truly, love, even the grass is gray."

Alea smiled. "At least there's grass at all." Cold blanketed the air and dulled everything but the dusty scent of stone and smoke from peat fires. The mountains plummeted to a plateau made of more scree than grassland. Somewhere a bird croaked. The town clustered in the crook between mountain and plain, distinguishable only by the series of flags flapping from the single post at the entrance. The timelessness crawled up Alea's spine like a chill.

The hillside was not dotted with dead trees, as she first thought, but strange sculptures. She drew up to peer at one erected just at the roadside. *Bones.* The skeleton was not recognizable as a person. Rusted wire bound sun-bleached long bones into a spindly tower. Tarsals fanned over the battered skull in a stark headdress. "Arman," Alea began.

"I know." Wind buffeted his words. His hand tightened on the reins. "We'd best keep going. No sense in staring at this thing longer than needed."

"No, look." She nodded to the skull. "Look at the plates. It's not fossilized. It's a Rakos." Sadness was a dull ache mixed with horror in her chest.

"My suggestion still stands." Arman nudged his horse into a trot. He wore an expression she had not seen since the Gods' War. Ahead, his shoulders rose in a defensive hunch. Acrid smoke and the scent of creosote drifted in his wake.

Their approach seemed to go unnoticed, but eerie quiet made Alea feel watched. They drew up at the walls. These, too, were made of bones. Flags hung in a column flanked the open gate and bore crudely painted portraits. All were plated in stone, all with green eyes. "I can't tell if this is a shrine or a threat."

"It's both." The voice rang from stone and bone. A man in the town's center was the only sign of life. His clothes were as worn as the mountains and sewn in the Berrin fashion. Faded purple of his changsang was the single spot of color. "A shrine to those who made us. A threat to those who would destroy us." He approached, apparently not willing to invite them in yet. "What do you want? No one visits. No one trades. This road only leads to cold and death."

"We're looking for someone," Arman offered. "Someone we were told is here."

"Many people live here." The man's dark eyes were wary, but not accusing.

Alea glanced at the houses, half of which seemed in disrepair or abandoned. "Many is a generous word, Master. I'm looking for the woman."

"Which woman?"

"The woman in my visions." The words clattered in the stillness, and Alea brushed mental fingers over her power. She felt her skin cool and marble. Darkness yawned under the surface. Understanding flickered in the man's face, but also fear. "I've come to learn more of the heritage of my people."

His gaze panned over her face before skittering down to the bare plains on his left. "You're her. The one who stole our ocean."

Φ

The 27th Day of Lumord, 1272
The City of Ceir Athrolan, Athrolan

An'thor peered through the doorway into Keplan's room. "Your Majesty?" Evening's chill sank into the stone. Curtains eddied in the breeze like a shroud. "Keplan?"

A mutter drifted from the dark study. "In here."

The king perched on the broad sill of the study's open window. A long jacket, buttoned at the waist, covered his otherwise bare body. He seemed caught in a staring match with Tzatia's portrait over his desk.

"You were supposed to meet me half an hour ago."

"Why did you want me on the throne?" Keplan did not look from the portrait. "A man ill-made for the throne is worse than no king at all. I was so terrified of war, balancing who I was and who I thought my parents would be in my boots. And everything happened so quickly."

An'thor leaned on the door frame. He wanted a drink, but these were not his rooms and he was not even sure if the boy drank. "You're ill-prepared, not ill-made. When you've burnt the place to the ground, I'll swallow my words." He did not smile. "Athrolan will fall."

The younger man turned, eyes wide into the cavern of his unlit room. "What?"

"Athrolan will fall. The Laen fell. The gods fell. Claimiirn fell. Mirik fell and rose again, changed. I don't know if it will be in a year or in a thousand. I don't know if it'll be by our own hands or another's. All I know is if you're King, she won't fall today."

Keplan stared at him. "No grand sweeping plans? No brilliant dreams?"

"I always have plans, but I change them as much as I make them. It's different, I'll agree, actually being here. During the Gods' War, I traveled so much I missed the intricacies." An'thor traced the lines of Tzatia's face in the portrait.

"It's the only one I let them leave. I can't stand a dozen dead folk staring at me." Keplan swung his leg back into the room and rested his head in his hands. "That war was different. You knew my mother would win."

"I knew the terrible mess war makes and the incredible cost. I didn't understand the sweeping nature of her power, or your father's. I saw it, but couldn't really fathom it." He leaned on the desk. "Tell me, what stories do you know about history?"

"The old ones."

An'thor snorted. "Right. Well, when a kingdom survives war, or uncertainty, who rules? When a nation drags itself from the mud, who is the monarch?"

"Heroes."

"People who didn't study the numbers, or studied them and didn't care."

"You're the legendary hero, Domarriigo. You do it."

"I love Athrolan like a father, but I'm covetous and I think you, listening to all those thoughts you don't own, know why I'm not the man to lead a Golden Age." He watched expressions flit across Keplan's ice-chip eyes. Calculating as An'thor did, but wrapped inside the mania was a shred of hope. An'thor saw shadows of who he had been, who Mel'iend once was. *Who my son could have been.* Perhaps if he saved Keplan from bitterness, every piece of the puzzle An'thor worked at for the last two hundred years would finally fit. "I'm trying to make amends for some stories the legends don't include."

"I'm a king at seventeen. Pretend as we might, this isn't peace, not by a league. Ban and Mirik are breathing at our heels." Keplan glared up at him. "I wish you hadn't roped me into your scheme."

"Your parents' blood roped you in, not me. You couldn't have a normal life no matter what you did, not with that power burning through you." One pale hand fiddled with his shorn, capped horn. "Some of us are born to these roles because we're better suited to them. I was made to protect this world. Your parents were made to mend it. And you, perhaps you're made to rule it."

Keplan pulled a flask out of his coat and took a deep draw before handing it to the general. "You think humans couldn't do it without us?"

"When you've seen as many kingdoms fall as I have." An'thor shrugged and took a gulp. It was fire ale, and cheap at that. *He drinks, but has awful taste.* "I didn't think you were much for drinking."

"I'm not. But it quiets things. Helps me sleep. And I've been tired."

"Watch that habit," the general cautioned.

"Wouldn't want to end up like you."

"You really wouldn't. You ought to have someone teach you meditation. I think it helped your mother." An'thor looked back up to the portrait. "You made good promises to Athrolan, at the coronation. Think you can keep them?"

"I didn't promise anything to Athrolan." Keplan's eyes were fixed on his ungloved hands, nail-bitten and chapped, bleeding from where he worried cracks in the callouses. "I promised it to Firas."

Φ

Cheap wood groaned under the weight of letters and missives on Reka's desk. She shuffled through them again, burning those no longer pertinent. As much as Bren offered an office of her own, she could not bring herself to accept. *It would ingrain me in that house, that kingdom more than I ever want.* She snorted, realizing she thought an office more tethering than sharing children.

Unfurling another missive, she tilted her chair back. It was short and from one of her Border friends. Though Ikel fought in the Gods' War too, she chose to move into the prairie years ago. Now with war brewing, she was more spy than friendly correspondent. Reka bent over the letter. She preferred it this way.

> *Reka,*
>
> *Something is brewing in Ban. A different war than that with Mirik. It centers around the Hall of the Purple Throne, but it's spreading. I think revolution is coming. We've flirted with it before, but this smells different.*

I see flashes of jewelry, hand signals that have too much of a pattern to be nothing. I fear the country will be torn asunder between two wars. I should clarify — this country needs change, but I fear what it will look like afterward if we are not careful.

I know your position in the Mirikin court gives you no peace. Perhaps it's time you returned to your people — our way of life isn't with hierarchy and taking orders.

If you ever change your mind about Bren and Mirik, I hope you'll come to us.

We miss you,

Ikel

Reka frowned, read the letter again, then burned it. Another war would be catastrophic. Athrolan was barely recovered from its taste of civil war. Now Ban hovered on the brink and did not even realize it. *It's as if the world rots from within.*

It was not enough to tell Bren, and she wondered if a library's worth of documents would be enough. She had plenty to share with him tonight over drinks. Foregoing her cloak, she stepped into the warm autumn evening.

Bren ushered her up the rear stairs when she arrived. She swore there was another white streak in his beard or hair at each meeting. Now he raked his hands through it. "Can I get you anything? Fireale? Wraith?"

"Wraith is my least favorite of the various habits you adopted from General Domariigo."

Bren rolled his eyes. "I drank it long before I met him. It's Mirikin."

"Doesn't mean it's not swill." She took the glass of wine from him and crossed one knee over the other." How are things in Mirik ?"

"Isn't that what you're supposed to tell me? Famous spy network and so forth."

"I was trying to make conversation. Besides, half of what I do is determining how people think the world looks as much as what actually happens." She took a slow sip.

"I think peace is coming, at least on this side of the ocean."

"You mean for Athrolan. Ban is almost half this continent, and if your wife has her way, they'll certainly not have peace. Whoever thinks peace is on the horizon is simply not paying attention."

Bren looked away. "I'm just being hopeful. Athrolan's more stable with Keplan on the throne. Perhaps once they see Daymir doing so well as Regent, they'll release Keplan of his duties."

"Now you're really not listening. Keplan wouldn't have walked out of there alive if the city didn't want him." She sat back. "Which brings me to our actual conversation for the evening."

"Has there been an attempt on Keplan?"

Reka waved her hand at him. "That would warrant more than a casual talk over drinks, and you are certainly not the first person I would bring that news to. I'm more worried about your sons, and yourself. Azimir in particular. Anyone who aided Keplan has become a target. It was a few street folk at first, people he talked to in the market and were friendly. They were given warnings, bloody ones. Told it was because they 'sided with the usurper.' Most don't even know Keplan's him."

"You're worried they will target us? The Smythesens?"

"The general, your household. Hard to say who. There's little sense involved." She nodded to the window overlooking the garden. "I'd double your guards and tell them there's added threat."

"Consider it done." He followed her gaze to the shadowed garden, but he seemed unseeing. "Any news from Ban?"

"They continue to prepare for war, bolstering their border forts. Part of running a successful empire is always having an army at the ready, whether it's to maintain peace or fight for it during war. Nothing Kemmer's captains couldn't tell her." She paused. "I know war is hard, but sometimes it's necessary. What's more important, Bren: doing the right thing, or peace?"

He shook his head at her with a faint smile. "I've lived through it, Reka. Peace is the right thing. Where do you get these questions?"

She looked away. She loved Mirik, and her position as Spy Master for Brentemir kept her mind and body honed. *But the network could practically run itself.* She knew it was unwise to create a system in which she was unnecessary. *But how can I retire when I'm vital?* She did not see retirement the way Brentemir might, or Daymir even, or Hylier. She did not want to stagnate in an armchair before a hearth for the last twenty years of her life. Any passing interest she had in family was quenched with surrogacy of Kemmer's sons. Her skin itched to move, to travel, to wander and learn. She eyed Brentemir, peering into his glass as if its depths held answers. War was a poor time for one's Spy Master to resign. "I might have to travel soon. Explore some rumors that have surfaced in the west."

"I thought you said nothing was heard from Ban. Are they mobilizing?"

"It wasn't from Ban, exactly, and I don't know enough to relay anything with confidence. At any rate, I received a letter, and I wish to see the evidence for myself."

"Surely you could send Billan or Cas. Or any of the two dozen subordinates I don't know about." The wiry line of

Bren's salted auburn brows curled together. "I need you here, especially with threats from Athrolan's resistance."

"You need a go-between to my Athrolani contacts. You don't need me. With all due respect, Bren, Kemmer and this world need me more than you do."

Bren mouthed silently, walking himself through some argument in which he changed her mind, surely. Frustration in his eyes was too close to that of a lover rather than a commanding officer.

"Bren, please understand." She ducked her head to catch his gaze. "I have a few weeks to lay groundwork for my absence. I'll still be in contact with yourself and your wife." She forwent Kemmer's titles, hoping it would remind the ambassador of his loyalties. She stretched and rose. "You wouldn't keep your navy harbored during war, would you?"

"Toar, I know you're right. I just feel like I'm in need of allies."

"Perhaps your allies need of you, instead." She paused at the door to drain her glass before fixing him with a pointed stare. "Double the guard, Brentemir."

"I promise."

She shut the door behind her, listening to the clink of the bottle's mouth on his glass. Already her limbs tingled with the possibility of travel, and her heart ached for change.

Φ

The 29th Day of Lumord, 1272
The City of Ceir Athrolan, Athrolan

"I can't breathe." Keplan clawed blankets from his body, pushing himself upright.

Beside him, something darker than lust shadowed Firas's smirk. "I had to close the windows."

Keplan was aware, in a distant sense, they were not in the Wise Hare. "Are the warehouses burning again?"

"It's the blood, 'Lan." His voice gurgled. Thick, black blood welled under the door, fountaining between the brown stone. It poured from his lover's mouth, his eyes. Acrid smells of sickness and rot joined the sweet tang of fresh blood.

Keplan body dragged as the walls crumbled beneath the wave of gore. Firas reached for him, but not for rescue. His hand clawed, gouging lines down the younger man's forearms. "It's the Gods' Blood. It'll rot us all."

Sweat drenched the sheets tangling his legs. He smelled blood, felt Firas's nails dragging across his skin, his arms were unmarked. He curled into the expanse of thick down and clean linen. *All the larger due to its emptiness.* Instead of Firas, he spoke to the silence in his room and the heavy darkness surrounding his curtained bed. "Do you think I'll ever get used to this? Solitude around the chaos and noise in my skull?"

Exhaustion was lead on his eyes and chest, but he dragged himself upright. The idea of meditation seemed simple, though he had yet to ask about it. His eyes lidded, thin chest rising with each billow of breath. Thrumming of his heart was steady under the thin skin of his throat and wrists, a familiar tap dance between his ribs. Underneath a second pulse thundered, a roar turned whisper by distance. Frowning, he followed the sound through his body, through the rush of his own blood, into a deeper crimson.

Caution screamed in the back of his thoughts, but he pushed on. *I've never explored my mental self the way my parents once did.* Red-brown lines mirrored his veins. Copper laced his arteries. Lines entwined his form, feathering where capillaries lay, through his skin, through the stone, into the groaning earth. *Is everyone connected to the world?* Twisting strands lead to the heaving center of the world, through a burning magma core to the metal sphere grounding the world. To his mind's eyes, it blazed black and copper, shadowed with warm blue and greens. He brushed against it. Pain exploded. Fire seared his skin and throat. Images thundered to the fore, filling his head to brimming. Screams pressed the aching inside of his skull.

All of Athrolan and her neighbors lay below. Instead of a map, he looked upon the rolling hills, grasses and trees waving in a wind he could not feel. Thunder rumbled around his body. Hot rain pelted the ground, each drop red and greasy. It dribbled over rocks and spread through the rivers and lakes.

Blood.

The earth twisted into an ancient face, the bloody tracks turning to frown lines, the tangled trees a mess of snarled hair. It was a woman, and she screamed. "Your blood clots the earth, strangles! Give it back! Give back the Gods' Blood!"

Keplan shoved away, tripping over thoughts and images. He scrambled toward the surface of his mind. His eyes opened on darkness. After a moment he recognized the dim bedroom, the night sky through his open bedroom window, the face of the soldier shaking him.

"Your Majesty!"

"Captain?" His throat ached, and his mouth tasted of blood. "What're you doing here? It's late."

"Early, actually. Almost dawn." She stepped back, hands still out as if ready to soothe or restrain. "We heard you scream."

"We?" Keplan's gaze roved to the three other guards panting in the doorway. Their weapons were drawn, expressions plainly saying he was the most frightening thing in the room. "Right. Thank you. It was just a dream."

"You are bleeding, Your Majesty."

He followed her gaze. Blood drenched the sheets knotted in his hands. "I must have scratched myself. That will be all, thank you, ma'am."

"Yes, Sire. Also, a letter came for you, I've left it in your study." She followed the others out.

Keplan glanced out the window. "I don't even recall falling asleep." *I don't think I ever did.* Stars dimmed in the face of sunrise. He shoved himself from the tangled sheets. The privy tiles were cold, and the eddying wind drew gooseflesh from his sweat-drenched skin. Tepid water filled the washbasin and he braced himself for the sting of new scratches. It never came. Scrubbing the clotted blood from his hands and forearms, he held them to the rising light. No wounds marked his bare body either. But for the pink water and jelly-like clots in the basin, he would have thought it a dream. *So whose blood is on my hands?*

Muttering wind banged shutters against stone and rattled him from his thoughts. It was a council day, though there were few actual issues during the audience earlier that week. Most came to gawk at the new king, not raise complaints. No doubt that would change. A clean tolstovka and loose breeches waited on his wardrobe and he tugged them over still-damp skin. He missed the days when none of his clothing bore embroidery.

As much as he wished to ignore the letter the captain brought, he knew better. *It's probably from Barrackborn. Or Azimir.*

Keplan froze in his study doorway. There was no beige military missive or smooth parchment of noble correspondence. Instead, it was the stiff vellum of a Banis scroll. *Of course.* It made all the sense in the world—an empire reaching out to a new king, clawed fingers scrabbling to gain him as an ally before their enemies did.

Anxiety stuttered his heart. Lighting the lamp on his desk spurred his motivation. Wax sealed ribbons unraveled under his fingers.

> *His Majesty Keplan Wardyn, King of the Nation of Athrolan,*
>
> *We rejoice at the news of your coronation. Athrolan has long been a beacon of strength and progress, and we look forward to our long future as neighbors. We hope, too, we will meet this future as allies.*
>
> *We look forward to your response regarding negotiations and wish you luck and a most smooth transition into what is sure to be a prosperous reign.*
>
> *His Eminence Emperor of Ban and the Jade Forest, Jamun-Ilta the Holy Emerald Throne*

Keplan's skin crawled with the saccharine tone. He brushed a hand over the signature and seals, ones he recognized.

A door banged and something clattered to the ground. Keplan glanced up. A maid stood in the doorway, eyes wide, hand pressed to her gray-blond hair. "Forgive me, Your Majesty, I thought you already gone."

Keplan waved her concern away. "Who do I call for tea?"

"I'll fetch Jaria for you." She ducked out, returning a moment later with a young woman bearing a tray.

"Fates, that was quick."

"It's our duty to be ready whenever Your Majesty wishes for something."

"Right." He drained the tea and asked for another. The letter joined the stack of economic reports from the past decade.

An'thor arrived with the mid-morning bells. "You were up late, I see."

"Early, actually." Keplan slumped back in his chair. "Is it that obvious? This is my fourth cup of tea since dawn."

The general was dressed for state, eyes as tired as Keplan felt. "The usual preoccupations?"

"Not really, no." *Add some ghostly blood and an alliance with the nation who tortured me.* "I need to ask your advice, actually."

"I thought Blackhouse was for these sorts of things."

"Blackhouse hasn't seen what you have."

"And what is that?"

"War. You've watched cities—Athrolan even—crumble. You saw Azirik drag Mirik into ruin."

"And you're worried you'll do the same?"

Yes. "This is about Ban."

An'thor sat back with a heavy sigh. He fumbled a flask from a small case on his belt. After a slow sip, his gaze returned to Keplan. "You mean to go to war with her as Mirik's ally. Freedom's a noble cause, surely."

"I was considering an alliance, actually."

An'thor's snowy brows rose. "I'd have sworn to the gods you wanted blood from the Empire."

"You're confusing war with revenge."

"Revenge." An'thor peered at Keplan's face. "So your scars are Kisses."

"Did you think I got them from running too quickly through a briar patch?" Keplan fiddled with his gloves.

An'thor looked away. "I just hoped. And when you're King, revenge often looks like war."

"I know it was the Emperor who shed my blood, not his people. But I still want Ban to crumble, want its wealth drained. I want the grasslands burnt to ash." He shook his head. "And I took this throne to avoid war."

"You don't think we'd win?" An'thor asked.

"We've cavalry and navies and fantastic strategists. They've numbers and the cold stones to throw their warriors away. If we won, it wouldn't be worth it."

An'thor hummed, though it was unclear whether he agreed. "I suppose it doesn't matter right now, anyway."

Keplan held up the letter from the emperor. "It does."

Snatching the scroll from the king's hand, An'thor bent over the elegant words. After a moment he tossed it back on the desk. "If you agree, it won't be easy. Politics aside. You'll be no good to us mad."

"I'm already there, Domariigo."

"Not fully, not yet." An'thor's lips were so tight they were almost purple. "You have nightmares about it? What happened?"

"Yes."

"What do you intend to do? Mirik has declared war."

"Well, we aren't Mirik. I'll continue to trade with them, and if they use our goods for war, that's on them. We'll profit, surely." He stared at his hands. In his mind's eye he saw the Banis soldiers who caught him. "I don't want war. I want to negotiate with Ban. I want to take their gold, their gems, their horses. I want to learn them like I know myself."

"And then?"

Keplan did not meet An'thor's gaze. Instead, his eyes were fixed on the city, irises bleached to colorless by the dawn.

CHAPTER TWENTY

The 28th Day of Lumord, 1272
The City of RoBal, Ban

RIH'S DOOR SLAMMED OPEN at dawn. Ceramic shattered when her mug cracked to the ground. Two guards loomed in the narrow doorway. Both were male.

"Rih-elte?"

She nodded once.

"You're summoned to the palace where you will be honored by His Eminence's presence."

She reached for her dropped tea but saw the guard slam the butt of his glaive on the ground. She glanced back to his mouth.

"Now."

A net and shawl were all she grabbed before rushing after them. Burning knotted high in her chest. Surely her heart had stopped. *Not this way, please.* It did not matter that the gods were dead. People prayed before they died, and every step was a blow of the executioner's axe. *I can't even think "rebellion," lest it show on my face.*

Now war loomed. Guards swarmed through the palace. Each level of the pyramid was locked with a different set of keys and passphrases. She stopped memorizing them after the first eight and wondered how often they changed. She remembered the opulence of her last visit. After months of dry, dusty weather, the lush potted plants and indoor garden in the center of the building made her mouth water.

The rebellion can't run without me — there are too many gestures to learn. Another voice, deeper in her heart, promised Ki-elte and Il-fald were enough to keep the movement going. *And what of Majilah Ag?* She signed an alliance. Would she go to war to avenge Rih's death?

Don't think "rebellion," lest it show on your face.

The sloping hall wound up to the fifth floor from the peak. She recognized the dark doors, again, emblazoned with the winged horse. Pale green jade panels flanked the door, visible only when the doors were slid shut. The finery soured her twisting stomach. Clenched teeth bit back her rising bile.

The doors slid apart. It was all she could do to kneel on the mirrored tiles instead of run. Red now accented the usual greens, for war. The emperor himself wore a rusty silk sash. Passed down to each emperor, older than the palace she stood in, it was dyed with the blood of enemy officers. *How many were the foremothers of the Vales?*

Mosil knelt at the emperor's jeweled feet, head bowed, nodding to instructions Rih could not hear. His gaze darted to her, though he did not look up, and the corner of his mouth curled. Perhaps he was no longer angry.

Hard fingers gripped her arm, and the guard levered her to her feet. "He wants to see Mosil-ten-Ebal's handiwork." He twirled his finger, and Rih turned in a circle, eyes fixed on the floor. The guard shoved her back onto her knees.

Don't think "rebellion."

She fixed her gaze on Mosil.

"Yes, Your Eminence. Of course." Most of his words were concealed as he bowed. "I'm glad you think she'll do."

She'll do? This did not feel like an execution, but her pulse still trembled in her throat. Another moment passed, then she was pulled upright and ushered into the hall.

Her cousin met her a minute later and signed, "Come with me." He strode down the ramp, descending to the third level. Subdued decorations told her it was a residential wing. He unlocked a door at the end of a narrow hall, fingertips pressing designs until the wood slid aside. "This is my study," he explained. "Sit." He turned to stare out the window. She sat, toes tapping against the tile. She hated not seeing his face, not knowing if he spoke to himself, knowing she could not hear him.

Finally, he turned and handed a heavy letter and tablet to her, face unreadable. She glanced at the parchment and seals, none of which were Banis, and frowned at him. The tablet bore the translation to the Trade words.

"Just read it."

She tilted the parchment toward the pink light of dawn.

Esteemed Excellence, His Eminence Emperor of Ban and the Jade Forest, Jamun-Ilta the Holy Emerald Throne,

Athrolan is honored to announce the coronation of His Majesty Keplan Wardyn of the Hartland, son of Lyne'alea ir Suna, Dhoah' Laen and Aud'narman Wardyn, the Earth Shaker Arrowlash. He is supported by His Highness Regent Daymir Blackhouse, and we wish to accept negotiations with your mighty empire.

We have learned of your ongoing war with Mirik, and while we are on peaceful terms with the aforementioned nation, we do not wish to engage Ban in warfare. Instead, we hope to seek trade with you. We

*look forward to your response and hope to discuss terms
further in person before the month is out.*

In friendship,

*His Majesty Keplan Wardyn, King of Athrolan
and the Hartland*

*His Highness Regent Daymir Blackhouse
and the Council of Athrolan*

Rih placed it carefully back on the desk. Her heart hammered. *"She'll do."* When Mirik declared war, she thought herself free of the duty of wife, at least for a time. She hoped to be forgotten like so many of the other imperial daughters. "I'm to marry this king? The child of the Rakos and Dhoah' Laen?"

"It is one of the terms of negotiation that His Eminence put forth. Enough resources were invested in your training, and I think His Eminence would rather it not be a waste. I doubt he will let the boy decline the offer."

"Boy?"

"His Majesty is seventeen."

Rih frowned, drawing the letter close again. "I know his name. I've read it before."

"There have been missives regarding his presence in Athrolan for some time, though this is the first official declaration from their own pens."

She could not place the memory. *Hartland. I've read it.* "When will we go?"

"I'll leave in a week. With them." Her cousin's dexterity left much to be desired. He waved to the window. "You'll leave once negotiations are finalized."

"With them?" She went to the window. The palace loomed above the dust-cloaked city. Ebony and silk shaded the room from the worst of the sun. At dawn, however, the brilliance lanced through the slats, spilling red light across the clay and wood.

Golden plains were lost in a haze of dust. Lean yellow flanks flashed through the clouds of dirt as captains trotted along the ranks of soldiers. Soldiers were a dark shadow under the thunderheads of dust. Rih marked the flags of the First March, the Fourth, her eyes counting women she once marched beside. She stopped at thirty-seven Marches, though there were easily twice as many. Her body shook. *The entire First and Second Arcs are out there.* The last time all the armies were called to the capital was for the coronation of the Emperor long before she was born.

If all the women below joined, her rebellion had a chance. *They own us, own our children, our husbands, our bodies. They learn our plans, and they will strike there first.* She jerked her chin at the gathered force. "Is this a display against Mirik?"

Most of his words and signs were lost to his nervous fiddling. She caught the spelling of Athrolan. "Two of those marches are my diplomatic entourage."

"I thought we meant peace with Athrolan. Or did I read a different letter?" She no longer cared about respect or deference.

"The best way to maintain peace is to remind your allies — and your enemies — of war."

Her thoughts paused on the map still on her desk, the tick-marks beside each country. The tick marks beside Athrolan. Adrenaline was a fire in her gut, thunder in her chest.

Rebellion.

"I'm going with you."

"You can't. It's negotiation. Nothing is finalized." He looked back to the army.

She yanked on his sleeve to bring his attention back to her hands. "I'm going with you. If you bring the bride, this boy will know you're serious." She pointed to the army amassed outside. "They remind Athrolan of war. I will be proof that you want peace."

Φ

The 29th Day of Lumord, 1272
The City of Mirik
Kemmer held the long wooden pole she used to arrange her war-pieces, but she did not look at the map inlaid on the table. Instead, her eyes were fixed outside. The ocean was sullen, and the sky seemed to sulk under its flat blanket of clouds. Bren was still gone, and a part of her wondered if he would refuse to return without Keplan in tow. The boy resolutely refused to answer her plea for an alliance. The half-read letter on her desk arrived an hour before and shattered all of her hopes.

She listened to the creak of the balcony encircling the room. "What are we going to do, Al?"

Her son sighed, descending the ladder two rungs at a time. "Damned if I know. That letter from Pa?"

"Keplan."

The young man groaned. "I'm fairly certain he's mad. Like, well and truly."

"But can he lead a country?"

Alleanthus frowned. "You think he can?"

"His decisions are not ones I would make, but they worked. From without he seems reckless, selfish, unstable. Yet nothing crumbled. I am starting to think he's a mastermind."

"You don't sound pleased."

"A Banis march arrives on his doorstep before winter. Not to wage war, but to negotiate a treaty."

Alleanthus groaned and rested his brow against the window. "He's our enemy?"

"Don't be foolish. Politics are far more complicated than 'my enemy's friend is my enemy.' Rather, I fear his choice to ally means I've missed something vital. I fear he sees something I haven't, something none of us have." She scanned the colored tiles marking Ban on the floor. "You said his relationship with Ban was complex."

"Interrogator's Kisses mark his cheeks, though whether he received them officially or at the hands of some zealot mimic, I couldn't say. If he was their victim I can't see why he would negotiate."

Kemmer shrugged. "Perhaps he saw enough violence to wish for no more. Perhaps he has moves yet to make. Perhaps An'thoriend is forcing his hand. There are as many possibilities as there are waking hours in a year."

"So, what is our move?" He leaned on the balcony ladder, dark face tilted.

"Athrolan and Ban are separate problems until they prove they're not." She jerked her head at the map. "I, too, have moves yet to make, and not all of them are kind."

"Does Pa know?" Alleanthus's voice lowered, as if his father could hear the words across the ocean.

"Know what?"

"We might face Athrolan in war."

"Despite his stubbornness, he's not stupid. He can add the digits."

"What side will he choose?"

Her eyes sharpened on her son. "Your father is sentimental and idealistic, but he is no traitor. I don't care who sits on their precious white throne. If you make those accusations, refrain from doing so aloud." She turned back to the window. "Go riding. The forest will do some good for the clutter in your head." When his faltering steps faded, she returned to her perusal of the map.

War hardened her. As stern as she must have sounded to Alleanthus, she was scared. Brentemir always put Alea first. Now, Keplan might take his mother's place in the ambassador's loyalty. *And he might well supplant Mirik.* She loved her husband, and his determination and morality was an inspiration to her more pragmatic mind.

But now she was Hetmir. If forced to choose between her people and her husband, Mirik would win.

Φ

The 30th Day of Lumord, 1272
The City of Ceir Athrolan, Athrolan

The entire room stank of blood. The voices in Keplans's head were as real—sometimes more so—as tolling bells, birds chirping, all the distant city noises drifting on the wind. A loud knock sounded on the study door, and Keplan realized someone had been knocking for a while. He pulled it open to find one of his guards.

"Your Majesty, forgive me for disturbing you, but Captain Hylier is here, claims to have been invited."

"I told him to come after lunch."

"It's midafternoon, Sire." She offered him a faint smile.

Keplan glanced at the sky. "Right, of course, I lost count of the hours. Show him in, please, and would you send for tea and some of those pastries, too?" He cleared his desk and arranged himself in his chair.

"Right away, Sire."

Hylier bowed as he entered, cap in hand. "Your Majesty, good afternoon."

"Captain, have a seat." He propped his elbows on his knees. "Thank you for meeting me."

"It's my pleasure, Sire."

"How do you like your position in the army?"

Hylier frowned. "I like it fine. My commission is up soon, though."

"Do you no longer wish to work for the Crown?" Keplan tilted his head. Hylier struck him as clever, if optimistic. *I need someone who blends in, who people trust.* Mirik's Spy Master set his mind turning, and with a kingdom the size of Athrolan, information was more valuable than coin.

Hylier tilted his head. "I was hoping for something a bit more challenging." He did not elaborate until tea and pastries arrived, and then only after Keplan had doused his food with syrup. "Is there something you needed me to do?"

"When Blackhouse asked, how did you find me?"

"I started with what I knew and asked questions. I've always liked puzzles and people."

"I'd like you to work on another puzzle. You'll be compensated for your time, of course."

"I find my schedule abundantly clear." Hylier grinned, and Keplan was reminded, for a moment, of boyish glee. "I'd like you to look into the networks of the resistance, as well as those who support me. The attempt on Dorcal's life was not an isolated incident, and my reign will not be colored by violence, at least not any more than it has to be."

"Peraan as well?"

"I've heard nothing of him since the ceasefire," Keplan realized. The fact sent a chill down his back. *I've been so wrapped up in ruling and keeping my head I never thought to check.*

Hylier's lips thinned. "You've not been listening then, begging your pardon. He wants you off the throne, and soon."

"I'm not even fully king." Tangles caught around his fingers as he raked a hand through his hair. If only his opposers gave him the chance to make mistakes before blaming him for them.

"As good as. Peraan is dangerous, and surely it looks like peace, sire, but city rumors rarely lie. Well," he risked a wink, "I'll still deny knowing the daughter of the Nel Corner baker if anyone asks."

Keplan offered a grin, but it felt limp on his mouth. "I promise not to tell."

"Peraan's current plot involves those who supported you, or aided your ascension to the throne." Hylier took a second pastry, but refused another cup of tea. "Gives me the winders."

Cold uncurled in Keplan's stomach. *Firas could be on that list.* "Do you have the names?"

"I can acquire them."

Keplan fished a coin purse from his drawer and slid it across the desk. "Find whatever you need. I'll see your commission is renewed, but only as guise. Learn his plan, the names he has. Is a week long enough?" Hissing rose in Keplan's ears, a crackle of burning gore. Red filled his vision, eyes stinging. "What was that?"

"I said I would look into it," Hylier repeated, "and report back in a week or as soon as I have news, whichever is first. Is there anything else?" He paused at the door. "Are you well, Your Majesty?"

"Distracted. Thank you, that'll be all." He did not hear the door close, and when he next glanced at the window it was dusk. When rare sleep came, it brought dreams of blood and writhing earth. He missed the nights wrapped in Firas's arms, tangled in the sheets in the too-hot attic of the Wise Hare.

He turned down the study lamp. Fetching a cheep bottle from his desk, he slipped into the bath waiting in the privy. It did not matter the water tumbling into the copper tub was cold. Metal bit into the nape of his neck when he rested his head back. Exhaustion clogged his thoughts about the kingdom, about Peraan and his plots, about Ban or Mirik's war. *Dorcal was afraid I'd succumb to whatever my parents left in my blood.* Water sloshed around his chin, and he fumbled the faucet closed again.

Magma roiled into life under his thoughts. His eyes flew open. Steam bubbled around him, water rolling into a boil as it deepened to crimson, to burgundy, to the black of clotted blood. Keplan scrambled out, breath heaving. Clear water filled the bath, unmoving, save for gentle sloshing from his escape. He dipped a tentative hand in.

Cold.

He was dashing through the slums before he could think better of it. Adrenaline burned through his limbs. If any guards followed, he lost them in the twisting maze of the market. It was quiet at the Wise Hare, and he heard a storyteller's murmur. He ducked through the front door. Most of the damage from the cannons was repaired, new wood garish and white against the smoke-stained gray beams and boards. *Did Mirrel hire someone or is Firas good at carpentry?* He tucked himself into the farthest barstool.

After a moment Mirrel caught sight of him. Her eyes widened and glanced at the room. Those who noticed his arrival either did not care that the heir was in their midst or had not recognized him. "You shouldn't be here."

"I know, but I need to talk to Firas."

Her lips thinned. "I don't suppose you'd believe he's with someone."

"It's still important."

"If you make a scene, barging in with dramatics to woo my brother, I'll never hear the end of it. We have trusted patrons here, ones that rather us not have such a reputation."

"I'll be discreet, I promise."

"Next time, just come through the back, will you?" She stepped away, grabbing a mug in one hand and a bottle of thick green alcohol in the other.

Keplan took the stairs several at a time, slowing only when he stood before Firas's door. He paused, shifting from foot to foot. Lack of sleep made him reckless. He knocked.

"Mirrel, I've not the energy for your shite. It's quiet, handle it yourself."

"Do you have energy for a friend?"

A bedframe groaned, and the floorboards creaked. The door opened. "'Lan?"

"I'm sorry this is unexpected, but I needed to talk to you."

Firas's beard was shorter, his hair messy. "I can scarcely advise a king."

"It's not about being a fucking king!"

The bartender sighed. "If I let you in will you stop shouting about it?" When Keplan nodded, the older man stepped aside. "What do you need?"

"I haven't slept in days. There's too much noise in my head, too many things in my mind. Every time I try to rest, I simply stare at blood rushing over my kingdom for hours and come to feeling even worse than before."

Firas sat back. "You smell of alcohol."

"It's the only thing that quiets things. I still hear them, but it's less. Garbled almost."

"I can't fix this, 'Lan."

"You did before! Lying next to you, talking to you, listening to your stories, it helped." Pleading twisted his voice brought a tremor to his hands.

"Keplan, you're the ruler of a kingdom. I care for you, but you realize what having you here does to us?"

"Mirrel said I'd give you a bad reputation."

"You aren't loved, not yet and certainly not by all. Someone sees you here, we're in danger. We've been threatened simply for sheltering you. And now you beg to sleep with me because you have nightmares."

"I'm sorry." Keplan sat back. *You were compassionate before.* But the bartender was right. "I didn't know where else to go."

"I can't do this. I can't watch you up on that throne, in your gilded palace, and let you come slum here with us when it could get us killed." The crack in his voice said how much the words pained him.

Keplan nodded, fingers tugging loose threads from his new gloves. "I'm sorry," No matter how many times he said the words, they did not make his heart stop racing. "I hope you have a good evening." When he left, he took the rear door to the alley. The dark crouched over the city, turning pale stone to the bleach of bone. He was abruptly aware he had, in fact, lost his guards.

A second, more desperate, surge of panic carried his numb, stumbling feet back to the lights of the palace. Leaving had been easy. Now ranks of guards on the wall watched the king stumble, weeping, into the courtyard. *"You aren't loved, not yet, and certainly not by all."*

CHAPTER TWENTY-ONE

The 31st Day of Lumord, 1272
The Town of Tut Kunis, Berr

MOANING WIND EDDIED SULLENLY around Alea, lifting grayed locks more from habit than interest. She leaned on the wall, shoulders hunched, staring at the expanse of salt flats. "There's something more going on here." The past weeks gave her face more lines than the twenty years prior.

"Is it the Laen you sense? This is the closest we've come to one of their cities since the war."

Her pupils were blown, the surface knotted with black power. "It's always her." Alea's voice changed, steadied, as she recited the most recent message from a madwoman. "'The Blood flows, clotted and putrid. Blood clogs the city streets. Poisons the trees. Erodes the mountains. We came first, they came second. Blood comes last.'"

Arman sighed, warm breath silent against Alea's icy cheek. "I don't know what it means any more than the last one."

Power drained from her features. "I wish we could get news. I wish we knew what was happening in Athrolan."

She stared at her hands, fingers tangled in the tattered hem of her shirt. "The map wasn't wrong."

Arman's gaze flicked to her, though he did not turn from the glint of dusk. Whatever urgency drove Alea into the mountains seemed replaced by patience. It was a patience he did not share and made worse by the avoidant townsfolk. "Daymir's map showed a lake."

"Do you remember when you took the sun in? Just as you opened to the fire of the earth and the sky, I opened to the water, the power of the oceans and the air. I dragged water from all corners of the earth. I could taste where it was from, heavy on the tongue of my mind. Some tasted dusty and spicy from the desert oasis, some hot and sweet from the grasslands. Most tasted of cold salt and ice. And some tasted of blood and bone."

"From here."

"I suppose." Her eyes narrowed on the flats, a general surveying grassland seeded over an ancient battlefield. "They don't trust me."

"Should they?" The words were out before he could bite them back. What honesty their relationship had was not always spoken.

She did not seem offended. Instead, she chewed absently at her lips, chapped to bloody. "No. No one should." The insinuation that even she did not trust herself was too heavy for thin mountain air.

"Dhoah'." The chief's voice cracked from the hooded doorway into the rest of the house. "Supper." He ducked back in, and Arman watched him go.

"Not talkative, eh?"

"Their land is dry and bitter, thus so are their words."

Arman hummed in response, taking her hand for the first time since they entered the town. "We should eat. Who knows what comes tomorrow or the day after." After a gentle tug, she followed him down into the darkness of the house. He imagined her mind stayed perched on the wall, overlooking the bone-white bed of salt.

The houses were the poorly insulated slats of a shanty town, those farther downslope built on stilts for a flood that would never come. Faded colored walls blocked the stark white light lancing off the salt flats.

"Are you going to kill us?" The tiny voice cut through the rattle of wind.

Arman turned, Alea's gaze following his a moment later. A girl, no more than nine, stood in the doorway to the kitchen. "What, little one?" he asked.

She fiddled with the buttons of her blue changsang. "Da said you were Death. You're going to take our souls like you took the ocean."

Arman's shoulders ached with the weight of those words. He caught the scent of damp, sullen ashes as the wind eddied. "No, we're just visiting for a bit. We'll be gone soon."

"Bu, go see your mother." The chief emerged from the kitchen and placed one chapped hand on his daughter's black hair. When she was gone, he handed Arman a large plate. "You can eat out here. I trust you'll be gone once you're through."

Arman thanked him, glancing down at the food. Gray salted meat and beige rice covered anemic lichen. Alea took a distracted bite. If she cared about the flavor, Arman could not tell.

"Sir, when can I see her?" Alea's voice rasped over the bitter air.

"She doesn't want to see you. But she said you will find it in the city." He gestured to the hills in the west.

Arman peered out the window. A narrow track wound up the scree of the mountainside before disappearing into a crevice. The meat was dry and flavorless, save for the bite of mineral salt. He looked back at Alea.

Her unfocused eyes stared through the mountains. "Find what?"

"The question you don't want to ask."

Φ

The 33rd Day of Lumord, 1272
The City of Ceir Athrolan, Athrolan

An'thor's footfalls were a ghost's whisper across the flagstones. Hearth to desk to hearth. Letters crouched on his desk like the monsters in his mind. Unlike monsters, however, letters were not chased away by alcohol. *Not for lack of effort.* He downed the dark liquid and drew a breath through his teeth. It was difficult to let go of all the duties he took over after Tzatia's death. *Besides, nothing good comes of saddling Keplan with everything at once.*

A scroll glowered where he left it on the polished wood. Three lines in and he had downed his drink. By the end, he tossed the offending thing away and started pacing. Dread erased the effects of alcohol.

He tugged on the bell by his door. "Tell His Highness Daymir I need to see him. Now." At the man's startled look he rolled his eyes. "We're not at war, I'm just impatient."

He did a circuit of his room, shoving discarded clothing and disarrayed papers into order. The rumors were bad enough, he did not need to help them with his poor housekeeping.

"General?"

"Ah, Daymir." He took in the regent's training uniform. "I see I did not wake you."

"Indeed not," He gestured to the chairs. "I doubt this is a social call."

"Not at this hour."

"Not from you," Daymir corrected as he took a seat.

An'thor smoothed his frown and handed Daymir the letter. "Tell me what you make of this."

"This is for Keplan."

"I still receive half his mail. Besides, I did not think it wise to bother him with it." An'thor poured them both a glass of wraith.

"You mean, you did not think he was stable enough." Daymir's eyes were clouded with something, exhaustion perhaps, or sorrow.

An'thor's nerves sharpened. "I don't know what you mean."

"Don't be an ass. All the cleverness and blood-power in the world can't counter trauma. We saw it with his grandfather at a distance. Now we are privy to every mood swing."

"I've no patience for lectures, Daymir. I'm tired."

"You're drunk is what." He waved An'thor's retort away and finally turned to the letter, reading it aloud.

> *"Your Majesty King Keplan of Athrolan and the Hartland,*
>
> *We have been blessed with news, and thought, as a show of goodwill, to share it with you.*
>
> *A prophet lives in our village, a woman once like your mother. She tells of a great wave that will wash the world clean of those who do not believe the truth. The blood of all that came before will birth a new deity, the One True God.'*

"An'thor, this is absurd. We get enough ravings from town idiots and false seers."

"This one isn't false." He pointed at the letter. "Keep reading."

"'The Dhoah' Laen herself has arrived, joining our prophet in the search for the Gods' Blood — ' fates ' — soon she will return west bearing the truth on her lips. We tell you this in hopes that you will erect temples to the One True God so your people are not swept away in the approaching storm.
    Respectfully,
    Orabon Marum'"

Daymir sank back into the chair, eyes more fogged than before.

"While the bits about Lyne'alea are clearly falsified, the words this madwoman uses are the same Keplan screams in the dreams the guards pretend not to hear."

"What makes this prophet a madwoman when our king sees the same visions?" Daymir still refused to look away from the letter. His hand shook.

An'thor looked away. The words were too close to home. "No sane person calls themselves a prophet. That's for the histories to decide." He took the letter back and ran a finger over the name. "Tut Kunis. It's on the border of the Northlands, and I've never even heard of it."

"What did you say?" Daymir stared at his hands, dark brows almost touching. "The town. What did you say it was called?"

"Tut Kunis?"

"They aren't lying." Daymir finally met An'thor eyes. His face paled. "The second part, about Lyne'alea. They aren't lying, because I sent them there."

"Who?" An'thor's gut churned and soured.

"A few weeks before I rode to meet with Keplan, two riders paid me a visit. I was surprised anyone let them through, but this squall descended —"

"Who were the riders, Daymir?"

"Lyne'alea and Arrowlash. They came seeking the answer to visions she was having. Said the world was rotting, or poisoned, I think. Tut Kunis was once a guard city for a Laen citadel. I forget the name."

"Lymorda." An'thor's gut settled like lead. "The Nenev fought them once, centuries ago. I forgot until now." He leaned forward. "You never managed to tell me? Or Keplan, for that matter."

Something dark flitted across Daymir's features, almost anger, not quite shame. He paced to the hearth. "It slipped my mind."

"The Dhoah' Laen and Earth Shaker came to tea in your manor — while you were exiled — and it slipped your mind." He growled the last three words.

Daymir's hand smacked the mantle. "I was a little preoccupied raising their son to the throne, Domariigo! You think he could handle knowing his parents are traipsing across the country, his mother half-mad with visions?"

An'thor stepped back. Daymir did not shout. Even when Tzatia stripped his titles he had not raised his voice. "What did she say?"

"They've heard nothing from Keplan since he left. I suppose I wouldn't know what to write were I in His Majesty's boots either." Daymir heaved a sigh. "They're looking for answers. Lyne'alea said something is coming, something worse than the gods. Something she caused."

An'thor turned to the window, drink forgotten in his pale hand. "I can smell a storm miles away. I can sense war. This feels like neither, feels worse than both. I just don't know what we can do against something that mighty."

"We already have our weapon."

"If you spout some 'we have each other' nonsense, I swear I'll shoot you where you stand."

"I'd like to think you know me better." Daymir rolled his dark eyes. "I meant Keplan. We have no idea what he is, but I bet my life he can face whatever is coming. It's our duty to see he's ready when it arrives."

"I feel ill."

"I think that's the wraith." Daymir rose. "If that's all, An'thor, I think I'll head to bed. I'm an old man." He paused in the doorway. "I'll think on this letter, and why don't you think on trusting our madman?"

An'thor watched the regent leave before turning back to his window. Dread crouched in his heart. The last time his body felt so much wrongness was watched the girl he thought was the Dhoah' Laen bleed out in his hands.

Something was coming. Alea knew, Keplan knew, even a mountain madwoman knew. Gold lanterns lit the city. The wind was quiet. On the eastern horizon the hills were lost to the night.

Φ

Keplan moved down the rack of bows, testing the weight as he went. In the early morning, the training hall was dim and smelled of sawdust. Azimir always touted the relief he felt after training, and though swords were far beyond Keplan's skill, archery was not. He drew a pale ash hunting bow down and strung it. His muscles protested, but it was faint, and the heat in his forearms was a pleasant, distracting burn. He found the corresponding arrows, tipped with dull metal nubs, and took up position. The first went wide, the second struck the quintain in the gut.

He drew back again, strengthening his stomach and steadying his breath. The straw of the quintain twisted before his eyes. It shrank, gray-streaked black hair lank about its shoulders. Skin marbled white, laced with blue veins. Vacant gray eyes bore into his own. His mother's mouth dripped sea water and clotted blood. "Kill me!"

He shrieked, arrow flying wildly off the mark and shattering against the stone wall.

"What are you doing?" An'thor stood in the doorway, dressed in training gear.

Keplan whirled on the general. "Did you see that?"

"I saw you losing your mind over missing a target." The general tilted his head. "Why, what did you see?"

Lifeless straw once more made up the quintain. Keplan sank to his knees in the sawdust. "I'm losing my mind."

"I thought you already had." An'thor's words were not mocking, but neither were they kind. "What did you see?"

"I saw my ma. She was bleeding, rotting, almost. She begged me to kill her."

An'thor glanced at the quintain. "But you didn't. That arrow flew wide."

"It wasn't a dream. She was there, I could have sworn." He scrubbed his hands on his thighs. "I didn't kill her, but something in my bones told me I should."

An'thor frowned. "What do you mean?"

"Under all the noise, the images, the memories that aren't my own, under all of it there's a voice. It sounds like me, looks like me, but different."

"You said you had dreams. Unpleasant ones." An'thor folded himself cross-legged on the floor beside the boy. "Visions. Let's call them what they are. There's no point in maintaining the pretense."

Keplan sighed. "They come and go. Always, though, there's blood. The smell of copper."

"Have you spoken to anyone else about this?"

"No one."

"Not even Firas?"

Keplan's eyes tightened. "No." He stared out the dark window high on the wall. Under his pounding heart blood and flesh heaved. Roaring was an approaching storm, the changing wind that brought the rain. "Every dream—vision—I have is warning. Blood, the smell of rot. Half the time I wake drenched in sweat and blood, but without wounds." He paced along the benches. "I think they made a mistake."

"Who?"

"My parents. They did what they were born to do, but it's only in hindsight that we see what side we were on and whether it was the right one."

"Keplan, you weren't there," An'thor rebuked. "You didn't live it. It wasn't easy. What your mother did almost destroyed her. There's a reason they disappeared into the woods for twenty years. A person can't live with the things they did, to the world, to themselves, to the gods, to the Laen. The only thing left is to run."

Keplan's bloodshot eyes swiveled to the general. He was angry. Angier than he supposed he ought to be. His mind filled with the face of a young ageless boy, harsh words tossed into icy wind. "Is that why you've gone north all of once since Claimiirn fell? Is that why you sent Mel'iend away?"

"Excuse me?"

"Never mind." Keplan stalked toward the door. "I'll see you tomorrow." His skin writhed on his body, anxiety humming like lightning. *I need to know what my parents did to the world, to the gods.* He broke into a jog.

Like the training court, the library was dark and deserted. The books muttered at him. Histories of the war looked new, compared to the tattered bindings of the older tomes. *Twenty years is just seconds in the life of a book.* He scanned the titles: *Fire and Lightning: How the World Ended,*

Death of a Deity, A Squire's History of War Volumes 16-19: The Gods' War. Keplan grabbed the second and another thin tome seemingly unread.

"Kill me!" Dust exploded from the shelves.

Keplan ducked, books tumbling from his arms. Torches guttered and went out. The library was empty and dark as before. Gathering the books again, he tried to ignore his hands shaking around the stiff canvas. Instead of lighting the torches again, he chose a table by a window.

He glanced back at the shadowed shelves. Nothing loomed in the darkness. Nothing whispered in his ear. The bindings creaked as he opened them. His fingers traced the author's name. It was not one he recognized.

> *Nothing survived the war. Our beliefs were shaken to the ground. The creatures we put our faith in, in the absence of the gods themselves, were gone. The world was whole again — and we knew it, like an animal senses a change in the weather. The air was different, fresher. But there was an impermanence to it as well. The sky was brighter, but in turn, cast darker shadows. The world is no longer unraveling. Instead, now, it seems to be suffocating.*

Keplan looked up. *"Your blood is strangling the world."* He thought they mended the world improperly or made a mistake in killing the gods. Perhaps it was not something they destroyed. What if their powers created something? Together. Something strangling the world, rotting it from within. He turned to the faint image of himself in the window.

What if it's me?

Perhaps it was the old, waving glass, but he swore his reflection grinned.

Φ

The 34th Day of Lumord, 1272
The City of RoBal, Ban

Dusk settled around the wagon train, a protective mother's arm as they prepared for the journey to Athrolan. Anticipation was a cloud over the guards and workers. Rih recognized the emotions before a march to battle. These were at once the same and entirely foreign. Soft scents of leather and the long-horned oxen underscored the tang of sweat and too much perfume.

A dozen of the Banis riahs accompanied the wagons, a gift to Athrolan's new boy king. The fore and rear were made up of ranks of soldiers, more than she expected for peaceful negotiations. Rih both hoped and feared her March would be among them, but saw few familiar faces. *It's better that they aren't. I need them here. I need allies in this city more than in Ceir Athrolan.*

She would have double checked her wagon held her baskets and a thousand gifts she only received now, to look the part of a princess. Instead, she stood at the head of the stairs. The days leading up to this were her chaos. Now was for stillness, the breath before the dart flew.

A hand clasped hers for a moment. She did not have to look to recognize Il-fald's dry, rough palm or the smoky, spicy scent of her muscle rub. "Il-fald."

"Rih." The gesture held a tenderness, a new deference. "I will miss you."

"You too. I'll write. And I'm sure you'll hear enough through servants and guards."

"I'll pass news to you as well when I can." She watched the wagons, but it was clear her mind was far distant. "I worry for you. Alone in a new country, with a strange husband."

"I worry for you, here, in our homeland, with a dangerous emperor." She squeezed her teacher's hand before asking, "Where are you headed next?"

"Baniol Hev ordered us north. To the coast. He fears Mirikin invasion by sea."

They put our women on the front lines. Her heart ached at the thought. "Be careful. I love you." She had never used the gesture for love to Il-fald, but the sorrow in Il-fald's eyes told Rih she understood.

The older woman repeated the gesture, but added another. "I love you, my queen."

Rih found her hands trembled too much to respond. She squeezed Il-fald's fingers hard and turned to the wagons. The layers of silk and netting drew back from the cushions within. They were ready for her. Curtains closed around her and the wagon lurched.

Bricks and wood rafters rolled past. It was rare she simply stared at her home. Soldier's errands distracted her, then fear and fury colored her view. There was still hate aplenty, and she would use it to fuel revolution, but for a moment she laid it aside.

I will miss this. The red of the clay. The black of the teak. The mound of the city, a fist against the colorless sky. She looked back once as they passed under the gate tower. *I'll return.* But it would be at the fore of an army, she promised herself. She would wrest change from the streets, and reap victory from the golden fields.

CHAPTER TWENTY-TWO

The 36th Day of Lumord, 1272
The City of Ceir Athrolan, Athrolan

THE NIGHT'S TEETH GLIMMERED with winter's bite, but Hylier left his thicker, guards' cloak tucked safely in his room. The Lily and Ahonsa was large, but the rooms were mostly let by those staying months, even longer. Coupled with the fact that many of Daymir's supporters chose it, had led him to stay there. Now, however, he could not use the door. Peraan left not long before Hylier made a show of going out for the night. If the barker's schedule held, Hylier had two hours. His fingers found purchase where mortar fell free between the stones of the alley wall.

After a moment's investigation, he hoisted himself up, the soft toes of his boots lighting only long enough for him to find the next hold. Heavy weathered wood of the window frame boosted him high enough to swing a long leg onto the narrow ledge surrounding the third storey. It afforded a view of the backside of a butcher shop and the dingy walk that ran along the wall between the Silver Apron and the Merchant Tier. *Not a pleasant view, for someone who can "hold court" in a place as established as this.* It deserved some thought, but at a later time. Gripping it tightly for silence, he eased open the metal window latch.

The room beyond was dark, but the smell of linen and smoke told him it was a bedchamber rather than a study. He slid his feet along the smooth wood of the floor, pausing to lift them as they brushed against discarded clothing. He suppressed a sneer. Of course, a man as fanatic as Peraan would keep a messy house.

Only then did he realize the window's latch was warm, despite the cold night. The soft sound of air was not from the window, but breath. He raised his face and sniffed softly. *Sandalwood. Musk.* "It Event File 9

K

Event Tag: Mission Compromised

Timestamp: 3:13-2-29-2157/ 10:30-2-29-2157 3:13-2-20-2157

seems our goals are crossing more often, Elang."

The low, familiar laugh was far from friendly. "I'm encouraged. It shows we're on the right paths." She stepped into the faint orange glimmer from the alley's guttering lantern. It was a few years since he last saw her, though that too had been under dim light in morning's early hours. Time did little for the twisted lines on her face or the slick white scars surrounding her eyes. They narrowed on him. The milky blue somehow seemed to see more than the brown. "Why are you here?"

"You think I'll tell?" His scoff was soft. "Neither of us are paid by him, it seems. Enemy of my enemy and all that?"

"Spoken like a child playing war in the street." Her murmur was almost lost in the noise of the common room below.

"We both know politics are more complicated." He shifted his weight carefully off a loose board.

"So, politics brought you here, then," she quipped.

"What, you didn't slip in through the door to leave a perfumed love letter?" he asked with a smile of his own.

Her mouth quirked. "Not this time, no." She brushed past him, lips warm and dry when they grazed his cheek. "I've found what I came for."

He watched her silhouette fade from the doorway then bloom again. "The center of the second rose on the left leg of the desk might be worth a fingering." He could not see her face, but he knew she winked before disappearing. "Good evening, Hylier."

"Evening, Elang."

When the bloom of cold from the window opening faded he began his own exploration. Blades, too expensive for a man of Peraan's background, decorated the shelves. Empty bottles crowded each surface. Their labels looked expensive, but most smelled cheap. The desk held a dozen letters that could warrant an invitation to the gallows in two provinces. Hylier crouched before the desk, thumb tracing the carved wood. It depressed, and a soft click heralded a hidden drawer dropping from underneath. There were several stacks of paper, mostly details of rebel troops and nobles who still did not support Keplan. Hylier copied each name into the tiny booklet in his pocket.

Underneath them all, however, was a letter and a penned list. The handwriting of the first was plain, but legible, and apparently gave the list its final name. Hylier froze at the signature. It was a simple commoner's name, but an old one. One he knew.

Dam Ornsen.

Confusion bloomed in his heart, chased by dread. The penmanship of the list matched the untidy rooms. *Did you find this as well, Reka? Or were you looking for something else?* Though Ambassador Barrackborn might think she was his, heart and pocket, Hylier knew her long enough to realize her loyalty was not always paralleled by her interests.

He scanned the list, chest growing cold. The last two names were both crossed from the list: *Smytheson (Wise Hare, Slummer), A'hane (Azimir, Noble District).*

He shoved it back under the stack of papers and slipped from the room as quickly as silence allowed. He bet gold whatever kept Peraan out had to do with the crisp lines crossing the names. How was he supposed to choose between protecting the son of an ambassador, and the man clearly keeping the king sane? He did not trust Reka, not when it came to lesser goods, not when it came to love or any other emotion beyond contentment. He glanced at the orange glow of the Slummer above the navy dockyards before turning up the street and sprinting toward the noble manors. Firas's death would bring pain, but Azimir's would bring war. Ancient poets and romantics be tossed, some lives were more important than others.

Φ

Had Bren been more sober, he would be concerned wraith no longer burned his throat. The view from his study changed much since his last visit. Even the lanterns were darker. Barkers and marching guards no longer drowned Azimir's boisterous voice as he updated Alleanthus on the past week. The silence was sullen, beaten.

A soft knock interrupted his inebriated observation.

"Father?"

He glanced over his shoulder. "Al, come in. I was just admiring how much better Athrolan looked without the shadow of war."

His son let out a hard breath, as close as he came to a scoff. "Ceir Athrolan looks rough. You can't tell me she's whole, not by a longbow's shot."

Bren scowled. "You never saw Mirik during the war. You never saw her streets filled with trash, her people starving, living in a rats' warren of derelict houses." He smelled the rank, damp corridors even now.

"No. I didn't. But Ceir Athrolan is not Mirik. A city can be broken without being in ruins." Alleanthus moved to the desk, fingers pausing on the bottle of alcohol. "Are you attempting to achieve General Domariigo's level of dependence on this stuff?"

"Just because you don't drink doesn't mean I've become reliant." Bren sighed. The remark took the fight from his words, though. This was the most he drunk in years. "Seeing Athrolan perched on the edge of disaster, and our own country preparing for war.... It hurts my heart."

"Ma sent me with a letter." Alleanthus's words were careful, and he was not a man to change the subject without segue. "It was to the both of us, and I took the liberty of reading it first, on the sail here." Trembling betrayed his nerves as he extended the open parchment.

Bren pinched sobriety into the bridge of his nose. "Ought I read this when I've slept?"

"I think you'll want another glass when you've finished."

Bren groaned and raised the wick of the lamp by his chair.

> *Brentemir and Alleanthus,*
> *I hope your time in Athrolan is safe. I am glad to hear the city is settling after her time of unrest. I look forward to seeing it myself soon.*

I fear I write with business in mind, and not simply to send my wishes. Our warships sail to Ban in a month. You will stay in Ceir Athrolan for a longer time than you both originally planned. I need my ambassadors there to keep an eye on this new king, and hopefully remind him of the need to remain close allies.

I trust you, Bren, to respect my choice in this matter. Alleanthus, I know I can count on you to remind your father of our values should he become blinded by his kind heart.

All my love,
Kemmer

He tossed the letter onto his desk with a sharp sigh. "Toar. This isn't a world I recognize anymore." *I don't recognize my wife anymore, either.*

Alleanthus turned away. "We knew our relationship with Ban could come to this."

"It's not about Ban. It was, originally. But this world, in my lifetime I've seen it rise from darkness. And now I'm afraid she's standing on the edge of this, this chasm, about to plunge down into something deeper and more terrible than before. I keep thinking if we just take a breath and look around, we'd see a bridge, somewhere to the other side." He ran a hand through his gray hair. "I sound like An'thor."

"General Domariigo is a fair bit more bitter than you."

"He did not use to be. He was this mighty force, full of hope and certain about the good in the world. Alea and Arman too. Where did our heroes go?" Bren sank into the chair by the window. "And now my own wife doesn't trust me to think of Mirik without your supervision."

"Ma just knows you lead with your heart. And this isn't the time for that. Hard choices must be weighed carefully in our minds—you taught me that. Adding Keplan to the mix doesn't help."

"I know." He nodded to the door. "Please inform the household we'll stay another few months. I'll need to see the steward, as well, to send for some things I left back home."

Alleanthus paused in the doorway. Worry weighed his dark eyes. "Should I tell Azi when he gets back?"

"I'll do it." Bren listened to his son descend the stairs, heard the steady low tone as he relayed his father's message. Alleanthus was a very different man from Bren. *And he'll make a better ambassador than I ever did.*

The front door banged downstairs, and Alleanthus's tone grew sharp. "What is this?"

"I need to see the Ambassador. It's urgent." The voice rasped with overexertion, but the accent was Athrolani. "It's about his son."

"I am his son," Alleanthus bit back.

Bren went to the doorway and tried to shake the fog of drink from his head. "What happened?"

The man in the foyer below was blond and beaded with sweat. "I'm Captain Hylier. His Majesty asked me to look into those behind the resistance, and I found evidence that your family is in immediate danger. Where is your son? The younger one, Azimir!"

Alleanthus looked up at his father. "He said he was going for a drink. He didn't say where—" A crash outside interrupted the rest of his words.

Panic burnt sobriety into Bren's limbs. "Stable!" He grabbed his sword from the table and dashed down the stairs. Bren motioned for the soldier to circle the stable as they surged into the courtyard. Azimir was on his back, hay matted against the velvet of his tunic. A heavyset woman with shorn hair pinned him to the stable floor. A thick fist had him by the hair, while she pressed a needle-thin blade to a gap between his heaving ribs.

"Let him go!" Bren could not keep the tremble from his voice, but beside him, Alleanthus snarled, hand perfectly steady around his raised blade.

The woman glanced back. It was only a second, but Azimir shoved a booted foot between her breasts and managed to skitter back enough to wrest his hair from her hand.

She scrambled atop him, standing and pulling him with her. The blade now dug into the soft brown flesh between his clavicles. "You aided the Usurper. Treason is punishable by death!"

Azimir glared at the pockmarked face of the woman gripping him. "It's not! We're not Athrolani, so it can't be treason."

Behind, Hylier eased through the partially open door, feet featherlight on the straw. Bren forced himself to not look away from the woman.

A shadow peeled from the darkness of the loft and dropped. In the same moment, Hylier lunged forward. It was a blur of limbs and flashing steel, then a gout of blood doused the fray. Azimir shoved the woman's body off himself and allowed Reka to help him to his feet.

Reka wiped gore from her cheek with a grimace. "Honestly, I've only got the one good eye, Hylier. You could stand to be a bit more careful."

He grinned. "Just imagine how poorly it would have gone without me."

Bren pulled Azimir into his arms. "If it's all the same to you, I'd rather not." He glanced at Alleanthus. "Double guard, around the whole manor, and send a message to the general and Captain of the Guard explaining what happened. They'll want to inspect the body." He squeezed Azimir once more before drawing away. "I've been lenient about your excursions, but as of now they're finished." He glanced up. "Reka, a word?" He watched her eye track the soldier and the others as they filed from the stable. When her gaze returned to him, he caught her up in an embrace. She was warm, and he was drunk. As he pulled away, he found his mouth on hers.

"Fates, Bren, enough." She shoved him away. Her arm wiped her mouth like she cleaned blood from her face.

"What? It's not as if we never have before." He raked a hand through his hair. "I'm sorry. The nerves got to me."

"And drink. We haven't lain together in years, and the last few times included your wife." She pointed to the manor. "You're being a rubbish husband right now. The least you could do is go be a good father."

He mouthed a response he had not formulated, then felt the fight leave his body. "You're right."

"I know I am."

He watched her leave. *I truly don't recognize this world.* He would tell Keplan, and write to Kemmer, but both could wait until morning. He turned back inside, calling for his sons.

Φ

"Can I talk to you?" Hylier's voice cut through the quiet and dark of the alleyway entrance to Reka's rooms.

Reka rested her head against her door. "We're not even on the same side." The words were only an echo of their earlier conversation, but she did not have the strength to think up another excuse. It felt like weeks, not hours had passed since they met in Peraan's rooms.

"We're not on opposite sides either, not yet, at least."

She opened the door, and unloaded her pockets and belt onto her desk. Muffled clunking of weapons on wood was a lullaby to her ears.

"I learned something today and need an opinion." He sank into the chair at the foot of her bed without invitation.

"Please, have a seat," she drawled, unclouded eye rolling. "Can't you process it without a sounding board?"

"Cut the shite." He ran a hand across the booklet in his hand. "Say you spent your whole adulthood fighting for something, for peace, then discover the person you hold in highest regard, whose orders you've followed, who is your friend and supposed confidant, did something terrible."

"Daymir or Keplan?" She crossed her arms, unsurprised. Daymir was noble, and therefore impossible to trust, and Keplan, for all his boyhood, was unfathomable.

"I can't tell. As you said—we're not completely on the same side." He looked at the fire. "What should I do? Do I move against them, or do I trust their actions as I always have?"

She sighed. It was not difficult to figure out of whom he spoke. "We spend all our time concerned with people trusting us, we forget whether or not we trust them. I've forgotten how to trust. You've forgotten how not to, it seems." She ran a finger around her mug's rim. "You go with your gut. That's what I always do."

His frown deepened, but he rose. "All right. Thank you. I won't find you again."

"I won't be here." She did not offer a goodbye as he left, only locked the door behind him. She understood the man's conflicted feelings. She loved Bren. Not in the conventional sense, but in the sense that people like her depended on people like him, idealistic people too kind and good to see the darkness, the twisted plots that writhed under the surface.

But those plots were necessary to the survival of the world, just as the beauty was necessary for her to hide behind. "Go with your gut." She whispered it to the dark room. She swore an oath to Bren. But before that, all those years ago when the Borderlands were caught between Azirik and Alea, she swore an oath to herself. *Do the hard work, the dirty work, so others won't always have to.* It took a moment to gather her things and clean the room until it seemed disused for days. It took another two hours to find a Banis stall still standing in the battered Thread.

The shopkeep was folding his silks, but the guard outside caught sight of Reka loitering. Leather armor and brown skin gleamed in the low light as she straightened. "Sorry, you can't go in. We just closed for the evening, but you could come back tomorrow."

"I actually hoped to talk to you. I heard a rumor." She made a gesture with her hand, a fist that opened from her chest. "I heard Liberty is coming."

The woman froze, then her face broke into a grin. "Meet me in a quarter of an hour, round back."

Excitement thrummed through her veins, and something bloomed in her gut for the first time in years. *Hope.* Some wars were worth fighting.

And if you won't, Bren, I will.

Φ

The 37th Day of Lumord, 1272
The City of Ceir Athrolan, Athrolan

Firas stumbled downstairs, rubbing rough hands over his arms. It was cold. He hated the mornings Mirrel went to market before getting the fire ready. The kitchen was dark and quiet, and he set about stirring the coals. The smell warmed his heart before his skin. He piled on the logs and nestled the kettle on its hook. Eggs. Today he wanted bread and eggs. It was unlikely they would have much if Mirrel was at the market. He slid open the pantry door and perused his options.

The shelves were well-stocked. Distant bells tolled, marking midmorning. *Hasn't she set about lunch?* He frowned and, kettle forgotten, traipsed back upstairs. Mirrel's focus meant more than once she lost track of time while mending. Fate's knew the common room curtains needed several days' attention. He nudged open her bedroom door. The room was empty, the bed cold and made. Her day's dress was laid across the coverlet. *She never got dressed?* Firas's hangover burned in the wake of dread. "Mirrel?"

He pounded back down the stairs. Every room on the second floor was deserted. "Mirrel!" His search carried him into the common room. He peered under the tables, into the pantry again, as if she could have tucked herself between the wheel of cheese and block of salt.

Then he heard a bump in the courtyard. He shoved open the door, shivering dramatically at the crisp breeze. "Mir, you got water? I couldn't find you—"

Blood splattered the cobblestones. Mirrel's body slumped against the looming gray wall. Red ruined the starched white neck of her underdress. Her head swung against the stable door with soft thumps. He scrambled over to her, fingers fumbling with the rope tangled in the locks of her hair. He pressed her head to its place on her butchered throat as if the ruined flesh would somehow mend itself. His voice broke on her name each time he screamed. He curled around her body, light hair tangling with her bloody, black curls.

His stomach seemed intent on vomiting, but his body was too tense. Gooseflesh peppered bare arms and chest as the cold sun edged toward noon. Disbelief was replaced with horror, then numbness. He did not stir at the distant bang of the inn's front door, and the soft creak of the rear one a moment later.

"Fuck."

Firas glanced up.

A blond soldier stood on the stoop. His pale lips clenched. "Master Smythesen?"

Firas's mind drifted far from his body, unwilling to feel the chill of Mirrel's flesh, or the stickiness of drying blood on his hands. He whispered the first thing he could think of to say. "Can you find a doctor?"

Φ

The knock was urgent. Keplan's drink splashed across his front, staining the pale blue brocade with the black alcohol. "Damn." He patted at the spot, not truly caring about his forced finery. Hylier stood in the hall. The man's head was bowed, his back straight.

"What? You have information?"

"Your Majesty, you're needed in the Slummer."

"Excuse me?"

"The master of the Wise Hare needs to see you."

"Why are you doing his bidding?" Keplan spat the words before finishing off what drink he had not spilled. The thought of seeing Firas twisted his chest, but he could not stomach another rejection. "He said as much that he didn't want to see me."

Fatigue weighed on Hylier's eyes when they met Keplan's. "He didn't send me, Sire. You asked me to check into the threats on your allies from Peraan and his men. I'm afraid to say I was too late for one. Mirrel is dead. Firas needs you."

Keplan's stomach revolted, and he was sick all over Hylier's boots. "Forgive me."

"No need, Your Majesty. I'll send for a horse and guard while you tidy yourself."

"I don't need a guard, dammit!" Keplan snarled as he staggered into the privy.

"You most certainly do." The door clicked shut behind the captain. Keplan stared into the mirror. His belly still heaved, but there seemed to be nothing left to vomit. *I haven't eaten in two days.* He wiped his face and rinsed his mouth twice before changing into his old shirt.

Moly waited in the courtyard. It seemed the stablehands had tried to groom her, but there was little to be done about the scruffy coat or hairy ears and nose. Keplan ignored the two guards who fell in behind him. He did not care about the spectacle he made, a tall man on a too-small horse, racing through the streets of the city at high noon. The Slummer was subdued, and he felt the heavy weight of accusation from the faces peering through the curtains. War was one thing. An assassination of one of their own, a daughter of blood as old as Athrolan, was personal.

Keplan trotted into the courtyard, dismounting before Moly had drawn up. The space reeked of blood. Pink stains marred the plastered walls and white stone. Sawdust scattered across the ground to soak up the worst of the gore. He shoved through the rear door. The common room was dark and cold. He took the stairs two at a time. Firas's room was deserted, but Mirrel's cracked door emitted the faint hitch of weeping.

Firas was curled on the bed, wrapped around a pillow. Keplan faltered in the doorway, but only for a moment. The mattress dipped and creaked under his weight as he tucked himself behind Firas, his knees folded into the hollow of the other man's, nose pressed against the nape of Firas's neck. "I'm so sorry."

"It's not your fault."

Yes, it is. "I'm still sorry." The bed smelled of roses and straw. *Mirrel.*

Firas's voice rasped over the expanse of his grief. "I don't know what to do. She took care of everything. I was a stupid child, through all of it, even when she needed me, I never did enough."

"You loved her."

"That's not enough." He sniffed, shoulder shuddering. "How do I run an inn? How do I look our patrons in the eye? How do I do any of it — live — without her?"

Keplan brushed a kiss across the mess of hair in his face. When faced with Daymir, with Brentemir, with An'thor, he always had the perfect, powerful response. *It's just honesty.* Another person's grief was a far more difficult challenge. He slipped an arm over Firas's chest, lacing their fingers together. "I don't know."

Light crept across the room and faded from the sky. They did not speak. Suppertime came, and Keplan pried the other man from bed. The common room was still dark, still cold, still a void where hard wit and sharp laughter used to be. Keplan dismissed his guards before finding food.

By midnight, the lamps sputtered with too-little oil. Empty plates and two battered mugs decorated the bar between them. Keplan glanced out the window. "It's no longer the worst day of your life, you know."

Firas followed his gaze. "You're right. Perhaps the second worst." His sigh was older than the wind. "What do I do today?"

Keplan traced the old lines of laughter and the new lines of grief on his lover's face. Firas needed purpose, needed strength. *He needs Mirrel.* "We'll start here. We'll tidy everything. You'll set the soup to cook for tomorrow, you'll go through the pantry and make sure you have everything for the week while I deal with the courtyard. We'll clean the common room, we'll scrub every last corner of this place. And then, when you're finally exhausted enough to sleep, you will."

"They left this." He slid a coin across the bar.

Keplan tilted it. The markings were those of an Athrolani mint, but Daymir's profile replaced Tzatia's. "May I keep this?"

"Do what you want." Firas's frown deepened at the mention of the courtyard. "I'll arrange for her burial soon. Maybe in four days, the First Frost was always her favorite festival."

Keplan looked down. Details of a funeral had not occurred to him. "I can ask for a place for her in the memorials."

"No." Firas shook his head. "We've a family plot. It's high up on the hill. We're one of the oldest families in Athrolan, you know." He ran a hand over the bartop. "I appreciate your offer to help and grateful you're here, but I'll want to tidy things alone." He met Keplan's eyes for the first time that night. "Yes, even the courtyard. I'm her brother. I ought to do it."

Keplan felt excluded, then immediate guilt followed. *I've done enough harm.* "Of course. I can help with whatever you need, whenever, just ask."

"You're a king, 'Lan. You've got bigger responsibilities than my grief. I meant what I said the other day. The roots of it, at least. I could have been kinder, but I meant it."

Keplan shook his head. King's responsibilities were nothing in the face of grief. "I want to help, I love you."

Firas's snort was too kind to be a scoff, but only just. "You can't."

"Doesn't matter. And I don't understand, but I'll respect it." Keplan rose, brushing his hand over Firas's. It was a ghost's touch. He wanted to fill his days with the business of the inn, with helping Firas, organizing the Hare's future without Mirrel. None of those were his tasks, after all. He was not family, even if they were his, not in the way that mattered when death arrived. "Could I say goodbye?"

"She's in your room."

Except, when Keplan climbed the stairs of the Wise Hare for the last time, he found it was no longer his room. Walls stood, and the roof stooped, and the window overlooked the city, but something had left the place.

It was the same with the body on the coverlet.

Sheets swaddled her, wrapping all but her face and head. Bloodstains spread from her throat, but her wounds were covered. A faint frown wrinkled her brow, but it was the only expression left, as if she forgot something important, but could not place what.

Hunting and the general brutality of nature prepared him for death. Nothing prepared him for grief. *She protected me. She never even liked me, but she protected me.*

He sank onto the bed beside her. Beetle

"I'm sorry. Firas denies it, but I had a part in this. The minute I shadowed your doorstep your fate was set—" Tears did not come. He wished they would, wished something would release the ache building between his ribs. His brow pressed to her wrapped shoulder. It was the most they ever touched.

Fear, fury, exploded in his mind. Rough hands gripped his shoulders. Ribs cracked against the wall. Pressure seared across his throat. Hot blood pulsed from his body. He lived it twice, thrice, until his pain-blurred eyes fixed on the man standing over Mirrel's body.

Foreign adrenaline jolted sense from his mind, erased his faint control over his emotions. Torrents of pain broke through the floodgate of his mind. *Peraan.* There was another man, but it did not matter. Emptiness came in the wake of grief, of exhaustion, horror, and most of all love.

Stumbling steps took him back across the bloodstained courtyard. Through the kitchen window he heard pans rattling through the too-empty inn as Firas cleaned. Walking to the palace seemed insurmountable and familiar streets only ripped at his grief-cracked heart. Instead, he turned left. Twisting alleys led through leaning, water stained compounds above the naval yards. In the small hours of the morning even torchlight seemed tired, guttering against the ocean air.

A narrow walk jutted between harbor towers, a spider's thread of battered stone over the black waves. Keplan staggered across. White scars marked where the harbor gates scraped closed weeks before. Keplan pressed his cheek to the damp wall. Everything smelled of salt. *Ma.* He understood, now, why she always smelled of storms, of an ocean he never saw. *And Da was woodsmoke and stone.* He wanted to settle on the floor by the fire and listen to his mother's terrible singing.

Small wonder they wanted him to lead a quiet peaceful life. *I should have listened.* Staring down at the darkness of the open ocean only echoed the yawning grief, the horror at every choice he made. He pushed himself upright and wandered down along the wall of the navy barracks. Muttering sailors and creaking rigging drifted over the dockyard.

"I'll see you when I'm next in town." A voice more suited to shouting over crowds cut through the quiet darkness. Peraan shouldered a pack and waved off another question from his companion. "No, errands. It'll be weeks this time."

Keplan no longer needed books to describe a Rakos's rage, or the fathomless cold that overtook the Dhoah' Laen.

Frozen fury pulsed through his heart. His feet followed Peraan's steps up the Tzama to the glittering coin-tiled basin of the Fountain of Starflies.

The man paused, and Keplan fell back into the shadow of a brothel.

"I already know you're there, whoever you are."

Keplan pulled his cowl farther and stepped up beside the barker. An empty city square was a terrible place for a king to meet a murderer, but the void where his reason once sat swallowed every instinct. Silence reigned while they stared at water dribbling over the mosaic of silver coins.

Exhaustion. The ache of old joints in winter. Blood washing into a basin. Keplan winced at the last image from the man beside him. *Scare him, make him run and never return to Ceir Athrolan.*

"You one of Luben's boys?" Peraan hazarded. "You can tell him I'll pay him when he takes care of Salt-tongue."

"I'm here about this." Keplan placed the calling coin bearing Daymir's head on the fountain's rim. "We know it was you."

"That was rather the point," Peraan snorted. "And it's scarcely a crime, the bitch was betraying our kingdom, tupping the usurper himself."

Rage melted the ice in his gut. He whirled, one arm cracking across Peraan's shoulders and sending the older man crashing into the fountain.

Sloshing water drenched them both as Peraan rolled onto his back, gasping. Keplan scrambled onto him. One knee ground into the man's groin. The king pinned the barker's hand against the cold coins. His red palm slammed into the man's throat, fingers digging into the fleshy veins. Peraan's free arm pounded against Keplan's face, his shoulders, fingers gouging at the boy's eyes. They scraped down his cheek and Keplan whipped his head, catching the clawing digits between his teeth. His jaw tightened, flesh and gristle grinding, blood spurting into his mouth.

His fingers ripped skin, worming their way behind the choking man's windpipe. Peraan thrashed, trying to buck the thin boy off, but slumped over the fountain's rim was not advantageous. Rage and adrenaline hurtled Keplan beyond the threshold of normal strength. *Let him think this isn't luck. Let him think I have power on my side.*

Let him think I'm a god.

Thrashing subsided. Spasms ceased. Water stilled to a ripple as twitching hands and feet slowed. Keplan gripped tighter for another moment before extricating his fingers from the crushed trachea and bruised wrist. He spat the dead man's gore into the blood-black water.

Peraan's discarded pack tangled his shaking legs as he stepped away. Papers and clothing tumbled out, followed by a bottle of whiskey. Keplan stuffed them back in, glancing at the body in the fountain, bumping against the spout in the center. Nausea writhed up his throat. He grabbed the bag and ran.

Blood's tang filled his mouth, but now it was fresh, and no amount of spitting erased it. He fumbled the bottle out and pried the cork out. Sickening spices of whiskey only set his stomach aflame. *Tell An'thor.* He knew the general had no grounds to judge him for murder, but the moment a confession slipped from his lips it would be real.

Fates, there's a body. The nearest street corner held a closed perfumery and the gleaming front of a Banis bathhouse. Already lantern light bloomed brighter, exposing every shadow as dawn approached. He recognized nothing. Two right turns and a faltering climb up a narrow alley brought him within a block of the fountain. All he needed to do was hide the body, just long enough to give him time to return to the palace and bathe before the crime was discovered.

I've killed a man.

"Murder!" The shout arced over the hard, white stones. "Guards! Someone: call the guard!"

Keplan's pulse stuttered to a halt. Breath hitched and he staggered back. He tossed the dead man's pack away and bolted down the nearest street. Darkness hid his flight through the Thread and back toward the Slummer. Market Square was sinister without its usual stalls. Beggars and prostitutes replaced performers on the corners. Keplan sank against a closed meat vendor to catch his breath. Another swig of whiskey burned through him.

"Boy, you look like you need to forget a fair few things."

Keplan turned. A dust-dealer hunched on a stoop.

"Whatever you're drinking over, it'll be gone from your mind in seconds. You'll forget all your dreams, your thoughts. Copper for a palm, silver for a box."

Keplan crossed the street, where a ladder led up the pillar of an aqueduct. The rusted metal was loud in the darkness before dawn. Cold stone bit through the thin fabric of his finery. His mind tumbled, knocked loose from its tentative moorings. *Something's missing.* Something more than Mirrel's life force, or Peraan's vitriol.

The only innocence he still had was in tatters. He should be panicked. He should be horrified.

His mind was silent. Power over another life was intoxicating. No alcohol rivaled extinguishing that spark with his blood-colored palm. It terrified him. It was not for him to decide who lived. It was not for men and women to make that choice for others. An'thor teetered over that line. Already the surge of energy, the sweeping peace of taking a man's life, of revenge, faded. There was no divide between the roaring noise, the churning images in his head and reality. How could he rule with chaos under his skin? How could he focus on war beyond his borders when he cast justice with his own hands? How could he keep the silence without murdering every person who did wrong?

"Whatever you're drinking over, it'll be gone from your mind in seconds. You'll forget all your dreams."

The liquor bottle splintered on the cobblestones below, but Keplan did not flinch. His trembling hands fumbled his way down the ladder. Staggering steps returned him to the stoop. Keplan stared at the tiny leather bags arrayed between them. He wondered if any other kings faced the same fears.

The dust-dealer's rheumy eyes fixed on the king. They were devoid of both recognition and judgement. "Change your mind?"

He would be a good king, he would keep Athrolan from war. *I'll protect them, even if it's from myself.* He jerked a nod at the man.

"All of my dreams, you said?"

END OF BOOK ONE

ACKNOWLEDGEMENTS

With each book the list of people for whom I am grateful grows exponentially, and the words I have seem ever more inadequate. But I will try.

Thank you to Marissa, for your hardwork, your infuriating optimism, your genius. Our business would be lost without your dedication, and my writing would be nothing without your friendship.

Thank you to the Indie Author Support group, for all your advice and – of course – support, especially Krista. You're a superhero, and totally saved this book!

And thank you to Brad, for your unwavering love and understanding, even when I'm hunched in the corner with my computer way past the time we were supposed to start watching a movie together or eat dinner. And thank you for reminding me that I need to take a break, even when I have "a thousand, goddamn" deadlines.

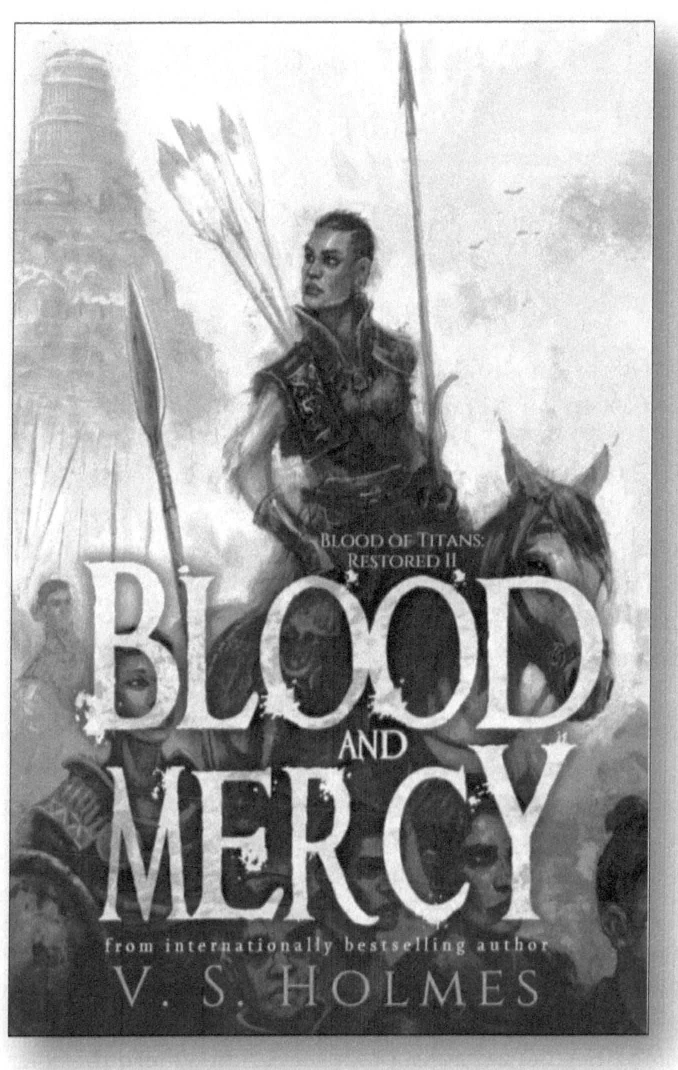

BLOOD OF TITANS:
RESTORED II
BLOOD
AND
MERCY
from internationally bestselling author
V. S. HOLMES

CHAPTER ONE

37th Day of Lumord, 1272
The Eastern Banis Prairie

THE FOURTH NIGHT ON the trail, wolves circled the tents. At the camp's edge, where cookfires burned, they crept even closer. Rih leaned over, peering past the licking flames at the bright eyes blinking at the edge of the firelight. Already the weather was colder, the air carrying teeth as sharp as those glinting several paces away.

"You'd think they'd be frightened, with this many people," she signed to the woman beside her.

The guard spared a glance for the predators. "War makes everyone hungry. It's been centuries since wolves were seen this far west. They've probably come to eat our dead," she turned back to her bowl with a shudder.

Rih winced and looked back to the camp's boundary. The glittering eyes were gone, just a memory lit on her eyes when she closed them. It would take another week to reach Athrolan's capital, more if the river crossing tomorrow went poorly. Even marches as a foot soldier didn't take this long, thousands of pounding feet beating their steady way across the dusty grasslands. It was hard to manage the transition from soldier to dignitary, but the differences in the march made the gulf between the two yawn wider. When she saw that Bimet was through with her food she leaned forward. "I have something to ask of you."

"Are you certain that's a good idea?" Bimet's gaze moved from Rih to the looming tent of the Emperor's Ambassador. Vi-baln shadow paced the tent wall, pausing when a runner appeared.

Rih raised the spear beside her. It was decorative, mostly but the blade was sharp. "I'll be quick," her fingers curled with ease, forcing casual comfort into the conversation to ease her guard's worry.

The guard's shoulders heaved in a sigh and she fell into step beside her. Fire lit the makeshift road between the linin tents.

Once out of eyeline of Vi-baln's tent, Rih ducked between the gently waving fabric walls of the larger barrack tents. Guards paced the edge of camp. Already she caught sight of armbands, caught glimpses of a fist, rising, opening. Liberty. She settled on the outcropping, legs tucked beneath her, and raised her face to the soft air. There was little time to acquaint herself with the surrounding women, but there would be chance enough upon arriving in Athrolan, where they would be watched more, but understood less. Bimet found an outcropping still within whistle distance of the camp, but outside the reach of firelight. Of Rih's half-dozen attendants, Bimet was the only one she had known before any of this. Their troops had worked together often, and the red armband she donned on the second day of their march told Rih enough.

"I don't like this," Bimet signed, lips pursed.

Rih shrugged. "There's no other option. I can't trust letters yet, not until I am safely in Athrolan. There're too many eyes on me. And not only Vi-baln's."

"Then I assume it's important?"

"Fourth Riding is being transferred to a nearby town," she said by way of answer. "A little one I can't remember the name of."

Bimet watched the glowing orbs in the trees bob and slink for a moment. "And?"

Beneath Rih's hand the rock was rough, ragged, and gray. Gone was the smooth red of home, the earth stained red by rust or blood. Her fingers curled in the crags, a tether to this changing world. "They're led by Baniol Desfal, of the Third Arc. I don't want him to leave the town alive. I know there are sympathizers there." She fixed Bimet with a pointed expression. "Understood?"

"Understood. I'll get the word out now. It'll go out with the morning progress runners tomorrow at dawn." Bimet rose, hand pressing the small of her back when she straightened. "I'll walk you back to camp."

Rih shook her head, "I can manage myself. The messengers' tent is on the other side of the camp from ours."

When Bimet was gone, Rih's attention drifted to the darkness before her. A small piece of her wished, fleetingly, that she could disappear in the makeshift roads and slip away into the night. She would not, no matter how inviting the dark woods and winding trails might be. But for a few moments, she could pretend. In a fortnight's time she would be in a different type of forest, one of cold white stone and looming duties.

Already she missed Ki-elte. Already her heart ached for home. *A woman will bleed and die for Ban.* She would see them again, in a year, perhaps two, on the field of battle, somehow, she would find a way, find those who would join their cause. In Athrolan, isolation would be their greatest ally. She just hoped she could survive it long enough to see her rebellion through.

Coarse grass pricked her feet through her silken slippers as she wound back to her tent, beside Vi-baln's. She turned the corner and froze. Vi-baln stood in the opening to his tent. Lanterns glowed behind him, gleaming off his broad, bare shoulders. His attention was fixed on her. "You'd best mind your slippers," he called, grey eyes never leaving hers.

She risked a nod, knowing he knew few, if any, of her signs.

"Wolves and all."

It was only after she had ducked into the illusion of safety inside her tent that she let herself shudder. Bimet was right to be cautious. The emperor's reach was long. Even here his ambassador served as sharpened claws. *This is temporary.* He would be gone once she married. Even as Athrolan's bride, however, safety was not guaranteed. Not for the first time, she wondered what His Majesty looked like. How he might act. Would she wish to sew his mouth shut as she wished so often of the baniol? Would he learn her signs? Would he be kind? She drew a long, slow breath. She was a soldier and marriage was war.

Φ

38th Day of Lumord, 1272
The City of Ceir Athrolan

Keplan staggered into his room, rain puddling on the wool carpet from his coat. A void opened in his chest, swallowing his nerves, his terror, the blood staining his hands. He looked down. A shred of tissue, remnants of a trachea perhaps, clung to the edge of a ragged nail. His empty stomach convulsed. His sleeves, too, were black with blood.

His tore the garment off, tossing it into the hearth with shaking hands. It was too damp, however, to do much more than smother the sullen flames. "Toss it!"

Even Azimir's swears felt like an inadequate response. The wooden box weighed in his purse, and he fished it out. He moved through the parlor to his study and sank into the chair without bothering to light a lamp. What he had become? He did not want the weight of his people on his mind. He did not want the grotesque mantle of divinity, nobility, on his shoulders. He wanted only peace, and Firas, and the distance to escape what he had just done. If holding the world's thoughts in his mind allowed him to end lives, then he would silence them.

All my dreams.

A part of him, the part currently struggling to keep its head above the churning guilt, told him this was not a solution. Not a true one. The box clattered open on the desk's polished top. Inside was a plain waxed pouch, a wide bamboo straw and slim, sharpened stave the length of his thumb. Once each was arrayed across the king's desk, he leaned back. Firas never tolerated his patrons using drugs — dust or its gentler cousin, black leaf. But it was hard to escape in the Slummer. The beggar had not told him how to use the substance, nor had he bothered to ask, or even wonder until this moment. *Fates.* This was a mistake, he was sure, a cliff jump from which he could not recover. Azimir's face flashed through his thoughts, followed by Firas's. His lover's expression morphed from tenderness, however, into the knotted snarl of fury, of grief, the one loneliness Keplan could not comfort. Keplan blinked. Blood. Skin and sinew rending beneath his grasping hands. He reached out, awkward but certain as he tapped the powder on to the gleaming wood. Before Firas's echo could talk him out of it, he bent over and inhaled.

He knew enough to pace himself, to circle his room and lock each door before returning to his study. He hated the portraits on the wall, the looming figures he would never live up to, the exhausted gaze of the queen now reduced to burnt bones in the mausoleum. He paced the balcony, emotions flashing through his chest like cannon fire— immediate and violent and inconsequential.

One after another he torn the portraits down, the hard, ancient wood of their frames clattering together. His gaze was caught by a landscape, hanging just above his fireplace, and he paused. A forest. *Like home.* The frantic energy faded, replaced by something bright, but too sharp for relief or happiness. He sank back into his chair, lidded eyes picking out each detail of the painted tree trunks. A thousand thoughts crashed through his mind, plans and ideas and fears, but not one lingered. Instead his battered psyche was left in unfamiliar silence.

Look for *Blood and Mercy* anywhere fine books are sold.

The taste of the ocean was the same salt as Nubon's blood. The waves beat in the pulse at her wrist, her throat, her thighs. Battered wood bit into her clenched hand. *Thirteen years and three days. I've heard the sounds of this sea for thirteen years and three days.* She absently wondered if the sounds of the womb she heard before were the same, an echo of this, much larger, water.

"It's almost dawn."

Nubon glanced at the man beside her. His sprawled stance lacked its usual playfulness. "Are you excited, *urhun?*" She had uttered the Berrin title for teacher a thousand times more than that for "father," and it held the same tenderness.

"No. Not today." His voice was as wave-beaten as the city bobbing at the horizon.

She heard Berinnal's streets from here, smelled the tar and kelp that kept the city afloat. The ships bearing the seven other potentials for the throne were visible, dark blots appearing occasionally through the morning fog. Nubon mentally ticked off her list. *Tua from the east. Buen from the south-east. Lebon from the south....* She continued, the words familiar in her mind, a touchstone she worried when her mind stormed. The snap of the junk's rigging dragged her eyes to the mast. The plain, dusky-orchid flag rose, the color of a warning sky. *And Nubon, from the north-east.*

A skiff slapped into the water. She followed Urhun down the ladder. This would be the last time they took to the sea together, at least, with her as his pupil. He pushed off from the ship, allowing her to simply be the passenger for the first time since they departed Berinnal a year ago.

"I think I'll miss this." She watched the knots of wrinkles in his beige face soften.

"I know I will." He paused in his rowing and looked at her as if her features were a map he needed to memorize. "Nubon Northeast. Remember everything."

"You taught me all I needed, I'm sure. I'll remember, I promise."

"You'll have to." Something darker shadowed the sadness in his voice. They could not speak about the week to come, the trials that would decide which of the eight scions could bear the weight of the Warlord's title.

Nubon forced herself to sit straight. Her tarred wooden armor was suddenly cloying. They were close enough to hear the smack of the others' oars. Close enough to see their faces were as apprehensive as hers. By the end of the day they would be enemies. Nubon looked to the city, glimmering like the inside of a shell in the sunrise. She wondered, for the first time in thirteen years and three days, what happened to the scions who failed.

**Read the rest of Nubon's story in *Out of the Darkness*
or at vsholmes.com/tempest**

ABOUT THE AUTHOR

V. S. Holmes is an international bestselling author. They created the BLOOD OF TITANS series and the NEL BENTLY BOOKS. *Smoke and Rain*, the award-winning first book in their fantasy quartet, became an international bestseller in 2018. *Travelers* is also included in the Peregrine Moon Lander mission as part of the Writers on the Moon Time Capsule. In addition, they write game content for Stone Blade Entertainment.

As a disabled and non-binary human, they work as an advocate and educator for representation in SFF worlds. When not writing, they work as a contract archaeologist throughout the northeastern U.S. They live with their spouse, a fellow archaeologist, their dog Rory, and own too many books.

www.vsholmes.com